Throne of Lies

Lovecraftian Mythical Urban Fantasy Thriller

John Corwin

Raven House

Copyright © 2020 by John Corwin.

Paperback Edition ISBN 978-1-942453-21-5

All rights reserved. Except as permitted under the U.S. Copyright Act of 1976, no part of this publication may be reproduced, distributed, or transmitted in any form or by any means, or stored in a database or retrieval system, without the prior written permission of the publisher.

The characters and events in this book are fictitious. Any similarity to real persons, living or dead, is coincidental and not intended by the author.

LICENSE NOTES:

The ebook format is licensed for your personal enjoyment only. The ebook may not be re-sold or given away to other people unless expressly permitted by the author. If you would like to share this book with another person, please purchase an additional copy for each recipient. If you're reading this book and did not purchase it, or it was not purchased for your use only, then please go to a digital ebook retailer and purchase your own copy. Thank you for respecting the hard work of this author.

(KENPC 581 V2)

WELCOME TO THE MULTIVERSE

Hannah will return to Cthulhu by week's end to become his eternal minion, and there's nothing Cain can do to prevent it.

Though he still has Soultaker, Hannah won't let him trade it for her freedom. The sword can summon an army of the dead and Cthulhu wouldn't hesitate to use it. It turns out Soultaker wasn't the only thing from the armory to survive. A mysterious cube was stolen by the mechanists. When Cain tries to retrieve it, he and Hannah end up in a parallel world where the mechanists reached the armory first and plundered it.

Using apocalypse weapons, the mechanists destroyed most of the coastal cities with tsunamis and have ground others to dust. To avoid destroying the world altogether, they're fighting a conventional war with airships and a small army of demigods. And if that's not formidable enough, they're also allied with Cthulhu.

Cain discovers the only way back to his dimension is by finding a device called the Tetron. To do that, he'll have to infiltrate the mechanists and steal it from them. But then he discovers a nasty twist-the mechanists of this dimension plan to use the Tetron to invade other parallel dimensions. Cain's dimension is considered the original-Prime. And the mechanists have their sights set on it.

If Cain can't save this dimension, then his will also be doomed, and Cthulhu will ascend to true godhood.

Books by John Corwin

Books by John Corwin

Join the Overworld Conclave for all the news, memes and tentacles you could ever desire!
https://www.facebook.com/groups/overworldconclave
Or get your tentacles via email: www.johncorwin.net
Fan page: https://www.facebook.com/johncorwinauthor

AMOS CARVER THRILLERS
Dead Before Dawn
Dead List
Dead and Buried
Dead Man Walking
Dead By The Dozen

CHRONICLES OF CAIN
To Kill a Unicorn
Enter Oblivion
Throne of Lies
At The Forest of Madness
The Dead Never Die
Shadow of Cthulhu
Cabal of Chaos

THRONE OF LIES

Monster Squad
Gates of Yog-Sothoth
Shadow Over Tokyo

THE OVERWORLD CHRONICLES

Sweet Blood of Mine
Dark Light of Mine
Fallen Angel of Mine
Dread Nemesis of Mine
Twisted Sister of Mine
Dearest Mother of Mine
Infernal Father of Mine
Sinister Seraphim of Mine
Wicked War of Mine
Dire Destiny of Ours
Aetherial Annihilation
Baleful Betrayal
Ominous Odyssey
Insidious Insurrection
Utopia Undone
Overworld Apocalypse
Apocryphan Rising
Soul Storm
Devil's Due
Overworld Ascension
Assignment Zero (An Elyssa Short Story)

OVERWORLD UNDERGROUND

Soul Seer
Demonicus
Infernal Blade

OVERWORLD ARCANUM

Conrad Edison and the Living Curse
Conrad Edison and the Anchored World
Conrad Edison and the Broken Relic
Conrad Edison and the Infernal Design
Conrad Edison and the First Power

STAND ALONE NOVELS

Mars Rising

No Darker Fate

The Next Thing I Knew

Outsourced

Seventh

ENJOYED THE BOOK?

JOIN MY READER GROUP ON FACEBOOK
HTTPS://WWW.FACEBOOK.COM/GROUPS/OVERWORLDCONCLAVE

Chapter 1

I'd only been in Voltaire's for five minutes when trouble found me.

Aura looked up from mixing a drink, brow furrowed with concern. She set my mangorita on the bar counter and shook her head. "Gods damn it, Cain. Maybe I shouldn't have lifted your ban." She plunked a curly straw in the drink. "Don't blow up the parking lot this time."

I sensed the presence lurking behind me before I turned around. "I'll do my best." Holding the mangorita in my hand, I faced the lurker.

A man with a pale complexion and thick head of hair offered a curt nod and a smile before settling into a chair next to me. There were fifteen chairs at the long counter, but the ones near me had cleared out the moment I sat down. It wasn't that I stank. I just wasn't the most popular person in the supernatural community.

Aura narrowed her eyes at the man. "Who are you?"

The man's aura was masked, but even without the true sight scope on my staff, I sensed more than a mere mortal hiding behind that face. I'd felt something similar when approached by a disguised Hermes not so long ago "You're a god, or close to one."

His eyebrows rose. "How did you know?"

I pursed my lips. "It's just a feeling I get when I'm in the presence of someone powerful."

He frowned. "Not possible."

"Thought you'd come in here all smooth and put us in awe?" Aura scoffed. "We're not nubs." Someone waved at her from the far end of the bar. She shot me a look and went to help them, leaving me alone with the unknown deity. That was probably for the best, considering she wanted vengeance on the gods that cursed her.

"Who are you, and what do you want?" I swirled my drink with the straw and took a sip.

"I am Skrym." He looked expectant, as if the name should be strike fear and awe into my heart.

I let an awkward silence ensue, waiting for him to get to the point.

He cleared his throat uncomfortably. "You have something my master desires. I am here to offer you something in trade."

I groaned. "Look, Skrym, Hannah isn't just some object to trade."

"We are not interested in the girl." Skrym seemed to recover some of his earlier confidence. "We desire the sword, Soultaker."

I almost shot him down outright but reconsidered. "What can you offer in trade?"

His eyes grew eager. "What do you most desire? Great riches? Power? A harem of beautiful women?" He leaned an elbow on the bar and smirked. "Eternal life?"

I flicked my hand. "Nah." I maintained eye contact and took a long sip of mangorita. "I want Hannah free from Cthulhu's service."

Skrym blinked a couple of times. "Only the god responsible for a bargain can nullify it."

"Surely you have something to offer Cthulhu that would be of greater value than my ward."

He leaned back in his chair, eyes lost in thought. "Perhaps, but I would have to ask my master."

"There will be no trade," said a cold feminine voice.

I flinched and flicked my gaze right.

A tall woman stood behind the barstool on my right. With her black leather attire, shaved temples, and long topknot hair, she looked ready to murder anyone who got in her way. The woman sneered down her nose at Skrym. "Be gone, servant."

Skrym's face paled. "I have every right to be here." His quavering voice didn't sound so sure of that.

She swung a leg over the barstool and considered the drink specials on the chalkboard. "Bartender, I desire an ale."

Aura shot an annoyed look from the far end of the bar where she was just serving a drink to another patron, no doubt peeved by the woman's condescending tone. Aura took a deep breath and held up a finger. "One moment and I'll be with you."

The woman responded with a regal nod and scowled at Skrym. "Why are you still here, minion?"

"Why are you here?" he shot back. "You have interrupted an important conversation between me and Cain."

"There will be no further conversation." She rotated in her stool as if to direct the full brunt of her glare on him.

I leaned on the bar to block her view. "Who are you to say that?" I didn't know who or what she was, but pissing her off seemed like a bad idea.

"Watch your tone, mortal." Her lips peeled back in a scowl. "You will address me with respect."

"Maybe if you stop talking out of your ass." I held her cold gaze for a moment before turning back to my mangorita.

Her fist clenched. "I am Kara, direct liaison to the gods."

"So, a low-ranking messenger girl?" I already knew the gods couldn't touch me directly, but I didn't know if that held true with their messengers.

Kara's face turned scarlet. "Do not tempt my wrath, mortal."

Judging from her jabs about my mortality, that meant she was a minor deity of some kind. I shrugged. "Then take your self-righteous attitude elsewhere."

Skrym snickered.

Kara moved so fast I barely saw a blur. She gripped Skrym by the shirt and flung him across the room. He slammed into a wall above a table of witches. Vibrations from the thud reverberated around the room. He then slid down the wall and landed heavily on the table, splashing drinks everywhere.

"The peace is broken!" Durrug, the bridge troll doorman rose from his stool. "The fae seal has been defiled."

Aura nearly dropped a drink she was carrying when the ruckus broke out. The witches scattered, not wanting anything to do with a fight. They, like everyone else, knew that fighting within a fae safe zone was subject to brutal punishment, even if in self-defense.

If Kara felt confident enough to fight within a fae safe zone, that meant she was almost certainly not just a simple messenger. She was a demigod at minimum. Whether she knew it or not, she'd just given away a lot about herself in that instant.

Skrym groaned and pulled himself upright, one of his arms hanging at an unnatural angle. He grimaced as the arm snapped and popped back into place. "You dare break covenant?"

"Covenant is not broken, catspaw." Kara raised a fist. "I will not let you have Soultaker."

I leaned against the bar, drink in hand, and watched the drama unfold.

Aura groaned behind me. "Cain, I'm going to ban you again."

"Not my fault," I said.

"Of course, it's your fault." She gripped my arm. "Trouble follows you like fleas on a dog."

I grunted. "You'd miss out on all the excitement."

Minute changes in air pressure rippled across my senses. It seemed the cavalry had arrived. Durrug flung open the only door into and out of the pub as a group of grim-faced beings in black mithril armor stormed inside. Two were dark elves, three were lesser fae, and the last was a woodland elf. They reached over their shoulders and oblivion staffs materialized in their hands. Though I'd once served in the Oblivion Guard, I didn't recognize any of them.

"The peace has been broken," the woodland elf said. "The price must be paid."

Kara stared down her nose at them. "Fae law holds no sway over me."

The other guardians exchanged glances, apparently uncertain what to do. I'd had my ass kicked by the last demigod I fought, so I had no advice to offer them.

The woodland elf stiffened her shoulders. "There are no exceptions. You are on fae territory and have broken the law." Her thumb pressed a sigil on her staff and the brightblade hummed to life. "Submit or double your punishment."

Kara's leather clothing morphed to shimmering metal armor and metal wings spread from her back, razor-sharp tips flashing dangerously. If those weren't enough, she drew a longsword with a golden hilt and held it menacingly before her. "Fight me, and the punishment will be yours."

"A Valkyrie," someone murmured from the tables on the right.

Holy shit, a Valkyrie? I maintained a confident façade. "Kick her ass!" I shouted in support of my former brothers in arms.

The woodland elf's eyes found me, and her eyes filled with anger. "I should have known you would be at the center of this, Cain Sthyldor."

I held up my hands helplessly. "I'm just here for a drink. This Valkyrie is the one who started making trouble."

"She attacked me." Skrym limped pitifully from where he'd been thrown even though he'd fully healed within minutes. "She is insane and must be killed."

"There will be no more violence." A commanding voice reverberated throughout the room, as a tall, fair-skinned man stepped inside. He was thick, muscular, and uncommonly handsome.

Durrug gasped and stumbled back out of the way.

Kara's face lit with fright. She sheathed her sword. The wings folded back into the armor, the armor reverted to leather, and she dropped to a knee. "Thor, I bow before thee."

The woodland elf did a double take at the newcomer. But she didn't even consider dropping to a knee. She was Oblivion Guard, after all. "Is this being your underling?"

Thor turned his blue eyes on her. "She is."

"She has committed high crimes by defiling the peace within this safe zone." The elf deactivated her brightblade but held the staff at the ready. "She must pay the price."

"Not by your hand." Thor spoke matter-of-factly without a hint of condescension. He said it the same way someone might say water is wet, or bacon is delicious. This guy wasn't used to dissent.

The elf narrowed her eyes. "Fae law—"

Thor waved a hand to quiet her. "Does not apply."

"Your Jedi mind tricks won't work here," I said, though not quite loudly enough that he might hear me.

His blue eyes locked onto me in an instant.

Oops.

"Valkyrie are not above the law," the elf said.

"You are correct." Thor turned back to her. "We are outside your laws. We answer to another order."

I noticed Skrym slinking away into a corner. He didn't want anything to do with Thor, and I couldn't blame him. I felt like slinking away myself before Thor noticed me.

The Nordic god seemed to sense I was thinking about him because his eyes immediately found me again. "You have come into a source of dangerous and unnatural power, Cain. It will remain safe in Asgardian hands."

I held up a hand. "How in Helheim do you people even know I have Soultaker?"

"Word gets around divine circles." Thor pursed his lips. "Your adventure to Oblivion did not go unnoticed."

Gasps rose around the room. A group of warlocks murmured among themselves. A pair of vampires made signs of the cross with their fingers as if to ward against me. Aura performed a feat I thought impossible by groaning and sighing at the same time.

"Hold up." I held up both hands. "Hephaestus said it was best for me to hold onto Soultaker. I didn't keep it because I wanted to."

More gasps and murmurs about Greek gods rippled across the room.

"I know Asgard is supposed to be"—I made air quotes—"good, but your messenger girl left a foul taste in my mouth."

"Kara is zealous in her duties." Thor patted her shoulder. "She is doing what is best."

"Zealots are bad news in my book." I took a sip of my mangorita. "Hitler's zealots murdered millions."

That comment drew a round of groans.

"Cain, are you really comparing Valkyries to Nazis?" Aura thumped the back of my head. "Just give them the stupid sword."

Skrym recovered some of his courage at the mention of the sword. "I beseech you not to give Asgard the weapon. They only wish to unleash Ragnarök."

"We wish to guard against Ragnarök," Kara spat. "The forces of Hel want nothing more than the army of the dead contained within the sword."

The room went quiet just as I slurped the last tidbits from my glass. I set it on the counter. "Another one, barkeep."

Aura huffed and snatched my glass. "I hate you sometimes."

"Love you too." I nodded at Thor. "You guys keep talking. This is the most entertainment I've had in a while."

"The Valkyrie must answer for her crimes!" the woodland elf stated again.

Another figure stepped into the pub, a black travelling cloak hanging from his shoulders like a cape. This person I knew all too well, primarily because he'd raised me. My adoptive father, Erolith, glanced at me with suspicion before intervening in the argument.

Part of me wanted to find a place to hide. My upbringing by high fae parents had not been easy or kind. They'd convinced me they were lesser fae, nobodies in the grand scheme of the fae courts, but I'd seen through their deceptions eventually. Erolith commanded the Oblivion Guard and perhaps other fae forces, though I'd never discovered the entirety of his duties. The last time I'd seen him, he'd tried to have me arrested on suspicion of destroying a fae peace seal and murdering a dwarf and a wizard.

My former commander, Torvin Rayne, had been the real culprit, but I didn't think any amount of proof would change Erolith's mind about it.

"Let us step outside and resolve this," Erolith said in his deep, sonorous voice. The tone was commanding but suggestive all at once. "There are things best discussed out of earshot of lessers."

I imagined rumor was rampant by now, especially among those recording the incident with their smartphones. It seemed clear to me that Kara was going to get away with her crime, much like Sigma, the demigod I'd killed in a park not far from Voltaire's. Sigma had been exempt from the laws—something I hadn't even known was a thing. Kara, it seemed, would get off scot-free, especially since her boss vouched for her.

Thor headed outside with Kara close on his heels. Erolith and the Oblivion Guard filed out after. Skrym remained in place, apparently afraid to join the group. I got up and followed them a moment later because I really wanted to hear what they had to say. But when I stepped outside, they were gone. I turned in a circle and shook my head. They'd only been a few seconds ahead of me. Had they been kidnapped by aliens?

I summoned my staff and flicked up the true sight scope. There in the parking lot was a shimmering bubble with all the complainants inside. Thor's aura crackled like bottled lightning. Kara's boiled cloudy red like the blood of a divine warrior. Erolith's aura glowed bright white. The guardians varied in intensity but had nothing on the big players inside the circus tent.

That was when I realized my scope could now penetrate fae glamour. It could see the auras of fae and gods alike. When Layla, Hannah, Aura, and I had broken into Hephaestus's original armory, I'd found an orb made for the original oblivion staffs and used it to replace the one on mine. It had been a bigger upgrade than I'd realized.

Thor's gaze settled on me. He seemed to know that I could see them. He held up a hand and motioned me over. I abruptly shot across the parking lot, passing between cars, and ended up inside the bubble with the others.

"Gods be damned!" I staggered and managed to keep my feet. "What in the hell?"

"You have something that does not belong to you," Erolith said. "As the watchers of mankind, the fae will hold Soultaker for safekeeping." His eyes flicked to the upgraded orb on my staff, but he didn't comment on it.

"No." Thor shook his head. "Asgard has domain over such a weapon."

"Ares last wielded the sword," Erolith said. "The souls do not belong to Asgard, but to Olympus."

Thor shook his head. "All warrior souls belong to Asgard."

Apparently, they'd moved way past the subject of safe zone violations. It was up to me to get them back on track. "What about Kara tossing Skrym across the pub?"

"The matter has been settled." Despite being my height, Erolith looked down on me. "The resolution is none of your concern, son. As your father, I command you to turn over Soultaker to me."

I was still a bit shaken by my sudden summoning into their circle, but I maintained a neutral façade. "I will certainly turn it over to the winner."

Thor raised an eyebrow. "Winner?"

I nodded. "The winner of an all-out cage fight between Asgardians, Olympians, and fae. I'm expecting to make a mint off the pay-per-view proceeds."

No one cracked even the faintest of smiles.

"The human is disrespectful to his betters." Kara glared at me. "Smite him and take the sword."

Erolith shook his head. "There will be no smiting within the safe zone."

"Smiter, no smiting," I said. "Besides, unless the rules are different for Asgardians, you can't directly smite me."

Thor didn't answer, so I decided it was best to put matters to the test. After all, I needed to know for sure before I said something completely stupid.

I smirked at Kara. "See? You couldn't smite me down if you wanted to. For all your bluster and superiority complex, you're just a messenger girl."

A scarlet-faced Kara raised both fists over her head. "I will destroy you, human!"

It seemed I was wrong. Dead wrong.

Chapter 2

Kara's fists came crashing down on my head—and stopped a hair away from touching me. Face contorted with rage, she tried to drop the hammer on me again and failed.

"Crazy." I pretended I hadn't nearly wet myself. "I guess I was right."

Thor motioned with two fingers and Kara slid back and away. "I held her hand, impudent mortal. Had she struck you, it would have broken covenant and allowed the forces of chaos to strike a blow that might very well have taken us to the end days."

"Which one? Ragnarök? Armageddon? The apocalypse?"

"All of them," he said grimly.

I shrugged. "Guess you learn something new every day."

Erolith pursed his lips. "What do you wish in exchange for the sword?"

"Hannah, freed from Cthulhu's service," I said at once. "If anyone can do that, the sword is theirs." Hephaestus, for whatever reason, deemed me a safe person to hold the sword, but if I could free Hannah from servitude by trading it, I figured Asgardians or the fae were responsible enough not to use it for evil.

They frowned back at me.

"What's to keep you from taking it from me?" I held out my hands. "I'm a mere mortal."

"You have named it and claimed it," Thor said. "It would break covenant to steal it from your grasp. The weapons must be freely given."

The ground just outside the safe zone erupted into flames. A dark pit bubbled and boiled. Normal humans—nubs—walked right past it, completely unaware, though some wrinkled their noses at the sudden stench of brimstone. A thin man sporting black jeans and a black button-up shirt rose from the pit, an amused smirk on his face. He looked harmless and unassuming on the outside, but something dangerous lurked behind his eyes.

He entered the bubble.

"It seems my emissary has not been dealt with fairly." The newcomer snapped his fingers. A moment later, Skrym ran out of Voltaire's, eyes wide with fear.

He stumbled into the bubble and fell to his knees before the other man. "Oh, great and mighty master, forgive my failures."

The man chuckled. "No." A pit of bubbling lava opened outside the safe zone. "Go to your punishment, minion."

Tears poured down Skrym's face, but he made no attempt to beg. He walked into the pit and began screaming in agony as flesh melted from his body, revealing a blackened, twisted creature beneath.

I whistled. "That's gotta hurt."

Thor sighed. "Can you please hurry this up, Loki? I don't have all day for your theatrics."

The man smirked. "Do you not love the sound of screaming, brother? Are you not a warrior?"

"I will take the meeting elsewhere, if need be." Thor held up two fingers. Judging from what he'd done to me earlier, he didn't need to do much to move people around.

Loki rolled his eyes and held up a hand. "Fine." Skrym's screams faded into the distance as he fell into a seemingly bottomless pit. The hole vanished and all was mostly silent once again.

I still hadn't adjusted to the presence of the newcomer a mere twenty feet away from me. Fae schooling had only taught us that the gods were bad when alive, but the fae had killed them and saved mankind. Except it was all a lie because the gods were very much alive. They simply hid their activity from mankind. The gods let the fae become the stewards of humanity only because they were off doing god things, not because the fae defeated them.

Which was to say I didn't know much about Loki or Thor except what I'd seen in the movies. My best bet was to keep quiet and observe.

Thor got us back on track. "You will not have these souls, Loki."

"My daughter, Hel, shall admit them to the underworld." He smiled magnanimously. "They will have a chance to earn their place in Valhalla come Ragnarök."

Thor shook his head. "I will not allow that."

"Is Asgard really so desperate for soldiers?" Loki said in a mocking tone. "I have more than enough. I'd be happy to send a few up to Odin."

"It is not the quantity, but the quality," Kara said. "Soldiers of the underworld are trash."

Loki feigned surprise. "Are you saying dear Odin created substandard soldiers? Say it isn't so!"

Kara trembled with rage. "You sit on a throne of lies, Loki!"

Thor sighed and flicked his fingers. Kara shot into the sky like a bolt of lightning.

I agreed with Kara. Everything about this felt staged, manipulating us to achieve an unknown goal. I cleared my throat. "What, exactly, is this really about?"

No one supplied an answer.

Thor stared at Loki without speaking for a long moment. Erolith seemed content to wait it out. I realized I still held my staff in my hand, so I banished it. I caught angry glares from the guardians. The fact that I'd been allowed to keep my staff after everything I'd done, was a major sore point among them.

As the silence persisted, I finally broke it with a sigh. "Look, the souls in the sword were claimed by Ares. If he slew the people, that means they're Greek and outside of your dominion."

Erolith shook his head. "That isn't the point, boy." He didn't elaborate.

Neither Thor nor Loki offered an answer either.

I offered one of my own. "Is this how you ward off the end days or should I begin post-apocalyptic planning?"

Still no answer.

I wondered if Loki and Thor were talking telepathically. Despite staring intently at each other, they hadn't uttered a sound in several minutes. I took the opportunity to address a matter with Erolith.

"Did you ever find out who destroyed the safe zone seals near Shipwreck?" I knew it was Torvin, but Erolith would never take my word on it.

"We did. You were exonerated of the crime."

I scoffed. "Exonerated? I was never proven guilty in any sense of the word."

"But you did resist arrest," he continued. "That is something I cannot overlook."

"Try it again, and I'll continue to resist," I said. "I will not submit to false charges."

Loki's chuckle broke the silence between him and Thor. "This is *the* Cain?" He gasped mockingly. "The last of his kind?"

I blinked. "In case you hadn't noticed there are plenty of humans."

The trickster smirked and glanced at the nubs strolling down a nearby sidewalk. "Oh, those creatures?" He nodded. "Yes, there are plenty of roaches, but only one of you." His eye settled on Erolith. "That I know of."

For once, Erolith looked uncomfortable. "Keep to your own business, Loki."

"Mankind is my business." He shrugged. "For better or worse, they must be shepherded properly."

Thor frowned. "Cease with your nonsense. Cain is clearly nothing more than a mortal."

Loki continued to speak, but all I could do was focus on what he'd said a moment ago. *Why did he refer to me as the last of my kind?* Was it one of Loki's deceptions, or had he meant it literally? Erolith's flicker of surprise at those words led me to believe there was yet one more thing he and my mother hadn't told me.

No one told me how my parents died, or where. My adoptive parents ignored or deflected any questions I ever asked about them, so I'd eventually given up. Erolith convinced me the death of my family was tragic, but unimportant in the grand scheme of things. He'd thrust me into magic and weapons training when I was old enough to hold a sword and a wand.

I'd never considered joining the Oblivion Guard. As a human, I couldn't hope to compete with elves and lesser fae. But when Erolith discovered my ghostwalking ability, he'd insisted I enlist.

Why adopt me? Why care at all about a roach?

Erolith glanced at me from the corner of his eye. It seemed a good time to have a long-overdue father-son chat.

Thor held up a hand to quiet Loki. "We are at a stalemate. The sword will remain with Cain for now." He held out his hand and a silver blur slammed into his hand. It was silver, carved with intricate runes, and looked like an ornate boat anchor with a blunt head.

I did a double-take. "That's Mjolnir? I thought it would be more hammery."

Thor spun the hammer until it blurred and thrust a hand skyward. A bolt of lightning struck the end and he vanished. Nearby nubs jumped at the crash of thunder, confused since it was a bright sunny day.

Loki smirked. "He always was the impatient one."

"Well, for obvious reasons, I won't ever hand the sword over to you." I shrugged. "The world sucks, but I'm pretty sure it'd suck harder if you had Soultaker."

"Why do you have such a bad impression of me?" Loki feigned sadness. "I do not demand fealty from humans. I did not create them for the sole purpose of stroking my enormous ego. You need look only to Odin or Thor for that. I want people to be happy and enjoy life."

"You called them roaches," I said.

He nodded. "Yes, but I meant it in a good way."

I'd only just met Loki, but I felt like I could really trust the guy. He cared about the roaches and especially me. Which meant his charismatic aura was off the charts. He hadn't even tried to make a compelling argument and instead used his considerable will to overpower my reason.

Despite years of training to resist compulsion and glamour, it took great effort to shake my head. "Stop what you're doing right now."

The pressure abruptly relented.

"How did you do that if you can't directly affect me?" I said.

Loki smiled. "Let's just say that some things slip through the cracks." He sighed and shook his head. "If you think Thor has given up, I'm afraid you're wrong. Though neither he nor I can act directly against you, we do have avenues available to us."

"Minions," I said.

He nodded. "Watch your back, Cain."

I raised an eyebrow. "For you or him?"

"Yes." Loki grinned. A black pit opened beneath his feet and swallowed him whole.

I stared at the place where the pit had been, wishing I'd had that available to me on embarrassing occasions. I turned to Erolith. "Going to arrest me now?"

He pursed his lips. "Perhaps it would be safer if you were in our custody."

I began to wonder if there was an ulterior motive to his actions. "When you tried to arrest me the last time, did you know what I was up to?"

"I did," Erolith said. "We found evidence that had not been destroyed at the scene of the murders. It mentioned the lost armory and Oblivion."

"You wanted to arrest me to stop me from seeking the lost armory, and not because you thought I'd murdered the dwarf and wizard."

He nodded. "As usual, Torvin was playing you, Cain. You've let your emotions for the girl, Hannah, cloud your judgment."

I abruptly changed subjects. "Why did Loki say I'm the last of my kind?"

"I cannot say."

Fae couldn't directly lie, but they could misdirect all they wanted. "You don't know, or you can't or won't tell me?"

"This is not a matter for discussion, Cain."

"You know, but you won't tell me." I nodded. "Loki isn't the first to suggest such a thing. Another god hinted at something unusual about my past as well." The clockwork owl, Noctua, had actually been the one to mention it, but he didn't need to know that.

The briefest hint of emotion flickered across Erolith's face. "There is nothing I can tell you." He summoned his staff and the other guardians did the same. His was identical to theirs with one notable exception. The orb at the top of the staff was golden like mine, the one I'd taken from the armory.

He slashed his staff downward. The other guardians mimicked him precisely. The air rippled in front of each of them, bulging out and swallowing them whole. The privacy bubble shimmered and vanished, and the sounds of the city washed over me. A woman shouted in alarm as I seemingly appeared from nowhere. She dropped her Starbucks cup. White liquid and ice spilled across the pavement.

I looked down at her drink. "If that's what I think it is, it's disgusting." I turned back for the pub.

"There's nothing wrong with milk and ice!" she shouted in a hurt voice.

I glanced over my shoulder. "It is when you're paying Starbucks prices for it!" I went downstairs to the speakeasy door and Durrug let me in with the password *Feary*.

Conversation died down the moment I entered Voltaire's. Aura glared at me from behind the bar, and I wondered how much time I had before she banned me again.

One of the witches who'd been at the table upended by Skrym's flying body stepped in front of me. "Cain, what horrors have you unleashed on us?"

Angry murmurs echoed around the room.

"He's nothing but trouble," a man said behind me.

"Butcher," another said.

I almost stepped around the witch. Almost ignored her and the others like I usually did. I didn't care what people thought about me, but sometimes it was just fucking exhausting. And seeing this new mess spawn right in front of me triggered something.

But first, I needed a drink. "Aura, is my fresh mangorita ready?"

She narrowed her eyes dangerously and set the yellow concoction down on the bar.

I offered something of a smile to the witch. "I'll be happy to tell everyone once I have my hand wrapped around that little piece of heaven."

Someone scoffed. "What kind of assassin drinks mangoritas?"

"You've obviously never tried one before," I shot back. I went to the bar, picked up my drink, and then turned to face the audience. For a moment, I was at a loss of how to start. Since these people were still stuck in the past, that seemed like a good place to begin.

"When I was barely a toddler, my family was killed. I was adopted by fae parents and raised as one of them." I took a sip of my drink and set it down. "My father insisted I apply for the Oblivion Guard, so I did. I trained under a dark elf named Torvin Rayne."

Hisses and curses echoed around the room. The Human-Fae War had ended over ten years ago, but emotions were still raw.

"He was merciless and cruel," I continued, to shouts of agreement. "He sent me on a mission to kill a cell of resistance fighters using fae poison. I was to sneak beneath the house, release the poison in the air vents, and leave without confirming the kills. Instead of leaving, I went back to ensure the soldiers were dead. But there were no fighters there, only their families. I found nothing but the bodies of women and children inside."

A man bolted to his feet and raised a fist. "Gods damn you, Cain. You expect us to believe you didn't know?"

I held up my hands helplessly. "I can't prove it, so believe me or don't. Shortly after this, I confronted Torvin. He laughed in my face and called me weak. It was then that I decided to leave the Oblivion Guard."

The witch who'd confronted me looked confused. "This is nothing like what I've heard. Later accounts claimed that house was only the start. That you went on to find more safe houses and murder even more families. When they discovered your crimes, you fled prosecution."

"Those are the rumors the fae propagated." I leaned back against the bar. "How could one man possibly murder so many innocents across long distances in less than a week?" I cast my gaze across the room. "Many guardians were sent on such missions. Most performed them without reservation."

"Lies!" the angry man shouted. "You're a murderer!"

"Unknowingly or not, I am a murderer." I looked around the room. "But if I am guilty of such a crime, why did they not arrest me when they were here only moments ago?"

"Because you made a bargain with them," the witch said.

I nodded. "But why would they bargain with a traitor?"

No one could answer that.

I filled in the blank. "The fae didn't want me spreading the truth about how Torvin prosecuted the war." I picked up my drink. "They would never want you to know that I spawned a new rebellion in the heart of Feary and forced their hand. I left their land having made enemies of all sides."

The witch frowned. "A rebellion in Feary? Why haven't I heard of this?"

"The fae don't like humans knowing their business." I shrugged. "Gryphons, hippogryphs, and other sentient creatures were enslaved by ogres, goblins, and even dark elves. I found shelter with gryphons and learned of their plight. I saw an opportunity and began assassinating slave traders and masters, freeing their captives. We built an army of liberated monsters and threatened war on Faevalorn itself. We couldn't have won, but we would have wreaked massive damage and claimed countless lives. The fae queens knew this and bargained their way out of it."

Looks and murmurs of confusion rose around the room. An elf at a back table rose. "I can confirm this to be true. The fae suppressed news of the Beast Rebellion, but I was in Faevalorn when Cain approached with his army. I never knew the truth of the matter until now."

"And we're supposed to believe a fucking elf?" the angry man said. "Cain is a liar and should be hung!"

Some of his companions pounded the table and howled in agreement. I should have known from their pack mentality that they were werewolves. And from the looks on their faces, they were more than ready to string me up.

Chapter 3

Durrug pounded a fist on the door loud enough to wake the dead and shut up the living. "It is true! Cain slew many slave traders. Freed the woman who became my wife."

My mouth dropped open. "Your wife?" Durrug had said more tonight than I'd heard him say in the past ten years. Bridge trolls weren't exactly known for their sparkling conversation.

The werewolves settled back down at their table. Their leader, the angry man, glared at Durrug. "You vouch for Cain?"

Durrug grunted and nodded. It was hard to tell from his ugly troll face if he was disturbed by that or not.

The witch glanced at her companions and exchanged words unspoken. She looked back at me. "That still doesn't explain the disturbance today."

I wasn't about to get into all the details, so I kept it simple. "I went to Oblivion and fought Torvin Rayne. After I separated his head from his shoulders, I took a dangerous weapon he'd stolen from the lost armory of Hephaestus. I am now in possession of that weapon, though not by choice."

The angry man blinked. "Torvin Rayne is dead?"

I nodded. "His body presumably eaten by scavengers."

A raucous cheer rose. Humans clapped each other on the backs, hugged and raised their drinks to one another. I couldn't blame them. Torvin had been the face of fae oppression long before war broke out. He'd struck down a human that had accidentally touched fae royalty and sparked the war.

"Three cheers for Cain!" Someone shouted. Drinks rose to shouts of "Hurrah! Hurrah! Hurrah!"

I certainly hadn't expected this reaction.

The angry man still looked angry. But he offered me a terse nod before sitting down while others rose around him in celebration.

One table broke into a terrifying rendition of "Black Heart," a campfire song about Torvin and dark elves. The humans had come up with countless songs about the fae during the war as they were wont to do in times of hardship. There were even a couple of unflattering ones about me.

The witch pursed her lips and nodded at me. "Perhaps you are telling the truth, Cain. Perhaps you're even something of a hero for freeing the beasts of Feary."

I shook my head. "No. I did what I did for my own personal gain. The Beast Rebellion helped me bargain away my troubles with the fae."

She chuckled. "Fomenting rebellion seems like an awfully inconvenient way to solve your problems."

I shrugged. "Gods know I've done more for far less."

"What in the name of the gods is going on here?" A familiar voice shouted above the singing and cheering. Layla Blade shoved her way through the throng and blinked when she saw me. "I should've known you'd be at the center of a riot."

I shrugged. "It happens."

She dropped onto a barstool. "Why aren't they tearing you apart?"

"Because, for once, all this isn't angry shouting." I sat on my stool and turned around. "I told them Torvin Rayne is dead."

Layla's eyebrows rose. "You actually told them that? The Cain I know doesn't tell bedtime stories."

The witch sat down to my left. "Cain, I'm a historian for the Atlanta coven. I'd love to sit down with you, hear your side of the story, and learn more about the war."

"Not interested." I sipped my drink.

"I think it would go a long way toward repairing your reputation in the community." She patted my hand. "Please."

Aura paused wiping down the bar. "I think you should do it. It'd really help business if you didn't drive off half the patrons when you showed up."

Layla barked a laugh. "Yeah, consider Aura's bottom line, Cain."

"You're a fascinating figure, infamous in most circles," the witch said. "It would be a real treat if I could interview you."

"I said no."

Aura snatched my drink before I could pick it up. "Cain, you let the nice witch interview you, or so help me gods, I will never let you set foot in here again."

"B-but—"

She shook her head. "No buts. Do it or get lost."

I'd been to most of the other supernatural bars in metro Atlanta. Only Shipwreck had come close to the quality of Voltaire's. Unfortunately, I'd beheaded the bartender during my stint on Oblivion. I blew out a long sigh. "Fine."

Aura flashed a smile and set down my drink. "Good boy."

I showed her my teeth.

"How's next week work?" the witch said. "My name is Glinda, by the way."

I snapped my gaze toward her. "Glinda, the good witch?"

She smiled. "That's my great grandmother, but I was named after her."

Her great grandmother was the protector of the human city, Oz, on Feary. Despite all odds, the place still existed even with its troubling past.

I sighed. "Next week is fine."

Glinda slipped me a piece of paper with a date and address on it. "We can meet at our coven house."

I shook my head. "No way." I pointed at the bar. "We meet here on neutral ground. Last thing I need is your coven collecting my hair or blood." Which reminded me that I still hadn't heard from my druid acquaintance yet. Humans First had a sample of my blood and were using it to track me. I needed a way to stop that from happening again.

"We wouldn't do that." She smiled reassuringly. "I promise."

It was healthy not to trust witches, warlocks, or others who could wreak havoc with organic samples from someone. "I don't care what you promise. We're meeting here."

She wrinkled her nose. "But it's noisy."

"We'll get a room," I said.

Layla snickered. "Already trying to bed her, eh, Cain?"

I gave her some side glare.

"Fine, we'll meet here in a private room." Glinda patted my hand again. "Thank you, Cain. This means a lot." She left to rejoin her friends.

The death of Torvin turned into a bigger deal than I thought. The crowd grew as word spread through social media, and soon Voltaire's was teeming with heavily inebriated supers.

I decided I'd had enough of the noise and headed out. Durrug barely looked up from a romance novel he was reading when I reached the door, so I interrupted him. "I didn't think trolls were taken as slaves."

He looked up and grunted. "They weren't." He didn't elaborate.

I prodded him. "But I freed your wife?"

"She is cecrops."

I blinked at that revelation. Cecrops were reptilian humanoids with multiple ways to poison the living. Ironically, they were generally peaceful people who primarily ate rodents. I was tempted to ask him how that worked, or if they could even have kids, but Durrug had already gone back to reading.

"Well, thanks for backing me up," I said.

He grunted and that was that.

I walked outside and toward my car, half-expecting an ambush by Mage Guild knights. I hadn't seen Sir Colin, Henry, or Francis since the last ass-whooping I'd given them which was very strange. They tried to arrest me at least once a month, always failing miserably.

I reached Dolores without incident, slipped inside her, and drew in the wonderful fragrance of old vinyl seats. Then I shifted into gear and headed to Sanctuary.

Hannah was on the couch watching TV when I walked inside. Fred was perched on the opposite armrest. I stopped in my tracks and tried to make sense of the scene. Hannah had never liked Fred because he was a creeper, but even more so because he was a minion of Cthulhu.

"What the hell is this?" I said.

Hannah plucked a handful of popcorn from a bowl in her lap. "I'm showing Fred *Star Wars*."

Fred's golden eyes met mine.

"Since when do you let him anywhere near you?"

She used the remote to pause the movie. "I decided to get to know him when he's not being used by Cthulhu, and I actually feel bad for him. He's a nice guy."

"You mean octopus."

Hannah shrugged. "Whatever." She tilted her head. "You look concerned about something. Did anything happen at Voltaire's?"

"I don't look worried about anything."

"Cain, even you have tells." Hannah pointed toward my forehead. "You get a tiny little wrinkle there when you're stressing."

She'd been training with me for three weeks now. The grasp on her powers had only improved somewhat, but her weapons training and skills of perception had skyrocketed. I imagined it had to do with her demigod heritage, because even my hyper-training spells didn't allow someone to learn skills that quickly.

I sat next to her and glanced at Fred. "What did you two talk about?"

Hannah pointed to a pentagram on the floor formed from carefully aligned bird corpses. "He told me how he does that."

I sighed. "More importantly, why does he do it?"

"It's ritual magic," Hannah said. "He's trying to free himself from Cthulhu. Unlike me, he didn't enter into an agreement willingly. He was drafted."

"Rough gig."

She nodded. "Yeah." Hannah put the popcorn bowl on the end table and leaned against my shoulder. "Do you think Cthulhu will be happy with my progress?"

"Let's not talk about him, okay?" I nodded at the TV. "How about we keep watching the movie?"

"Cain, I only have a week left before I go back to him." Hannah wiped a tear from her cheek. "I'm going to miss you so much."

I cleared my throat and swallowed a lump. "I'll miss you too." I didn't like emotional attachment, not even a little bit. It was enough to make people do crazy things. As the time remaining until she had to leave forever ticked toward zero, the more depressed I felt. But I kept that to myself. "I'm meeting with a witch next week. She wants to interview me."

Hannah blinked. "Since when does anyone in the super community want to talk to you?"

"Oh, yeah." I leaned back. "I have a few things to share with you."

By the time I finished telling her about the night's events, Hannah was in shock.

"You're a hero now?"

I shook my head. "They won't stop hating me just because I killed Torvin." My phone buzzed. I slid it out of my pocket and read a new text.

Meet at lake house tonight at 9. -C

"Your forehead is wrinkling again," Hannah said.

I checked the time and discovered I had only thirty minutes to get to the meeting place. "The druid finally contacted me. I've got to go meet him."

Hannah's eyes brightened. "Can I come?"

"Yep."

She threw on a coat and we headed to the door. I glanced back at Fred and wondered if he wanted to come too. An octopus wasn't the most ideal pet in the world. Then again, as a minion of Cthulhu, he was hardly an actual pet. Fred dropped off the couch, slithered across the floor, and slid into the deep pool I'd had made for him when I began living in the church.

I disabled the wards on the inner and outer doors so we could exit. We went to the garage, hopped into Dolores, and headed out. Traffic was light so we reached my cabin on Lake Lanier right on time.

My druid acquaintance once lived at the lake house. The living earth had granted him protection, infusing the ground with silver and iron to protect the land from vampires, zombies, and werewolves, but mostly to keep him off the faes' radar. The Atlanta area was rife with Feary portals and one of the largest travel hubs between the planes. That made it a bad place to live for anyone wanting to avoid contact with the fae.

He'd thought hiding in the area was the last thing they'd expect. It'd worked for a while, but a disagreement with a coven of witches forced him to leave or risk being exposed. I'd discovered the land on my own while searching for safe houses in case my own residence was compromised and realized it was the perfect place for a backup hideout.

The house was dark when I pulled into the driveway. I parked and we got out. I sensed a presence lurking near an old oak tree to our right. I could have summoned my staff and viewed the lurker through the scope, or cast a light spell to illuminate the area, but decided to let him come out on his own.

"Why are we just standing here?" Hannah whispered.

I put a finger to my lips. "Patience, grasshopper."

"Hello, Cain." The voice didn't belong to the druid, not unless he'd figured out how to turn into a woman.

I cast a light ball and readied myself for a fight. A lovely red-haired woman stepped boldly into the light and smiled. "Do you plan to attack me?" She had a pleasant Irish lilt to her voice.

"I'd like to take a look at you." I summoned my staff. She didn't flinch as I aimed it at her and looked through the scope. Her aura glowed a healthy green. Sigil tattoos lit up like hidden ink under a black light. Unlike mine, hers were visible.

Hannah tugged my sleeve. "Can I look?"

"What a pretty lass." The woman smiled at her. "I didn't know you had a daughter, Cain."

Hannah peered through the scope. "Whoa, she's glowing green! Those are some serious tattoos."

I took back the staff and banished it. "You're a druid. I thought Caolan was the last of his kind."

She frowned. "Is that the name he gave you?"

"He's protective of his identity." I shrugged.

"That he is." She flourished a hand and bowed. "Nice to meet you Cain. I've been Caolan's apprentice for nearly twenty years. You can call me Grace."

"That's not your real name?" I said.

"Close enough." She shrugged. "Living under assumed identities is safer for us. Too many fae would love to exterminate the last druid."

"Is there a reason Caolan didn't come himself?" I asked.

"Naturally." She shrugged. "Few fae know I exist, so it's safer for me to do the meet and greets. Despite his mostly clean living, Caolan's made many enemies over two thousand years."

Hannah's eyes widened. "How can a human live that long?"

I couldn't imagine such a long lifespan. "I'm actually confused as to why you came here at all. I was prepared to go to him."

Grace grimaced. "That's because something terrible has happened and we need your help."

Chapter 4

I'd expected to owe the druid for his services, but this sounded major. "So, I help you and then I get the protection I asked for?"

"No, that's not how he operates." She walked over to us. "You'll receive what you need regardless."

Hannah gasped. "You've got the most beautiful red hair! And you're so pretty!"

Grace beamed. "Aw, thanks. You're a lovely little thing yourself."

"Are you Caolan's girlfriend?"

Grace snickered. "We tried that for a time. Let's just say that it wasn't good for my apprenticeship."

I grunted. "Good to know Caolan has a backup plan. Be a shame to lose the last druid."

"I agree, and that's why I forced him to take me under his wing." Grace skipped the final step to us. "I'm nowhere near his skill level, of course, but I'm not exactly helpless." She touched a thin iron necklace around her throat, and I found my eyes wandering lower across her milky white skin.

Hannah elbowed me. "Cain, are you looking at her boobs?"

I blinked out of it. "Was that an enchantment?"

Grace giggled. "Heavens no. That's just the power of cleavage."

I sighed and shook my head, trying to come up with some reason for my behavior, but decided there was no excuse. "Sorry."

"Oh, don't apologize to me." Grace reached into her jeans pocket and produced a thin, gray chain. While hers looked decorative, this one was rugged and plain. "Put this on a wrist or around your neck and it'll block most tracking spells."

I took the chain and fastened it around my neck. It felt oddly cool, but not uncomfortable. The fit was tight, but the sensation faded until it was like I wasn't wearing it at all. "Why do you say most?"

"It's not bonded to your aura," she said. "Very powerful spells could still penetrate the protection."

"Thanks." I nodded my head at Hannah. "Any chance she could get one too?"

Grace frowned. "There's something different about her." She took off a sandal and dug her toes into the dirt, eyes narrowed in concentration. "There's a dark presence leeching on her aura." She gasped. "Ancient, twisted, and not of this world." Grace snapped out of her spell. "What have you done, lass?"

"First of all, my name is Hannah." Hannah straightened up. "I saved Cain from a terrible fate by taking his place in an agreement with Cthulhu."

"Oh, my." Grace took off her other sandal and dug both feet into the dirt as if for comfort. "Your aura is bonded to the creature. You still have free will, but you're chained."

Hannah nodded. "Cain is training me so I can be a good little minion for my new master."

"Training her?" Grace's voice rose. "What evil are you perpetrating, Cain?"

I held up my hands. "Whoa, now. I'm not doing it by choice."

"Cthulhu threatened to kill me if I don't learn how to use my powers." Hannah slumped. "It's a no-win situation."

Grace took a deep breath and nodded. "I'm so sorry. Perhaps I should relay Caolan's request another time."

I shook my head. "No, it's fine. How can I help?"

She bit her lower lip. "Some years ago, Caolan fought off a demon in a forest. The fight killed the land and not even the elemental of the region could sense it anymore. It's taken him years to return life to the land."

I grimaced. "Sounds awful. How can I help?"

"He sent me on a cross-country journey so I could introduce myself to other elementals."

Hannah frowned. "What are elementals?"

"They are spirits of a sort that reside in and protect regions of land." Grace closed her eyes. "The one here was angry for a long time, when Caolan first arrived. But after spending time tending the land, the elemental accepted the changes humans had made. Caolan convinced it to use the new resources it now possessed and to make the best of it."

Hannah knelt and patted the dirt. "Wow, I never realized the land was alive."

"I was passing through here some months ago when I sensed a dead spot forming near the southeast end of the lake." She frowned. "I tracked it to an area near a waterworks building. But not long after arriving, it faded and healed itself."

"You think it's related to demonic activity?" I said.

She frowned. "None of the animals sensed a demon, and they're usually the first to know when something unnatural is prowling nearby."

Hannah blinked. "Wait, how do you know what animals saw?" She gasped with excitement. "Are you like the Beastmaster?"

Grace smirked. "Something like that."

I tapped a finger on my chin. "You want me to investigate the waterworks building?"

"No." She bit her lower lip. "An elemental in Alabama communicated with others of its kind to pass a message along to Caolan. It reports a growing section of land that it can no longer sense."

It sounded outside my realm of expertise, but I asked anyway. "How can I help?"

"Caolan left Gaia to help an old friend repay a debt." Grace shrugged. "He left me orders to meet more elementals and maintain relationships in his absence, so that's what I'm doing. But if there's a demon stirring up trouble in Alabama, I'm not equipped to handle it."

"We'll definitely help." Hannah took Grace's hand. "I've only got a week of freedom left, but this sounds like a good way to spend it."

"A week?" Grace looked horrified. "What happens in a week?"

"She has to return to Cthulhu." I steadied the tremble in my voice. "I've been searching for some way to cancel her agreement with him with no luck."

Grace studied Hannah for a moment. "Your aura has a strange silver lining to it." She reached out and traced her fingers through the air. A gasp. "I've seen this before. You're a demigoddess, aren't you?"

Hannah nodded. "To Cthulhu I'm just a weapon."

"Yes," Grace said, "I imagine you are, love."

I sighed and patted Hannah's shoulder. "One last adventure, kiddo?"

She looked up at me and smiled, a tear forming in her eye. "One last adventure before goodbye."

Grace seemed to swallow a lump in her throat. "Are you certain, Cain? Perhaps you'd like to take her Disney World and we could pick up this task later."

Hannah burst into laughter. "Disney World would be a major letdown compared to what we've done."

I chuckled. "Yeah, it would." I looked at Grace. "Let's go on an adventure, shall we?"

Grace smiled back. "Sounds splendid."

"No reason to waste time. Let's start tomorrow." I looked around. "How did you get here?"

"I took a bus and walked the rest of the way." She patted her legs. "Good exercise."

"You can stay with us unless you have other plans."

She nodded. "I'd like to see Sanctuary. Caolan said it's a nice refuge in the middle of the city."

"It is."

"And you let the place grow wild?" she said.

I nodded. "Except for the church, there are eight acres of wilderness."

She put on her sandals then we climbed into the car and left.

Grace leaned forward in the back seat. "Caolan told me you tracked him down years ago and asked him to protect the land around Sanctuary as he'd done at the lake cabin."

"Doing it myself would've taken forever." I shrugged. "When I discovered the ring of iron and silver guarding the cabin, I knew I had to find out who did it and how. I wasn't surprised to discover it was a druid."

"He was surprised as hell, I can tell you that." Grace chuckled. "Caolan still doesn't know how you tracked him."

"Maybe I'll tell him one day." I turned onto the main road. "He wasn't exactly happy that I found him, but after we got past the awkward introduction, it wasn't too bad."

"Awkward is one way of putting it." Grace snorted. "He knew of you by reputation and wasn't thrilled that an infamous member of the Oblivion Guard found him."

"Former member." I shook my head. "Anyway, it was a good visit. I learned some things, he learned some things, and we help each other out from time to time."

"Aww, what a sweet story." Hannah patted my shoulder. "You made a friend."

I gave her the side glare. "An acquaintance."

Grace groaned. "Gods, he sounds just like Caolan. Emotionally unavailable."

"So how does this elemental stuff work?" Hannah asked. "Are they like dryads or the men with hoofs and goat horns?"

"No, they're living parts of the local biome." Grace pursed her lips. "Some elementals are limited in what they can control. Some only influence iron or copper, for example. Others control all aspects of the land. The elemental who helped protect the cabin at the lake and Sanctuary is Oreic, a small elemental who can move silver, iron, and copper."

Hannah frowned. "How did he get that name?"

"Caolan named him that because he can move around multiple kinds of ore."

"The regional elemental is called Atlanta," I said. "Don't expect originality when it comes to naming elementals."

Grace snorted. "It's just easier naming them after something in the region."

"Must be tons of elementals like Oreic," Hannah said. "What are you going to do, start numbering them?"

Grace began listing them on her fingers. "Well, there's Oreic, Oreca, Oregami, Orec, and Karen."

"Karen?" Hannah burst into laughter. "Why Karen?"

"Because she's a fussy elemental who complains to Caolan when another elemental invades her area." Grace winked. "He's the manager."

Hannah giggled. "He has a sense of humor."

"You might call it that," Grace said with a chuckle.

When we reached the gate to my land, Grace lowered the car window, took in a deep breath, and smiled with pleasure. "This is happy land. I can't wait to touch it."

"Druids are weird." Hannah crossed her arms. "Why did you dig your feet in the dirt?"

"That's how we draw power," Grace said.

Hanna's forehead wrinkled. "You're like land mages?"

"They're much more than that," I said. "Druids are more about protection than destruction. They're powerful because they draw power straight from Gaia. Druids can also live forever. The ancient ones were nearly as strong as high fae, which made them a threat."

"So, their minions hunted druids ruthlessly." Grace's smile faded and she pulled her head back into the window. "Caolan was the last, at least until he trained me."

Hannah's eyes lit. "Anyone can learn to be a druid?"

"Only those with extreme patience, lass." Grace leaned back in her seat. "And only those the land accepts. The longer you do it, the easier it becomes. But once my name is known, then I too will have a target painted on my back."

"That's not fair!" Hannah said. "Why can't the fae just let you be?"

"Because it would undermine their superiority complex," I said. "A human that is equal in power to a fae is anathema to them."

"Well said, Cain." Grace sighed. "It's a burden, but one I gladly accept."

The moment I parked in the garage, Grace hopped out of the car and ran into the yard. She kicked off her shoes and closed her eyes in contentment. She was only a couple hundred feet from the tombstones lined up on either side of the road, but that didn't seem to bother her in the slightest.

Hannah watched her curiously. "Should we wait?"

I shook my head. "She could be here for hours."

"But how will she get past the door wards?"

"I'll leave them disarmed for her."

We went inside and started getting ready for bed. I figured we could discuss Grace's mission over breakfast. But she came inside moments later and went straight to Fred's pool, dipping a hand inside.

A few moments later, a tentacle hesitantly rose from the water and wrapped around Grace's wrist. She smiled and nodded. This went on for some time as Hannah and I watched.

Hannah couldn't take the silence anymore. "Are you talking to him?"

"I am," Grace said. "I temporarily suppressed his link to Cthulhu."

"How is that possible?" I sat down next to her. "Cthulhu is powerful."

"But his attention can't always be on every single minion," Grace said. "I asked the Atlanta elemental to suppress the link so Fred can speak his mind."

Hannah put a hand on the tentacle on Grace's arm and gasped.

Another tentacle appeared from the water and touched my arm. *I am sorry, Cain. I was put into that shop as bait. Cthulhu hoped to collect an army of loyal mages by cursing them with enchanted pearls. I was the first minion used to test the plan. But the pearl did not infect you as quickly as Cthulhu hoped, nor did it bind you to him. So, he did not proceed with the plan.*

"Wow, he can really talk now!" Hannah said.

Communication is not a problem for me, Fred said, *but I do not speak out of fear Cthulhu will hear me.*

"I don't think your ritual magic with the dead birds and rodents is working," I said. "And it makes an awful mess."

It helps me pass the time, Fred replied. *I am a prisoner here, and the pool is dreadfully boring.*

"I wish you talked like this all the time." Hannah stroked the tentacle. "You must be the smartest octopus in the world."

I am not an octopus, but a spawn of Cthulhu himself.

Hannah gasped. "You're a baby Cthulhu?"

Yes, you could say that. But Cthulhu's link suppresses my growth, so I will never grow beyond this.

Hannah's eyes teared up. "Grace, can you sever the link permanently?"

The druid narrowed her eyes as if focusing on something we couldn't see. "The link between Fred and Cthulhu is different from Hannah's connection. It's one-sided, like a master to a slave."

I grunted thoughtfully. "Cthulhu can directly control Fred. He can't do that with Hannah."

Grace pursed her lips. "Because Fred was enslaved by Cthulhu there's no bargain enforcing the power of the link."

"So, it's weaker?" Hannah asked.

"In some ways, yes." Grace closed her eyes. "The link travels through water, even the water molecules in the air. I could request that Atlanta permanently disallow the link."

Hannah's eyes widened. "You can do that?"

Grace opened her eyes and nodded. "Elementals don't usually pay attention to such things, but if Atlanta is willing, she can prevent water within her region from allowing Cthulhu's link to Fred."

I gave it some thought. "Would Cthulhu realize what was happening?"

Grace nodded. "I'm sure he'd realize the link was gone, but not why."

"Then do it." I liked the idea of Cthulhu not peeking into my home whenever he wanted.

Grace closed her eyes again. "I sent the request. It may take some time for Atlanta to respond."

Thank you, Fred said.

"I want to be a druid," Hannah announced. "This seems way cooler than blowing up stuff."

"I don't know." Grace shrugged. "I think being a demigoddess sounds way cooler."

"Yeah, but I still can't use my powers at will." Hannah slumped. "I'm just stupid, I guess."

"I don't think that's your fault," Grace said. "You've had a lot happen to you in a short amount of time. Being linked to Cthulhu so shortly after coming into your powers might have inhibited the learning process."

Hannah looked hopeful. "Do you really think so?"

Grace nodded. "The link probably has had unintended consequences."

"Somehow, I don't think Cthulhu will care about excuses," Hannah said. "He'll probably kill me if he's displeased."

"Is there a way to trace Cthulhu's link back to the source?" I said.

Grace raised an eyebrow. "You want to find R'lyeh?"

I shrugged. "Maybe. I'd like to see if Cthulhu is as impressive in real life as he is in dreams."

His true form is close to what you've see in your dreams, Fred said. *His true form drives some beings mad. You do not want to experience him in person.*

The fear in his thoughts was palpable. But if I were to save Hannah, a physical confrontation with Cthulhu seemed unavoidable.

Chapter 5

I looked at Fred. "Do you know where R'lyeh is?"

No. I was there for a time after birth, but I was unconscious when they sent me away.

"They?" I frowned. "How does Cthulhu mate if he's asleep?"

He produces asexually, Fred said. *Slumber is no obstacle for him.*

Hannah's nose wrinkled. "That's gross."

"How many children does he have?" I asked.

I don't know, Fred replied.

Grace pursed her lips. "What does R'lyeh look like?"

I can show you. Close your eyes.

I closed my eyes and suddenly I was underwater. I opened my eyes and I was back in the church.

Hannah gasped. "Whoa, it's just like virtual reality."

"Impressive," Grace said.

I closed my eyes again and looked around. Hannah and Grace floated next to me, Fred's tentacles tethering each of us to him. We jetted forward leaving a wake of bubbles. A school of monstrous fish parted before us. We sped through a forest of kelp and coral trees, the way lit by a path of brightly glowing algae.

Beyond it rose structures of mind-bending geometry. Spikes and spires rose at odd angles. Curving rectangular buildings jutted between the spikes. Stone tentacles wove between the formations as if to lay claim to everything within. The bones of long-dead underwater giants rested among the graveyard of the city. In the center of the enormous structures rose a conical citadel with a gigantic rectangular slab on it. Alien symbols had been etched in the stone and all over the outside of the citadel.

A stone column rose crookedly from the silt near the entrance. The likenesses of bizarre and alien creatures were etched into the surface. Beneath each illustration was a string of symbols. They reminded me of Egyptian hieroglyphs, but instead of canine and feline beings, the monsters had tentacles.

A ring of several etchings bisected the column, each one of them depicting a bipedal creature with wings and the head of an octopus. That creature was undeniably Cthulhu. He stood with arms upraised in one, in the next he crouched. No matter which way his body was oriented, his face always looked out, as if to say Cthulhu was always watching. Only one etching was different. In it, only his head was visible, and his eyes were long slits, not open, not watching.

I looked away from it and up at the citadel. Dread rose in my chest, snaking down through my bowels and constricted around my organs. I hadn't felt such primal fear in a long time. My spirit had been forged in the fires of violence and fear but tempered with logic and reason.

Even as a child, Erolith had often thrust me into frightening situations and said, "Recognize that which deserves fearing, accept it, and realize that it too knows fear."

At seven years old, I'd learned quickly to repress my natural urges or suffer the pain of failure. Even so, the intense dread roiling in my guts was nearly enough to overwhelm my training.

Hannah and Grace screamed and vanished in a puff of bubbles.

Welcome to R'lyeh, Fred said. *That is the citadel of the Great Ancient Ones in the center.*

"Do others live here?" Despite being underwater, I had no problems talking as usual.

Many others, but they all sleep. Fred turned his serious gold eyes on me. *Pray they continue to sleep for eternity, Cain.*

The world went black.

I opened my eyes and found Hannah and Grace panting and trembling, both well away from Fred and the pool.

"T-that was horrible." Hannah wiped tears from her eyes. "I've never felt so scared, not even when Cthulhu talks to me in my mind."

That is why you could never go there, Cain. Fred's tentacle tightened on my arm. *If the sight of the city does not strike you senseless with fear, Cthulhu certainly will.* His tentacle went slack, and he slid back into his pool.

Grace fanned her face with a hand. "I wasn't ready for that."

Hannah shook her head. "Weren't you frightened, Cain?"

"It affected me, sure." I shrugged. "It's like looking death in the eye. Once you've done it a few times, it's not as powerful."

"It felt worse than that though." Grace shivered. "It was pure, existential dread. Like looking into the pitch black of oblivion."

I nodded. "And the world would be better off if we annihilated the entire city of R'lyeh."

Hannah scoffed. "I don't think that's possible."

"Anything that exists can be destroyed." Unfortunately, I'd rid the world of the weapons that could have done the trick. I went into the kitchen and poured a glass of water. "Grace, where's that dead spot in Alabama?"

She leaned against the kitchen counter. "It's near a town called White House Springs."

I blinked. "Did you say White House Springs?"

"Yep." Her brow furrowed. "Why?"

I exchanged a confused look with Hannah. "Because we were there a few months ago. Humans First was trying to wipe out the Human-Fae Alliance with their prize demigoddess, Daphne."

Grace raised both eyebrows. "You think it's a coincidence?"

I gave it some thought but had no dots to connect the Firsters with dead land. "Maybe, maybe not."

Grace leaned forward as if trying her cleavage magic on me again. "Then I guess that will be our first stop."

"You okay with flying?" I said.

She nodded. "Caolan hates it, but I'm a modern kind of girl."

"Gotcha. I'll get us tickets and we can leave early tomorrow." I finished my water. "I'm headed to bed."

Hannah hugged me. "Goodnight, Cain."

It felt awkward, but I mussed her hair. "Goodnight, Hannah."

She went to her room.

Grace smiled, but there was a sadness in her eyes. "I hate that you're losing her so soon."

"Yeah." Talking about emotions wasn't exactly my strong suit. "Well, night."

"Goodnight."

I almost left her standing there when I realized what a terrible host I was being. I pointed to the other guest room. "You can stay in there. There's a linen closet in the hallway. Help yourself to anything in the kitchen."

She smiled. "Thanks."

I went to my room and locked the door, then sat at my desk and turned on the laptop. I must have stared at it blankly for quite a while because power-save mode turned it off before I even thought about buying tickets. All I could think about was that every minute ticking past was a minute closer to losing Hannah forever.

"There's got to be something I can do," I murmured. "Fucking hell, this can't be the end of the road. There must be something Cthulhu wants."

But there was nothing he wanted that he could have. Not unless I wanted to do the unthinkable. I looked toward my walk-in closet. A hidden trapdoor inside led down a ladder to miles of twisting tunnels. Somewhere in that maze, I'd locked Soultaker in a mithril vault. Only a complex combination of sigils could open it. I stood and started walking toward the closet without realizing it until I stood before the table hiding the trap door.

Surely Cthulhu would take an army of the undead over a demigoddess. Then his minions could duke it out with the other gods and old Tentacle Face would be happy as a lark. All I had to do was make the proposal and see what he said.

My hand was on the bedroom doorknob when I remembered Grace had cut Fred off from Cthulhu. Without that line of communication, I couldn't even bargain with him.

"Son of a bitch," I muttered. If I asked Grace to enable the link, there was no telling how pissed Cthulhu would be. He might kill Fred. I had to find another way to talk to the ancient god.

I sat back down at my laptop and purchased tickets to Alabama, then reserved a car at the airport. This was deja-vu all over again. White House Springs, Alabama hadn't been on my radar, much less my thoughts, since our showdown with Daphne and the leaders of Humans First. Was it just coincidence there was a spot of dead earth in that town, or was it somehow linked with the Firsters' attempted massacre of the HFA?

After breakfast the next morning, we headed to the airport and caught the first flight to Huntsville. Despite Grace's assurances that she was fine with flying, I noticed she constantly stroked a metal charm on her iron necklace when we boarded.

I gave Hannah the window seat so I could talk with Grace across the aisle. "Do you know exactly where this dead spot is?"

She blinked and looked at me. "I'm sorry, what?"

"The precise location of the dead spot?"

"Oh." She stroked the animal charm. "I only have a general sense. Talladega, the local elemental there, senses a place it can't reach anymore."

I reached over and took her hand off the charm so I could get a look at it. "What is that?"

"A honey badger." She smiled as if remembering something pleasant. "Caolan told me it was a perfect representation of my personality."

"Because you don't care about obstacles and bulldoze over them?" I said.

Her smile widened. "Exactly. I store earth magic inside so I have reserve when I can't touch the ground."

I let go of her hand, but she squeezed mine tighter. "The more I learn, the harder it is to go back to my old ways." She sighed. "Flying in airplanes does make me a bit claustrophobic now."

"Still the safest way to travel." I shrugged. "How large is Talladega?"

She took a deep breath as if calming herself and spoke. "He controls the northern part of the state and reaches all the way into Mississippi."

"That's a big region," I said.

"Not nearly as large as some in the Midwest." Grace looked down at my hand and blinked as if surprised she was still holding it. She smiled sheepishly and let go. "Sorry."

I smiled back. "It's okay."

Hannah nudged me and whispered, "Already romancing another one, Cain?"

I leaned back in my chair and gave her a disapproving look. "You know I'm not a romantic."

She scoffed. "That's for damned sure."

After landing in Huntsville, we picked up the rental car and headed toward White House Springs.

Grace fidgeted in the back seat for about ten minutes before reaching forward and grabbing my arm. "Cain, can we stop for a few minutes?"

I pulled off an exit and parked on the side of a backwoods highway. Grace hopped out the instant the car stopped and kicked off her sandals. She closed her eyes and drew in a deep, relaxing breath.

Hannah watched her for a while and shook her head. "Druid powers are really cool, but having to touch the ground all the time would get tiring."

"Caolan isn't like that," I said. "I think Grace is going through a period of adjustment."

"Maybe so." Hannah opened her mouth to say something else when she froze. White light pulsed in her eyes and goosebumps spread up her skin. "Oh, shit." She jumped out of the car and ran into the field.

"Remember what I taught you!" I got out of the car and followed her. "Don't let it control you."

Hannah sat cross-legged on the ground and closed her eyes as a white nimbus around her skin grew brighter. Her mouth moved as she recited a mantra I'd given her to focus her mind. The glow around her skin grew brighter and her body began to shake.

"Keep calm, Hannah." I wanted to touch her but didn't want to break her concentration. "I'm with you." I backed away and glanced at Grace who was staring with awe at Hannah. "Better get back," I told her. "I don't think she's going to control this one in time."

Grace retreated a few steps. "Control what in time?"

"Hannah sometimes gets a buildup of power and it's too much to control." I patterned a shield sigil even though I knew it wouldn't be enough.

"No!" Hannah pounded the ground with her fist. "No!"

Grace ran over to her and pressed her hands against Hannah's temples. She closed her eyes in concentration. Currents of power flashed across the ground. Hannah's trembling slowed and the light began to fade. A moment later, episode had passed.

Hannah stood and hugged Grace. "What did you do?"

"I redirected some of the power into the earth," Grace said. "Talladega thanks you for the energy and says it will help him persevere in a fight against developers."

Brilliantly green grass sprouted from the ground where Hannah had been sitting, growing until it was nearly a foot high. Hannah and Grace were facing away from it and didn't notice.

"He's what?" Hannah squinted as if processing the thought. "How does an elemental fight off people?"

"Not easily, I'm afraid." Grace pointed west. "They're preparing to clear a forest for a subdivision not far from here. Talladega has tried rusting their machines and using animals to chew through cables and hoses, but it hasn't helped much."

"Only way to stop nubs is to make it too expensive for them to make a profit." I shrugged. "If you kill or sabotage them, someone else replaces them."

"It's true, I'm afraid." Grace sighed. "I sabotaged an entire fleet of construction vehicles once and they were back up and running within a week because insurance covered it."

Hannah bared her teeth. "It's an awful feeling when you're defenseless and have no rights to protect you."

"Sounds like you're speaking from experience," Grace said.

A breeze blew Hannah's long black hair from her face, revealing tears on her cheeks. "People used and abused me when I was an orphan. Now Cthulhu is the one pulling my strings."

I pointed to the new grass behind her. "Well, that's kind of cool."

Hannah and Grace glanced back and cooed with pleasure.

Hannah knelt and stroked a blade of grass. "Wow, did I make that?"

Grace blinked a few times then examined the grass. "Uh, that was unexpected. I don't even know what kind of grass this is." She closed her eyes. "Talladega says no seeds in her domain sprout this kind of grass."

"Oh." I shrugged "Maybe we brought some seeds on the bottoms of our shoes."

"Doubtful." Grace shook her head. "More realistically, a bird pooped them out and the extra magic I redirected made them grow super-fast."

Hannah stood and clapped her hands. "I didn't destroy something for once!"

"Good job." I motioned my thumb at the car. "Let's get back on the road."

Grace nodded and recovered her sandals. Hannah skipped back to the car.

We rode in silence for a while, Hannah staring out the window and Grace reading a novel she'd brought along.

Hannah pounded the window with a fist. "No."

I raised an eyebrow. "No what?"

"Let's stop them." She turned to me. "I don't want them to bulldoze the forest."

"How are we supposed to stop them?" I said. "We could destroy their machines, but then what? Insurance will have them back up and running in weeks."

She thought about it. "We could curse the forest, so people get sick when they go inside."

"Think about what you're saying." I glanced at her. "These people aren't evil. They need to make a living."

Hannah scowled. "But the developer is exploiting the land out of greed."

"Maybe."

"She's right," Grace said. "This developer is known for hiring day laborers and paying them next to nothing to do the work. He practically owns the local politicians and can get away with anything."

"How do you know so much about him?" I said.

"It's a nationwide company," she said. "Owen Reynolds, the owner, has his fingers in a lot of pies across the country."

"I wish I had Earthmaker." Hannah clenched her fist as if holding the mighty world-shaping hammer. "I'd build a stone wall all around the forest."

Grace raised an eyebrow. "He'd probably just blast it down."

"Look, can we just concentrate on the mission at hand?" I said.

Hannah folded her arms over her chest and slumped. "Fine."

I felt guilty about it, but as a teenager, Hannah was prone to being impulsive and unreasonable at times. "The best way to handle this would be to bankrupt the corporation, but that would take months. And even if we did, another company would eventually come along. The only way to stop them is to kill off demand. But there are simply too many people who need homes."

"Then let's kill a bunch of people," Hannah said. "It's time for an apocalypse."

I thought back to Thor's and Loki's words and wondered if that was such a far-fetched notion right now. "Maybe so, but don't ask me to start it."

Hannah sighed and stared out the window. "You've got a lot of money, Cain. Maybe buy the land so they can't use it."

I was too busy pondering thoughts about the real possibility of the end days to respond.

We reached White House Springs within the hour. I drove straight into the center of town, curious to see if the town had recovered from the major assault all those months ago. I probably shouldn't have been surprised when we arrived and found A New Hope Bar and Grill was unscathed and open for business.

The fae had covered up the entire incident.

Chapter 6

The restaurant and surrounding buildings looked spotless.

In fact, the only sign that a major supernatural battle had taken place was a tall metal fence surrounding the car junkyard across the road from the grill. I was hungry so I parked in front of the restaurant. "Let's get a bite to eat, then we'll poke around." The parking lot was mostly empty, but I noted a windowless black van sitting on the far edge of the asphalt near the neighboring car dealership.

Grace stepped off the parking lot and into the grass for a moment. She closed her eyes and nodded a few times, then put back on her sandals and followed us inside.

I recognized the hostess and one of the waitresses from our last time here. It wasn't that they'd made an impression on me, but I habitually memorized faces, places, and details because it came in handy when planning an assassination and when remembering how much I tipped the server last time.

We got a booth and ordered water while deciding what to eat.

I looked at Grace. "Talladega have anything useful to say?"

"The dead spot is close," she said. "But it's hard to pinpoint since he can't detect it."

"Just visualize a map with a black space," Hannah said. "Easy peasy."

"Elementals don't visualize overhead maps." Grace bit her lower lip in thought. "They sense geography and everything living in it, but it's not like a body that they can examine."

"Can they see through animals?" Hannah said. "Or maybe pinpoint a landmark near the blank spot?"

"Elementals also don't talk, at least not like animals do." Grace tapped a finger on the table. "You sort of feel what they're conveying to you, like gaining knowledge without words."

Hannah's nose wrinkled. "Sounds complicated."

As they spoke, I observed a table with a pair of individuals in black suits devouring buffalo wings. When the waitress returned, I nodded my head at the pair. "Looks like the CIA is in town."

She chuckled. "Naw, they're with the EPA. There was a toxic spill across the road so they're studying how to clean it up."

"A toxic spill?" I feigned concern. "What happened?"

"They just said one of the cars in Mater Thompson's junkyard must've had a barrel of chemicals hidden in the trunk." She shrugged. "They put up an iron fence and won't let anyone in there."

"Did Mater report it?" I asked.

She shrugged again. "He left town to visit relatives about the same time and hasn't been back."

Grace frowned. "How many EPA agents are in town?"

"Just them right now," the girl said. "There were more, constantly in and out of the place, but I ain't seen them since the first few days."

"Guess we'll stay away from it, then." I pointed to the mild buffalo wings on the menu. "I'll have ten of those, and can your bar make mangoritas?"

She blinked. "Mangorita?"

"Yeah, like a margarita, but mango flavored."

"Oh." She wrote something on her pad. "They can make anything you want, sir."

The others ordered and the server left the table.

"I think we found the spot," Grace said.

Hannah and I exchanged a look.

Grace narrowed her eyes. "What was that look?"

"We fought Daphne and the Firsters in that junkyard," I said. "I blew away Digby, Ingram, and Mead right across the road. That can't be a coincidence."

Hannah turned to Grace. "Would killing bad guys create a spot like that?"

Grace shook her head. "No. Demon magic is the typical cause, which means those two in the black suits might be agents of the Catholic church."

"They don't look it," I said. "If anything, they look like a couple of people who don't have the first clue how nub government officials dress."

"Well, they don't have priest collars." Grace pursed her lips. "And EPA agents don't dress like the Secret Service."

The fake agents didn't have smartphones that I could see, but they cast furtive glances at a nearby table where a man was reading something on his tablet. Most supers adopted the ways of nubs, carrying smartphones, using technology, and so forth because it was easy and helped them fit in. This dynamic duo seemed to have disdain for what they saw. A look inside that van I'd noticed would probably tell me all I needed to know.

"What else besides demons can kill the land?" Hannah asked.

"That's a good question." Grace tapped a finger on her chin. "There are a lot of nasty creatures in the world, but most of them depend on the land for survival. Skinwalkers, werewolves, and even dropbears need a healthy ecosystem or they won't have prey."

Hannah blinked. "What's a dropbear?"

"Pray you never find out," I said.

The waitress returned with our food. I was starving, so I dug in.

The supposed EPA agents paid and left about five minutes later. I wondered how upset they'd be if we tried to peek at their operation behind the fence. I doubted there was anything they could do to stop us.

Hannah finished her meal. "Grace, what's a dropbear?"

Grace ate a French fry. "They look like koalas, but they're carnivorous. They like to hide in trees and drop on people."

Hannah's eyes flared. "That sounds awful!"

Grace nodded. "You can thank Australia for one more thing that'll kill you."

I paid for the food and we went outside. The EPA agents stood next to the black van, both smoking cigarettes. I summoned my staff and took a peek through the true sight scope. Their auras were gray, but a strong magical aura emanated from the van.

Grace frowned. "You look confused, Cain."

"I am confused." I let her look through the scope. "They're not supers, but they seem to have something magical in their van."

"Like magical weapons?" Hannah asked.

I shrugged. "Maybe. Wait here." I strode toward the van.

The woman narrowed her eyes when she realized I was coming toward them. She tapped the man on the shoulder, and he turned around to face me. Neither said a word as I approached.

"I hear there was a bad chemical leak over yonder." I put on my best redneck accent. "What you think happened?"

The woman took a long draw on her cigarette while staring at me. The man leaned against the van. "Why do you ask?"

"There's a sixty-nine Ford Mustang I wanted to buy and restore." I shrugged. "But I was told they ain't letting no one inside."

The woman dropped her cigarette on the ground and squashed it with the toe of her shoe, then walked around to the other side of the van where I couldn't see her. Both agents looked fit, and they had the appearance of seasoned security professionals. They weren't nubs and they weren't supers, but they had some kind of connection to the supernatural world.

"The junkyard is off limits." The man glanced toward the junkyard. "Sixty-nine Mustang is a sweet ride. Does the one you want have the two-eighty-nine v-eight?"

He was testing me. "Sixty-nine Mustangs didn't have two-eighty-nines."

He grunted. "My bad."

The woman returned from the other side of the van. "Hey, Farlow, they said it's okay for them to go inside, but only for a little while."

The man's eyes flicked toward Grace, Hannah, and back to his partner. "You sure about that?"

She nodded. "All of them." There was a bulge under her suit jacket that hadn't been there a moment ago. These two were trying to be slick, but it was obvious they were up to no good.

I flashed a grin. "Thanks, fellas."

A family of four glanced curiously our way as they entered the bar and then we were alone again in the parking lot. I held a hand behind my back and patterned a sigil. The woman's eyes flared. I cast a camouflage blind between us and the restaurant just as she drew a bronze pistol.

In that instant, I knew who we were dealing with. I powered the sigil tattoos on my body for extra speed and strength. A quick flick of a spell knocked the pistol from her hand. The man reached inside his suit jacket. I chopped his elbow right on the funny bone. He cried out in pain. I flicked my fingers through another pattern and jammed the woman's neck, sending a gentle electric shock into her nerves. She dropped like a sack. I twisted Farlow's arm behind his back and perp-walked him to the sliding door on the other side of the van.

Hannah and Grace looked shocked by the sudden violence, but quickly came and dragged the unconscious woman to the other side.

I threw up another camouflage blind to hide us from prying eyes at the neighboring car dealership as we opened the sliding door and shoved the pair inside. The tall cargo van was nearly empty except for a rack with bronze pistols, rifles and an assortment of gadgets confirming who I thought the agents were.

A monitor mounted on the wall displayed the feed from cameras watching the outside of the junkyard fence from every angle. It was the sole example of nub technology inside the van, probably because the faction they were with despised it.

I knew why they wore black, I knew why they were in good shape, and I knew why they didn't have supernatural auras. These people were mechanist constables. The upper crust of their society consisted of apprentices, engineers, and the crème de la crème, inventors. The worker class, the grays, were treated like sub-humans. These two were the security and soldiers of the guild. They were babysitting the junkyard, hiding whatever secret waited inside.

I sat the man down on an office chair in front of the surveillance screen and bound his hands behind his back with a quick spell.

He looked at the woman. "If she's dead, I'll fucking kill you."

"She's fine, just unconscious." I sat down in the chair next to his and motioned the others inside the van. Once Hannah and Grace were inside, I closed the sliding door and had them sit in the driver and passenger seats.

I studied him for a moment. "What are mechanists doing in White House Springs, Alabama?"

His eyes flared. "I don't know what you're talking about."

I stood, picked up one of the pistols from the rack, and fiddled with the clockwork magazine. "Nubs don't make anything like this. Let's cut to the chase, shall we? Why are mechanist constables guarding a junkyard?"

He continued to glare but remained silent.

I picked up a device with an antenna on it and flicked the switch on the side. Clockwork gears ticked. The antenna rotated and bent until it pointed at Hannah. I switched it off and the antenna straightened. I turned it on again, this time orienting it toward Grace, but the antenna once again pointed at Hannah.

Concern flickered in Farlow's eyes.

I raised an eyebrow. "What's got you worried?"

He shook his head.

I picked up a bronze case with smoothly rounded edges. Farlow flinched, obviously not wanting me to open it. He didn't seem concerned enough that it might blow us to pieces, but it probably held information. The latch was secured by a sigil pad. I plucked revealer mist from my utility belt and sprayed it. It adhered to the oil from the fingers of those who'd used the pad, revealing only a single pattern.

It wasn't a pattern I was familiar with, but I didn't really need to be to trace it.

The man clenched his teeth and strained against his bonds. "Leave it."

I traced the pattern and the latch clicked. A small lens rose from the bottom of the case, angling to point at a screen on the inside of the top of the case. "What's the point of such antiquated tech?" I shook my head. "Laptops are so much smaller and more convenient."

He bared his teeth. "Fuck the nubs."

Hannah snickered. "It's no wonder mechanists don't have smartphones."

There were several small reels of film tucked into a space on the bottom of the case. I pulled a lever and an arm emerged from the mechanism beneath the lens. The reel slid onto the arm and another flip of the lever pulled the reel inside the machine. I flicked a switch and a clockwork mechanism began to tick. A light projected from a pinhole in the projector and was magnified by the glass lens, which then cast the image on the screen.

I turned to Farlow. "I hope this isn't a porno."

He glared at me. "You're Cain."

"At your service." I looked at him expectantly. "And you are Farlow."

He glared silently.

I wasn't terribly surprised he knew my name. Layla and I had infiltrated a mechanist stronghold a little over a week ago in search of a map leading to the lost armory of Hephaestus. Then we'd stolen a mechanist submarine and used it to travel Cthulhu's deepways to Oblivion, destroyed the weapons in the armory, and stolen another submarine the mechanists used to pursue us.

Instead of fighting me, however, they'd ended up fighting Torvin Rayne and an ogress named Norna. As far as I knew, there had been no surviving mechanists. Torvin and Norna died later by my hand.

"Oh my god, Cain." Hannah drew my attention back to the projector. "Horatio survived!"

I turned back to the projector. Horatio's bruised and battered face was on the screen. He appeared to be in a hospital bed. A timestamp in the upper corner showed it to be from three days ago. He was talking, but there was no sound.

I fiddled with the controls and found a slider that increased the volume. I turned a knob to rewind to the beginning of the video so I could hear what I'd missed.

Horatio drew a rasping breath. "My brethren, what I am about to say has been a closely guarded secret. Several months ago, I received a letter detailing information about a device within the armory that would grant us immense power. Unfortunately, the letter had been damaged in transit, and for reasons that will soon become clear, I could not request more information. What it hinted at would allow us to conquer not only this world, but all the worlds."

Farlow's eyes flared.

I paused the recording. "You haven't seen this?"

He shook his head. "The inventors who visited the site left it with us. They went over to the junkyard and came back looking like they'd just stared death in the face. They ordered us to build a wall immediately, so we did."

Now that I didn't need him for info, he was all about spilling his guts. "Cool story, bro." I resumed the video.

"According to a surviving paragraph of the damaged portion of the letter, there were instructions that would allow us to easily find and defeat the guardians of the armory. Had those not been missing, we would have conquered Gaia long ago." Horatio groaned and took a moment to breathe before continuing. "You might wonder why I would trust such a letter. At first, I did not. But after careful, scientific analysis, I realized that this letter must be telling the truth. Because this letter was sent by an individual I trust above anyone else in this universe or any other."

He took another shuddering breath. "It was sent by me."

Farlow gasped. "That explains it then."

I held up a hand to quiet him and continued to watch.

"In a dimension closely resembling ours, I was already successful in raiding the armory. Inside the armory, I found a device that allows inter-dimensional communication and travel." Horatio smiled as if he just won the lottery. "Obviously, my other self didn't know how to travel with the device but was able to send across an inanimate object. He transmitted it into the castle at Deepvale, but it materialized where an apprentice had moments before spilled a bottle of ink." He huffed. "Thus, making much of the letter unreadable."

"This is crazy," Hannah said. "Noctua mentioned the multiverse but to know that someone like Horatio conquered Gaia on one of them is scary."

I paused the recording, stunned by the reality we now faced. "Yeah. And if he's sending messages across dimensions, that's even scarier."

"I'm feeling a bit lost." Grace looked from the frozen image to me. "There are multiple dimensions?"

"Yeah." I waved off the question. "We'll talk more about it later." I resumed the recording.

Horatio scowled. "Because of Cain, our plans were foiled. But I survived and was able to sneak into the armory after the ogress left me for dead. I found part of the device mentioned in the letter and hid it on my body before stowing away on the submarine Cain stole from us. The fool released me without ever realizing what I had on my person."

I grimaced and paused the video. "Oops."

"I can't believe you just let him go, Cain." Hannah tutted.

"What was I supposed to do, imprison him in my basement for eternity?" I shook my head. "Not my job." I'd considered other options after taking Horatio prisoner. With his faction all but destroyed, killing him didn't seem necessary, and I didn't want to be responsible for clothing and feeding a prisoner. The Guild Knights might have taken him off my hands, but they might have been just as likely to try to arrest me again.

Two days after capturing him, I'd taken him across town and dumped him. I hadn't searched him because, as far as I knew, everything in the armory was destroyed. I resumed the video.

Horatio held up a cube of finely woven silver mesh. Tiny gears clicked and rotated beneath the surface. It was an intricate work of art. "This will grant us victory, but to use it, we must find the blood of a god. There are rumors a battle between gods happened months ago in a small town called White House Springs. You will take the device there and pray that the blood of a god was spilled. I've included the rest of the instructions in written form for you."

He coughed again. "Once I am well, I will rejoin the project, and together we will march to victory against the gods."

The projector clicked and the screen went white.

Chills ran up my spine. I turned to Farlow. "Where is the cube now?"

He didn't answer, but his eyes flicked in the direction of the junkyard.

"They must have found Daphne's blood." Hannah looked out the front window of the van toward the junkyard. "They must have opened a gateway to another dimension!"

"I feel like I'm in way over my head." Grace looked at me uneasily. "You think this cube could be causing the dead spot of land?"

"Maybe." I looked at Farlow. "Tell me everything that happened."

Now that the video was over, he wasn't talking anymore. He just stared at me blankly as if he didn't know what to think anymore. I suspected he didn't know much of anything. Mechanist inventors must have brought the device here and found Daphne's blood. Layla had hit the girl's shoulder with a thrown dagger so there'd been plenty of it.

I suspected the mechanists had used the device, but things hadn't gone as planned.

I stared at Farlow. "Tell me what happened."

He continued staring at me defiantly.

"Tell you what," I said. "I'm going to knock you out. When you wake up, you'll be lying in a ditch somewhere with a thick purple dildo shoved up your ass, and I'll have sent pictures to mechanist headquarters."

He looked taken aback by the threat but shook it off and glared at me again. "Do your worst."

Grace giggled. "Cain, I don't know about you, but I'd love to see this torture technique of yours."

I raised an eyebrow. "Is there a sex shop in this town?"

Farlow paled. "You can't be serious."

Hannah smiled menacingly at him. "Oh, you bet your ass he's serious."

Grace giggled again. "I see what you did there."

I picked up a metal rod from the desk with the laptops. "When's the last time you had a colonoscopy, Farlow?"

His face grew even paler. "We drove here with Inventors Darby and Chadwick, but they didn't tell us anything. They had us search the junkyard inch by inch until we found a dagger with blood on it. Then they told us to leave them while they ran an experiment. Moments later, they ran out, faces pale as ghosts, and told us to barricade the junkyard."

I sensed he was telling the truth. Something had gone horribly wrong in the junkyard, and it seemed the only way to know for sure was to go over there ourselves.

Chapter 7

"I remember seeing that cube from the film on the bottom of Noctua's pedestal." Hannah's forehead wrinkled. "I'll bet she'd know more about that cube."

I nodded. "One way to find out." The little owl had given me a whistle I could use to communicate with her. Now seemed like a prime time to do it.

"I feel a little lost," Grace said. "Who's Noctua?"

I shook my head at Farlow. "I hope what your people did isn't permanent. There's a reason I destroyed all the weapons in the armory. No one should have godlike power."

Farlow bared his teeth at me. "The gods least of all, may they burn."

"Maybe not, but at least they haven't destroyed the world yet." I checked the other three films in the case, but they were blank.

"Burn the gods?" Grace scoffed. "What insanity is this?"

I sighed. "These mechanists are part of the Pandora Combine, a faction that wants to enslave or kill the gods."

Grace's eyes widened. "Impossible."

Farlow growled. "Not with the weapons from the armory. If Cain hadn't interfered, we'd already have the gods on their knees."

"Along with most of the world," I said. "I practically rearranged an entire region of Oblivion just so I could destroy those weapons. I knocked down an entire mountain with a hammer." I shook my head. "There's no way anyone, especially someone hell-bent on revenge, should have that kind of power. What your people want to do with the cube is a perfect example of that."

With a roar, Farlow struggled against his bonds, cursing and shouting. "You ruined everything, you bastard!"

I knocked him out with a jolt to the neck and he slumped in the chair.

Grace shuddered. "I feel so out of the loop on everything. Maybe you should give me a quick rundown."

So I did, going all the way back to my decision to save Hannah. I figured it was important she know about the various factions vying for power.

When I was finished, Grace stared at me for a long moment. "I can't believe you were able to repeat all of that with a straight face. It sounds like something out of a madman's dream."

"Which part?" I said.

She laughed. "All of it!"

Hannah patted Grace's back. "You don't get out much do you?"

"Apparently not." Grace looked at the unconscious mechanists. "What do we do about them?"

"Kill them, obviously." Hannah cracked her knuckles. "And hang the corpses from street-lamps to strike fear into the hearts of their comrades."

Grace's mouth dropped open.

Hannah burst into laughter. "Just kidding! I might have felt like that at one time, but Cain showed me it's not always about killing your enemies."

"Strange lesson coming from an assassin," Grace said.

"I'm not an assassin anymore." I studied the slumbering mechanists. "First things first. We need to find out how to counteract whatever these bozos did." I reached into my utility belt and withdrew the owl-shaped whistle Noctua had given me. She'd told me to simply blow on it and I could communicate with her.

So I gave it a toot.

When I blew into it, it hooted like an owl in the night. I lowered the whistle and waited. And waited. And waited some more. A good five minutes passed before I decided to give it another toot. But as I lifted it to my lips, I heard a faint voice. At first, I couldn't figure out where it was coming from, and then realized it was emanating from the tip of the whistle. I put it up to my ear.

"Hello? Cain?" Noctua said.

I wasn't sure where to speak, so I just talked into the whistle. "Yes, it's Cain. We need your help."

The reply came two or three minutes later. "There is a significant time lag since we are on different planes. I suggest you ask everything at once for more efficiency."

I paused to formulate an efficient question, and then spoke into the whistle. "Horatio, the mechanist, found a clockwork cube that may have come from your pedestal. His followers used old blood from a demigoddess to activate it. Now the land where they tried it is dying. How can I stop it? What does this cube do?"

The answer came nearly five minutes later. "That is quite odd. There is no function of the cube that I'm aware of that would blight the land." She paused. "The device did not perform its function because they used old blood. Simply use fresh godlike blood, Hannah's will suffice, and the device will function properly. The cube is a multidimensional transceiver that allowed me to observe other realities and record significant developments, but it is only one of three parts to the Tetron that adorned the base of my pedestal. There is a sphere that allowed me to observe other planes, and a pyramid that linked the cube and sphere so I could perceive planes in other dimensions. Hephaestus told me that the devices were activated by the blood of gods so that if they fell into the wrong hands, they would not be able to restart them. Now that I consider it, I do not remember him ever putting blood into it. Perhaps when the devices were separated after the destruction of the armory, they ceased to function."

Her answer troubled me, mainly because if Noctua didn't know why the cube was killing the land, then only Hephaestus would have the answer. I digested the information and formulated another query. "There must be a correlation between the cube and the dying land. Are you certain there's nothing in its function that would cause this?"

"Not that I know of," Noctua replied after the delay. "I suggest finding the cube and using Hannah's blood with it to see if that counteracts the effect."

Hannah nodded. "Let's give it a shot."

"Thanks, Noctua." I tucked the whistle back into my utility belt.

Hannah frowned. "I thought Noctua knew everything."

"Yeah, so did I." I idly tapped projector case. "Maybe we should revisit Oblivion and make sure the other parts of the pedestal didn't survive. We don't want anyone else gaining universal surveillance."

Grace paled. "That would be catastrophic. There would be no safe place to hide."

I held up a hand. "We don't know that it works quite like that. I suggest we try to fix the dying land and go from there."

Hannah nodded. "I hope it works."

"So do I." Grace shivered.

I unbound the spell holding Farlow to the chair and sprawled him out on the floor next to his companion. They'd be out for a few hours—plenty of time for us to do what we needed to do, I hoped.

Hannah studied the tracking device that pointed to her. "I don't like knowing they have a god tracker."

"Yeah, as backwards as they are about some things, their inventions are pretty impressive." I took the tracker, summoned my staff, and slashed it in half with the brightblade. "There are probably plenty more where that came from."

"I hope not." Hannah opened the passenger door and climbed out. I left through the sliding door and left the slumbering mechanists inside. We walked across the street to the junkyard fence.

A gate with a clockwork lock guarded the entrance. The mechanists had somehow erected heavy plates of steel all around the perimeter, probably with the help of their clockwork exoskeletons, or exos, as they called them. I skipped the front gate and walked around the perimeter to the back. In addition to the plate steel, rings of razor wire guarded the top. I didn't really feel like trying to scale ten feet of smooth metal and dealing with razor wire, so I summoned my staff.

A press of the sigil on the hilt and the brightblade hummed to life. I pressed the tip against the metal and the energy blade penetrated the steel like cold butter. Once it was through, I slowly carved a nice wide door. Molten metal hissed and dropped to the ground. The sliced chunk toppled inward and thudded into the dirt.

"Watch the edges, they're scalding hot." I slipped inside and the others followed. There were far fewer cars in the junkyard than last time, and most of them were stacked against the northern side of the enclosure.

The cracking sound of shifting ice drew us around a stack of cars. We didn't find ice, but we did discover the source of the dying land. The ground was gray as ash for nearly twenty feet in diameter. A crack a foot long and an inch wide occupied the middle. The silver cube hovered a few inches above the blight, the only spot of color in the area.

Black vines, some thick as my arm and others thin as veins, spread from inside the crack across the ground and to the edges of the blight. They seemed to pulsate with darkness and cold. The cracking sound seemed to emanate from the air around the phenomenon.

"What in the gods' names is this?" Grace knelt next to one of the vines and gingerly touched it. She snapped her hand back with a hiss.

"What happened?" I stepped back from the vines.

She showed me the tip of her finger. The skin looked burned. "No, they're so cold, they killed the skin on contact."

"Whoa." Hannah backed away a step. "This one's already an inch closer to my foot than a moment ago."

I noticed one of the veiny vines was inching toward my foot as well. "Let's fix this before it gets worse." I tentatively tapped a foot on the blackened land. When my foot didn't fall off, I figured it was safe to step onto. I touched my brightblade against one of the vines. The energy sparked and popped like water in hot oil. Most notably, the vine wasn't even singed.

Grace grimaced. "My gods, they must be too cold for your weapon to affect them."

"Whatever this is, it's really bad news." I stepped into the blackened area, careful to avoid the vines. Even then, I felt coldness emanating all around me, and the air seemed thinner and harder to breathe.

Hannah and Grace followed close behind. When we reached the crack in the middle, I examined the cube. A fleck of crimson near a tiny hole in the top seemed to indicate where the blood went. I produced a small dagger. Hannah extended a hand without me asking. I poked the tip of a finger and blood welled on the skin. Hannah dripped blood into the tiny hole in the top of the cube.

The cube flared. Bright energy pulsated from within it. The ground beneath our feet trembled, and the vines began smoking and hissing. The crack rumbled shut and the blighted earth began to resume a normal color.

Grace breathed a sigh of relief, and we did the same.

"Thank the gods." I blew out a breath. "I have a feeling that thing would've spread until it killed the entire planet."

"What gods-awful weapon would unleash those vines?" Grace shivered. "I've never seen anything like them."

Hannah turned in a circle. "Uh, where did the cube go?"

It was no longer hovering where it had been or anywhere else nearby. "What the hell?" I banished my staff and used a spell to dig a shallow hole in the ground where it had been. "Did it fall into the crack?"

"Definitely not," Hannah said. "It was on the ground. I looked away for a moment and then it was gone."

"I'm afraid I wasn't looking." Grace put a hand on the ground and closed her eyes. Her forehead pinched into a V and she yanked back her hand. "This can't be right."

Hannah frowned. "What can't be?"

"Talladega is acting strange." Grace shook her head. "She doesn't seem to recognize me."

"Maybe the damage to the land gave her amnesia," Hannah said.

Grace shook her head. "No, I don't think it's that." She turned to walk away and abruptly stopped. "Where's the fence?"

I'd been so focused on finding the cube I hadn't even noticed that the steel-plated fence was gone. The cars were still piled up, but not in the same pattern as before. I looked across the street at the restaurant. The black van was gone, and the building was dark. The car dealership was boarded up, the lot was empty and overgrown with weeds. The town looked deserted.

"Oh, shit." I dropped to my knees and started looking under nearby cars in case the cube had rolled under there. But it hadn't. It was nowhere to be found.

Hannah turned in a circle, eyes widening as she realized what I'd just seen. "What did we do? Did we destroy the town?"

"Where did our rental car go?" Grace hopped atop a junk car and looked around. "Everything's changed."

I took out my phone, but there was no signal. Hannah and Grace did the same with identical results.

I spotted a minivan next to a motel down the street. "I don't know what happened, but we need to find out." I weaved between junk cars and headed for the road.

Hannah stopped outside an abandoned mini-mart. The windows were broken, and the place looked as if it had been ransacked. She ducked beneath the inside door handle and returned with a newspaper that was several months old.

The headline read: *World Leaders Reject Ultimatum.*

Hannah read the body of the article. "The mysterious organization known as Umbra issued a demand that world leaders cede authority to them. The UN called an emergency session in which they unanimously rejected the demand. Shortly after that, a massive tsunami wiped Sydney, Australia completely off the map. New York, Washington, D.C., London, and many other major cities near large rivers or other bodies of water were also struck. Electricity and most communications along the east and west coast of the United States are down. The US military issued a statement that all citizens should shelter in place."

Hannah read the rest in silence. "Cain, I don't think we're in Kansas anymore."

Chapter 8

Hannah was right. Either we'd destroyed the world as we knew it, or using the cube had caused an unintended side effect. But I wasn't ready to jump to conclusions just yet, as likely as it seemed. There was only one being who might provide answers. I took out Notcua's owl whistle and blew it.

The owl answered a few minutes later. "Who is this?"

"It's Cain. Who else would it be?"

"Cain?" A moment of silence followed, exacerbated by the minutes-long lag time from being in separate planes. "How very interesting."

Grace and Hannah frowned in confusion.

"You just talked to us a little while ago," Hannah said.

"Is that Hannah?" Noctua sounded surprised and intrigued.

Hanna scoffed. "Yes, of course it's me."

The lag time between messages was maddening, so I gave my next question some thought before sending it. "The mechanists used old blood from Daphne to activate the cube they took from your pedestal. It created a crack in the ground that was killing the earth. There were black vines coming from the crack and they were so cold, they killed skin on contact. Hannah used her blood on the cube from your pedestal to fix the problem. The ground repaired itself, but the cube vanished and everything in the world has changed. Did we corrupt the timeline?"

Noctua's reply addressed Hannah's last statement since she probably hadn't gotten my question yet. "You sound very much like your old self, Hannah."

I put a finger to my lips to cut down on confusion from the communication lag and waited on Noctua's response to my question. I wasn't surprised by the answer.

"Cain, if you did not have the pyramid and sphere to regulate the cube, then it seems you inadvertently created a rift in the dimensional barrier between your world and this one. The cube was at the precise origin of the rift and did not cross over with you, so it's still in your dimension. D-d-dimension." Noctua repeated the word, her voice slowing like a toy with a dying battery. "Apologies. I was damaged and am not myself." She continued where she'd left off. "You are not the Hannah and Cain of this world." There was a whir and clicking as if she fluttered her clockwork wings. "It seems the bad blood from Daphne only partially created a rift, instead opening a hole to the u-u-underverse, a d-d-dimension of negative energy. The freezing vines you saw would have sapped energy from your dimension until a-a-all life ceased to exist. It is good you repaired the damage."

Realization dawned on Hannah's and Grace's faces at about the same time my brain accepted Noctua's information. We had crossed over into an alternate dimension where a group called Umbra had apparently destroyed civilization as we knew it. I wondered if this was the universe the other Horatio lived in, or if the same calamity had befallen other parallel dimensions.

I asked the next question that came to mind. "Noctua, how do we get back to our dimension?"

"You must retrieve the Tetron from my pedestal," she said. "I'm afraid the armory was ransacked, and the pedestal was taken with everything else, so I don't know where it is."

"Oh, gods." Grace put a hand on her mouth. "Who ransacked the armory?"

"I am having d-d-difficulty speaking." Noctua's words slowed. Static hissed and the whistle went silent.

I spoke into the whistle again. "Noctua, please repeat. Are you okay?"

We waited and waited, but no response came.

"This isn't good at all." Hannah stared at the whistle. "What's the Tetron?"

"Must be the name for the cube," I said.

Hannah threw up her hands. "We've got to find the cube in this dimension and steal it from whoever took it from the armory?"

"Sounds like it." I nodded at the minivan. "Let's see if I can get that thing running."

The windows to the minivan were cloudy with filth. I tugged on the door and was greeted by a fully clothed skeleton slumped over the steering wheel.

Hannah gasped. "Oh my god."

Grace peered at the body. "Whoever it was has been dead for months. I think it must have happened around the time that newspaper was published."

I looked around. "Judging from the absence of cars, I suspect the people here evacuated. Looks like this guy didn't make it."

Grace nodded. "Looks like it."

I gingerly tugged on the clothing and managed to get the skeleton out of the car, much to Hannah's dismay. The key fob was in the jeans pocket.

"Eww!" She watched me dust off the seat with my hand. "That's dead body dust! You're okay driving a car with death cooties?"

I waved a hand around at the abandoned town. "I don't see any other viable options." The car had a push-button start which did nothing when I pushed it. I popped the hood and used an electricity spell to trickle life back into the battery. While we waited on the battery to charge, I took the skeleton's driver's license and examined it. The man in the picture was grossly overweight, if his face was anything to go by. He also had a medical emergency card listing a heart issue and diabetes.

I imagined the stress of evacuation had probably killed him. The poor son of a bitch apparently stopped at the local bank to empty his accounts and never made it out of the parking lot.

The dashboard indicators flickered on within ten minutes. The fuel tank was half full, which came as a surprise. I'd figured the man had died while the engine was running.

Hannah pointed to the man's cell phone. "Can you charge that?"

I shook my head. "It's not quite as straightforward as a car battery." I looked in the center console and found a cord hooked up to the USB port inside. "But this ought to work." I pushed the starter button. The minivan sputtered and came to life. I blew on Noctua's owl whistle again and set it on the console so I'd hear if she responded, but the ensuing silence seemed to guarantee we were on our own.

"What now?" Grace opened the sliding door and grimaced at the clothes, furniture, and other odds and ends stuffed into the back.

I opened the sliding door on my side and started tossing stuff into the parking lot. "Now we drive back to Sanctuary. Hopefully the me in this dimension has more information about what happened."

Hannah shuddered. "That's so weird to even think about. There's another version of me walking around this world."

"Presumably," Grace said. "Noctua sounded surprised to hear from you. Maybe you're dead here."

I sat in the driver's seat and browsed through the rest of the newspaper. It was a very thin edition with mostly local stories about how the disasters in major cities were affecting the lives of citizens in Huntsville. "Were there any other newspapers in the store?" I asked Hannah.

She shook her head. "The place was cleaned out. If apocalyptic movies are anything to go by, I think the scavenging happened after everyone left town."

"Probably." I displayed the map on my phone. The GPS seemed to work, but there was no cell signal. That meant the nub satellites orbiting Gaia were still functional. I checked the route. "We'll head east and then south through Birmingham. Keep an eye out for places to get supplies. I have a feeling food will be scarce."

Hannah grimaced. "I love reading apocalypse stories, but I don't want to live one!"

"What if the gateway is still there?" Grace pursed her lips. "Maybe we can go back where the cube was and walk back through?"

"I walked back and forth over the same area ten times while looking for the cube." I shook my head. "It was a one-way door."

"Gods damn it." Grace squeezed her eyes shut. "We're going to be trapped here for a while, aren't we?"

"Don't think about it." I patted the steering wheel. "Put one foot in front of the other, and we'll be home before you know it."

Hannah scoffed. "Not if our last adventure is any indication."

I took the highway south and then turned southeast so we could reach I-65 south into Birmingham. The highway was mostly empty aside from a few abandoned cars here and there, but once we got on the interstate, things changed. The northbound and southbound lanes were clogged with abandoned vehicles that had been heading north away from the city.

Hannah rolled down a window and stared at abandoned cars along the roadside. "This is starting to feel a lot like the zombie apocalypse."

I nodded. "Yeah it is." I was able to navigate past much of the traffic jam using the median and shoulders, but we were still twenty miles outside of town when a clogged bridge prevented us from going any further.

Grace frowned. "How are we going to get through this mess?"

That was a damned good question. I stopped the van and checked the map app on my phone for alternate routes. If we backtracked five miles there was a highway that also went south, but I felt certain it would be just as jammed up as the interstate.

"What now?" Hannah said.

I turned off the van and got out. "We walk."

Hannah grabbed the deceased van owner's cell phone from the center console. "It's got fifty percent charge. Maybe he took some video before he died."

"Maybe so." I climbed on the hood of the van and looked across the blocked bridge. The cars sat in relatively neat rows, doors closed and glass intact. The windshields were filthy from neglect, so I summoned my staff and looked through the true sight scope. A semi-truck cab held a corpse. The other vehicles were empty. There were no signs of magic use, but those would have faded by now anyway.

Grace climbed up beside me. "Thoughts?"

I gave her a peek through the scope. "In a mass panic situation, people will flee by any means possible. Windows would be smashed, doors would be open, and cars would be in the median and on the shoulders." I waved a hand at the bridge ahead and the traffic on the road behind us. "But it looks to me as if everyone calmly got out of the cars, closed the doors, and just left them."

"No zombies?" Hannah sounded disappointed.

"Don't get your hopes up." I banished my staff and hopped to the ground. "Tidal waves might have destroyed coastal cities, but something less catastrophic happened here."

"Maybe armed soldiers forced everyone out at gunpoint," Grace said.

I waggled a hand. "Maybe. But I think we would've seen signs of panic or damage to the cars."

"What if it's mind control?" Hannah pressed fingers to her temples and made an eerie sound. "It's got to be something magical."

Grace nodded. "I agree."

"Well, if Umbra took all the weapons from the armory, there's no doubt they found something that allows them to use mind control." I blew out a breath and shook my head. "This is why we can't have bad things, people."

Grace narrowed her eyes. "You mean nice things?"

"There's nothing good about the shit in the armory," I said. I tapped the cell phone in Hannah's hand. "What's on that?"

She turned on the screen and flicked through the picture gallery. There were countless pictures of food and video reviews of restaurants the man had visited. Hannah chuckled. "Looks like this dude was all about Instagramming his food."

Hannah backed out of the album and found a few images and videos sitting in the main folder. She clicked on the most recent one.

The chubby face of the dead man filled the screen. "Hey followers, I hope everyone is alive and well with all the shit going down. Even people here in my podunk town are talking about leaving and heading further inland. But a man's gotta eat, even when he's running from impending doom. So stay tuned to my Instagram for my apocalyptic road trip food review." He gave a thumbs up and the video ended.

Grace scoffed. "The nubs are so self-absorbed it's a wonder their society even functions."

Hannah nodded. "True story." She flicked through the other videos, but none of them contained useful info. "I guess this phone is a bust." Her forehead wrinkled and she looked at the bridge ahead. "But if all those people willingly got out of their cars and left, I'll bet they left behind some phones."

I grunted. "I'll bet you're right." I walked to the nearest car and opened the door. A purse held a large phone with a bedazzled pink case. I pulled off the case and took the phone and charger. An SUV held three phones, two of which looked like they belonged to kids, if the cases were anything to go by.

I brought back my haul to the minivan. There were several USB ports in the car, so I was able to plug in all the phones at once. I started the engine and let it idle while we waited. Most of the phones came on within ten minutes, so we started going through them. Hannah checked the kids' phones first.

"I don't know what's happening!" An exasperated man with a beard sat in the driver's seat of the SUV where I'd found the phone. He peered through the windshield and shook his head. "Traffic just stopped moving."

"What's that sound?" The woman in the front passenger seat leaned forward.

The microphone picked up a faint discordant melody.

"God, why did we even leave home?" The view panned to a teenaged girl in the seat next to the holder of the phone. "There's no way a tidal wave could hit Birmingham and now we're stuck in stupid traffic!" She moved her hands through patterns as she spoke, apparently directing them at the person holding the camera.

Hannah paused the video. "Is that sign language?"

Grace nodded. "Looks like it."

Hannah resumed the video.

"My god, what's that behind us?" The man turned, facing the camera.

The camera turned. Sunlight glinted off a bronze nacelle. The vessel was perhaps half a mile away but there was no mistaking the shape. It was a small airship and almost certainly of mechanist design, if the bronze color was any indication. A basket hung beneath the gondola and inside it stood a person.

The eerie music steadily grew louder. The camera panned back to the girl who was staring slack-jawed at the airship. Suddenly, her eyes went blank. She calmly turned, opened the car door and slid out. Her door closed in unison with the front two doors as her parents did the same thing.

"Mom?" a young boy said. "Dad?" His voice was slurred like that of someone who'd once had their hearing but lost it.

The camera faced out of the rear window. The airship was close enough to make out a man standing in the basket beneath the gondola turning the crank on a brass box that hung from a leather strap around his neck. It looked like the kind of music box buskers used for their dancing monkeys.

Droves of people calmly climbed out of their cars and followed the airship. Their faces were completely slack and void of emotion.

I paused the video. "Oh, shit. That's one of the music boxes from the armory."

Hannah frowned. "I don't remember music boxes."

"Layla dumped a cartload of them in the furnace after you left to fight Torvin." I looked away from the phone. "Hephaestus made them for Ares. They were supposed to allow his commanders complete control over their soldiers, but instead, they just made the people passive and compliant, so they were dumped in the armory."

I resumed the video.

The boy gasped and dropped his phone. It landed at an upward angle on the seat, showing a young boy with hearing aids clambering from the car as he shouted for his parents. He slammed the door and the top of his head bobbed past the window.

The rest of the video was an endless parade of people mindlessly following the gondola. I stopped it after a few minutes.

Grace grimaced. "My gods, a music box that steals your willpower? What other horrors were in the armory?"

"Too many to list," I said.

Hannah sucked in a breath between her teeth. "Do you think Atlanta is empty just like Birmingham?"

I nodded. "Probably so, but we need a home base and Sanctuary is the best place for that."

"What if the Cain from this dimension is there?" Grace asked.

"Then we tell him what's up and try to gain his help." It felt strange considering such an option, but it wouldn't be the strangest thing I'd ever encountered.

Hannah looked out at the cars. "What do you think happened to all those people?"

I bit the inside of my lip and gave it some thought. "I have no idea. If Umbra didn't hesitate to destroy major cities, then there's no telling what they did to those people."

"Those music boxes remind me of the Pied Piper of Hamelin," Grace said. "They could have led the people into the river and drowned them."

"Yeah." It was a grim thought, but likely. Umbra, whoever they were, had taken over Gaia with the most dangerous weapons in the worlds.

Chapter 9

I grimaced. "I hope this alternate dimension has made my point about why we destroyed the weapons from the armory."

Hannah laughed. "Lesson learned. Can we go home now, please?"

"I wish." I blew out a breath. "Too bad Layla and Aura aren't here to learn the lesson too."

Hannah tapped a finger on her chin. "Why did Umbra bother giving the UN an ultimatum? Why not just use the music boxes to mind-control them into signing over power?"

"Because the music boxes don't use mind control." I tapped the boy's phone. "They make people passive and compliant. Those people left the car and followed the music without any verbal cues. Grace is right—it's like the pied piper."

"But we learned something." Grace rewound the video to the boy. "The music boxes don't work on deaf people."

"I don't think he was completely deaf." I zoomed in on the hearing aids. "He was hearing impaired. The music didn't seem to work on him through his hearing aids."

"The music in the video also didn't affect us." Hannah quirked her lips. "Let's find some earplugs just in case."

"Good idea." I turned off the van. "In the meantime, let's get walking." Unless we figured out how to get through the car logjam, it was going to be a long walk.

We were about an hour into our journey south when I spotted a possible solution to our dilemma. A pair of Harley cruisers sat next to each other beneath an overpass. It seemed the riders had pulled over to rest before the music box called to them. The batteries were dead, but the gas tanks were half full.

I trickle-charged the batteries. When we tested the ignition minutes later, the motorcycles roared to life.

"You comfortable driving one?" I asked Grace.

She nodded. "I love motorcycles."

Hannah sighed wistfully. "I want to drive one."

"Have you ever driven before?" I asked

She shook her head.

"Maybe we'll start you off in a car." I mussed her hair. "I'm not ready to die just yet." I handed her a helmet.

Hannah laughed. "At least it would be an exciting death." She climbed onto the bike behind me and we rolled out.

Thanks to the neat rows of abandoned cars, we were able to drive down the right shoulder for much of the distance. Rail guards and bridges narrowed the shoulder in places where a car wouldn't have been able to pass, but the motorcycles fit easily.

We reached the outskirts of Birmingham late in the afternoon, at which point I was starting to get hungry. I pointed toward an exit with several gas stations and restaurants and we pulled off to take a look around and see what we could scavenge. A massive Costco offered the best chance of finding food that might not have perished in the months since the mechanist takeover.

The parking lot was still packed with cars. It seemed shoppers had been lured away before finishing hoarding toilet paper and other necessities. Abandoned shopping carts still full of items sat in the parking lot. Any food items had been picked clean by scavengers and birds.

The doors to the store were boarded up and locked. A quick slash with the brightblade opened them right away. It seemed strange the doors would be locked, but it was likely preparations to close down had been in progress once everyone learned of the tsunamis destroying coastal cities.

The first thing I noticed once inside were the numerous globs of crusted bird crap on the polished concrete floor and displays. There were only a few pigeons in the rafters, not nearly enough to have caused the mess. I thought back to the locked doors and realized I'd come to the wrong conclusion.

This place wasn't abandoned, and whoever lived here was probably supplementing their diet with pigeons. The hairs on the back of my neck prickled. I sensed eyes watching us from nearby. Movement atop one of the tall shelves caught my attention.

"We're not alone," I murmured.

A man stepped from concealment behind a shelf, a shotgun held at the ready. He was balding, and a patchy beard covered old acne scars. His gaze drifted to Hannah and a nasty grin spread across his face. "Well, would you look at this? Strangers bearing gifts!"

I flicked my hand in a pattern and cast a revelation spell. It drifted out in a radius, a barely visible vapor that sensed everything in the vicinity.

"I see that itchy trigger finger." The man smirked. "My boys are locked onto you from three different positions."

Apparently, he'd mistaken my spellcasting for wishing I had a gun. I pointedly turned my gaze to each of the high spots where his snipers lurked. "There, there, and there."

He frowned. "Well, shit, boys. We got ourselves a former military man."

"You could say that," I said. "Perhaps we could exchange information. We're new in town and would like to know what happened to all the people."

That drew a round of guffaws from the man and his concealed crew.

"You been hiding under a rock, boy?" The man shook his head. "Ain't nowhere that wasn't fucked by Umbra. Not unless you and those pretty little girls with you been hiding out in Antarctica for the past five months."

"You look like a child molester," Hannah said. "And not the good kind, either."

The man did a double-take and burst into laughter. "The good kind?"

"Wrap it up, Tommy!" one of the men on the shelves called.

Tommy nodded and licked his lips hungrily. "All right. You little ladies come to me." He motioned at me. "You got to the count of ten to run for it, and then we come for you."

"Let me get this straight." I folded my arms across my chest. "You plan to hunt me down for sport and then rape my female companions?"

"Aw, don't make it sound so harsh," Tommy said. "It gets awful boring around here. A man's gotta have some sport."

"I'll make you a counter proposal." I dropped my arms to the sides. "You tell me what I want to know, and I won't kill every last one of you."

That predictably drew another round of guffaws.

I sighed. "Look, you think we're easy targets, but I'm really trying to settle this without a lot of bloodshed."

"Yeah, we're from an alternate dimension," Hannah said. "I'm a demigoddess, she's a druid, and Cain here is a former assassin for the fae. So, you really, really don't want to fuck with us."

"Did she say the fae?" someone hidden said. "Maybe we ought to—"

"Maybe you ought to shut up, Slim!" Tommy held up a hand. "Start running, boy, or the moment I lower my hand, they'll riddle you full of holes."

I sighed. "Fine. Let's do this."

"Your funeral." Tommy dropped his hand.

My body sigils flashed with power. I summoned my staff and the brightblade hummed to life just in time to deflect the first three bullets. Someone cried out as the deflected bullet hit them.

Tommy saw my blade and his eyes flared with fright. I didn't think the shooters would aim at Grace and Hannah, but I threw up some small shields just in case.

"Get behind cover," I shouted.

They dove behind a cash register.

Blade whirring and blurring, I intercepted another volley of hot lead and dashed toward Tommy. He flinched and looked down as if suddenly remembering the shotgun in his hands. No amount of skill would be enough to deflect an entire load of buckshot, so I dodged left down an aisle and nearly ran into another shooter with a pistol.

He'd been running to the corner for a shot, but I put an end to that real quick. I slashed down, removing both of his hands, and the pistol clattered to the floor. His screams cut short as my brightblade removed his head. I booted the body to the side so it wouldn't topple toward me. The next closest guy was on top of the towering shelf to my right.

It was a good twenty or thirty feet to the top where the man perched atop a pallet of plastic-wrapped toasters. I banished my staff, vaulted six feet up to the first level, and clambered like a monkey to the top. The man was up on one knee, eye to the scope of a gun as he scanned the store for me. He'd probably lost sight of me the moment I dashed toward Tommy.

I cast a camouflage blind to hide us from the other snipers, then tapped him on the shoulder. He whipped around, a surprised look on his face. I yanked the gun from his grasp and threw it over the side. Then I gripped his neck and squeezed. He struggled and flailed, but there was nothing he could do against my magically enhanced strength. I crushed his windpipe and tossed him over the side after his gun.

I summoned my staff and pressed another sigil, switching to sniper mode. There were four more guys roosting atop shelves, two to my right, and two more to the left. One on my right peered with almost comical confusion right at me. He was probably wondering why he couldn't see his comrade anymore. Or maybe he'd caught a glimpse of me just before I cast the camouflage screen.

I flipped up the scope, aimed, and sent a blast of magic through the staff. His face imploded as the energy ripped through him, sizzling brains and flesh. Just for variation, I blasted through the next guy's neck, then charbroiled the guts of the guys to my left.

I took a sort of perverse joy at watching them die in agony. Shit stains like this deserved to suffer. My revelation spell was still drifting across the store, revealing another group of people not far from Tommy's original position. The spell didn't have the range to spread across the entire store, but I imagined there were probably even more who hadn't joined in the fun just yet.

I banished my staff and slid down the side of the shelf, then ducked and peered through a giant stack of glass cleaner multipacks. I didn't see any movement on the next aisle, so I squeezed between that and king-sized bottles of toilet bowl cleanser.

The neighboring aisle was completely empty. I figured out why when I looked at the sign overhead indicating this was the toilet paper aisle. Anytime there was a major crisis in the world, people bought all the milk, bread, and toilet paper they could carry. This dimension was no different in that aspect.

Urgent whispers and the clomp of boots on concrete gave away the position of Tommy's reinforcements. I ducked past the empty shelves on this aisle then squeezed between mega-sized products for a peek at the next aisle. It was there I found him rallying seven men armed with a variety of rifles and pistols about fifty feet from my position.

I slid out and summoned my staff, igniting the brightblade at my side. "Tommy, Tommy, Tommy." I tutted. "Why didn't you accept my proposal?"

The group of ruffians shouted in surprise. Rifle barrels clattered against one another as they collided in their haste to turn on me.

I whirled the brightblade, letting the energy hum menacingly. "I once thought killing wasn't the answer." I shrugged. "Turns out, it's a great answer depending on who's dying."

"Good thing you'll be the one dying!" Tommy shouted. "Kill that fucker!"

I cast an illusion of myself and ducked back between the crates out of the way. Bullets whizzed past, going right through the illusion. Within seconds, they'd emptied their guns and were scrambling to reload.

The pigeons in the massive store suddenly took flight from the rafters, dive-bombing Tommy and gang and unleashing an ungodly amount of shit on them. Bullets ripped into the men.

"Take that, you child-molesting mother fuckers!" Hannah screamed.

I drew my dueling wands and hurled destruction down the aisle. Within seconds, we'd reduced Tommy and pals to a pile of twitching corpses.

"Cleanup on aisle eighteen," Hannah called.

I cast another revelation spell and jogged down the aisle to rejoin the others.

Hannah and Grace exchanged a high-five.

I raised an eyebrow in Grace's direction. "Was that you with the pigeons?"

She nodded. "They were happy for a little target practice."

I looked at the pistol in Hannah's hand. She'd apparently picked it up off the first guy I'd killed. "Nice shooting."

Hannah shrugged. "It's easy when they're all bunched together."

"True." I walked around the blood pooling on the floor and confirmed everyone was dead. My revelation spell found more warm bodies further back in the store, so I put a finger to my lips and motioned the others to follow me.

We encountered the first blip on the radar near the back—a man hiding behind crates near the entrance to the stock room. I ended him with a blast of energy to the temple. The vapor from the spell had drifted into the open door behind him where it detected more people. It was hard to accurately count them since they were all crouched near each other, apparently readying a last stand.

Hannah had picked up a rifle from Tommy's men even though the thing was nearly as tall as she was. She held it awkwardly with the butt against her chest instead of the crook of her arm. I didn't have time to instruct her on proper usage, so I took the lead and went to the next corner. I peered around it and found the people. Except they weren't crouching in defense, they were huddled together, bound by ropes and chains.

"Shit." I motioned for Hannah to lower the rifle. Using my true sight scope, I scouted the vicinity for any other armed lurkers, but found none. The prisoners were women and children, a mix of boys and girls. There wasn't an adult male among them. Most of them wore next to nothing, and what little clothing they had was filthy.

"Oh my god!" Hannah's rifle clattered to the floor. "What did those bastards do to these people?"

"Help," a woman said in a trembling voice. "Please."

I walked over and knelt next to her. The foul stench of body odor and human waste was nearly overpowering even though Tommy's men had opened packets of air fresheners nearby. A long chain connected most of the women, wrapped around their ankles and padlocked to keep them secure. Rope prevented the children from escape.

"Where are the keys?" I asked the woman.

She shook her head. "Tommy keeps them in his pocket."

I didn't feel like running back out to Tommy's corpse. "I'm about to draw a weapon. Don't be alarmed."

"We see weapons all the time." A woman with several scars down her cheek rose unsteadily to her feet. "You won't alarm us."

"This weapon is a little different." I summoned my staff and ignited the brightblade.

Women and children gasped in unison.

"He's one of the magic people," a little boy said.

I carefully cut through the padlocks securing the women, then banished the staff and used a dagger to slash the ropes holding the children. The prisoners cried out in relief, rubbing formerly bound ankles and wincing in pain at the blisters and calluses on the skin.

"Gods be damned," I said. "Did they ever unchain you?"

A crying woman latched onto Grace, hugging her as if she'd found a long-lost relative. Hannah soothed another woman. As for me, I was the brunt of suspicious and frightened stares, all except for the little boy who'd proclaimed me a magic person.

He limped over, favoring the formerly bound ankle, and looked up at me with hope. "You're one of the good magic people. The ones who tried to stop the evil ones, right?"

It wasn't entirely accurate, but close enough. "We're the good guys," I said. "Well, mostly at least."

"Mostly?" The woman motioned at the boy. "Ty, come back to me."

He shook his head. "No. I want to learn magic so I can fight too."

Ty's ribs showed through the skin and his arms were practically skeletal. Some women looked healthier than others, but they all looked malnourished, bruised, and abused.

I'd seen some bad shit, but this place was a living hell.

Chapter 10

I pointed toward the exit. "I want everyone out of this room. I'll find food and clothes for everyone."

The woman who'd spoken to Ty looked at me and shivered. "No disrespect, but that look in your eyes frightens me."

Hannah smiled, her eyes lighting with pride. "That's his killer look. We just wasted Tommy and all his baboons."

"T-they're all dead?" the woman asked.

"Yes, they are." Hannah walked over and took her hand. "Cain looks scary because he used to be an assassin for the fae. But he's pretty nice once you get to know him."

Grace snorted. "What a glowing endorsement."

"Wow, that's cool!" Ty shouted.

Looks of concern and alarm indicated the women didn't think so.

I sighed. "I know you've been beaten and abused by animals posing as men, but I'm not one of them. So, please follow my instructions and start moving out."

Ty was the first one to leave, followed by other children. Little girls looked up at me with big eyes, circling as far out of my way as they could. It made me feel like a monster, like the person I'd once been all those years ago. I hadn't killed anyone for so long until I met

Hannah. Then I'd killed Sigma. He was just a kid himself, brainwashed and used by the Divine Council to murder other demis like him.

I'd lost count of how many had died at my hands since then.

Hannah gripped my hand. "Cain, I know what you're thinking."

I raised an eyebrow. "Yeah?"

She nodded. "They were righteous kills, okay? Some people don't just deserve to die, they need to be violently ended like the scum they are."

I snorted. "I like that philosophy."

"Hey, I'm a teenager." She grinned. "I know everything."

Eventually, all the former prisoners shuffled past me and out into the store. Grace and Hannah located a patio furniture display complete with hammocks and tables and got everyone settled. Then Grace went to the pharmacy and looted some healing ointments, bandages, and other supplies to help with the physical harm the prisoners had suffered.

I knew from experience that these people had scars running much deeper that would never heal. But if Hannah was any example, those wounds could be forged into strength and courage. I just had no idea how to accomplish that. My specialty was hurting and killing, not helping.

A four-wheeled cart from the lawn and garden section helped me ferry canned food from the stockroom to the people. I was able to ignite the gas burners in the former bakery and heat up the contents before serving it.

All the perishable items in the meat and frozen sections had been cleared out, probably eaten or thrown away by Tommy and gang. While the others ate, I scouted around the store looking for more supplies we could take with us to reach Sanctuary. I stuffed what I could in backpacks and piled it near the front of the store.

On my way back I paused out of sight of the former prisoners. Some of the children were running around, laughing and playing. Most of the women talked excitedly, many in tears, hugging and laughing. Hannah was engrossed in conversation with a girl her age. Judging from the scowl on Hannah's face, they were talking about the girl's captivity.

I walked into sight and much of the conversation and activity quieted to a somber mood.

"Oh, for fuck's sake!" Hannah threw up her hands. "He's a good guy!"

"I'm sorry," one of the women said as I approached. "It's just been so long since I've seen a man who didn't have his way with us."

I held up a hand. "Look, it's fine. I understand. All I want right now are some answers."

The woman pointed to her chest. "I'm Betsy." She pointed to others, naming them as she went. I already knew some of their names from overheard conversations. As with most details, they stuck in my mind.

She didn't give me the names of the children, which was fine with me.

When she was done with introductions, I sat cross-legged on the ground to make myself smaller. "Tell me how the apocalypse started."

Betsy frowned. "How do you not know already?"

I bit my lower lip and considered what to tell her. "I assume you all believe in magic now, right?"

They nodded.

"My friends and I are not from this dimension." I spread my hands to indicate the world. "We come from another reality, another Gaia where none of this happened."

Murmurs and confused looks rippled across their faces, but some of them simply nodded as if resigned to believe every crazy thing now that they'd witnessed magic.

"Gaia?" someone asked.

I nodded. "Nubs—that's what we call normal humans—refer to it as Earth." I made a fist. "This plane is Gaia." I held up another fist. "There are more planes, other worlds as well. One of them is Feary."

"Did he just call us nubs?" a young woman asked.

"I've heard the word Feary," Betsy said. "Tommy's men captured one of the Umbra soldiers and they tortured him for information. He said that once Umbra captured this world, Feary was next."

Grace's forehead pinched. "I can't believe one organization could take over the entire world. It sounds like the plot to a bad movie."

"Everything happened so fast," Betsy said. "Umbra took over our televisions one night and announced that they'd given the UN and other leaders of the world an ultimatum. Either acknowledge them as their masters, or they would unleash the horsemen of the apocalypse."

Terry, a petite woman with dirty blond hair nodded. "They showed a man demolish a mountain with a hammer. And a woman used a trident to overturn the Chinese navy. But we thought it was all special effects like in the movies. No one believed them."

A black woman named Cherie shivered. "A week passed and then all these natural disasters started destroying cities. The news showed videos of five people on these flying metal horses wreaking destruction on the world. They wore black cloaks and these awful golden masks."

Hannah gave me a confused look. "I didn't see any flying metal horses in Hephaestus's armory."

"Me either." I motioned them to keep going. "What happened next?"

"An earthquake swallowed Washington, D.C., and Los Angeles was wiped off the map." Betsy hugged herself. "My husband and his brother packed our families in our cars, and we left, hoping to get to Montana or North Dakota where it was less likely they'd come for us. But we hadn't even made it past Birmingham when the airships appeared."

"I remember hearing music," Terry said, "and then I started walking toward it. I remember everything, but all I cared about was getting closer to the music."

"This lunatic in a van crashed into us and pinned our SUV against the concrete guardrail of a bridge," Betsy said. "When the music came past, we couldn't get out of the car. That was the only reason we didn't follow the others."

Angela, the teenaged girl Hannah had been speaking with, nodded. "That's what happened to my family. After the airships were gone, my dad managed to smash out the windows and we crawled out. We spent a month hiding out in this area and looting supplies from the stores. Tommy's gang showed up one day and killed my parents."

Tears trickled down Betsy's cheeks. "We stayed closer to Birmingham, but supplies were running low, so we came out here. That was when they killed my husband and took me."

Other women told similar stories even though I really didn't want to hear them all. I finally held up a hand. "What happened to the people lured away by the music?"

Betsy pointed to a woman in the back who'd remained silent. "Claire?"

The woman slowly raised her eyes, face twisted as if looking at me caused her pain. "I was lured by the music, but somehow I twisted my ankle and crawled after the others, but eventually fell behind until I was out of range of the music. The airships led everyone to a big warehouse, and I don't know what happened to them after that."

"Where was the building?" I said.

She pointed north. "Straight out on interstate twenty, southeast of here."

"Did any of you come from Atlanta?" I said.

A couple of women nodded. One answered. "I left before the general panic started, so I don't know what happened. There were rumors that monsters with squid heads were coming out of the Chattahoochee River and killing people."

Hannah flinched. "Can you describe them more?"

The woman shrugged. "That's all I know."

Ty raised his hand. "Hey, Mister Cain, can you take us to your dimension?"

I exchanged a look with Hannah. "We don't know how to get back yet, so I don't know."

Everyone tried to speak at once, most of the women begging us to take them to another world where it was safe. I had the sense that most of them didn't quite believe it but were willing to take the chance on anything at this point.

I couldn't imagine how many people were in the same situation and would be trapped in this hellhole for the rest of their lives.

Tears welled in a little girl's eyes. "Promise you'll take us when you go back? I don't want the airships to get me."

"I promise," Hannah said before I could inject a dose of reality.

Grace winced but didn't add her two cents.

Betsy tilted her head curiously. "Why did you ask about Atlanta?"

"That's where we're from." Hannah glanced at me. "It's where Cain lives anyway."

Betsy looked at me, then Hannah, and Grace. "Are you a family?"

Hannah grinned. "Not really, but sort of. Cain's like a big brother to me because he saved me from a demi who was trying to kill me."

That predictably opened a new can of worms that Hannah spent the next several minutes explaining, going so far as to talk about the old gods, demigods, and the various factions vying for power.

While some looked skeptical, most seemed ready to accept the bizarre truth.

Betsy was a believer. "Out of all the factions, you didn't say anything about Umbra."

"That's because we've never heard of them," I said. "Horatio, the leader of the Pandora Combine in our dimension must have renamed their faction to Umbra. Maybe he thought it would sound cooler to world leaders when he demanded their fealty."

"We need to find Cain in this dimension and find out all we can," Hannah said. "Maybe we can fix things."

I held up a finger. "Don't get ahead of yourself. This is way beyond our control."

Grace nodded in agreement. "The best we can do is find the cube and get back home."

Hannah sighed. "Leaving Umbra in power is wrong. We've got to stop them."

I scoffed. "How? They've got the most powerful arsenal in the worlds at their disposal, and if we get close to them, they could use a music box to subdue us."

"Cain, you infiltrated Count Dracula's castle, stole a map, and found the lost armory." Hannah gripped my hand. "You faced your greatest fear and killed Torvin on the shores of Oblivion. If there's anyone who can stop an evil organization from world domination, it's you."

I noticed a lot of wide eyes and open mouths in the audience. Even Grace looked impressed and she already knew the story. "Gods be damned, Hannah, it's not that easy. Layla helped me."

"Then let's find the Layla of this universe and get her to help!" Hannah squeezed my hand tighter. "We could even get Aura to help us."

A flock of pigeons near the front of the store burst into flight, cooing in alarm.

I tensed and held up a hand to quiet everyone. "Everyone hide. We've got company."

Grace closed her eyes. "I'll try to make contact with the pigeons to see what's going on."

"Wait here. I'll go scout the situation." I looked pointedly at Hannah. "That includes you."

She sighed. "Be careful."

I set off down the aisle, using displays and intersecting shelves for cover. Aside from pigeons, there were no other signs of life on my way to the front, nor did I find anyone when I arrived. But just outside the broken doors, I saw what must have spooked them—a motorcycle that hadn't been there before.

Whoever parked it hadn't been concerned about being noticed. The lack of caution hinted that it was one of Tommy's men who'd probably just gotten back from patrolling or perhaps scouting for more women to kidnap. I summoned my staff and scanned the area with my scope. The infrared mode picked up on the huddled mass of women and children hiding on aisle twenty.

I caught a hint of something down near aisle seventeen where I'd slaughtered Tommy's men. The newcomer probably saw all the blood and was freaking out. My scope was powerful, but there were too many full shelves for me to detect a heat signature. I cast a camouflage blind in front of me then quickly and silently made my way toward aisle seventeen.

I took cover one row over and paused for another look. I heard whispers but couldn't make out what they were saying. Whoever it was sounded upset, which made sense considering they just found their buddies' lifeless bodies in a lake of blood on the floor. They were probably on a walkie-talkie radioing for help.

That meant I'd have to keep this guy alive for questioning and find out how many more of his friends we could expect to kill when they showed up. The hairs on my neck prickled. I spun and blocked a dagger with the haft of my staff then lashed out with a foot and caught the attacker in their stomach.

A familiar face bared her teeth in a fierce grin. "Cain, you're easier to track than a wounded fawn."

I blinked a couple of times, unable to believe who it was.

Chapter 11

My eyes definitely weren't deceiving me. "Layla?"

She sheathed her dagger somewhere in her yoga pants. "Now you look like a confused puppy."

"Are you my Layla, or the Layla from this world?"

Layla blinked a couple of times. "What kind of drugs are you on? And what in the hell happened to this city?"

I sensed another presence and turned to see Aura watching us. "This makes even less sense now." I shook my head. "Aura is with you?"

"The girl sent me a text yesterday explaining that you were going back to sweet home Alabama." Layla smirked. "And not just any part of Alabama, but the very town where we killed those Firsters."

I shook my head. "Why would Hannah tell you that?"

Layla sighed. "Because, Cain, she thought it was a good idea to have backup in case something went wrong. We arrived in White House Springs a little while after you did and found the van with unconscious mechanists in it. Then we tracked you across the road to the junkyard and found a weird cube on the ground. I walked over to pick it up and it vanished."

"It didn't vanish," I said. "It's still on the ground, but it's in our dimension."

Aura's mouth dropped open. "That was the cube from Noctua's pedestal, wasn't it? The one that allowed her to observe other dimensions."

"The very one," I said. "But what makes even less to sense to me about this is why Layla brought you along."

Layla chuckled. "Your elven sweetheart is the one who convinced me to go in the first place."

Aura sighed. "Layla was drinking at the bar when she got Hannah's text. She thought it was laughable that Hannah thought Layla would care enough to watch your back, Cain. I told her it would be more exciting than sitting around drinking."

"And she was right!" Layla's eyes brightened. "What kind of fuckery have you gotten us into, Cain?"

An unexpected laugh came out of my mouth. It wasn't a happy laugh, but the kind where a person realizes life has veered wildly out of their control and they're powerless to stop it.

Aura blinked. "This isn't funny, Cain."

I laughed harder. "Oh, but it's hilarious!" I blew out an exasperated breath and motioned for them to follow me. "Hannah was just talking about you, Layla."

Layla paced alongside me, eyebrows raised. "Oh, really?"

"Yeah, really." I shook my head. "Despite her knowing what kind of person you are; she still has faith in you."

"Hah." Layla cleared her throat. "Stupid girl."

I opened my mouth to say something and decided against it. Layla had proven time and time again she was selfish and acted in her best interests, but she occasionally did something unexpected that went against the very grain of her character. But mentioning she might have a soft spot for Hannah would only make her deny it even harder.

Layla noticed my hesitation. "What were you about to say, Cain?"

I shrugged. "Just that I feel bad for Hannah. She thinks you're a better person than you are even though you treat her like shit."

It was very telling that Hannah had contacted Layla but not Aura. Aura had betrayed us and Layla, despite her faults, was brutally honest about what she planned to do, whether that meant abandoning us or just calling us names. One thing was for certain—this was a second chance for Aura and Layla to lay their hands on apocalyptic weaponry. I hoped the sad state of affairs in this dimension would persuade them otherwise.

"You found her already!" Hannah burst from hiding when we walked into view. "And the Aura from this dimension is here too?"

"This is our Layla and Aura." I dropped onto a patio stool. "Your text convinced them to follow us to White House Springs. They found the cube, but when they tried to pick it up, it transported them here."

"Oh, snap." Hannah winced. "You mean we left an interdimensional portal wide open back in our reality?"

"Yep," Layla said. "And it's apparently not two-way because we walked back and forth all over the place looking for that cube and didn't go back to our Gaia."

Hannah sighed. "We have to find the same cube in this dimension and use it to get back." She looked back. "It's safe to come out, everyone."

Women and children began drifting out of hiding, drawing confused looks from Layla and Aura.

Layla did a double take. "What in the gods' names is going on here?"

I blew out a breath. "Hannah, you tell them." My throat was tired from earlier. As Hannah caught them up on our adventures, I considered the paradoxical problem of the clockwork cube. It had transported us here through a one-way gateway that was now wide-open back in our realm. That meant those mechanists would eventually wake up and go investigate the junkyard, whereupon they'd likely end up here as well.

But that didn't worry me so much as the alternative. If and when we acquired the same cube here, would we open a gateway between realities that would allow Umbra and their ilk to come to our world? Their grand plan according to Horatio's recording was to invade all parallel universes. I certainly didn't want to enable that.

One way or another, I had to make sure that using the cube here wouldn't open a permanent gateway back to Prime that could be exploited by Umbra.

When Hannah finished her tale, Aura and Layla were predictably upset.

"Gods be damned, Cain." Layla bared her teeth and hissed. "Now we're trapped in this gods-forsaken world!"

Aura slumped. "You were right about those weapons from the armory, Cain. All they did was bring pain and suffering to normal people."

Ty tugged on Hannah's sleeve. "Why do they say gods be damned instead of God damn it?"

"Because they grew up knowing there are multiple gods, not just one." She mussed his hair. "It still sounds weird to me too."

Layla dropped onto a patio chair and propped her feet on a table, drawing looks from the other women. "I suppose Cain was right about the weapons, but you can be damned sure if I lay my hands on one, I will pound Umbra to a bloody pulp and claim this world for myself."

Uncertainty flashed across the faces of everyone who didn't know Layla.

Betsy hesitantly spoke. "B-but what could one woman do against Umbra?"

Layla sprang to her feet, a wolfish grin on her face. She tucked her hair behind her ears to reveal the slightly pointed tips. "I'm half-fae, half-human, and all woman." She picked up a nearby chair and flung it a hundred feet down the aisle as if it weighed nothing. "And I will ram my fist up Umbra's ass and turn them inside-out."

A little girl cheered and was joined by the other children. The women looked frightened, impressed, and somewhat hopeful.

"And I'm an elf." Aura pushed her red hair back to reveal even pointier ears than Layla's.

"Pssht." Layla flicked her hand dismissively at Aura. "Don't let the tits fool you. She's an elf, not a woman."

"You're really crude, but I kind of like you," Betsy said.

The others murmured in agreement.

"I'd rather see her in control of the world than Umbra," Terry said.

Layla's flashed a wide grin at me. "I think I found my new calling, Cain." She cracked her knuckles. "Let's go take over the world."

"I'm glad you're here, Layla." Hannah smiled. "You're such a bitch, but you're a badass bitch."

Layla opened her mouth but seemed at a loss for words. She closed her mouth and pursed her lips. "I like that description. I'm a badass bitch."

"Just a straight-up bitch," Aura murmured.

"I heard that, elf." Layla cast a maniacal wide-eyed grin at Aura. "Don't make this badass bitch come for you."

"Oh, please." Aura dropped into a seat. "What's our first move, Cain?"

"Atlanta," I said. "We need to find the Cain in this dimension and see if he can help."

"Ooh, you think my doppelganger is wandering around too?" Layla said. "I might have to kill her, because I don't want competition for the throne."

"I'll let you two work that out." I had bigger issues to consider.

"What about us?" Betsy said. "Will you take us with you?"

I shook my head. "If this city is any indicator, the trek to Atlanta will be too dangerous for a large group. There's no way I can guarantee your safety if we're ambushed by another gang. Plus, you have everything you need here."

Terry shivered. "But we'll be all alone."

I stood. "Tommy's gang owned this store and the territory around it. I doubt any other gangs will violate this territory as long as they think Tommy is still around. We can also arm you with their weapons and show you how to take care of yourselves."

Ty raised his hand. "Will you come back for us, Mister Cain? Will you take us to your world?"

"If we can't make this world safe, then we'll take you with us," Hannah said.

Layla scoffed. "Don't make promises you can't keep, girl. We might be dead by tomorrow and these people will be waiting for a rescue that never comes." She put her hands on her hips. "Learn to defend yourselves instead of relying on others. That way if we don't come back, you'll still survive."

Cherie nodded. "She's right. Cain is going up against powers none of us can even begin to understand. We need to prepare for the worst and hope for the best."

Betsy watched Layla as if trying to draw strength from the other woman, but tears trickled down her cheeks. "Tell us how, Layla."

"Gladly." Layla looked at the children. "Just because you're kids doesn't mean you get a pass. I'm gonna turn you all into little killers, okay?"

"Yeah!" Ty raised a fist. "Layla's little killers!"

"Oh, my gods." Aura face-palmed.

Hannah shrugged. "Whatever it takes."

Grace gave me a concerned look but said nothing.

Layla led the group to Tommy's dead men first. "Gather all the weapons from the bodies and stack them over there." She pointed to an empty shelf. "Then I want you to pick up the bodies and body parts and haul them outside. We're going to make a nice bonfire."

Many of the women and children recoiled in horror, but with some fierce glares and prodding, Layla got them to work. When the bodies were dumped outside, Layla had them mop up the blood with paper towels and take them outside. There were stacks of wooden pallets in the back of the store, so we gathered those and made a woodpile around the bodies, then lit them on fire.

There were cheers and lots of tears. These people had been through hell. Burning their former tormentors would be cathartic to some, but these scars would be with them for the rest of their lives. Experience taught me that some would be forged stronger and others would be weaker. Time would eventually weed out the weak.

The fire raged on until well after dusk by which time there wasn't much left but ashes and bones. During that time, I confirmed all other entrances to the store were chained and secured, found Tommy's gun and ammo stash, and had the survivors make a list of the food stores available.

Around noontime the next day I felt like we'd given the survivors as good a chance as any to defend themselves should another gang decide to encroach on Tommy's territory. Even so, I felt guilty when we climbed on our motorcycles and drove away, leaving behind a ragtag force of heavily armed women and children who had almost no idea what they were doing.

Grace looked over her shoulder a few times, expression guilty. "I hate this."

Aura had doubled up with Grace since Layla wanted to ride solo. "I don't like it either, but it's the best we can do for now."

"They'll be fine!" Layla shouted over the roar of the engines.

"Why am I the only one wearing a helmet?" Hannah said, voice muffled by said helmet.

It took a moment for me to come up with an answer. "I just feel better if you wear one."

Hannah wrapped her arms around me and squeezed. "You're so protective."

Layla smirked and rolled her eyes. "Overprotective father."

Hannah flipped her off. "He's my brother not my father."

"He's an assassin, not a daddy!" Layla gunned the bike and took the lead. We'd abandoned the interstate and taken to city streets and backroads since they were easier to navigate without traffic. Burned out shells of vehicles and skeletons littered an area in downtown Birmingham. Bullet holes and black impact marks from explosions marred the area.

"Looks like they put up a fight," Hannah said.

"But how did they resist the music boxes?" I slowed and stopped next to a barricade with six bodies behind it and found the answer. Several sets of earmuffs lay on the ground near the skulls. I picked up a pair and inspected them. They weren't the ordinary foam-filled kind that went over the ears. These actively canceled incoming noise.

I opened a slot on the side and found badly corroded batteries inside. They popped out after some prying, but the electronics inside the earmuffs were rusted from sitting in the elements too long.

The others parked their bikes nearby.

Layla swung a leg and slid off her bike. "What is it?"

"Protection against the music boxes." I showed her the inside. "We need to find where these came from."

Aura tore a swatch of cloth off a skeleton and held up a nametag from Gus's Gun & Pawn. She turned in a circle and pointed to a damaged building a block away. A sign on the ground bore the same name as the nametag. "If there are any to be found, they'll probably be there."

We walked to the store. One wall had partially collapsed from a direct hit. The rest of the store was intact, but the guns and ammo were all gone, probably scavenged by local gangs.

"Looks like whoever looted the guns didn't care about their hearing." Hannah plucked a package from a shelf and removed a pair of the earmuffs from the box. "Or their eyesight." She pointed to the packages of eye protection on the shelf above.

"Batteries over here," Grace said. "And they left a whole section of pistols and ammo here too."

I walked over to her and examined the discovery. "These are twenty-two caliber guns. Not enough firepower."

Hannah picked up a western-style revolver. "Ooh, I'm taking this!"

"Don't forget these." Grinning, Grace tossed Hannah a belt with holsters.

"Yes!" Hannah buckled it on and put a revolver in each holster. "Dude, this is so cool."

I chuckled. "Better load up on ammo. You're going to need all of it to take down one person."

"It's not that bad," Grace said. She hunted around and found a duffel bag under collapsed shelving, then shoved all the twenty-two ammo inside of it.

I grabbed the entire supply of fifteen noise-cancelling earmuffs and put batteries in five of them so we could use them at a moment's notice. As we prepared to head back to the bikes, my body tattoos tingled. Layla held up a fist before I could do the same and put a finger to her lips.

She looked at me and pointed diagonally up to indicate the rooftops across the streets. "We've got company," she whispered.

Chapter 12

I'd suspected we wouldn't make it out of the city without another confrontation. There was no telling how many gangs roamed the streets between here and the countryside.

The gun shop was only one story while the neighboring buildings were three- or four-story stores and apartments. "Grace, can you scout with birds?"

She shook her head. "There aren't any nearby, and I used up most of my magic reserve back in Costco. I meant to recharge, but every square inch around here is asphalt."

Layla grinned. "Let's go hunting, Cain."

"Come out with your hands up," a man shouted from outside. "We've got you surrounded."

I walked to the employees only area of the store and peered through the dirty window. A narrow alley separated us from the next building over. I looked at the others. "Wait here. We'll be back." I cast a camouflage blind around us, then Layla and I eased open the back door.

"Someone's coming," a voice hissed from the left side of the door.

Being so close, the blur in the air would be highly noticeable. But nubs weren't accustomed to such things and probably wouldn't know how to react right away. Then again, these nubs had been exposed to quite a bit, so underestimating them would be a mistake. I cast the camouflage blind ahead of us to test it.

"It's a concealer!" someone else shouted. Bullets ripped through the air, pinging off bricks and ricocheting into the gun shop door.

Layla scowled. "Sounds like these nubs aren't completely stupid."

"Nope. But I know where they are now."

Hannah and the others rushed into the back, eyes wide and full of concern.

"Oh God, I thought you were dead!" Hannah put a hand to her heart. "Why did they shoot?"

"They've seen camouflage illusions before." I held up a hand. "Just wait here. Layla and I sort of know what we're doing."

"Do not attempt to escape from the rear," the man outside shouted. "Don't try your magic tricks on us, because we've seen them all before."

"Can't wait to shut him up," Layla growled.

The back wall was bare brick, so I walked over to it.

"Want me to go outside?" Aura said. "I can draw fire while you take them out."

I shook my head. "I don't feel like hauling your dead body around for the next few hours."

Grace's mouth dropped open in horror. "Wow, some friend you are, Cain."

Hannah giggled. "Aura can't die. Well, technically she dies, but she revives around midnight. It's pretty weird."

"Huh?" Grace rubbed her temples as if that might help absorb the information. "How?"

"It's personal." Aura gave Hannah a pointed look then turned to me. "Fine. Just be careful."

"As if you care," Layla said.

Grace shook her head. "I can't decide if you all are friends or if you hate each other."

"Friends with these people?" Layla scoffed. "That'll be the day."

"Aura's a traitor, so I don't trust her even though she did die for us once." Hannah shrugged. "And Layla's cool sometimes and a complete bitch most of the time, but she's also a badass, so it's nice having her around for times like this."

Layla blinked a few times and worked her mouth but didn't seem to have an immediate response. She made a raspberry. "The girl's not wrong."

"Hey." I snapped my fingers. "Can we do this?" I summoned my staff and peered through the scope. The brick was thick, but I picked up two faint heat signatures on the other side. I activated the brightblade. "Toss something out the back door to distract them."

Layla picked up a ball cap with the gun store's name on it and flicked it into the alley. Bullets lit it up almost instantly. I plunged my brightblade through the brick and a man screamed as it cauterized his insides. The gunfire stopped. Layla sprang outside. Someone gurgled as blood filled their throat.

I went out back and observed the two fresh corpses. Someone shouted from the rooftop of the neighboring building. A metal door near the bodies hung open. Layla and I sidled up to it and checked the inside. A stairwell led up. I went first and sprinted four stories, Layla close on my heels.

We reached the roof access and peeked outside. A man with a semi-automatic rifle peered over the edge and spoke into a radio. "Greg and Jonas are down! I repeat—" An arrow from Layla's bow ended the conversation.

I cast a camouflage blind to hide us and the body before the people on nearby roofs noticed.

Layla smirked and folded her black bow, then pulled a golden rod from her backpack. "I've been dying to test this out." She flicked it and the golden rod turned into Apollo's golden bow, a trophy from the armory.

The other buildings were of equal or lesser height, each one populated by more men with more rifles. One of them shouted down at the gun store. "Come out now or we'll start lobbing grenades in there."

"There's that mouthy bastard." Layla nocked an arrow. The shaft glowed with energy.

I flicked my staff into longshot mode. "Ready."

Layla loosed the arrow at the speaker. I sniped a man on the roof to the east and another to the south by the time the arrow hit the man. His body exploded spectacularly, flaming pieces flying in arcs all over the street below.

More men below shouted in panic and began to run. I sniped four and Layla exploded another three of them. After the echoes from the explosion died down, the streets were once again silent.

Layla grinned wildly and planted a hard kiss on my lips. "Gods, that was fun." She kissed me again, then smacked me on the ass and walked away. "You know how to show a girl a good time, Cain."

I groaned and adjusted myself. "You really are a bitch."

She looked over her shoulder, eyes smoldering, hips swaying. "Yep." Then Layla vanished down the stairs.

I blew out a breath and followed.

Hannah looked relieved when she saw me. "Is this going to be a thing everywhere we go?"

"Probably." Layla rubbed a spot of blood on her yoga pants. "How in the hell did that jackass bleed on me?"

I shrugged. "We were standing right next to the body."

"It's a bit disconcerting that we can't trick them as easily with magic," Aura said.

"Why do they have to be so hostile?" Grace shook her head sadly. "Post-apocalyptic humans are just awful."

Hannah scoffed. "They suck even in the best of circumstances." She looked at a nearby body. "Can I have one of their rifles?"

I shook my head. "Stick with the revolvers, please."

She sagged. "Okay."

We loaded the saddlebags on our motorcycles with the loot from the gun store and set out once again. We finally reached I-20 but the ramps were too clogged with vehicles for us to squeeze past, so we took our chances with a highway that paralleled the interstate. The going was slow but uneventful until we reached another damaged section of town where the residents had put up a fight.

A wounded woman propped up against the side of a car held out her hand. "Help me, please."

"Oh no!" Hannah tugged my sleeve. "Let's help her."

I held up a fist and we stopped about a hundred feet from her. Old retail stores and restaurants lined the side of the road. None were over a story tall, but I couldn't see on top of them. Even so, I didn't need the tingle of my tattoos to tell me that there were people waiting just ahead.

"We know it's a trap," I called out. "This is the oldest trick in the book."

"Please help," the woman called again.

"Look, we've already annihilated two gangs." I put down the kickstand and got off the bike. "Don't make me do the same to you."

A barrel-chested man stepped out from behind a car and the woman climbed easily to her feet, a smirk on her face. A belt-fed machine gun hung from a strap on the man's shoulders. He braced it against his waist and flashed a grin.

"That's a mighty tall tale there, stranger." He narrowed his eyes. "You part of Jonas's gang or Frank's?"

"Neither." Layla slid off her bike and stood beside me.

The man whistled. "Whoo, ain't you a juicy piece of ass, girl?"

Layla unholstered her golden bow and flicked it out to full length.

The man laughed. "Y'all sporting bows and arrows? That ain't even fair."

The woman burst into laughter and produced a submachine gun. "We got y'all covered from high and low. Heck, we'll even give you the first shot with that bow."

I sighed. "What the fuck is wrong with you people? Civilization ends and you think it's okay to be complete assholes?"

"We do what we have to," the man shot back. "It's survival of the fittest."

"More like the dumbest." Layla pursed her lips. "You have four people on the rooftops and at least six more doing a poor job of hiding in the stores on the left and the right. The first person who falls to their knees and shouts, 'Layla, you are a fucking goddess,' will be allowed to live. They will then go forth and spread the gospel of Layla and convince other assholes to stay out of my way."

The man and woman guffawed, but it was just a show. Even from this distance, the uncertainty was plain on their faces.

Layla drew the arrow. Energy gathered around the shaft, and she let it fly. It hit the building to the left and exploded against the wall. The structure crumbled and collapsed. A man on top cried out in surprise just as those hiding inside screamed when steel and concrete rained down on top of them. Another arrow collapsed the building opposite and another round of screams echoed.

The man and woman stared in awe, mouths hanging open as two arrows decimated their gang. They dropped their weapons and fell to their knees, both shouting, "Layla is a fucking goddess!" at the tops of their lungs.

I stayed alert in case there were stragglers as Layla and I walked across the distance between us and her new worshippers.

"Well, shit." Layla looked down at the prostate believers. "I guess you both did it at the same time." She collapsed her bow and drew a blade. "I think a game of spin the dagger should decide who dies."

"How many people are in your gang?" I said.

The woman sat up her knees. "Fifty-two men, and eight women."

I nodded. "Where's your hideout?"

"You gonna let me live if I tell you?" she said.

Layla shrugged. "Sure."

The man jerked violently. "What about me?"

"Shut your filthy mouth and let me think about it." Layla made a pinching motion with her fingers.

The woman spoke again. "We're two miles south at the old country club."

Hannah joined us. "I'll bet they have sex slaves too."

"That's what I am." The woman put on a sad face but couldn't quite make herself cry. "These men kidnapped me and make me do horrible things."

The man shook his head violently. "That ain't true, Laverne! You're the one who thought up the idea of robbing travelers." He looked at me. "We ain't got no sex slaves, sir, I promise."

"No?" Layla put her blade under his chin and lifted it. "Are you sure?"

"Y-yes, ma'am," he stammered.

"Answer me this." Hannah put on a stern gaze. "How many walkers have you killed?"

His forehead pinched in confusion. "How many what?"

Hannah ignored his concern. "How many humans have you killed and why?"

I snorted. "Are you quoting *The Walking Dead*?"

"We don't have time to dilly-dally around." Layla sheathed her dagger. "Let's get out of this shithole."

Lavern and her man sagged with relief. I was tempted to cut off their heads, but instead motioned for them to stand.

They did so uncertainly, bodies trembling with new fear.

I watched them silently for a moment, then leaned closer and spoke in a soft voice. "You will return to your gang and tell them that we're coming for all the gangs who think killing and stealing is the only way to survive now." I summoned my staff and the pair gasped as it appeared out of nowhere. They gasped and shrank back when the brightblade blazed to life. I sheared the roof off a nearby car with a casual swing and banished the staff again.

"Spread the word, Laverne. Because if you don't, there will be blood." I shooed them away. "Go! Get out of here!"

They bolted like a pair of freed pack animals.

I walked back to my motorcycle and climbed on.

Layla stood in front of my bike and watched me with a smoldering gaze. "Gods, I love your scary voice, Cain. It's too bad you're such a softie most of the time." She hopped on her bike and licked her lips. "I'm having fun. How about the rest of you?"

Grace stood barefoot in a patch of grass at the side of the highway, face relaxed. "I hate this world."

"Me too." Aura watched me for a moment. "You look like you could use a mangorita, Cain."

I sighed longingly. "Yeah, I could. Guess it'll have to wait until the next world over, though."

She smiled. "Unless we find a bar with fresh mangos."

We started our motorcycles and once again headed out. A few miles outside of the city perimeter we were able to get back on the interstate. It was smooth sailing until we reached the Coosa River where another gang had blockaded the road with school buses.

"Gods damn it." Layla didn't wait for introductions and loosed three blazing arrows at the bus on the right. The arrows struck the ground beneath the bus. The explosions flipped it up and over where it rolled down an embankment on the side of the bridge. A chorus of shouts and screams rose from the bus as it tumbled.

"Anyone else want to fuck with us?" Layla shouted.

A group of armed men fled from the back door of the other bus and kept running. We filed past and crossed the bridge. Over the next few hours of travelling, we encountered four more gangs, none of which stood a chance against us. At the very least, we were making the roads safer for other travelers.

At long last, we reached Atlanta. Except for the downtown connector, the interstate was oddly empty, relatively speaking. Judging from the sparse number of abandoned cars on the road, it seemed the citizens hadn't had a chance to escape before the airships came. It didn't take long to cross town and reach the outskirts of Sanctuary.

At long last we turned down the side road leading home and reached the gate. I patterned the disarm sigils with a hand and hoped the Cain of this world used the same ones I did. The gate rattled open.

"That was easy." Layla gunned her bike.

"Wait!" I gripped her arm. "Let me check it first." I summoned my staff and looked through the scope. The wards on the ground were dark as were the ones on the gate. I nodded. "Yeah, it worked." Even so, I let Layla go first just in case. Despite what I told her and others, the wards didn't kill, but they would knock out anyone who tried to cross them. I didn't mind letting Layla take the hit.

Layla passed without incident and the rest of us followed. I rearmed the gate behind us. Moments later, we reached the church. It looked identical to mine in every way, but there were a few new plots in the graveyard that I didn't have in mine.

A figure in a dark cloak and wide-brimmed hat waited in the shadows on the front porch, an oblivion staff in his hand.

I stopped my bike and turned it off. I got off the bike and summoned my staff. "I don't know how to tell you this, Cain, but I'm you from another dimension."

Cain tensed but said nothing.

Hanna tugged on my sleeve and whispered, "Cain, look at the grave to your left."

I risked a glance and couldn't believe the name engraved on it.

Chapter 13

I took in the names on the other graves and grimaced. Then I looked back at the figure on the porch. "Who the hell are you?"

The figure stepped out of the shadows and lifted the hat to reveal the face. "Gods be damned. Are you really Cain?"

Hannah, Aura, and Layla gasped.

Grace stared in horror at the graves.

The woman wore a patch over her right eye and had an extra scar down the right cheek. But otherwise, she was a complete match for our Layla.

I banished my staff. "Yes, I'm Cain, but not from this world."

The staff dropped from her hand and clattered on the porch. It was made of wood and fashioned to look like an oblivion staff, but it wasn't. The other Layla hesitantly walked down the stairs and lifted a hand to my cheek. She touched it and peered into my eyes. After a moment, she nodded and backed away. "You're real."

I nodded. "Yeah, for the most part." I looked down at the graves. The nearest one bore only my first name, Cain. The others in order were Harry, Nathan, Caolan, and Grace. "Gods almighty. Did Cain try to form the Justice League or something?"

She frowned. "The what?"

I waved a hand at the graves. "That's a lot of heavy hitters."

Alt-Layla nodded. "There were others, but gods only know what happened to them." She looked at Cain's grave. "I didn't even have bodies to bury, but it felt wrong not to have something to remember them by."

Layla scoffed. "What happened to your eye?"

Alt-Layla pointed at Hannah. Her jaw tensed and her body trembled with barely constrained rage. "She happened to my eye." She looked at the graves. "She happened to Cain."

"What?" Hannah's eyes widened. "No, I would never!"

Alt-Layla squeezed her eyes shut and shivered once more, as if shaking off the anger. "I know you're not our Hannah."

"Y-you call me by my name in this world?" Hannah said.

Alt-Layla stared at her for a moment, then looked at me. "How did you get here?"

"Long story." I nodded at the door. "Can we go inside? It's been a long day."

Alt-Layla turned and picked up the fake oblivion staff, then opened the front door and walked inside. The others started to follow, but Layla grabbed my elbow. "That woman is fucked in the head. Don't trust her."

I scoffed. "You realize that she's you, right?"

"Yeah, and that's exactly why I'm warning you." Layla sighed. "What are we going to call her, because I sure as hell don't want her using my name."

"I think of her as Alt-Layla."

Layla wrinkled her nose. "It's awkward."

I shrugged. "Well, deal with it."

Hannah took my hand. "Cain, I'm a little scared of the other Layla." Tears welled in her eyes. "Do you really think the Hannah here killed this Cain?"

I pressed my lips together and shrugged. "We'll just have to get the full story."

The inside of this Sanctuary was identical to mine in many ways, but with some significant differences. Fred's pool was filled in with concrete. A large portrait of Hannah hung on a wall, daggers embedded in both eyes.

Hannah gulped when she saw it. "This Layla doesn't like me."

Alt-Layla walked into the kitchen area. "Want a sandwich, Cain?"

"I'd like a story first." I opened the liquor cabinet and was practically giddy to find it still stocked with rum.

Alt-Layla opened the freezer and removed a pair of mangos. She took the rum from me and began mixing ingredients for a mangorita.

Layla sat down at the kitchen counter, a confused look on her face.

Aura stood over the other woman's shoulder. "I like to add a pinch of sugar."

Alt-Layla ignored her and used agave instead. She opened a drawer and removed a curly straw with more bends than I'd ever seen before in my life. She poured the concoction into a tall glass and plopped the straw inside.

"I don't have garnishes or I'd give you a pirate sword too." Alt-Layla handed me the frosty glass and watched me expectantly.

I took a hesitant sip. It was smooth, sweet, and oh-so mango-licious. "I'm impressed. This is probably the best mangorita I've ever had."

Aura huffed. "Are you serious?"

Layla watched her alternate self with horror building in her eyes. "You learned to make mangoritas for Cain? What kind of dull-witted fool are you?"

Alt-Layla's eyes narrowed, but she didn't respond.

Hannah hesitantly raised a question. "What do we call you? Other Layla?"

"I'm the only Layla around here, "Layla said. "We can call her One-Eye or Bar Wench."

Alt-Layla considered it. "Call me Hemlock."

Layla's mouth dropped open. "You traitorous little bitch!"

Alt-Layla—Hemlock—smirked at her counterpart. "Hemlock Breakstone."

Layla pounded her fist on the counter hard enough to shake it. "You fucking bitch!" A dagger appeared in her hand. "I'll cut out your tongue."

Hannah and Aura looked just as perplexed as I felt at that moment.

I held up my hands. "What in the gods' names is going on?"

Layla lunged at Hemlock, but the other woman dodged back and ran down the winding stone stairs to the basement. Layla ran after her and the rest of us followed. Aura reached the bottom first, the confusion on her face replaced with joy when she reached the bottom.

Layla and Hemlock faced off in an empty space that contained bookshelves and books in my Sanctuary. Judging from the clean rectangular marks on the stone floors, bookshelves had been there not too long ago.

Daggers clashed as the pair fought, mirroring each other's attacks and defenses almost perfectly. Layla leapt backward and threw a dagger, reached into her yoga pants, and produced another one from seemingly nowhere. Hemlock batted aside the dagger almost contemptuously with her own blade but didn't respond in kind.

Instead, she sheathed her dagger and stared at Layla.

Layla bared her teeth in a scowl. "Fight me, coward!"

"How, exactly, does one win a duel with oneself?" Hemlock raised an eyebrow. "Why fight at all, or hide behind aliases that mean nothing? Why forsake what life has to offer because you feel that you're above it all?"

"Shut up!" Layla's fist tightened into a white-knuckled grip around her dagger. "You're just saying that because everyone you know in this universe is dead!"

A tear glistened in Hemlock's eye. "Yeah, they're dead, and all the things unsaid can never be said to them now." She sighed. "Because I was exactly like you not so long ago."

Hemlock turned toward me and met my eyes for a moment, then pushed past and went upstairs.

Layla sheathed her blade and rolled her eyes. "I'll be so fucking happy when we get out of this dimension."

Aura narrowed her eyes. "What in the gods' names was all this about?"

"Wouldn't you like to know?" Layla pushed past us and went upstairs.

Hannah, Aura, and I looked at each other with puzzled expressions.

"Hemlock Breakstone." I bit the inside of my lip and tried to remember if I'd ever heard that name, but nothing came to mind. "Doesn't sound familiar, but maybe it's someone Layla used to know."

"I've never heard of it either." Aura sighed. "It's a fae name, and that's about all I can say for certain."

"Maybe it was her mom or something." Hannah shook her head and started walking upstairs.

"Maybe so." I shrugged and followed Hannah. Being explosive and unpredictable were Layla trademarks, and she was even more close-lipped than me when it came to her past.

Aura gripped my arm to stop me from going. She swallowed hard. "Cain, I just want you to know that I'm sorry for betraying your trust. I'm sorry for saying that I only slept with you because I was using you."

I blinked. "Why are you telling me this now?"

"Because Hemlock was right. I don't want it left unsaid in case you die."

I sighed. "I had feelings for you once, Aura, but I'm over it, okay? No need to apologize."

"You're over it?" Hurt glistened in her eyes. "What Hemlock said hit me hard. Don't leave things left unsaid because you never know if today will be your last."

"That's why you're telling me this now?" I laughed. "Gods, Aura, you picked a hell of a time to come clean. For what it's worth, I forgive you. But it's also sad that the person who

I considered a friend and a really cool bartender never existed. Then again, I guess that's normal with everyone. The person you first meet is never the same person when you peel away the layers."

Aura sagged. "No, I guess not. But the more layers I peel away from you, Cain, the more I like you."

I scoffed. "You wouldn't have liked me during my days in the Oblivion Guard. It wasn't until I murdered a house full of women and children that I found a conscience. And I still wrestle with that even today."

She took my hand and kissed the top of it. "I've said my piece, and I thank you for your forgiveness."

I still felt a spark of something when I looked into her sea-green eyes, but that spark had been tainted by betrayal. Aura had good reason for hating the gods, but I didn't appreciate being used.

"You're welcome." I reclaimed my hand and went back upstairs. Aura didn't follow.

Hemlock was making a sandwich with homemade bread when I reached the kitchen. Layla wasn't there. Sanctuary was powered by liquid mana, and if this Cain was anything like me, he had enough stores to last decades.

I sat on a stool at the kitchen counter. "Where's Layla?"

"Outside blowing off steam." Hemlock deftly sliced a tomato and layered it on the sandwich. "I kept up the garden. My Cain showed me just enough about sigils to maintain the pest control wards, but the protective wards on the doors and main gate are about fizzled out."

"They're complicated," I said, my mouth watering for a taste of the delicious looking sandwich she was working on. "I guess you've been using the golden ankh to get in and out when you want?"

She saw me looking at the sandwich and smiled. "Are you a hungry boy?"

I blinked at the affection in her voice and returned the smile. "I am."

Hemlock sliced the large sandwich and gave me half. "Hope you like it."

I bit into it and sighed in pleasure. "It's perfect, just like the mangorita." I'd left the glass up here during the duel downstairs but picked it up and resumed where I'd left off. "So tell me—"

"About the name?" Hemlock licked a dab of mayonnaise from her lip. "I don't know if I should antagonize my alternate self any further."

"It's a fae name that means something to you." I pursed my lips. "Your mother's name?"

She waggled a hand. "Sort of."

I took another bite of the sandwich. "Gods, you know exactly how much pepper to put on this to really make the tomato pop."

The left side of Hemlock's lip lifted into a lopsided smile. "Cain taught me how he likes sandwiches made."

"Tell me what happened in this world. How did it all go wrong?"

Hannah appeared from the guest bedroom. "Is it story time?"

Hemlock nodded. "Might as well be." She regarded Hannah for a moment. "You tracked her to a school and marked her, right?"

I nodded. "Yep, but then I regretted that decision and took her with me so the Divine Council couldn't kill her."

Hemlock grunted. "Then you trained her while we set up a hit on Digby, Mead, and Ingram so we could get you a beating unicorn heart."

I nodded. "Yep, that's how it happened."

"We got into a firefight with the targets. You took down Digby, Mead, and Ingram, but Daphne burned Hannah before escaping, leaving her to die."

Hannah's eyes widened. "No, that didn't happen."

Hemlock pursed her lips. "I guess that's the starting point for my story." She took another bite of her sandwich and chewed it thoughtfully. "Cain killed Digby and Ingram but was too weak to shoot Mead. Aura and I rushed her, and for some reason, Hannah followed. The girl tried to use her powers on Daphne, but she had no control. Daphne aimed at her and I threw a dagger. But a fucking bird flew out of nowhere and intercepted the dagger."

I suddenly saw where this was going. "Our Layla's dagger just missed a bird too."

"My second dagger caught Daphne, but not before she hit Hannah hard. Burnt off all her hair and her right side was nothing but exposed muscle and bone." Hemlock took another bite from her sandwich.

Hannah gasped. "Oh God."

"Cain got the final shot off at Mead and passed out." Hemlock shook her head. "I think the only thing that kept Hannah alive was probably her godlike blood. We escaped before the Oblivion Guard descended on us and drove the rental car all the way back to Atlanta. We took Hannah to my healer, but there was nothing she could do except soothe the pain so the girl could die in peace."

I cleared the lump from my throat. "I did something stupid, didn't I?"

"Something desperate." Hemlock sighed. "We came back to Sanctuary and you spoke with Cthulhu through Fred. You reached an agreement and we drove Hannah up to Lake Lanier. A group of people met us there and took her. That was the last we saw of her until about a month later."

I already suspected the answer but asked anyway. "What did I do?"

"Cthulhu said he could heal her completely, but the price would be that she accepts the bargain in your stead." Hemlock touched my left cheek. "When we arrived back here, you spoke with Cthulhu again, and the taint vanished from you.

Hannah had accepted the bargain.

Chapter 14

"And I killed Cain?" Hannah slammed the flat of her hand on the counter. "This is bullshit. I accepted the curse in our dimension too, and I didn't kill him. I love him like a brother!"

"The Hannah that left then was not the same one we met later." Hemlock reached over and touched Hannah's hand uncertainly, as if still unsure it was a different person. "She was full of rage. I think it's because the decision wasn't entirely hers. She felt as if Cain gave her up to Cthulhu without even trying an alternative. Our Hannah said a lot of things when we next met her, but it wasn't until after Umbra raided the lost armory of Hephaestus that the shit hit the proverbial fan."

I grunted. "As far as I know, we don't have an Umbra in our dimension."

"They were formerly known as the Pandora Combine, but changed their name to accommodate new allies." Hemlock sighed. "Let's back up the story a bit. Before we saw Hannah again, Cain, Aura, and I went to see the unicorn prize he'd won. He asked if the unicorn heart could be exchanged for Hannah, but Cthulhu wasn't interested. So Cain asked Shraya, the unicorn, for something, anything that might capture Cthulhu's fancy. Shraya gave him two options. One was about the lost armory of Hephaestus and the apocalyptic weapons stored there. The other was about an artifact of the Great Ancient Ones that Cthulhu would do anything to have."

I blinked. "I don't know anything about that."

"Shraya said there were rumors it was in the Pacific Ocean, not far from a deepway entrance." Hemlock shook her head. "Aura, of course, was still working for Eclipse at the time. What she didn't know was that Torvin Rayne had used a fae eavesdropping spell on her, so he heard everything."

"Well, shit." I stopped chewing for a moment. "Shraya didn't talk about any of this in our meeting. I just took a magical dagger in payment."

Hemlock's eyebrows rose. "You were still cursed?"

I nodded. "Let's talk about my event later. What happened next?"

"The Pandora Combine, an alliance between Dracula and the mechanists were already seeking the lost armory. Torvin allied with them and they raided the armory a week before Cain and I did." Hemlock quirked her lips. "After that, they allied with Cthulhu, rebranded themselves as Umbra, and enacted their plan for world domination."

"And this was months ago," I said.

She nodded.

I grunted. "The mechanist leader, Horatio, sent an interdimensional letter to his counterpart in our dimension, telling him they'd soon be able to raid other dimensions."

"Oh, how fun." Hemlock bit into her sandwich.

"I can't believe Torvin was the mastermind behind it all." I sighed. "He's such an asshole."

She smirked. "Before this happened, Torvin was playing all sides against each other. He used his organization to assassinate demis for the Divine Council, but he also undermined their power so he could seek vengeance on the fae. Once he formed Umbra, he didn't even need to pretend anymore."

"Is he their grand leader now?" I said.

Hemlock shook her head. "Something happened after they allied with Cthulhu. I don't know how, but Horatio and the mechanists are running the show now. Even the Hannah here follows his commands."

I grinned. "I'll bet Torvin isn't too happy about that."

"Probably not, but then again, all he cares about is killing the fae queens." Hemlock set down her sandwich. "He'll be happy as long as they take the war to Feary."

Hannah hissed. "Ugh, I hate Torvin!"

I snorted. "Can't escape the bastard, can we?"

Hemlock glanced at Hannah. "We saw our Hannah for the first time when we returned from Oblivion, completely empty-handed."

"What happened to Noctua and Korborus?" I said.

She frowned. "Who?"

"Oh, I guess you wouldn't know since you got there late." I shook my head. "I'll tell you about it in my story."

Hemlock pursed her lips. "You've been to the armory?"

"Yeah."

She sighed. "Gods, our dimension is such a failure."

I shook my head. "Mistakes were made, but you're still alive."

She flicked her hand dismissively. "Hannah paid us a visit at Voltaire's soon after we returned. Sigma showed up to kill her, but she was so full of rage, that the boy never had a chance."

Hannah blinked. "Wait, so this version of me can use her powers?"

"Oh, yes." Layla chuckled. "She's a fucking terror. Sigma attacked her in Voltaire's, a fae safezone no less, and Hannah literally threw him through the speakeasy door. The Oblivion Guard showed up and Hannah fought her way out. The next time we saw her, she came to Cain's doorstep, right outside the gates and tried to blow her way through them. But somehow, the fae magic kept her out."

"Jesus, the alternate me is a bitch!" Hannah said.

"Cain asked her what she wanted. She said the end times were coming and she wanted him to have the courtesy of knowing it first, even though he hadn't tried hard enough to save her and had sacrificed her to Cthulhu to save himself. Now she was nothing but a slave to Umbra."

I winced. "Well, I can see how it might look that way to her."

Hannah scowled. "Maybe, but still, I can't believe she went full evil."

Hemlock continued. "Two days later Umbra made their demands for world domination to the UN and other governments. Cain gathered an alliance of powerful magic users from all over the world to fight back."

I grimaced. "Didn't work out so well, did it?"

She shook her head. "We rendezvoused at Voltaire's with the other supers to formulate a plan. When we tried to leave, we ran into a squad of demis outside in the parking lot."

Hannah winced. "Oh, shit."

"The battle of the fucking century broke out in Little Five Points. Destroyed the safezone, Voltaire's, and most standing buildings within a one-mile radius." She stirred her drink again. "Cain was slicing and dicing with his brightblade, but his allies were dropping all around him. I was only able to take out this one demi and that was because her powers were dog shit."

"What do you mean?" Hannah asked.

Hemlock snorted. "The girl couldn't do anything but make flashing lights and fake explosions. It was pathetic, so I put a dagger through her eye. Then something hit me. I flew fifty feet into a brick wall that collapsed on me. I woke up gods only know how many hours later, missing an eye, and the fight was long over. All that was left of Cain and the others were piles of ash. Dozens of nubs and supers had died, burned to nothing but cinders."

"Where was Aura in all of this?" I asked.

"Aura was killed, but she came back to life. She saw the others die." Hemlock winced. "She went back to Feary, or at least that's where she claimed she was going."

Hannah blew out an exasperated breath. "This is so fucked up."

Hemlock nodded. "Welcome to the new world order, girl." She looked at me. "Tell me how things are in your universe."

The divergence in our timelines was amazingly simple but devastating. I almost hated to tell her that a bird decided the fate of her universe. "Our Layla hit Daphne on the first try before she could harm Hannah. I took out Mead, and the rest of the Firsters fled in their helicopter."

Hemlock swallowed hard, as if trying to get down a bitter pill in a dry throat. "Fuck me."

"I met the unicorn but refused to kill it for its heart." I looked down at my drink and swished it around in the cup. "Then I baited Sigma at Voltaire's. I fought him, Layla helped me, and I killed him with an enchanted dagger given to me by Shraya, the unicorn."

"Gods damn me." Hemlock leaned against the counter. "One little mistake and the entire world comes crashing down."

I touched her hand. "It's not your fault. I saw that same bird pass within a hair's width of the dagger in our reality."

She yanked her hand back and straightened. "Tell me the rest."

I told her about our adventure with the lost armory and continued to the present.

Hemlock finished her drink and began mixing another. "I guess we're fucked. There's no getting those weapons back, especially not with Cain and everyone else dead."

"The gods obviously don't care," Hannah said. "They're content to let this reality destroy itself."

"Except it won't, because with the Tetron, they'll be able to march across dimensions, join with their parallel selves, and conquer them as well." I shook my head. "With the apocalyptic weapons in their arsenal, no one will dare confront them."

Hannah slumped. "Well, when you put it like that, it's really grim."

"Sounds like a lot of bother for nothing." Hemlock scowled. "What's the point?"

"Good question." Noctua had explained multiple dimensions to us, but some of the concepts were difficult to grasp. Some divine beings existed as one across all universes while others didn't. As an outsider god, Cthulhu was a separate being in each dimension whereas someone like Thor was the same consciousness throughout.

"You've got that wrinkle again," Hannah said.

I nodded and told them my thoughts. "I think the push to claim multiple dimensions is being driven by Cthulhu because by uniting with alternate versions of himself, he might be able to ascend to one consciousness across all dimensions and become a true god."

Hannah pursed her lips. "I don't understand how that works."

"Me either," I admitted. "But it's all I can think of."

Hemlock shrugged. "Makes sense to me."

"I think we're missing a bigger picture." Hannah stepped back from the bar and looked at me. "Noctua said the Tetron allowed her to view other dimensions and make predictions about outcomes in Prime based on events in parallel worlds."

I nodded. "She said she could rewind past events and review them and use those to predict future possibilities."

Hemlock scowled. "I don't like the idea of someone being able to spy on me."

"I don't know how it works." I stirred my drink. "But if the mechanists have it, you can be sure they're using it to their advantage." I turned around and flinched when I saw Hannah staring blankly at us, a gentle white glow in her eyes. "Hannah?"

She didn't respond.

This wasn't like one of her typical accidental meltdowns where her powers burst out of control, but that made it even more alarming because I didn't know what to expect.

Hannah gasped and threw out her hands.

I dove over the bar grasping at Hemlock to pull her to safety, but she dodged to the side and I ended up thudding on the floor alone.

"Cain, it's okay!" Hannah walked around the counter and looked down at me. "It wasn't one of those kinds of episodes."

I looked up at Hemlock and Hannah staring down at me and felt pretty foolish. "Now you tell me." I stood and brushed off my pants, then nonchalantly walked around the counter and back to my drink. "What happened?"

"I was trying to think about the big picture and all this stuff started flashing through my mind." She sat down next to me. "It was like all the information from a hundred television shows hitting me all at once."

"Noctua said gods think about things differently." I shrugged. "Maybe that's what happened."

"Maybe." Hannah bit her lower lip. "One thing I kept seeing was you talking to Loki and Thor. I think that might be important to what's happening. Maybe them asking you for Soultaker is somehow linked to this."

I focused on the incident, thinking of the events that led to me and the gods standing inside the privacy bubble next to the parking lot. Loki's agent had approached me inside Voltaire's first, followed almost immediately by Kara the Valkyrie. If something linked that event to the events of this universe, I couldn't see it.

"I wish I'd been there to watch them," Hannah said. "Maybe then I'd know what was so important."

I was about to give up and finish my drink when something Thor had said popped back into my head. "I won't allow the lords of chaos dominion here, Loki."

Hemlock's eyebrows rose. "What's that?"

"Thor said that to Loki." I ran it back and forth in my head. "The key word is *dominion*."

Hannah touched my hand. "Are you certain he said lords of chaos plural?"

I ran it back in my head again. "Yeah."

Hemlock cackled with laughter. "Oh, this is getting better by the moment. You think not only do we have Umbra to worry about, but the lords of chaos?"

Hannah grimaced. "Yes, I do. I also believe we didn't end up here by accident."

I couldn't even begin to imagine how that was possible. Grace walked inside as we silently contemplated the possibilities.

Hannah turned to her immediately. "How did you find out about the dead spot in White House Springs?"

Grace flinched as if surprised by the hurled question. "Talladega told another elemental and they passed the message to me."

Hannah stood up and questioned her like a prosecutor in a murder trial. "You said elementals don't usually communicate that way."

"Technically, they don't ever pass messages along." Grace shrugged. "It surprised the hell out of me. Caolan would've dealt with it himself the moment he found out, but he's off on his own adventure."

"Leaving you, the apprentice to look into it." Hannah tapped a finger on her chin. "So you thought asking Cain for help was wise since you had to give him the iron charm anyway."

"It was the first thing that occurred to me." Grace held up a hand. "Why do I feel like I'm on trial here?"

"You're not." Hannah turned to me. "I submit to you that the elementals did not pass those messages to Grace. I don't know how, but Loki knew that Grace was going to see Cain. He also knew the mechanists had opened a crack to the underverse in White House Springs and saw it as an opportunity to get rid of Cain."

"How did he know so much? Loki isn't omniscient, is he?" I wasn't sure if that was a stupid question or not.

"You're asking the wrong person." Hemlock shook her head. "I think the gods can see what they want to. They've got minions all over the world, so anything is possible."

"Loki's chaos thrives on information." Hannah made sprinkling motions with her fingers. "He needed Cain out of the way in our dimension. We didn't get sucked into the underverse, but we're definitely not in his way anymore."

"How could I possibly upset Loki's plans for world domination?" I asked.

"Soultaker." Hannah pursed her lips. "That's why he sent a minion to ask for it. I don't think he actually wanted it. He wanted to verify you had it, and if so, get rid of you so you couldn't use it against him."

Hemlock frowned. "I hate to admit it, but the girl might be right. By sending you here, you can't use Soultaker to defend Prime."

"I don't see how Soultaker would defeat him." I pursed my lips. "Maybe Loki isn't as clever as we think. Maybe this was all an accident."

Grace seemed relieved. "And here I thought you were about to blame me for our situation."

"Not yet." I finished off my drink. "But if Loki is behind it, it means we're up against even longer odds than I thought."

It meant, in addition to Torvin, the mechanists, and Cthulhu, we might have the lords of chaos against us.

Chapter 15

Hannah groaned. "I thought I glimpsed something, but maybe it was just my imagination."

I shook my head. "I think your god powers offer insight none of us have. Maybe it'll become clearer later."

Layla walked inside and paused when she saw us. "You look like you've been huffing Cain's farts. What's wrong?"

I told her about our suspicions.

"Well, here's a simple solution," Layla said. "Make a deal with Loki that you won't go up against him so we can get out of this shitty dimension."

"Is it really that bad, babe?" Hemlock smirked at her counterpart. "Or you just don't like seeing an inferior version of yourself?"

"You're not inferior, Hemlock." Hannah took the other woman's hand. "If anything, I like you better. You're more honest and not as bitchy."

Layla barked a laugh. "Shut your trap, girl." She pointed a finger at Hemlock. "That's just a cheap copy of me. I'm Layla Prime, the real deal."

Aura appeared at the top of the basement stairwell. "Real full of shit."

Grace burst into laughter and clamped a hand over her mouth.

"Maybe we should tell Layla what happened to this world," Hannah said. "Maybe she'd be interested in knowing why it turned out this way."

Hemlock's shoulders slumped.

I shook my head. "Layla might be a pain in the ass, but she's not your enemy, Hannah." I turned to the others. "We've all been through hell together, even you, Grace." I let that sink in. "We don't need to make deals with Loki. We're perfectly capable of stealing the Tetron and returning home ourselves. We just need to rely on each other as always, okay?"

Layla looked at me like I was crazy. "Who in the hell are you? Because the Cain I know doesn't give inspirational speeches. He does what needs to be done, just like me."

"Sometimes even we need inspiration." Hannah looked at me hopefully. "And I'd listen to Cain before anyone else."

I cracked a yawn. "Look, I'm not trying to inspire anyone, but I need you all to remember where we've been and what we've done." I swirled the straw in my empty glass. "We assassinated the leaders of Humans First. We met a living unicorn. We killed a demigod, and we destroyed the armory of Hephaestus. Stealing the Tetron from Cthulhu will be child's play in comparison."

Grace nodded. "Well, when you put it that way, I feel pretty confident." Her nose wrinkled. "Let's keep the forces of chaos out of this, shall we?"

Aura nodded emphatically. "Agreed."

Layla crossed her arms and shrugged. "Fine."

"I'm going to sleep outside tonight." Grace sighed. "I don't feel connected to this world yet, and I really need to if I'm to be of much help."

"Want a sleeping bag?" Hemlock asked.

Grace nodded. "That would be nice."

"I slept outside a few nights myself." Hemlock looked as if she had more to say, but abruptly shut her mouth. She motioned to Grace and they went outside.

Hannah took my hand in both of hers. "Cain, I need to control my powers in case we encounter the evil me. There has to be some way!"

I nodded grimly. "There's a way, but it's not the right way."

"What do you mean?" Her eyes filled with pleading. "I've got to do it any way I can!"

Aura examined the liquor cabinet. "Cain isn't the brightest in the world, but he's not wrong about this."

I scoffed. "Thanks for that vote of confidence."

She smiled at me. "You sometimes let good intentions get in the way of seeing the truth."

"Like I did with you." I shrugged. "I get it. Won't happen again."

Aura started mixing a drink. "Especially not with Hemlock."

I raised an eyebrow but didn't know what to say.

Hannah squeezed my hand again. "What's the wrong way to control my powers, Cain?"

"You already know what it is." I finished off my mangorita. "Just think back to the parking lot in that high school. Think back to the time you burned down most of my library. Or when you sliced and diced the sea serpent on Oblivion."

"Or the time you threatened to light me up in the car," Layla said.

"B-but those were accidents." Hannah leaned back on her stool, eyes lost in thought. "I had no control."

"You had control, but it came from a bad source." I leaned my elbows on the counter. "What was the common thread?"

"I was angry, frightened, concerned." Hannah's eyes narrowed in concentration. "I also kind of hated Layla at the time."

"Anger, fear, anxiety." I tapped a finger on the counter as I listed each one. "Strong negative emotions allowed you to tap into your powers, but they don't give you control. When the Hannah here—"

"Can we give her another name?" Hannah shuddered. "I hate hearing my name associated with the person who killed Alt-Cain."

I nodded. "We'll call her Rana, then."

Hannah blinked. "Where'd you come up with that name?"

Aura stopped in the middle of mixing her drink. "Is that her middle name?"

"My what?" Hannah's eyes widened. "The headmaster of the orphanage said my middle name is Ann."

"It's not supposed to be." I really didn't want to go into a side story right now, but I'd inadvertently opened a can of worms and dumped them into the big bowl of worms we needed to discuss. "Your mother filled out your information as Hannah Rana Kabiri, but the hospital misfiled the paperwork. Someone later entered the information as Hannah Ann Kabiri and never sent your mother a copy of the birth certificate. The file was digitized not long after along with the original paperwork, and one of my assets discovered it."

Hannah frowned. "Well, I like it better than Ann. I was pretty young when Mom died, so if she used my middle name, I don't remember it."

"So this Hannah, heretofore known as Rana—"

"We could just spell my name backward and call her that," Hannah said.

I rolled my eyes. "You're so clever."

She smirked. "I know, right?"

Aura frowned. "Hannah backward is...Hannah."

Hannah giggled. "I know."

Aura plunked her drink on the counter and sighed. "Maybe you can let Cain get to the point sometime this century."

Hannah's smile faded. "I already know where he's headed. Rana was furious with Cain and felt betrayed. Powerful negative emotions allow her to access her power."

I nodded. "The same way you access them."

"But I saved you from a sea serpent!" Hannah threw up her hands. "It was eating you and I killed it!"

"What if you'd sliced me in half while I was in there?" I watched her expression. "Did you know exactly where to cut?"

Hannah's gaze lowered. "It just happened. I don't remember controlling it much."

I put a finger under her chin and lifted her eyes to mine. "Until you can control your powers without relying on negative emotions, you'll be a danger not only to enemies, but to friends as well."

"It was my lack of control that caused this world to happen." Hannah's shoulders slumped. "If I hadn't been afraid and tried to fight Daphne, Hemlock never would have had to throw that dagger. I wouldn't have been injured."

"Hold up." Layla dropped into a stool next to Hannah. "What about me throwing the dagger caused this?"

"Your counterpart hit a bird in this dimension." I put a hand on Hannah's shoulder. "Daphne nearly killed Hannah before Hemlock hit her with a second dagger."

"I fucking missed?" Layla's jaw went slack. "I caused all this?"

"No, I did, because I tried to fight Daphne," Hannah said.

"Gods damn it, just shut up." Aura huffed. "Any one of us could be to blame. All our decisions led to us being in that junkyard. Maybe if we'd just stayed put and let Cain get off his final shot, none of it would have happened."

I nodded. "We made our decisions, but events unfolded slightly differently in this reality."

Hannah angrily wiped tears from her cheeks. "I hate this, Cain. I hate that I'm useless unless I'm mad or scared, and then I'm just dangerous."

Layla slowly stood, her face white as a sheet. "I'm going to bed." She marched into the guest bedroom she usually occupied in our reality and closed the door.

Aura frowned. "I don't think she took that well."

"How is she supposed to take it?" Hannah looked glumly at the counter. "One of us caused the pivotal moment that destroyed the world."

"Enough with the pity party." I slapped a hand on the counter. "Do you want to set things right?"

Hannah looked up at me. "More than anything."

"Then let's figure out how to control your powers the right way." I pointed to the basement door. "I assume there are training rooms down there, so let's get started, okay?"

She stood slowly and trudged downstairs.

Aura studied my empty glass. "Was Hemlock's mangorita really better than mine?"

The concern in her eyes and the look on her face was adorable. I considered lying to her, but decided the harsh truth was the best. "Yes, hers was better."

"Shit." She huffed. "Challenge accepted."

"It's not a competition."

"Layla's a better fighter, she's snarkier, and you already like her better than me." Aura's eyes flared with indignation. "I will not let a Layla from any universe make better drinks than me. It's all I have left."

I rose from my stool with a snort, walked around the counter and kissed her on the cheek. "I've liked you a lot better since you died for me."

"Really?" her eyes brightened. "I'm not even all that keen on the Enders anymore. I mean, what's the point if we can't kill the gods?"

"True." I tucked her red hair behind a pointed ear. "Keep it up, and I might even trust you again someday."

Aura impulsively kissed me and jerked back as if she'd surprised herself. "I'd like that, Cain."

The feelings I'd tried to bury for her crept back to the surface. I'd known her for so long and had thought she was something of a friend. Then I'd discovered out she was secretly my Eclipse handler, Janice, and was also using me to get close to Hannah. Despite everything, I still liked her. Still wanted something more from her. In the end, it was foolish and wishful thinking.

I grunted dismissively and went downstairs to check on Hannah.

She was already performing a complex ballet routine in time with a training golem, perfectly mimicking its every move. The only dance I hadn't taught her was the shadow dance, mainly because it was too difficult for a golem to emulate. One didn't merely perform the shadow dance, they experienced it right down to their very core.

It had been an effective training tool for the Oblivion Guard. Most candidates scoffed when our first trials consisted of dance lessons, many of them centered around ancient fae rituals. By the time they'd winnowed down the candidates from hundreds to dozens, no one was scoffing anymore.

Hannah understood physical control. Coupled with spells to enhance learning, she'd picked up quickly on sword fighting techniques, dagger play, and martial arts. She could hold her own against me for a minute or two, which was impressive for someone who'd only been cumulatively schooled for a few weeks. Cthulhu's minions had tried punishment and deprivation to bend Hannah to their will but failed to understand that she couldn't use her powers even if she wanted to.

Why is that? I wondered. Surely, she'd felt anger and fear during the months in Cthulhu's grasp. I watched Hannah until she finished the routine, her face a stony mask of boredom, then motioned her to sit next to me on the stack of tumbling mats.

Hannah wiped sweat from her forehead. "I don't think dancing is helping."

I nodded. "Did you ever get angry or scared while you were with Cthulhu's people?"

Her forehead pinched. "I was scared at first, but mostly I was sad and depressed. I felt like I had no future."

"Hmm." I turned to her. "You were filled with despair."

"Yeah." Hannah seemed to swallow a lump in her throat. "That's how I feel right now. Hopeless."

I mulled that over. "Despair, anguish, and loneliness are different kinds of negative emotions. They're draining rather than filling."

Hannah considered it. "Anger fills me with energy, but despair makes me feel empty."

"What about happiness?"

She shrugged. "It fills me."

"So, we need to link a positive emotion to your powers." Unfortunately, there weren't many happy moments in Hannah's life. "What's the happiest moment with your mother?"

Hannah smiled. "Mom used to read me bedtime stories, but my favorite ones were when she made up something."

I felt like I was onto something. "Do you remember a made-up story?"

She tapped a finger on her chin. "Sort of, but it's hard to recall."

I patterned a memory sigil on her forehead. "See if this helps."

Her eyes lost focus and she went quiet for a moment. "Wow. The memory is so vivid right now."

"How does it go?"

"Once upon a time, a woman lived on a tiny planet surrounded by a sea of stars." Hannah's lips curved up faintly and her voice took on a deeper tone that wasn't hers. "She had simply woken up on the planet one day, all alone. Her planet aimlessly drifted around the universe but never encountered another planet like hers. One day, and I use the term loosely since there were no days yet."

Hannah giggled and spoke like a child. "How were there no days, Mommy?"

Her voice deepened again. "Just because."

Hannah spoke like a little girl again. "Okay, Mommy."

Apparently, my memory sigil had put her in a state of hypnosis. I hadn't intended for that to happen but decided to let things unfold naturally.

"One day the woman saw a star explode on the other side of the universe. At the time, the universe was still relatively small and surrounded by darkness. The woman had figured out how to make her planet move by using her mind, so she willed it to go to the exploding star." Hannah made a cradling motion with her arms and smiled down at them, as if holding a child. "When she arrived, she found a man observing the destruction of the star."

"She was frightened and elated to find another person in the universe but, at the same time, curious, so she asked him what happened to the star. The man was excited and happy when he turned and saw her, for he too had been so lonely, wandering the universe and learning its secrets. He told her that he had figured out how to destroy the star by controlling tiny little parts of it. By destroying the star, he hoped to learn more about why things existed and how they worked."

"By blowing up stars?" Hannah giggled in her girly voice. "Mommy, that sounds awful."

Hannah continued in her mother voice. "But it was exciting for the woman, so she helped him blow up star after star. But the stars were so large that their explosions simply created new stars. Chunks and pieces of destroyed stars began orbiting the new stars. The man wanted to destroy them, but the woman wanted to nurture them and see what happened. He hesitantly agreed. After a time, the stardust coalesced into something different than anything they'd seen before, new planets that were a thousand times larger than their own little planets."

"Giant planets?" Hannah looked up in wonder, as if into her mother's eyes.

"That's right, my darling." Her gaze returned to the imaginary child in her arms. "The man said that these planets were not like theirs. They warmed in the sunlight and their surfaces reacted and changed. He thought they could find a way to make more beings like them to live on these giant planets. And that was when a great voice boomed out to them from the darkness. It said, 'At long last, my children have learned their purpose. I give you this universe as yours to do with as you will. May it prosper.' The man and woman were frightened at first, but then the woman called out a question to the void. 'Why are we here?'"

"The voice answered. 'I have made many universes, and all have failed. It is because perfect balance leads to stagnation, boredom, and death. I made you to see if you could succeed where I have failed.'"

Hannah frowned. "But the woman was confused. 'How do we succeed if the man does nothing but destroy everything?' The man said, 'How do we succeed if the woman does nothing but coddle what exists until it stagnates?'"

"I'll bet they fought a lot," Hannah said in her girl voice.

She nodded and returned to her mother voice. "The voice from the void called back to them and said, 'This should be very interesting to watch.' And they lived unhappily ever after."

Hannah laughed. "Mommy, your stories are silly." White light began to glow within her pupils. "But I love to hear them." The light brightened and gathered in intensity.

She returned to the mother voice. "And I love you, little one."

Hannah blinked as if awakening from a spell as a soft, white nimbus warmed her skin. "I love you too, Mom." She held up a hand and stared curiously at the orb of energy in her palm. Then she touched it to the floor. A green stem grew from the stone, rising several inches until it blossomed into a white flower with glowing petals.

I rubbed my eyes in disbelief. "What the hell?"

Hannah flinched and the glow faded from her eyes and skin. The flower remained, somehow having sprouted from cold, hard stone. Tears filled her eyes. She buried her face in my chest. "I found my happiness, Cain, but it hurts so much to remember it."

I tried to clear the lump forming in my throat but was still overcome with disbelief. The flower had to be a conjuration or facsimile. It couldn't be real.

Hannah raised her face from my chest and looked up. "What's wrong, Cain?"

I separated myself from her and dropped to my knees next to the flower. It smelled sweet and my fingers tingled when I touched the petals. It felt real.

She knelt next to me and touched the flower. It glowed brighter where her skin met it. "It's so pretty. I can't believe I made it."

"Me either."

Hannah frowned. "What's wrong, Cain?"

"Hannah, if that flower really grew from stone, if it's real and not bits of stone made to resemble a flower, then you've done something even more impressive than switching the souls of those kids at your high school." I touched the flower once more and shivered at the pleasant tingles it sent across my skin. "It means you've created new life."

Chapter 16

Hannah stared at me silently for a long time. "New life? As in I created something?"

"Yeah." I wanted to get up but couldn't stop staring at the flower. "When you were angry, you destroyed. When you were happy, you created."

"This sucks!" Hannah threw her hands in the air. "How am I supposed to fight Rana if all I can do is make stupid flowers?"

I forced myself to my feet as possibilities filled my mind. What would Cthulhu do with a demi who could create life as well as take it? He would have power beyond reasoning at the tips of his tentacles. Did he even know what Hannah could do yet? All I knew was that regardless of the outcome, I absolutely could not let Cthulhu have her.

Hannah had been something of a gift to me, but what if she was meant to be a gift to the world?

"Cain, what's going through your mind?" Hannah gave me a concerned look.

"I don't know how you'll fight. We need to experiment a lot more before doing anything." I bit the inside of my lip. "Esteri, your mom, made up that story?"

"Yeah, that's what she told me. Although it was a lot better than the ones she usually made up." Hannah gripped the stem of the flower as if to pluck it.

"No!" I held out my hand. "Please don't."

"But it's useless."

I shook my head. "No, Hannah, it's beautiful." The word felt strange coming from my lips, but it demanded to be spoken.

A large tear gathered in the corner of her eye. "I'm glad you like it, Cain. I just hope it's not all I can do."

"Don't worry. We'll figure it out." I motioned her toward the door. "Go upstairs and get ready for bed. We've had a long day."

Hannah stood on tiptoes and kissed my cheek. "Okay, bro."

After she left, I summoned my staff and studied the floor with the scope. There were no signs of old seeds or other magical residue in the stone. I couldn't tell if the flower had roots or how it had sprouted without cracking the stone. There were spells that could make seeds sprout quickly, but from what I could tell, this flower wasn't the result of something like that. It simply hadn't existed moments ago.

I hesitantly left the training room and went upstairs to get ready for bed. I went to my room to shower and was startled to find Hemlock sitting in the corner of the room with a romance novel in her hand.

She looked up at me. "I never understood why you liked these things."

"It was how I learned about humanity," I said. "Human entertainment helped me adjust to moving from Feary to Gaia."

Hemlock nodded. "My Cain said the same thing, but I think he actually enjoyed the drama."

"I'm not ashamed to admit it." I shrugged. "I was taught to remain logical and not let emotion cloud my judgment. Romance novels were a way for me to experience emotion and drama without actually doing it."

She chuckled. "I wondered if you might come into my Cain's bedroom, having forgotten this isn't your home."

"I did." It felt extremely awkward to be standing in my room that wasn't really my room. Hemlock ran Sanctuary in this dimension, so it was hers. "I can go to one of the guest rooms."

"No, it's fine." Hemlock stood. "I'll sleep on the couch."

I stopped her with a hand as she tried to pass me. "I take it things developed differently with your Cain than they have with me and my Layla."

"That obvious?" She scratched around her eyepatch. "I talk too much now. I wasn't like that before. I still don't know what changed."

"Tell me more." I sat down on the edge of the bed and patted next to me. "I'd like to know more about myself from here."

Hemlock put a book marker in the novel and set it on the nightstand, then sat in the office chair across from me. "He was exactly like you. Stiff-lipped, stony-faced, but sometimes he'd slip up and show this other side to him that was..." She paused to swallow hard. "It was adorable."

I raised an eyebrow. "I've never heard Layla use that term except sarcastically."

"Yeah, that was me." She bit the inside of her lip. "He and I had a moment. We finally let each other in, and it was more than what I imagined and scary as hell." Tears formed in the corners of her eyes. "Then we went back to the old relationship, bickering, picking on each other. It was nice, but since I'd tasted what it could be, part of me wanted more, and another part wanted to run for the hills."

"You didn't run," I said.

"No, I didn't." Hemlock smiled through her tears. "The night before we went to Voltaire's, I came to him and told him how I felt. He hemmed and hawed and tried to make me leave, but I slammed him against a wall and demanded he tell me how he felt so I could be at peace one way or the other."

When I looked at her, I didn't see Hemlock, this other person from another reality. I saw my Layla, but instead of hints of emotion that sometimes flashed behind my Layla's eyes, I saw them loud and clear. And part of me knew what my answer would be if things had gone differently in my reality.

"He wanted to be with you," I said.

"And then he died." Hemlock stared blankly at the floor. "You and Layla have the old relationship. Something happened in my world to make it work. Maybe it was Hannah being torn away from him that gave him an emptiness to fill."

I reached over and took her hand. "No, it's not that. Layla is my biggest critic, she bitches all the time, makes fun of people, and is generally unpleasant. But ever since Hannah, she's always been there for me and saved my life even when she didn't have to. It's so bizarre to put this into words, but she's like my worst best friend."

Hemlock wiped her face and smiled. "That's what Cain and I realized too late." Longing filled her eyes. "You remind me of him in every way. So much so that it hurts."

"And you hate yourself for feeling that way."

She nodded. "You know me too well."

"I know my Layla."

"My Layla." Hemlock touched my lips. "I like hearing that again."

I reached over and touched her cheek. "Is that what he said to you?"

"Yes." Her voice was a rough whisper. "I like it and hate it when you say it." She lunged forward and shoved me backward then fell on top of me and pressed her lips to mine.

I'd kissed Layla before and it felt exactly the same, except for the hot tears. Hemlock pulled off my shirt and ran kisses up and down my chest. She bit my neck, my ear, and then kissed my lips once again.

"My Cain." Hemlock stiffened and sat up slowly. She wiped her face and moved back over to the office chair.

"What's wrong?" I asked, somewhat out of breath.

"Everything." She smiled sadly. "Cain, promise me that when we go on this mad quest, if it looks like I'm going to die, don't try to save me, okay?"

"Why not?"

Hemlock put a hand to her chest. "I'd just started feeling okay again recently, but having you here makes my heart a ball of burning agony. It'll only hurt worse if and when you go back to your world. This is why Cain and I avoided loving someone all those years. Because we both know it comes with a high price."

I didn't know what to say or what to feel. She was Layla but she wasn't. She was Cain's but she wasn't mine. And she was right—I avoided love like the plague until I met Hannah. That girl had forced me to open my heart maybe for the first time in my life.

"I understand, Layla." I stood and caressed her cheek. "But I've realized something. The pain and agony of losing a loved one isn't a price, it's a prize. Because never loving someone that much is the highest price of all."

I kissed her gently on the lips, and then went into the bathroom. I closed and locked the door behind me, then turned on the shower. I needed some space to think about what had just happened and what it meant for my time here.

When I got out of the shower, I found the walk-in closet still mostly full of my counterpart's clothing. Hemlock had claimed some space now that she lived here, but it wasn't nearly as much as I'd expected her to take considering her Cain was dead.

Hemlock was gone when I went back into the bedroom. A part of me had hoped she'd still be there despite sleeping with her being a horrible idea. I looked around the room and found it nearly identical in every way to how I'd left my room back in Prime. Just one stupid bird in the wrong place had changed everything.

Layla stormed inside the room and slammed the door behind her. "What were you doing with the other me?"

I played innocent. "Talking. Why?"

She scowled. "That woman isn't like me anymore. She's mentally unstable. If you think fucking her is the same as having me, then you're an idiot and I'll kick your ass for taking advantage of the other me, got it?"

Laughter sputtered from my lips.

Layla put her hands on her hips. "What's so funny?"

"You're so protective of your alternate self." I shrugged. "I think it's kind of sweet."

"I ought to kick your ass right now." Layla clenched her fists. "Cain, did you do anything with her? Did you fuck her?"

I walked calmly over to her until we stood nearly eye-to-eye. Layla stared at me with burning eyes. There was more than anger hiding behind her eyes. I sensed jealousy and hurt. Given what Hemlock told me, it made sense. I put a finger under her chin.

Layla slapped it away. "What are you doing?"

I put my finger back. This time she glared at me. I leaned in and gently kissed her, then stepped back. "We talked, we kissed, and that's it."

Layla blinked and wiped her eyes. "You swear it?"

"I swear it. I would never take advantage of your alternate self, Layla." I shrugged. "Despite what you think, she's every bit as strong as you. If anything, she might be stronger."

She didn't seem to know how to respond. "It's not my fault she fucked up. It's not my fault she destroyed this world because she missed Daphne."

"No, it's not anyone's fault." I sighed. "Are we done? I'm really tired."

Layla's eyes settled on something and she flinched almost violently. She gave me a troubled look then left the room as violently as she'd entered, the door slamming behind her. I locked the door since I'd had about enough of dramatic entrances and exits for the night. Then I cast my gaze around, wondering what she'd seen that rattled her so.

I didn't know how I'd missed it before, but a photograph lay in the chair where Hemlock had been earlier. Two people who I never thought I'd see smiling happily looked back at me. The other Cain and his Layla lay in bed, smiling up at the phone camera for a selfie. Layla still had her eye. I couldn't imagine what strange impulse caused them to take a picture, but they had.

And it had scared the shit out of Layla.

I picked up the picture and stared at it for a long while before putting it on the nightstand next to me, turning off the light, and going to sleep.

Hemlock was already up when I instinctually awoke to make breakfast. She smirked when I walked into the kitchen. "Figured you'd show up soon."

"Same habits as your guy." I shrugged and heated up the cast iron pan on the stove for the bacon. Hemlock was already mixing the pancake batter, so I watched her. "Tell me what happened to the population of Atlanta."

"Airships with music boxes started downtown near the capitol while the legislature was in session." She tossed almonds and walnuts into the batter. "Led them northeast from what I heard. Scuttlebutt has it that they took them to a holding facility. Rumors from other cities tell the same story. I think they're training humans to become mechanist soldiers, probably for a war on Feary."

I grunted. "Can't they just use the music boxes in Feary?"

"They don't work on fae or elves. Probably won't work on the other Feary races either."

"How do you know?" I said.

"Because I watched an airship lead a procession of humans." Hemlock sprinkled cinnamon into the mix. "All the human supers at Voltaire's followed the siren call of the boxes, but none of the orcs or elves responded to it."

I dropped the bacon into the pan with a welcoming sizzle. "Supers are affected, but not Feary folk. Interesting."

"Umbra plans to organize the humans into a fighting force." Hemlock shrugged. "Why they don't just use the armory weapons is beyond me."

"Because they're not idiots." I shifted the bacon. "They don't want to destroy the world they want to rule. Most of the armory weapons would leave the world in pieces."

"You said there were orbs and swords that cause plagues. Why not just wipe out the populations?"

"Same reason," I replied. "They want denizens to rule. Cthulhu needs worshippers to increase his power just like any god."

Hemlock poured batter onto the griddle. "I also heard rumors that people near rivers and shorelines were attacked by some kind of humanoid squid creatures."

"I heard that one too." I tapped the spatula against the edge of the pan. "If you were Umbra, where would you take the Tetron?"

"I imagine it's in the metro area somewhere near a cluster of Feary portals." She fetched butter from the fridge and set it near the griddle to warm. "If they're planning an invasion of Feary, then you can bet they're trying to tap into the Tetron to see what strategy will succeed."

"It's a big area to cover." I flipped the bacon. "But I have a feeling it'll be near Lake Lanier."

She raised an eyebrow. "What makes you think that?"

"Because there's a deepways tunnel there." I nodded grimly. "Which means we need to go there as soon as possible."

And pray the Tetron wasn't impossible to steal.

Chapter 17

"Deepways?" Hemlock tested the edge of the pancakes to see if they were ready to flip. "Those underwater tunnels, right?"

I nodded. "Cthulhu's minions use them to travel quickly around the world."

"Well, isn't this sweet?" Layla dropped onto a stool opposite us and watched with narrowed eyes. "Such a sweet, precious couple you make."

Hemlock didn't seem the least bit fazed by her counterpart's jabs. "Want to help with the eggs?"

Layla scoffed. "You want me to cook?"

"Don't pretend you're not good at it." Hemlock folded her arms and stared her down. "Or that you don't enjoy cooking because it helps you unwind after a long day of being a bitch."

"I ought to cut out your tongue," Layla said. "Because you can't keep it from flapping."

"Gods damn it, Layla." I produced a carton of eggs. "Can you scramble this dozen, please? I promise we won't take away your badass assassin card for cooking a fucking meal."

Layla flinched and narrowed her eyes. "Well, since you asked nicely." She found a metal bowl in a bottom cabinet and began cracking eggs into it.

Hannah and Aura emerged from a room, rubbing their eyes, and staring with confusion at the three of us in the kitchen. Grace came in a moment later but didn't know us well enough to be concerned by three assassins cooking breakfast together.

"Smells great!" She skipped over to the counter. "Can I help?"

Layla sniffed. "You could start by showering. Smells like you've been cuddling with a grizzly bear all night."

Grace laughed. "No, but I spoke with some coyotes. They bring news from the north. I also managed to get the local elemental, Atlanta, to start communicating. It sounds like there's a lot of activity up near the Buford Dam and Lake Lanier area."

Hemlock snorted. "Score one for Cain."

Layla stared menacingly at Hannah and Aura while she whisked the eggs. "Sounds like they're using the deepways."

"You can use my shower, Grace." I pointed to the room.

"Wouldn't hurt to groom a little too," Layla said. "Get those lady bits looking nice."

Grace snorted. "What does that have to do with anything?"

Hannah scoffed. "As if you've ever groomed in your life, Layla. I'll bet it's like a seventies porn show in your panties."

Layla and Hemlock burst into laughter simultaneously, and then exchanged concerned looks.

Grace grinned. "If it means that much to you, Layla, I'll get them looking nice and pretty for you."

Layla winked. "You do that, babe."

Hannah sat at the counter and shook her head at Layla and Hemlock. "One Layla is already too much."

"Agreed." Aura looked around the kitchen as if searching for something useful to do, then went to the liquor cabinet and began mixing drinks.

Grace stopped walking toward my bedroom and turned slowly toward the basement door. As if in a trance, she went downstairs.

"What was that about?" Hannah said.

I shrugged and started putting bacon on towels.

Grace emerged moments later, a wondrous expression on her face. "There's something amazing downstairs! Everyone, come with me."

I connected the dots. "Hang on, are you talking about the flower?"

She nodded. "How did you know about it?"

"Hannah made it," I said.

Grace's mouth dropped open. "She grew it from a seed?"

I shook my head. "No, she literally created it from nothing."

Grace leaned against the doorframe for support and fanned herself. "I've never seen anything like it."

Aura did a double-take. "Hang on, Hannah made something?"

Layla dumped the eggs into a pan. "Guess we'll start throwing flowers at our enemies now."

"It's actually a big deal." I carried the platter of bacon to the table. "Destruction is easy. Creation is a miracle."

"Agreed." Aura dashed downstairs.

Layla wrinkled her nose at Grace. "You still stink."

Grace rolled her eyes. "Fine, we can talk about miracles later."

Moments later, everything was ready, and we sat down to eat. Grace emerged wearing nothing but one of my bathrobes. She flashed Layla. "Clean enough?"

Hannah groaned. "Not while I'm eating, please!"

I paused with a slice of bacon hanging from my mouth. "Oh, I don't mind."

Hemlock and Layla laughed and once again flinched and scowled at each other.

Grace bounced on her heels a couple times for added effect, then closed up the bathrobe and sat down to eat.

After breakfast, I laid out the day's plans. "I need to scout Lake Lanier, but I want to keep the party small. Two or three people tops. I need another group to scout the local Feary portals, especially Little Five Points near Voltaire's. We need to know how much and what kind of traffic is going back and forth."

"The Midtown and Old Fourth Ward portals were some of the busiest besides the one in Little Five," Hemlock said. "We should probably check all of them."

I nodded. "You volunteering for that?"

"Sure." Hemlock paused eating her pancake. "I'd like Grace to come with me."

"Oh, I thought I'd be more use at the lake," Grace said.

"The urban landscape is more treacherous," Hemlock said. "Having someone who can talk with birds would be helpful."

Grace pursed her lips. "Sure, I'll come with you."

"I'm on urban duty too," Layla said.

Hannah shook her head. "No, you're going to Lake Lanier with Cain."

"I don't want to." Layla tore a piece of bacon in half and chomped it. "He'll be fine with you and Aura."

I shook my head. "Hannah, I don't want you going out."

"But—"

I held up a hand. "I need you to keep practicing. Your powers could be our ace in the hole."

She scowled. "Fine. I'll stick around and think happy thoughts. Maybe I'll plant an entire rose garden in the basement."

"I'd actually prefer you practice outside." I had given her act of creation a lot of thought. "I think you'll be more at peace if you're not underground."

Hannah sighed. "I'll give it a shot, Cain. But I'll be so pissed if you get caught or die."

"Me too." I turned to Aura. "I'll be fine alone."

"Well, if you say so." Aura shrugged. "I'm not entirely useless when it comes to stealth."

Layla scoffed. "No, just mostly useless."

"I'll go with Cain then." Hemlock tapped the plate with her fork. "He shouldn't go alone."

Layla jabbed her fork into her pancakes and muttered something.

"Or, Layla could go with him." Hemlock gave a meaningful look at her doppelganger. "Because no expedition needs two Laylas."

"Amen to that," Hannah said.

"Fine, I'll watch his sorry ass," Layla growled.

I caught a look from Hemlock and wondered why she was manipulating Layla into going with me. If she was playing Cupid, I didn't care for it. Just because things were different between her and Alt-Cain didn't mean they should be that way for me and Layla. I had plenty enough emotions to deal with thanks to Hannah. Even though the pain of her returning to Cthulhu was inevitable, provided we returned home, I was happy to endure it.

Once breakfast was finished and the dishes were done, we prepared to leave. I went to the garage out of habit and felt shocked and dismayed when Dolores wasn't there waiting on me.

"She's gone, Cain." Hemlock watched me from the front porch when I stepped out of the garage. "Hannah destroyed Dolores right as the battle started. I think she was trying to rattle Cain."

"Did it work?" I said.

Hemlock nodded. "He was pretty pissed. He ghostwalked and decapitated one of Hannah's demis before they even knew what happened."

"Good for him." I looked at the motorcycles parked in the yard. "They're going to hear us coming from a mile away."

"Use a muffling spell," Hemlock said.

"I plan to, but even that won't completely block out the noise." I checked the items in my utility belt, holstered my dueling wands, and checked the blades in my thigh sheaths.

Hemlock handed me a long-range two-way radio. "Its range is just enough to reach from Lake Lanier to here. I'll leave one with Hannah and she can relay any messages to us."

I tucked it into a saddlebag on my bike. "Sounds good." I cast muffling spells on the three motorcycles.

"You'll need to double up with Layla because we need the other two bikes."

I frowned. "Don't play this game with us, okay? Just because it worked for you doesn't mean it'll work for us."

"I'm not trying to play matchmaker, if that's what you think." Hemlock studied my face. "I just don't want you to have regrets."

Layla stepped outside. "Did I interrupt anything?"

"Always," I said. "You ready?"

She nodded. "Guess we need to take one bike and leave the other two?"

Hemlock nodded. "Grace, Aura, and I will be checking the portals."

Layla nodded. "Keep Grace safe. I don't care about Aura."

"Maybe I'll give you sloppy seconds on Grace." Hemlock winked at her.

Layla snorted. "Maybe if you stopped fawning over Cain long enough, you'd have a chance." She hopped onto the motorcycle and started it, then patted the seat behind her. "Don't poke me with your boner, Cain."

"What's the fun in riding behind you then?" I climbed on and wrapped my arms around her waist. "Isn't this romantic?"

"Gods damn it, Cain. I'll make you ride on the handlebars if you say that one more time."

"Have fun, kids." Hemlock waved. "Use protection because there's no telling where she's been."

Layla flipped her off and then gunned the bike down the driveway.

The roar of the engine was muted but still seemed loud in the dead city since the usual background sounds of other traffic weren't competing with it. We headed northeast and took the Friendship Road exit about thirty minutes later. I found it interesting and a bit concerning that we didn't encounter any opposition, whether from gangs or from Umbra minions the entire way there. I suspected there weren't many free humans left in the area, and Umbra probably didn't feel threatened enough to post patrols.

We were nearly to the eastern docks when Layla decided that was close enough. The muffled engine roar was probably already loud enough to hear for anyone on this side of the lake. She parked at a convenience store not far from the docks. An SUV sat at a gas pump, the hose still in the gas tank.

Layla unhooked a pair of mountain bikes and climbed on one.

"Why don't we just walk?" I said.

She raised an eyebrow. "Because this is fast and quiet."

I couldn't argue even though I'd look stupid riding a bike in my assassin gear. Layla was already pedaling away, so I climbed on my bike and hurried to catch up. Rather than take the main entrance to the campgrounds, we took a detour down a hill to nearby docks where a large warehouse held dozens of motorboats suspended from large rods.

There was movement at the docks, but the trees made it difficult to discern many details. We rode the bikes along the edge of the woods near the storage facility then hid them in the bushes and stalked quietly through the trees until we reached the ramp leading down to the floating docks.

There were usually houseboats and yachts docked in this area, but most of them were gone, now replaced by the bronze sails of mechanist submarines.

"Isn't this interesting?" Layla cracked her knuckles. "They've got an entire armada."

"But why?" I looked through my scope and identified men and women in the utilitarian uniforms of mechanists. The majority wore gray and were performing menial tasks, moving crates, unloading submarines, and maintenance. Those in navy blue paraded around the docks pointing this way and that and the grays scurried to obey.

I saw fewer teal uniforms, and only one man in an ivory uniform. I was no expert on the mechanists, but the teals were either apprentices or lower order mechanists. The ivories were worn by those with the highest title of inventor.

"Let me see." Layla took the staff and observed them for a while. "Let's say you became super powerful overnight and could suddenly take over the world. What would you do once you'd won?"

I shrugged. "I have no idea. What's the point of world domination anyway? It's too much responsibility."

"I get the feeling the mechanists don't know what to do either." Layla handed me the staff. "They swept in and gathered up gods know how many nubs, and now they don't know what to do with them all. If you're Cthulhu, you don't want to kill them, because worshippers give power."

I grimaced. "There are six billion regular humans on Gaia. What in the hell do you do with that many bodies? Surely they aren't going to invade Feary with them all."

Layla shrugged. "The important thing is that it doesn't really matter. All we have to do is steal the Tetron and leave this piece of shit dimension to die."

I flicked the scope through several modes. None of the grays had a glow about them, meaning they were barely a step up from nubs. The navy-clad people were mostly the same, with only a smattering of them displaying the glow of a mage. The teal and ivory mechanists had the aura of stronger mages, which made sense. Though mechanists despised magic users, their inventions relied heavily on liquid mana and other magical properties to function properly.

The wind gusted and a flag I hadn't noticed before flapped in the breeze. The background was black with a white symbol in the center, a white circle with an octopus in the middle. "Will you look at that? Cthulhu's got his own flag now."

Layla scoffed. "He's going all out, isn't he?"

The water at the end of the dock rippled and a green-skinned humanoid burst from the water, arced through the air, and landed on the platform. Four more just like it followed seconds apart. Tentacles dangled where mouths should be, and their heads were triangular like those of squids.

The leader tromped up to one of the gray cloaks, tentacles writhing.

"What in the hell are those things?" Layla hissed.

"They're salkos. I've seen sketches of them when I studied Cthulhu lore." I zoomed in and took pictures with my phone. "I have a feeling we're going to see some unpleasant creatures before this is over and done." I patterned a sigil and cupped my ear to enhance my hearing. The distance and ambient sounds made it hard to understand what was being said. The man in gray said something about a reeducation facility. The squid people eventually jumped back into the water and didn't reappear.

I hoped we didn't have to deal with Cthulhu minions. The mechanists would be obstacle enough without salkos jumping into the fray. Either way, our mission might have just become a lot more complicated.

Chapter 18

Layla peered at the docks with her binoculars. "Hear anything useful?"

"Yeah, maybe." I scanned the area for more activity but didn't see anything. "They mentioned a reeducation facility. That must be where they're keeping nubs."

"Oh, indoctrination." Layla tucked her binoculars into a pouch at her side. "Sounds like they have a plan after all."

"Be that as it may, it's not vital to our end game." I switched my staff to longshot mode and began patterning a tracking mark. I usually prepared them in advance but hadn't been expecting to use one anytime soon since I wasn't in the business of marking bounties or targets for Eclipse anymore.

Layla narrowed her eyes. "What are you doing?"

"I'm going to mark that inventor." I pointed at the ivory guy. "If he's anyone important, he'll go to the nearest mechanist headquarters at some point. That's probably where they're keeping the Tetron unless Cthulhu is keeping everything offshore."

"That would make things tricky." Layla sat down and leaned against a tree. "If it's at a mechanist facility, we can be in and out in no time. Easy as stealing a submarine from Dracula's castle."

"Oh, so easy," I said sarcastically. "We had to evacuate the castle through a toilet."

"Evacuate." She chuckled. "Nice pun."

"I wasn't trying to make a pun." I shrugged. "But I'll take credit."

Layla sighed. "That was fun, Cain."

An image of us splashing down in the freezing water flashed through my mind. Layla, so caught up in the adrenalin of the moment pressing her cold lips against mine, her hot tongue finding mine.

"Cain?" Layla snapped her fingers. "Did you forget what you're doing?"

I realized I'd stopped patterning the mark and was staring blankly at a shrub. "Sorry, got distracted."

"Well, you'd better get undistracted. That inventor is heading toward the parking lot."

I finished the pattern. It wasn't as unbreakable as my usual marks, but I didn't have the time to be perfect. I aimed at the inventor, held my breath a split second, and released the shot. It struck him invisibly on the skin of his neck. He swatted at his neck as one might swat a mosquito but seemed otherwise unconcerned.

A pair of teals strode to a bronze car resembling nineteen-twenties Rolls Royce Phantom. The lack of a tailpipe indicated it utilized a clockwork engine powered by liquid mana. One teal climbed in the driver's seat and the other opened the rear door for the inventor to climb in.

I hadn't even noticed the strange car sitting among the abandoned modern ones in the parking lot. Then again, I'd assumed people weren't driving anywhere these days.

"What now?" Layla said.

"We wait for a few minutes." Trying to immediately follow the car on our bikes would be stupid. I scanned the parking lot and spotted several clockwork vehicles about the same size as golf carts. They were the same vehicles the mechanists used in Dracula's castle in Romania.

The parking lot was a good hundred yards from the docks. Trees and other foliage hid it from the view of those down on the water. "We could probably procure one of those carts for ourselves if we so desired."

Layla grinned. "I so desire."

We crouch-walked along the edge of the woods, ducked behind a pickup truck, and made our way to the nearest cart. A small crank to the right of the steering wheel sparked the liquid mana and the gears beneath the hood began to click. It was practically silent compared to the Harleys, but I doubted it would be nearly as fun to drive. Layla, for once, didn't seem to care who drove and plopped into the passenger seat. I shifted into first and pushed forward the accelerator lever.

Layla looked at the levers and buttons and rolled her eyes. "These idiots like to overcomplicate everything. Why use a lever instead of an accelerator pedal? Why is the brake a lever? I'm surprised they use steering wheels at all."

"Mechanists are good at taking existing creations, replacing all the ergonomic features with switches and levers, and then calling it their own invention."

"Sums it up pretty well." Layla leaned back in the seat even though it wasn't adjustable. "We need some better disguises this time. The gray uniforms we stole at Deepvale didn't work very well."

"Unless there are a lot of rank and file mechanists in teal uniforms, stealing a set of that color won't be any better." I concentrated on the mark and felt the connection tugging us to the right toward Lanier Islands.

We were just passing the entrance to another marina when motion caught the corner of my eye. A cart bearing six gray-clad mechanists appeared over the rise. The driver did a double-take when he saw me and Layla. Mechanist constables wore black. Layla's yoga pants and t-shirt weren't enough to pass muster.

I yanked back on the brake lever and the cart slowed. Layla threw a dagger. It plunged into the front right tire of the other cart. The wheel popped and the vehicle veered out of control, rolling down a steep embankment to a chorus of shouts and cries of dismay. A tree shuddered and the cart crunched.

We leapt from our cart and looked down the embankment. The cart had come to rest upside down at the bottom. A pair of injured grays lay moaning near the cart. One was pinned between the cart and the tree, and the other three had fallen out on the way down.

"Can't let them report back," Layla said.

I nodded. "Make it look like an accident, okay?"

She snorted. "Already did."

I clambered down to the nearest mechanist. Aside from some dirt, he didn't look badly injured. I fixed that by powering my body sigils and throwing him head over heels down the embankment. His nearby comrade followed shortly after. Layla snapped the necks of two more mechanists then checked the vitals of the guy pinned against the tree.

I reached bottom and slammed one man against a tree until he stopped moving, then repeated the process with another. They were all too stunned from the accident to even beg for their lives. I didn't feel anything as we ended the lives of six people, not even a little bit of satisfaction despite the horrors they'd unleashed on the world.

Layla retrieved her dagger from the wheel of the vehicle. "Why don't we steal their uniforms and hide the bodies?"

I considered it. "Six missing people won't go unnoticed. Better to have it look like they took a plunge and died instead of sparking a manhunt that'll make it harder for us to get around."

She nodded. "Provided they don't think it's crazy that everyone died in the accident."

I snorted. "That's a lot of snapped necks and blunt force trauma for a thirty-foot fall, but stranger things have happened."

Layla chuckled. "That's for damned sure."

I used the true sight scope to scan the area as we climbed aboard our cart and followed the tracker. One accident might pass the bullshit test, but another one would raise alarms for certain. Thankfully, the mechanists assumed they were in complete control of the area. After all, all the regular humans had been taken to parts unknown, leaving them the masters of the world.

We passed a water park and crossed a bridge. A roundabout led to a fork. The mark had gone to the right. Most of the island was occupied by a golf course and amenities. If memory served, and it usually did, there was nothing at the end of the road except for a lodge. My scope picked up scattered heat signatures ahead, so we stashed the cart in the woods and continued on foot.

The Lake Lanier Legacy Lodge was a finely constructed facility, with stone arches and Dutch woodwork. Three clockwork Phantoms were parked beneath the fancy portico. A pair of grays stood outside the portico smoking cigarettes. A wheelbarrow and other nearby yard equipment indicated they were responsible for lawn maintenance.

"How sweet." Layla scoffed. "They created a new world order but still want a neat lawn."

"Always more of the same when it comes to conquerors." I studied the area with my scope. The body of the lodge was made with stucco concrete, making detection of heat signatures possible only where occupants were close to the outer wall. Remaining in the woods, we circled around to the back of the lodge and found a full-fledged pool party.

Athletic men and busty women frolicked in and around the pool, most of them doting on people with average and outright flabby bodies.

"Oh, sex slaves, how nice." Layla produced a dagger and fingered the blade as if itching to throw it. "Or maybe they're collaborators."

The mechanists had apparently rounded up the best-looking nubs from their prisoners and were exploiting them as servers and more. An old man whose skin hadn't seen the sun in a decade lounged in a pair of swimming briefs next to the pool while a pair of muscular young men rubbed him down with oil.

Another pair of mechanist men watched in amusement as a group of shy women slowly stripped naked for their viewing pleasure. A woman in teal watched disapprovingly from a balcony overlooking the pool, but it was doubtful her objections would hold much sway.

I pointed to the glowing lights. "They have electricity. Probably set up a liquid mana converter somewhere to power the place."

"Must be their headquarters if they went through all the trouble." Layla tapped a finger on her chin. "I say we grab one of the teals and question them. If they don't know anything, then we'll kidnap an ivory."

I nodded. "Good idea." I scanned the area for opportunities. It was broad daylight, so infiltration would be difficult without a disguise. Security was non-existent, which made our task more difficult. It would have been easy to take out a couple of unsuspecting guards and use their uniforms to pass initial scrutiny. The main difficulty would be in traversing the open space between us and the lodge. Once inside things would be much easier.

"We'll have to go in the front." Layla circled back around the side without waiting for my opinion.

I followed until the portico was front and center. The pair of lawn maintenance grays were still enjoying a smoke break and showed no signs of departing anytime soon. Layla watched them for a moment and seemed to arrive at a decision.

"What are you about to do?" I asked.

She pulled off her shoes and began tugging her yoga pants down over her generous bum. "Just the oldest trick in the book. Works every time until it doesn't." She stripped down to her panties and bra. Her torso was small-breasted and athletic, and her lower body looked muscular enough to leg-press a truck. "Just be ready to go on a killing spree if this doesn't work."

I looked appreciatively at her athletic form. Scars crisscrossed her back and she'd been stabbed in the calf on one leg and in the thigh on the other at some point in her sordid history. "Somehow, I don't think that'll be necessary."

She touched the ragged scar on her thigh. "You like that one?"

"I'm more interested in what happened to your back."

Layla tensed and leaned toward me. "I'm not saying. And if you go to Hemlock for answers, I'll kill both of you, okay?"

I grinned. "There's no one I'd rather have kill me than you."

The tension in her shoulders eased. "Gods you're a pain in the ass, Cain." She crept from the bushes, staying low and timing her movement for when the grays weren't looking.

But there wasn't enough cover for her to make it all the way. One of them spotted her and nudged his companion.

"Hey, what are you doing over here?" The taller of the two marched over to Layla.

She stiffened and stood up guiltily, shoulders slumped in defeat. "Please don't tell them. I just had to get away from the party for a while."

The tall gray smirked. "Fine, but you'll have to pay the toll."

Layla shrank back. "The toll?"

He grabbed her arm. "Yeah. Or I'll tell them you tried to run away, and you know what they do with runaways."

"Please, mister, don't tell them." Layla began to sob. "I'll do anything."

He smacked her butt hard enough to leave a handprint. "You're damned right you will." He turned to his comrade. "You want a piece of ass too?"

The other guy looked her up and down appraisingly. "Hell yeah."

"Right out here in front?" Layla looked around frantically. "Can we do it in the bushes over there? I don't want to be seen."

"Fine." The gray squeezed her breasts. "Barely enough tit to feel anything, but you got more than enough ass to make up for it."

Layla slumped and walked toward my position with the grays behind her. She grinned, eyes lighting with eagerness as she neared the trees. The grays chattered excitedly about all the nasty things they had planned for their prisoners, sounding like a pair of pubescent teens who'd watched too much porn.

Their fantasies were over in a flash the moment they crossed the tree line. She gripped the shorter one by the head and snapped his neck violently, then hoisted the other one up by his throat and grinned maniacally at him. "What was that you wanted to do to my ass, you little shit?"

He couldn't answer because he was too busy choking to death. Layla set him on the ground and clamped a hand over his mouth so he couldn't scream. She gripped his privates and squeezed until his eyes bulged.

I felt ill just watching it. "Just kill him and get it over with, you sicko."

Layla obliged and the body hit the ground. "Gods, I enjoyed that too much, didn't I?"

"Enough to make my balls hurt." I took the taller guy's uniform and grimaced at the odor. "Man, these guys haven't bathed in a while."

"I noticed." Layla yanked the uniform from the shorter guy and sniffed them. "We won't get far in these."

"Just need to cross the open space and we're golden." I held my breath and slipped into the uniform. "You can be pretty fucking insane sometimes, you know that?"

She shrugged. "I have issues. Being a half-blood isn't exactly a cakewalk."

"I'm surprised you even told me that much about you." I frisked the uniform I'd taken and found only a padlock key in the pockets.

"Me too." She put her clothes back on then slipped the uniform on over them. "Let's go."

We were eight murders into our little adventure and still hadn't learned anything. I hoped this venture wasn't a complete waste of time.

Chapter 19

A woman in teal stepped outside to smoke and barely even glanced at us as we walked back toward the lawn maintenance equipment. We'd quickly learned during our infiltration of Deepvale that the grays were just grunts and barely worth noticing. While these disguises might allow us to clean bathrooms without anyone complaining, they wouldn't get us into a room with the higher-ups.

I tested that by approaching the main entrance. The woman wrinkled her nose. "What do you think you're doing, scrubs?"

I lowered my eyes to appear subservient. "We were told to clean a bathroom in the lobby."

"Who told you that?" She looked around as if there might be a manager nearby. "They're only using the glitzy nubs for that. And you reek. Have you been swimming in sewage?" She shooed us away. "Go before I call a constable to come put you filthy scrubs in your place."

Layla's fist clenched, but she bowed. "Yes milady."

The woman stiffened. "You will address me as befits my rank of engineer, scrub."

"Yes, madam engineer." Layla bowed again and backed away.

The woman huffed and continued smoking as if we'd stopped existing the moment the conversation ended.

Even I wanted to punch the woman. "Man, they treat the grays like shit."

"You know life is bad when they call you a scrub." Layla cracked her knuckles.

I rolled the lawnmower around the corner from the portico. "The only other entrances are in the pool area. There's no way we'll sneak through there."

Layla looked up and around. There were windows all along the first floor but breaking one would be noisy and leave evidence that someone was up to no good. "No roof access that I can see from here. There must be an emergency exit around here somewhere."

"Let's walk to the other side." I pushed the lawnmower ahead of me and we walked across the parking lot. The teal beneath the portico paid us no attention as she stubbed out her cigarette and went back inside.

The left side of the building hosted a restaurant with big windows. There were people inside eating and drinking. A couple of people glanced at us as we walked past, but otherwise no one seemed to care. We walked around and came across a service entrance. An attractive young woman in a French maid uniform stood next to the dumpster bawling.

She saw us coming and stiffened. "Please don't report me!"

I frowned. "What's wrong?" This seemed like a good opportunity to gather some intel from a nub perspective. Maybe she could tell us what the mechanists were doing here.

Layla gave her a concerned look. "What did they do to you?"

Seeing that she had a sympathetic audience, her eyes brightened. "They said I wasn't pretty enough for the pool party and took that skank Jaden instead while I have to clean dishes and serve food! Even Hunter and Posy got to go."

Layla barely repressed a snort. "You're not upset that the world as you knew it ended and is now run by a bunch of weirdos in color-coded uniforms?"

The woman blinked. "Well, yeah, that totally sucks too, but what can I do about it? They took my parents and brothers to the re-ed center in Gainesville but picked me out because I'm pretty. Apparently, I'm not pretty enough."

Layla scoffed. "Damn, maybe it's a good thing the nubs aren't in control anymore."

"Why do you call us nubs?" The woman was no longer crying. "It sounds stupid."

"It's slang," I said. "It means you're a normal human and not supernatural."

She shuddered. "Well, I wouldn't want to be a squid man."

I nodded. "What's your name?"

A cautious smile spread across her face. "I'm Madison. You guys are nicer than the other mechanics."

"Mechanists," I said.

"Oh, whatever." She laughed. "I never knew people who fixed cars could, like, take over. It's so weird."

"Well, if people can't drive, they're powerless." Layla patted her shoulder. "And that leaves the mechanics with all the working cars."

"I'm surprised Jefferson isn't with them," Madison said. "He's, like, the best mechanic in town, according to Dad."

This girl barely had the brain function to walk, much less give us intel. I nodded. "Well, maybe Jefferson is with them." I cracked open the service door and peeked inside. "Are there a lot of people in the kitchen?"

"Bob and Margaret, mainly. They're ugly but they can cook." Madison listed off three more pretty people who'd been pressed into working as servers.

"What have the mechanists been doing besides eating, drinking, and partying?" Layla asked.

"I dunno." Madison shrugged and looked immediately disinterested. "A bunch of them in white uniforms go to a conference room every day and talk about maps or something. I serve them bagels and coffee and it's awful, because they keep touching me and slapping my ass like I'm a piece of meat."

"That's all they see you as." Layla scowled. "Dogs."

"Well, we've got to get to work." I stepped inside the kitchen. Meat sizzled on a grill and steam rose into a vent on the other side of a partition. The top of a chef's hat was all I could see of the person on the other side. Going right would take us to double doors and out into the restaurant. Thankfully, the kitchen had another exit.

Madison didn't follow us inside, probably so she could sulk next to the dumpster as long as possible.

I eased open the rear door and found a hallway with four doors. A locked metal door with a small glass window led to a stairwell, another opened into a large supply closet, and the third into a laundry room. The fourth led back to the lobby. We entered the third and began rummaging for disguises. A pair of ivory uniforms hung on the end of a rack along with a dozen teal and a handful in black. There were no gray ones to be found.

"Guess the scrubs are responsible for cleaning their own clothes," Layla muttered. She counted the black uniforms. "Judging from the numbers, it looks like there are more engineers than constables."

I frowned. "Constables are their foot soldiers. You'd think there'd be a lot more."

Layla tapped a finger to her lips. "So, would we go more unnoticed as engineers or constables?"

"Either one would be risky." I gave it more thought. "We might pass muster as nubs in hotel uniforms."

"That might be less threatening." Layla approached another rack, this one packed with French maid uniforms and burgundy tuxedos. "We also need a key to a room."

"I've got an idea for that." I took a teal robe that fit me and put it on. "Maybe I can go ask for one."

"Don't let another engineer see you," Layla said. "I have a feeling they know all the other engineers here."

"I'll be careful."

Layla dumped her gray uniform and put on a teal one. "I'd better go with you in case you fuck up."

I shrugged. "Let's just hope we don't run into our friend we met under the portico."

Layla bared her teeth. "Oh, if we do, you can bet she won't be making it out alive."

We went back into the hallway and took the door leading into the lobby. A couple of nubs walked past, but they kept their eyes on the floor when they passed us. Apparently, they'd also received a verbal drubbing from a snobby teal.

The female clerk behind the desk stiffened when we came into view. I glanced around to make sure there weren't other mechanisms in the vicinity and went behind the long lobby desk.

"I want a room closer to the conference room," I demanded.

The attendant shrank in on herself. "We don't have any more rooms there, master engineer. The master inventors took them all."

"I just arrived." Layla feigned a yawn. "Where is the main conference room?"

The girl looked confused. "Where the inventors meet?"

"Yes, of course."

"Down the hall to the left, master engineer." The girl took out a printed map of the hotel and drew a line from the lobby to the conference room. "The engineers meet in the opposite direction." She traced another line to the right.

I sighed. "Is there a room directly above this conference room?"

The clerk blinked. "Yes, but that won't make the room more convenient for you."

"It's fine. I'll take it." I huffed on my fingernails and polished them on my uniform.

"Yes, master engineer." She took a keycard, entered a number in the computer application, and programmed the card with a scanner.

"I'll take the one next to it," Layla said.

The clerk obliged.

I watched as she programmed another card. There was an option to make a key for housekeeping on the main screen. I spoke to Layla in Alder. "Distract her so I can make a master key."

Layla frowned, but got the gist of it. She turned to the girl and smirked. "Don't you need to see my ID?"

The girl went stiff with fright. "Absolutely not, master engineer!"

"You're a cute little thing." Layla put her arm around the girl and led her a few feet away, so she wasn't facing the computer.

I opened the list of housekeepers and clicked one of the names. The clerk was logged in as an admin, so it let me program as many keycards as I wanted. I made one card with one housekeeper's account, then made another with a second housekeeper account. I doubted these people even worked here anymore now that the mechanists controlled it.

A couple of mouse clicks closed the windows and returned to the main screen. When I turned, I wasn't surprised to see Layla making out with the clerk, or at least trying to. The girl was rigid with fright.

Layla backed away. "You're not into women, are you?"

The clerk replied in a quavering voice. "I'll do whatever you want, master engineer."

"Oh, I'm not a cruel mistress." She booped the girl's nose. "Don't worry your pretty little head about me, okay?"

"Y-yes, master engineer."

"I like the sound of mistress engineer better," Layla replied.

"Yes, mistress engineer." The girl looked at the floor.

I rolled my eyes at Layla. "Thank you for your help, clerk."

The girl didn't look up. "You're welcome, sir."

I went back to the service hallway and used the housekeeping key to unlock the stairwell door. "Now we've got the run of the place."

Layla rummaged through the housekeeping clothes until she found a set of gray slacks and matching shirt that fit her. "I don't see any French maid outfits in here."

I scoffed. "They probably found them in a lingerie store, because I don't know of any legitimate hotels that would make housekeeping wear them." I found another housekeeping uniform for myself and put it on. "Let's hope the real housekeepers are still wearing these." I grabbed a rolling laundry basket and put our stolen teal uniforms inside. I removed the ivory uniform from the rack and held it up to me. It was a bit short but could work in a pinch. I dropped it inside, then piled towels on top.

A service elevator in the stairwell took us to the second floor where we almost immediately ran into a pair of engineers strolling down the hall. They ignored us until the last moment when one held up a finger to his comrade and turned to us. "I need fresh towels in room two eleven, pronto."

I bowed. "Yes, master engineer."

He grunted and continued walking.

"We could probably stealth kill all these pricks and pile their bodies in a room," Layla whispered. "I'll bet we could get all of them before anyone noticed."

I snorted. "While I'd love to test your theory, let's try to keep a low profile for now." I went to room two eleven and dumped some fresh towels in the bathroom, then searched the room. An old leather chest held several fresh sets of undergarments and teal uniforms. A document pouch bulged at the seams with blueprints and letters. Some letters were addressed to inventors and others were attached to replies, most of them disparaging a design the engineer had submitted.

"I guess this is how you become an inventor." I dropped the pouch back into the suitcase. "Just keep submitting blueprints until you can't take the rejection anymore."

"Nothing about their current plans?" Layla said.

I shook my head. "Let's take a look in the other rooms."

We randomly inspected ten rooms and found nothing but teal uniforms and shoddy blueprints in most of them. It seemed all the inventors were staying on the first floor near their conference room.

"We should just kidnap an inventor," Layla said. "I'll bet they'd tell us where the Tetron is."

I gave it some thought. "Yeah, it's probably the fastest way. But I'm concerned that once we do that, it'll raise an alarm and it won't be so easy for us to move around anymore."

"We could make him disappear." Layla found the room the clerk had assigned me and opened it with her keycard. "That'll give us some time."

"We already killed six grays in the cart and another two here. We can hide those bodies and they'll probably go unnoticed. But if an inventor goes missing, they might link this sudden spate of deaths to an insurgency. Security will be increased and finding the Tetron will be even more impossible than it already is."

"What if the Tetron is right here right now?" Layla closed the room door behind us. "We could be out of here and back in Kansas with Toto in no time."

"You've got to work on your pop culture references," I said. "That one was pretty lame."

"Shut up, Cain." Layla jabbed a finger at the floor. "What if the Tetron is in that conference room beneath us?"

"Then we'll find out with some good old-fashioned spy work." I shoved the bed against the left wall then summoned my staff and scanned the floor with the scope. It didn't pick up anything from the floor below, probably because of thick insulation in the ceiling of the conference room.

I didn't want to set off a fire alarm, so I used a dagger instead of my brightblade to cut out a large patch of carpet and the foam padding beneath. The concrete beneath the padding presented an obstacle the dagger couldn't overcome. I activated my brightblade and pushed it into the concrete slowly, giving myself a wide margin between the sizzling blade and the carpet.

The edges of the concrete hissed and cracked. Insulation beneath it began to smoke. An alarm blared. Layla cursed and destroyed the smoke detector with a quickly thrown dagger.

"Let's hope that thing doesn't alert a computer." Layla removed her dagger. "Or we'll have company real soon."

I finished carving out a circle of concrete. The freed slab didn't fall far due to the insulation beneath it. Layla opened the sliding glass door to air out the room while we waited for the edges of the concrete to cool enough for us to move it. I peeked into the hallway to make sure there weren't any concerned hotel staff rushing to see what triggered the smoke detector. It seemed Layla had killed it quickly enough.

I dug into the laundry basket and pulled my clothes from the bottom, then plucked a pair of thick gloves from the utility belt. The slab was still warm, even through the material, but I managed to reorient it and wrestle it out of the hole while Layla watched with an amused expression. Gray foam filled the cavity below. I cut out a circle with the dagger, careful not to stab too deep lest I cut a hole into the ceiling below before I was ready. Thankfully, the foam wasn't glued down so it only took a moment to expose the drywall underneath.

"Finally." Now all I had to do was cut a small hole without raining dust down below.

Someone pounded on the door. "Constables. Open up!"

It seemed the alarm hadn't gone unnoticed after all.

Chapter 20

I grabbed the bottom of the bed and dragged it to cover the hole and the mess, then pointed urgently at the pierced smoke detector on the floor. Layla tossed the ruined device in the garbage and held up a finger as the constable pounded the door again. I took cover between the bed and the wall, still able to see the door with the help of a mirror on the back wall.

She stripped down to her undergarments and turned on the shower in the bathroom. Waited a moment, and then yanked open the door as the constable held up his fist again.

"What's the problem?" she said in a tired tone. "I'm trying to take a shower in here."

"A fire alarm was reported on the second floor." He looked at her suspiciously, his gaze not once wandering over her half-naked form. "Did you hear it?"

She shook her head. "No, I took a nap. Maybe that's what woke me up a moment ago."

He shifted his tight black uniform as if making sure she saw the color then stared at her for several uncomfortable seconds. His nostrils flared. "What smells in here?"

Layla backed away and pointed to the open glass door. "I don't know. Maybe they're cooking something outside."

He stared in that direction for several uncomfortable seconds, then nodded. "Good day."

Layla closed the door and huffed. "Guess my tits weren't big enough for him."

"Maybe he's not into women." I shrugged. "Close call."

"Yeah, for him." Layla put an ear to the door. "He's knocking on all the doors. I don't think very many people are in their rooms."

"Well, let's hope he gives up." I pushed the bed out of the way and summoned my staff for another look through the scope. This time I was able to see thirteen distinct heat signatures on the other side. They were about twenty feet below us, meaning the conference room had a high ceiling. I preferred seeing actual faces, but the scope couldn't see through objects.

As far as I knew there wasn't a spell that made objects transparent from one side. Such a spell would've made my life a lot easier, but the best way was to cut a small hole in the ceiling and use a flexible camera. It was nub tech, but it worked well.

I drew my wands from my clothes in the laundry basket and lay down on my stomach next to the hole. I cast a burrowing spell with one and a vacuum spell with the other. As the first spell slowly carved a hole, the second one drew the dust up and away so it wouldn't fall onto the table below. It took the space of several minutes but stealthily created a hole without showering the room occupants below with drywall dust.

The hole was no bigger around than my pinky—all the space I needed for the spy work. I produced the telescoping camera from my utility belt and fed it through the hole. The image fed into an application on my smartphone. Indistinct voices drifted up from below. I could have used an amplification spell, but the camera also had a microphone. I gave Layla an earbud and inserted the other one into my right ear.

"We're running out of time, and Cthulhu does not have infinite patience," said a familiar voice.

I oriented the camera until I found the speaker. It was none other than our old friend, Horatio. He'd made quite a name for himself in this dimension.

"The education devices still aren't working properly," another man said. "Nubs are dying or suffering permanent brain damage."

A woman stood. "I've said it before, and I'll say it again. Fervent belief does not come at the hands of a device. It comes from fear, love, and devotion. Cthulhu should reveal himself so the nubs will bow down before him."

"You've said your piece many times, Hilda." Horatio held up a hand. "I will hear that objection no more. An education device will allow us to program the nubs into doing whatever we want. We will certainly need their numbers if we're to keep pushing into the Midwest."

Layla and I frowned at each other.

"The Midwest?" I whispered. "Does that mean they haven't conquered the entire continent yet?"

Layla pursed her lips. "Rotate the camera around the room."

I did and was rewarded almost at once. Several maps were pinned to the wall, each one with a different continent on it. The coastlines of nearly every continent were shaded crimson. Asia and most of Europe were white beyond the coastline. Parts of countries in Central and South America were green and other parts yellow, but the vast majority was also white.

Canada was almost entirely green, as was the west coast of the United States. The Southeast was green with yellow pockets and the Midwest was almost entirely yellow. Arrows from the coastal states pointed inland toward Colorado, Kansas, and other midwestern states.

"The red must indicate where they slammed the coasts with tsunamis," Layla said. "Green means conquered, and yellow means in conflict."

I nodded. "The arrows must indicate where survivors and others fled. And if white indicates untaken territory, then it means this world isn't nearly as bad off as we thought it was."

"Or else those areas capitulated without a fight." Layla focused the camera on Russia. It was covered in brown dots. "I can't figure out what that one means."

I shook my head. "No idea. I doubt Russia went down without a fight, and I can't believe China would capitulate unless they directly overthrew the leaders."

"Doesn't matter anyway." Layla put a finger to her lips and tapped the earbud.

I tuned into what was being said.

"What does the military have to say, Commander Sars?"

A man in navy blue stood to speak. "The Firsters and Enders are a formidable alliance. Daphne and their other demis are not affected by the music boxes and our exo suits are no match for them. They also employ a small army of supers and nubs who were mutated with genetic material from demis. We simply don't have enough demis to fight them."

Layla scoffed. "Never thought I'd pull for the Firsters."

"Yeah, me either." I continued to listen.

Horatio slapped a hand on the table. "What, then, shall we do? Cthulhu grows impatient. Even though he desires to rule over an undamaged world, he will likely use one of the earth-maker weapons to annihilate everything in the Midwest."

"I see no issue with that tactic," Sars said. "Once we master these weapons, we can simply rebuild it as we see fit."

"I prefer not to waste so many beings, especially when they could be bodies for the war on Feary." Horatio shook his head. "We will consider using Soultaker against the enemy. Not even their demis can withstand an army of the dead."

Sars shook his head. "Who is strong enough to bear the sword?"

"Esteri for certain, though the other horsemen may also be strong enough."

I stiffened at the name. "Esteri? That was the name of Hannah's mother."

"Sounds like she's dropped her given name." Layla pursed her lips. "Now she's out for revenge against the world that killed her mother...or something like that."

The mechanists continued plotting, and Horatio called a vote. All the ivories voted for his plan. Those in navy blue didn't vote, which apparently, meant it was unanimous. Soultaker would be the next weapon wielded in the upcoming war, and the gods only knew what would happen next.

After the naval officers left, the inventors began discussing other matters.

Horatio motioned toward someone off camera. "I would call the observers to tell us what possibilities lay ahead."

I rotated the camera toward the entrance as a group of people in civilian clothes walked inside, the lead person bearing a laptop. Layla and I did a double-take at that since mechanists weren't fond of nub technology. Every last one of the people in the group looked sick and emaciated. Several bore sores and blisters on their skin as if exposed to extreme heat.

A man in glasses stepped up to a podium and attached a cable to his laptop. A projector blinked on and a pie chart appeared on a screen to the man's left. He cleared his throat and spoke.

"After more experimentation, we discovered a way to manipulate the Tetron, so it projects multiple possible branches in the space-time continuum. Combined with events from Dimension Prime Beta, since its events closely mirror ours, we've improved our model for predictions." He cleared his throat nervously. The slide on the projector changed to one with three spheres. The top sphere was labeled Prime, and the other two Prime Alpha and Prime Beta.

"How long after us did Beta reach the armory?" an inventor asked.

"Two months after receiving Master Horatio's letter," the man said. "We discovered Master Horatio in Prime was unable to read the entire letter due to an unforeseen ink spill on his desk that blotted the letter."

Horatio scowled. "One minor change and our paths have completely diverged."

"Do you think it coincidence?" another inventor said. "After all, we were assured of help."

"Loki would not profit from such a blunder." Horatio turned to the presenter. "Is there evidence of divine tampering in Prime?"

The man gulped. "Multiple instances, but nothing around the time the ink spill occurred."

Horatio pursed his lips. "You've rewound and examined the time period thoroughly?"

The presenter nodded assuredly. "We inspected the thread and found nothing, unlike the instances where Loki intervened."

Layla's brow furrowed. "Gods be damned, that Tetron allows them to rewind time and examine it?"

"I think the bigger news here is that Loki is actively helping them," I whispered. "I don't know how Prime survived when two other dimensions failed."

Horatio sighed long and loud. "It seems the ink spill was mere chance." He flourished a hand. "Continue, observer."

The presenter wiped sweat from his forehead and continued. "We projected over forty possible branches in which apocalypse weapons are used. In eighty-seven percent of cases where Earthmaker is employed, a chain reaction leads to the cooling of the Earth's core. With the collapse of the magnetic field, the ensuing havoc slowly kills all life on Earth until only the hardiest survivors remain."

Horatio looked unfazed. "Who did you project as the wielder of Earthmaker?"

The presenter cleared his throat. "Esteri wields it in twenty-nine percent of the projected futures. Other demis split the rest of the percentage almost evenly. When Esteri wields it, the destruction is far greater."

A female inventor raised a question. "How do these projections work?"

"In order to see an object's causality arc, we place it on a table near the Tetron, then each observer touches the object and the Tetron." The man rubbed at a sore on his hand. "The timeline splits into multiple threads, representing all the possible outcomes. We then grasp the timeline thread and view the projection until we've seen a sufficient period of time."

The woman pursed her lips. "So, Esteri might wield it in multiple branches, but other minor changes cause differences further out."

He nodded. "Yes, Master Inventor."

Horatio tapped a finger on the table. "In thirteen percent of the branches, Earthmaker is used successfully?"

The man winced. "I would not call those scenarios successful. In those branches, an unknown man wields Earthmaker and turns it against us."

Murmurs of disbelief rose around the room.

"Who is this man?" several demanded.

The speaker tapped a button on his laptop and switched to a grainy photo of a man holding Earthmaker aloft as an army of mechanists in clockwork armor descended on him. Another figure stood next to him, sword raised above their head. The speaker tapped a button, and a new photo appeared, this one of a massive boulder crushing a horde of mechanists. This time I could make out that the figure with the sword was female, but I still couldn't see faces.

The next picture was still grainy, but the faces were clear enough to make out. The man with Earthmaker was me, and the female was Layla holding Soultaker.

Horatio abruptly laughed. "That man is Cain and he's certainly no threat to us. Esteri saw to that almost immediately."

The speaker nodded. "Should I continue, master inventor?"

Horatio nodded. "Yes. What are the projections if Soultaker is used?"

The speaker nodded. "We observed eighteen possible branches. In forty-one percent, the ghost army massacres millions because the wielder is unable to sufficiently control them. The remaining probabilities have a mostly positive outcome."

"Oh, enough with the projections, percentages, and nub babble." An inventor with muttonchops rose, smacking his lips noisily. "We have been frozen in place for two months as we project favorable scenarios. I say we press ahead with Soultaker and finish off the Firsters and the Enders once and for all."

"Hear, hear!" a chorus of voices agreed.

Horatio held up a hand and rose from his seat. "Darby, need I remind you that this war is merely a practice run for the real thing? Once we have perfected our strategy, we will use the Tetron to attack Prime since Loki's machinations did not work there as planned."

Darby sighed. "Very well, Horatio. But I believe we've dawdled long enough, and I'm certain Cthulhu grows tired of our dithering."

"Two days." Horatio held up a pair of fingers toward the speaker. "Return with your predictions then and we will proceed with the war." He looked at Darby. "Agreed?"

Darby raised a fist. "Hear, hear!"

The other inventors raised their fists with his.

Horatio motioned toward the door. "Then go, observers, and bring us good news."

The speaker gulped. "Yes, master inventor." He and the other observers hobbled out of the room.

"How much longer for that group?" Darby asked once they'd left.

"Another week at most until they're of no use." Horatio yawned. "The shields in place are not filtering out enough of the peculiar radiation from the Tetron. As it now stands, we still have a sizable herd of intelligent nubs who have been tested and found compatible with the Tetron."

A woman slapped the table to draw attention to herself. "Why have we not found the bloody owl from the armory and used it? Surely the creature is still on Oblivion."

"It was heavily damaged and lost in a crevice." Horatio shook his head. "I'm afraid it would be a waste to send another expedition in search of it."

"But we still don't know how to use the Tetron to travel to Prime," the woman said. "That owl surely knows."

"Belinda, bringing a sentient creation of Hephaestus' into our midst would be a terrible idea," Darby said. "The owl could be a spy. Our ingenuity is boundless. We will find a way to protect observers from the radiation just as we will discover how to open the way to Prime with the Tetron."

Belinda scoffed. "Fine. Let us waste another month, the next, and the next until the year has died on the vine and we are no further along. Or let us send a small expedition back to Oblivion that the owl might be found and questioned. It was perfectly willing to answer our questions at first. Had we made sure the clockwork hound was destroyed in the first place, it would not have reignited the battle and led to the owl being damaged and lost."

A group of inventors raised their fists. "Hear, hear."

Horatio pursed his lips. "Very well, but it will be a small group. I will tell Sars to give you the *Archimedes* with only bridge crew. You may select two constables to accompany you as well."

"Most generous, Horatio." Belinda bowed slightly. "I will leave first thing in the morning."

"Perhaps we should ask the observers to look into the success of such a mission," Darby said.

Horatio shook his head. "Asking them to look into another dimension doubles the radiation. If we wish to proceed with the war in two days, we can't afford to divert their attention at this crucial moment."

"Any news from Torvin Rayne?" a woman asked.

"He returned from Feary last night and said the fae are gathering troops in Faevalorn." Horatio didn't look concerned. "He returned to Feary this morning to see if he could recruit potential allies. A tribe of ogres is considering the offer. Then he will travel to Oblivion to check on the progress there."

Darby clapped his hands. "Excellent. I hear ogre females are rather tantalizing."

"That reminds me." Horatio sighed and rose from his seat. "I have one more thing to discuss involving the glitzy nubs."

"Gods, not this again," Darby complained.

"Yes, this again." He stared at the man. "They are here for our enjoyment, but not complete disposal."

Several others murmured agreement.

Another man stood. "Taylee was my favorite, you royal ass. Yet you borrowed her and others and left a corpse when you were done with her."

Horatio raised his eyebrows disapprovingly. "Darby, you and your group absolutely must refrain from damaging the goods. There is no infinite supply of beautiful nubs, and some of us have a fondness for particular ones. If you cannot abide by that rule, then your privileges will be restricted or revoked."

Darby and a group of other men groaned in disapproval.

Darby held out his hands in pleading. "Horatio, then I beseech you to give us our choice from among the plain nubs in the reeducation centers. Surely no one will miss those."

Horatio pursed his lips. "I will submit it for a vote, but within reason. No more than three a week, Darby, do you hear me? They may be normal, but they are living, sentient beings."

"I hear you," Darby said.

"Very well, then." Horatio cleared his throat. "Provided Darby and company can restrain themselves, shall we allow them a limit of three plain nubs per week they may use as they see fit, but all others shall be preserved?"

The vote was all over the place with only Darby and a few other men passionately raising their fists in agreement. The others who voted for it seemed to hold that group in great distaste. Then Horatio adjourned the meeting and the room emptied.

I cast Layla a look.

She barked a laugh. "We're going to Oblivion, aren't we?"

"Yes, we are." Because we really had no choice.

Chapter 21

I told Layla my reasoning for the latest twist on our travel plans. "We need Noctua as much as we need the Tetron if we're to get back to Prime." I tapped a finger on my chin. "Let's find the location of the Tetron tonight and then stowaway on Belinda's submarine so we can ambush the crew and take it ourselves."

"Why not just steal a submarine of our own?" Layla said.

"Because we need our activity to remain off the radar until we're ready to snatch the Tetron." I grabbed the two-way radio and clicked the scramble button to encrypt the signal. "Hannah, you there?"

The reply came seconds later. "Cain! Are you okay?"

"I'm fine." I brought her up to date on what we'd discovered and told her our plan.

Hannah sighed. "I don't like that plan at all, but you'll do it anyway, won't you?"

"It's the best way forward. Stealing the Tetron won't get us home, but maybe Noctua can." I glanced at Layla, but she didn't seem concerned. "Heard anything from Hemlock?"

"Yes," Hannah said. "The Feary portals are heavily guarded, probably in case the fae send through troops, but it doesn't look like the mechanists are traveling through them."

"Probably because they haven't finished conquering Gaia," Layla said. "It seems they don't control as much as we thought they did."

"Why hit the southeast United States first?" Hannah asked.

"Atlanta is a major Feary hub," I replied. "They need to lock down all the portals to prevent the fae from sending troops. I'd be surprised if the fae didn't simply disable all the portals."

"Oh, they will." Layla scoffed. "The fae can be patient when they have to be. They'll wait until Umbra drops their guard and surprise attack."

"The humans have Torvin on their side this time, and he wants revenge." I shook my head. "Gods help this world if they put him in control of their armed forces."

Layla smirked. "Maybe you'll have the chance to kill him again. Wouldn't that be nice?"

"I wish there was something we could do." Hannah sighed. "It's awful leaving these people to suffer."

I hadn't mentioned what the mechanists were doing with their harem of prisoners, and I felt guilty about it. Hannah had suffered at the hands of sexual abusers and would demand we do something to free them. But even if we liberated this compound, what good would it do? If Torvin returned with an army of ogres, things would get even worse.

The only things holding the mechanists at bay were the Firsters and their squad of demis. I hated to even think it, but the humans would probably be better off if the Firsters won. But sooner or later the fae would respond and reclaim their prize.

I clicked the scramble button again. "Hannah, we'll be out of communications range for at least a day. If we're gone more than two days, then something went wrong. Adjust your plans accordingly."

"Don't you dare fail, Cain." Hannah's tone was steely.

"Aw, don't cry." Layla made pouty lips. "Cain's got me to rescue him when he fails."

"You be careful too, Layla." Hannah's voice softened. "Good luck." The radio clicked to silence.

Layla flinched, eyes uncertain. Then she looked at me and scowled. "I don't like it when she's nice."

"You don't like it when anyone is nice to you." I put away my gadgets and brushed off my hands. I went to the sliding glass door, opened it, and stepped outside. I had a nice view of the lake, but that was about it. I turned to Layla. "I'll be right back."

She frowned, then turned away and flopped on the bed.

I cast a camouflage blind around me, then leapt up and gripped the edge of the roof. The sloped metal roof was slick, but I managed to hoist myself up without too much problem. Even though the blind obfuscated the vision of anyone who might have looked toward me, I kept low to minimize the blur. Mechanists were well aware of magic and a mysterious blur would be a dead giveaway to those with a trained eye.

Once I reached the peak, I realized the roof wasn't completely sloped. There was a five-foot drop-off to a flat industrial roof, providing plenty of concealment when I dropped down to it. I made my way to the front of the lodge and located the observers just as they emerged from beneath the portico and approached a vehicle resembling a nineteen-thirties police paddy wagon.

Using the same mark I'd used on the inventor earlier, I took aim and fired a tracker at a female. She flinched and nearly fell over backward, but a stout constable gripped her by the arm and shoved her into the back of the paddy wagon with the other observers.

I took a few moments to scout the rest of the area from my vantage point. No one had noticed the two grays we'd hidden in the bushes out front, and it was unlikely anyone would anytime soon. But it wouldn't be long before the corpses started to stink, so we needed to do something about them before we started our journey to Oblivion.

The crowd at the pool in the back had grown with the arrival of the inventors. Darby and his group surrounded a young woman, hands groping roughly. My fists clenched, but there was nothing I could do without blowing the plan.

Another male inventor stalked over to them. "Darby, this one is mine!"

"They're all ours, Chadwick." Darby held up his hands as if to calm the other man. "There are plenty to choose from."

"Then choose another." Chadwick didn't look like much physically, but he pushed into the throng, took the girl by the hand, and dragged her away without the others making a fuss.

Unfortunately, that girl's reprieve was another's doom. Female nubs clung tight to any nearby inventor in the hopes of avoiding Darby's gang, but there weren't enough inventors to go around. A tall blonde of hearty Viking stock soon found herself in the crosshairs.

Layla appeared next to me. "Cain, what the hell are you doing?"

"Nothing." I turned away from the scene. "Absolutely nothing."

She shook her head. "Ever since Hannah, you've gotten this notion in your head that you need to be some kind of hero." She gripped my arm. "You're a killer, not a savior, Cain."

I smirked. "You said her name."

Layla's mouth dropped open. "Fuck. The disease is spreading."

"Don't worry, I won't tell her." I headed back toward the room. "We need to move the bodies from the front shrubs to a better hiding spot."

She nodded. "I take it you tracked an observer?"

"Yeah." I closed my eyes and felt the pull. "They're headed southeast." I went back to the sloped roof above our room and slid back down to the balcony. I left the sliding glass door open to let the smoky odor filter out, then moved the bed back over the hole.

We put our stuff back into the laundry basket and covered it with towels, then went into the hallway in our housekeeping disguises. Once back in the laundry room downstairs, we switched into our ninja gear and slipped teal uniforms on top of them. Gray uniforms might have been a better choice, but we didn't want to run afoul of any engineers for our next stunt. I took a nearby laundry bag and stuffed the ivory uniform inside just in case.

We left via the back exit next to the dumpster. The woman from earlier wasn't there which was just as well, since I didn't want to explain to her why we were in different uniforms now. The number of vehicles beneath the portico had multiplied and diversified. In addition to the Phantoms, there were other sleek vintage-looking cars of mechanist design.

Another paddy wagon pulled into the circular drive, its motor gently clicking like finely turned clockwork. A pair of constables climbed from the front and unlocked the caged box at the back to unload a fresh batch of male and female nubs.

These were certainly more plain in appearance and probably sent to appease Darby and his filthy cronies. The constables herded them around the side of the building, presumably to the pool area, leaving the portico empty for the moment.

Layla hopped into a Phantom and twisted the ignition crank next to the steering wheel. The engine clicked to life like a brand-new sewing machine. I climbed into the passenger side and bounced on the springy seat as Layla guided us down the driveway. She drove onto the grass and stopped near the shrubs where we'd stashed the grays.

I popped the trunk and we scurried to recover the bodies. There was just enough space to cram the bodies inside, which we did only seconds before a mechanist smoking a cigarette wandered out from beneath the portico. We climbed back into the car and drove off before the smoker had time to wonder what we were doing out there. Layla steered us into the road and away from the lodge.

Several more vehicles hummed past in the opposite direction when we reached the roundabout. A pair of teals waved as we passed, so we waved back, keeping our faces averted so they couldn't get a good look. An inventor in a long, black single-seater car thrummed toward us, his absurdly wide car requiring Layla to veer off the road so he could get past.

"I'm not hating their car designs," I said. "The mechanists could make a pretty penny if they went legit and sold those things."

Layla scoffed. "They wouldn't want to give the nubs the honor of driving such perfect machines."

I closed my eyes and let the tracker pull at me. We continued off the islands and back to the mainland. Layla pulled onto a gravel road leading down to houses. None of them looked as if they were in use, so we dumped the bodies in the woods down near the lake. With any luck, they'd stay hidden long enough for us to complete our mission.

Once back on the road, I let the tracker guide us. There was only one road leading out to the islands. All other avenues in the near vicinity ended at the lake. The signal changed from a southeasterly direction to northerly. The observers could have gone down any of the numerous roads nearby, so I had Layla slow down at each one. Once we reached North Waterworks Road, the change in pull was almost directly to my left.

I tapped pointed down the road. "This one."

About a mile down the road we reached the waterworks building. Four paddy wagons were parked out front and a pair of constables sat in chairs outside. Another five constable wagons were parked at the large house across the road. Civilians cooked at grills outside while others prepared dozens of lawn tables.

It looked like a typical American cookout, but there were no children, no pets, and no laughter. Constables watched from the front porch, bronze and brass rifles nearby in case any of the nubs thought about running.

Layla drove past and pulled into the driveway of an abandoned house just down the road. "Looks like we found the observers and the rest of the livestock."

"Well, now we know what's keeping the constables busy." I stepped out of the car and took in the nearby terrain. "The tracker is coming from the waterworks building." I thought back to the dead spot Grace had tracked to this location but in our dimension.

"You've got that worry wrinkle on your forehead, Cain." Layla poked it with a finger. "What are you thinking?"

"Grace tracked a dead spot in our dimension to this location, but by the time she arrived, it had healed." I shook my head slowly. "I think using the Tetron here is causing it."

"Freaky." Layla shuddered. "They're fucking around with forces beyond their comprehension."

"Probably incorrectly, too." I studied the building. "The waterworks building is all concrete. They hope it's enough to hold in the radiation they mentioned."

Layla grunted. "The building is solid concrete with metal doors. That might be the most secure place for them to keep their stash of apocalypse weapons."

"Maybe, but there aren't enough constables guarding it to indicate that."

She nodded. "True."

I peered through my scope, but the concrete obfuscated the heat signatures inside. "I can't get a look inside."

"Well, we've got all night to infiltrate." Layla looked to the west where the sun had begun its descent into the horizon. "We've got a few hours before dark. Let's see how far these teal uniforms get us."

I considered that for a moment. "How likely do you think it is for the constables to know all the inventors?"

Layla tapped a finger on her chin. "A better question would be, how likely are they to know the female inventors?"

"The split seems pretty even, so probably just as likely either way." I shrugged. "You can wear the ivory uniform if you want."

The corner of her lips curled into a sly smile. "You know I want to."

"I know all too well you like to be the boss." I retrieved the laundry bag from the backseat and tossed it to her.

"You're a strange one, Cain." Layla caught the bag. "You're so alpha one minute, then perfectly willing to play subordinate the next. Are you a switch?"

"I don't know what that means."

She smirked. "A switch is someone who can be dominant or submissive given the circumstances."

"One of your BDSM terms?" I shrugged. "Just because I let someone else lead doesn't mean I'm submissive. It means I respect their judgment. I trust them as much as I trust myself under certain circumstances."

Layla flinched as if I'd slapped her. "Oh." She looked at the ivory bundle in her hands, then shook off whatever she was thinking and changed uniform.

"Something wrong?" I said.

She stuffed the teal uniform into the bag. "You shouldn't trust me, Cain."

"Under certain circumstances, I do." I grinned. "I'm not stupid, Layla."

She laughed. "Good."

I climbed into the driver's seat. "Get in the back, Inventor Blade."

Layla hopped in. "Let's get this party started."

I didn't start the car. "We need a cover story."

"I'm Inventor Chatsworth," Layla said in a haughty British accent. "You are Engineer Paddington. We are studying the effect of the Tetron on human tissue as a side project."

"Kind of thin," I said, "but it might be enough to get us past the constables without killing anyone."

"I'll bet they won't even ask why we're there." Layla held up the hem of her uniform. "They're just there to keep the inmates from escaping."

"You're probably right, but I don't like making dangerous assumptions." I rapped my fingers on the steering wheel. "What if we run into other engineers or inventors inside? They'll know in a heartbeat that we're impostors."

"Worse comes to worst, we'll steal the Tetron and make a run for it." Layla motioned west. "Then we run to the docks, steal a sub and get Noctua. Easy, peasy."

"I really don't think it'll be that easy."

She leaned forward. "You trust me, right?"

I nodded.

"This is going to be so easy."

Famous last words, I thought. "I think I regret telling you that I trust your judgment."

"Too late." She leaned back and snapped her fingers. "Get it in gear, Paddington!"

I started the car and turned around in the driveway. Every vehicle in the vicinity of the building except for ours was a police wagon. I hoped that meant there were no inventors or engineers inside. The constables on duty in front of the waterworks stiffened slightly when I opened the rear door and Layla stepped out.

Layla didn't even look at them. She motioned me toward the door, and I walked past the guards as if they weren't even there. It looked like it was going to work. But just before I reached the door, another constable stepped from a side building and put himself directly in our path.

This is it, I thought. We were going to have to kill every constable here to reach the prize.

Chapter 22

The constable glanced at us, then turned away to face the door. He sorted through the keys on a ring, then used one to unlock the door. He pulled on the handle and held it open for us. I allowed Layla to precede me, which she did with royal flair. I followed her in, and the constable closed the door behind us.

Layla stopped in the empty front office and mimicked wiping her forehead with the back of a hand. "Holy shit, I thought it was done."

"Me too." I looked in the nearby rooms, but they were empty. "Let's find the observers."

Layla tapped a concrete wall. "They didn't even use drywall on the inside. This place is like a bunker."

I ran a hand along the rough wall. "Now I'm almost positive they bring the Tetron here or maybe even keep it onsite."

"What makes you say that?"

"There's plenty of concrete to block radiation." I rapped my knuckles on the dense wall.

"Makes sense." Layla walked around the corner and opened a metal door.

The structure looked like something built in the fifties to keep utilities safe in case the Soviets nuked it. Even if the building survived, I couldn't imagine what use it would be with an irradiated water supply, which also made me wonder if the mechanists had outsmarted themselves.

I snorted. "Those idiots."

Layla raised an eyebrow. "What?"

"They put the source of radiation inside the facility that purifies their water."

"Morons." Layla pursed her lips. "Then again, this is just the office building. The actual purification is done in the ponds out back."

"Maybe so." I eased open the next set of double doors and peered inside. A plain steel table sat in the middle of the floor of a large room. Flimsy cots lined a space on the other side. Dozens of vinyl aprons hung from the walls, each one overlapping the one below. I realized they were lead aprons like those used to shield the body during x-rays.

Brass video cameras on tripods encircled the steel table, presumably to record the observers while they did their work. I doubted any mechanists wanted to be near the building when the Tetron was in use.

The only thing I didn't see was the Tetron itself.

Most of the observers sat or lay on cots, most of them staring blankly into the void. I opened the door and stepped boldly inside, Layla close at my heels.

The observers stiffened, shaking their comrades awake and then standing at attention next to their cots.

The woman I'd marked stepped forward from the others. "I'm sorry, inventor, we were told the next reading would be in an hour."

"And so it will be." Layla walked around the woman as if inspecting her. "I'm simply here for an inspection."

"Yes, inventor." The woman bowed.

Layla looked around the room. "Are they following protocol when they remove the Tetron from this room?"

The woman glanced uncertainly toward the only other door in the room. "We weren't told of specific protocol. They bring it to us and leave, then retrieve it when we're done."

"How long are your sessions?" Layla said.

"Hours, usually." The woman looked at the man who'd given the presentation earlier. "Wouldn't you say, Tony?"

He nodded. "As Maria told the inventors, there are simply too many variables to sift through. The further we look into the future, the more inaccurate the prediction model becomes."

"The chronological variables are immense." Maria shook her head. "We could spend days simply tracking one chain of events."

It was obvious from the way they spoke they were well-versed in science. It was no wonder the mechanists were limited on the number of observers they could use. It probably took great intelligence to know how and where to look for the answers the mechanists wanted.

"I've never been versed in the workings of the Tetron, inventor." I bowed toward Layla. "May I ask for a greater explanation?"

Layla pursed her lips. "Very well." She motioned to Maria. "Answer his questions."

Maria bowed. "Yes, inventor."

Noctua had explained a little of alternate dimensions but seeing as we'd been in the middle of a crisis, I hadn't asked for a full science lesson. "I thought there were infinite dimensions. Is that not true?"

Tony answered. "Theoretical physics allows for the possibility, but what we've found is that there are only a few dimensions that closely parallel our own. What causes them to exist, we cannot say."

"The Tetron allows us a bird's-eye view of those closest to ours," Maria said. "We have tried to see beyond them, but we can barely control our glimpses into the ones near us. There are three local dimensions where events are almost identical to ours."

"It was shocking to discover a prime dimension, and we're not in it." Tony shook his head. "At first, I thought it meant we were merely copies and insignificant, but from what we've discovered, it seems we're just as real and important, but we're on a new ship sailing in a slightly different direction."

"I love that analogy," Maria said.

"How do you know which dimension is Prime?" I asked.

"When you look into the Tetron, you start in your physical location and pan out until you can see the entire world. At a certain distance, you see the other alternate Earths orbiting around a central dimension. That center one is Prime."

"And there are only three existing dimensions?" Layla asked.

"Oh, there are far more, but they're so different from ours that they've shifted far away from Prime." Tony held his hands apart as if holding a sphere. "It's mind boggling, really."

Another man hobbled over. His dark skin was spotted with sores. "An abnormal occurrence in Prime is the only reason it didn't suffer the same fate as our reality."

Maria winced. "But we're happy with that fate, right, Howard?"

He scowled. "No, but what are they going to do, kill us?" He laughed until he coughed. "We're dead men walking."

Layla shrugged. "Feel free to speak your mind to us. We don't agree with your treatment either. Unfortunately, neither of us are in a position to do anything about it."

"It's fascinating work." Tony sighed. "I suppose death is the price to pay for godlike powers."

Maria motioned to Howard. "Howard is a time specialist. I'm afraid the radiation is affecting him more than the others, possibly due to a predisposition to cancer."

Howard shrugged. "A fair price to pay for a peek at the inner workings of the very universe."

A look at the resigned faces of others in the room told me that was not a price they wanted to pay. "What's the abnormal occurrence that spared Prime from your fate?" I asked.

Tony fielded the question. "Matter is neither created nor destroyed, so theoretically, each dimension should have identical mass. All matter in a universe, especially sentient beings, are variables particular to that universe. If some matter were to shift from one universe to another, that would create a new variable."

I frowned. "Is that a bad thing?"

"We don't know," Maria said.

These people seemed honest enough, so I decided to take a chance with them. "Don't freak out, but we're not mechanists."

The trio blinked.

"Is this a test?" Maria asked uncertainly.

I shook my head. "We're from Prime, the dimension that isn't ruled by Cthulhu."

Gasps rose around the room and other observers approached us.

Layla hissed. "Gods damn it, Cain, what if they tell the mechanists?"

"We won't!" Maria clasped my hand. "I promise you we'll die first."

"That would explain a great deal!" Howard tapped a finger on his chin. "Events have become unpredictable because matter from another universe is now in ours."

"Absolutely." Tony rubbed his forehead as if it helped him think. "How did you get here?"

"The cube transported us here, but we don't know how." I shook my head. "It apparently created a one-way doorway, trapping us here. We need to get the Tetron and figure out how to return."

Maria cocked her head. "They don't keep the Tetron onsite."

Howard nodded. "They bring it to us when they need us to predict future outcomes."

I raised an eyebrow. "Do you know how to traverse dimensions with the Tetron?"

Howard shook his head. "It allows us to view our timeline and others with a bird's-eye view," Howard explained. "If there's a way to physically cross into the other dimension, we haven't discovered it."

Layla frowned. "Tell me more about the timeline. You can rewind and review past events?"

"The Pyradon controls the time function of the Tetron," Tony said. "It allows us to rewind the tapestry and review history."

"Tapestry?" I said.

Maria winced. "It seems impossible, but I suppose it's no crazier than a giant god with an octopus head ruling the world. Our lifelines weave a tapestry just like in Greek mythology."

Layla and I exchanged a glance.

Layla smirked. "You guys are scientists, right?"

The entire group of observers nodded.

"Hate to burst your bubble completely, but the Greek gods exist. All that shit you thought was myth is real." Her smirk widened into a grin at the shocked looks rippling across their faces.

I softened the blow. "That doesn't mean science isn't real, it just means it's not the only truth out there."

"Why haven't the gods helped us?" Maria made the sign of the cross. "I'm a scientist, but I'm also a devout Catholic. I prayed but God never answered."

"The gods don't really interfere much," I said. "I've learned that when they do, it's usually bad news."

"Meaning, we're on our own." Maria sagged.

Howard frowned. "I was a devout atheist, but the events of this past year certainly changed my outlook on life. Now I simply don't know what to believe."

"Do you plan to take our Tetron and leave us to rot in misery?" another female observer asked.

Layla patted her shoulder. "Of course not. We'll return with help and defeat the mechanists and Cthulhu."

Maria clasped her hands. "You can do that?"

Layla nodded confidently. "We have some demigods of our own to help."

The faint light of hope shone in their eyes, and I felt like shit because Layla was blatantly lying to them and I wasn't about to stop her. We needed these people on our side. We needed the Tetron. Most of all, we needed them to keep quiet about our visit.

Tony glanced at an old clock on the wall. "We're scheduled for a session in twenty minutes. Do you plan to steal the Tetron from them and get us out of here?"

I looked at the sickly faces, the sores and boils forming on some of them and felt angry. As an assassin, honor never held much sway with me. But what the mechanists were doing to these people was disgusting. And we were going to leave an entire world to suffer.

I shook my head. "We've got a lot to do before we steal the device. Do you have any idea where they keep it?"

"A lot to do?"

"We're dying! Can't you help us now?"

The other observers clamored for answers.

I held up a hand. "If we steal it now, it will put the mechanists on alert and our chances of getting you out of here alive drop to almost nothing. They stole powerful weapons from the lost armory of Hephaestus. We need to steal some of our own if we're to stand a chance."

"My God, this is insane." Maria rubbed her eyes. "Mythical weapons and Greek gods? I can hardly believe we're having this conversation."

"Yeah? Well vampires, werewolves, and wizards have been hiding under your noses all this time too." Layla barked a laugh. "So you're better off if you just accept it and move on."

Howard tenderly touched a sore on his face. "I'm afraid I'm done for no matter what. But I appreciate whatever you can do to save the others."

"Don't say that, Howard!" Maria squeezed his hand. "We'll get you help. Maybe there's a magic potion that can cure you."

I flattened my lips. "It's possible." I checked the wall clock. "We've got to go."

"Godspeed, friends." Maria took my hand and kissed it. "I will pray, and perhaps my god will miraculously answer."

Layla scoffed. "Doubt it. You're far more likely to hear from Lucifer."

A number of them cringed at the name, so I felt it best not to mention the devil was alive and well. They hadn't answered my question the first time, so I asked it again in parting. "Do you know where they keep the Tetron?"

They all shook their heads, which meant we'd probably have to see them again when we stole the device. And there was no way we'd be able to take them with us when we did. Not having to look them in the eyes when we left them behind would be so much easier.

On our way out, I started to worry about something else. "What if the constables tell whoever comes next about us visiting?"

"I'm sure mechanists visit all the time," Layla said. "Plenty of people want to know the future."

I hoped she was right.

The constables barely glanced in our direction as we exited the building and climbed into the Phantom. We drove back out to the main road. A single constable wagon was parked on the side of the road. A pair of constables looked down the embankment where the grays had wrecked.

I slowed the vehicle and rolled down the window. "What's the problem?"

"Bloody grays rolled their cart and killed themselves, sir." The constable removed a small brass tube from his pocket. "I'll have a report available on the voxograph soon."

I nodded. "Very well. Carry on." I continued down to the docks.

Layla chuckled. "They don't even care enough about the grays to investigate."

"Looks like it." I parked in an empty space right near the ramp leading to the submarines and scanned the area for a sign of other engineers and inventors. A few sailors wandered the piers, but most of the activity came from grays bustling about loading crates and boxes onto their little carts.

"No bigwigs," Layla said. "Let's go take a look around."

Most of the sailors and grays kept their eyes averted from us as we walked down the long line of submarines. The first few were much larger than the one we'd stolen, outfitted to carry large complements of soldiers and cargo. The equipment on the outside was similar but more advanced than what I remembered. Golden letters on the hulls displayed the names of the vessels. The *Archimedes* was moored at the far end of the dock alongside other smaller submarines.

It seemed the mechanists were slightly more advanced here, probably because they'd joined Cthulhu. His minions had probably aided their progress immensely. It also meant travelling the deepways should be much easier this time around.

The *Archimedes* was a smaller submarine docked at the far end with two vessels that looked much like the ones we'd stolen in our dimension.

Layla stepped behind some crates out of view of the workers. "What now? Do we slip onboard in full view of everyone?"

I was about to answer when streaks of light out over the water grabbed my attention. Plumes of water rose like rooster tails behind the streaks, casting mist high into the air. Sailors shouted. A claxon began to howl. Sailors ran aboard the submarines, manning the turret guns along the hull.

The far side of the dock where we stood was quickly abandoned by all personnel rushing to man the battle subs. I summoned my staff and peered at the incoming threat. The streaks of light resolved into people, each of them wearing Icarus wings. I didn't know who they were, but it was obvious we were about to be in the middle of a fight.

Chapter 23

I hadn't seen Icarus wings since the war. The only reason to use them instead of flying carpets and brooms was the speed. They were sleek and fast, but also flimsy as hell. Without proper training, most pilots would end up cratering. From what I could tell, the people using them knew exactly what they were doing.

Weapons turrets opened fire. Winged bullets flashed across the water toward the targets. A torrent of yellow light speared out and destroyed the projectiles before they ever got close. I zoomed in on the source, expecting to see Daphne, but found a young man instead, wearing clothes that reminded me of ancient Egypt.

Another blast from him destroyed the turrets on the submarine and rocked the vessel back and forth. The fliers were approaching from an angle that made it impossible for the other submarines to line up a shot, blocked as they were by the first one. Dozens of sailors poured from a warehouse up the hill, most of them brandishing the brass rifles favored by the mechanists.

The fliers landed. The young man in the lead held up a hand and his compatriots unclipped their wings and let them fall to the ground. Their bodies convulsed, rippling with muscle. Black fur sprouted from head to toe. Their ears grew long and pointed. Their mouths extended into long muzzles like those of Doberman pinschers. Within seconds, they towered seven feet tall, giant bipedal canines.

Layla gasped. "What in the fuck are those things?"

For a moment, I was at a loss for words. "They look like Anubis."

The only one in the group to retain human form was the boy. He thrust out his hands and incinerated a group of sailors as they opened fire. The Anubis soldiers raced into the mechanist ranks. Bodies flew. Blood spattered. Innards rained down as the hapless mechanists screamed and died. Another thrumming vibration drew my attention to the water. A brown Apache helicopter soared around an island and aimed for the submarines as they moved into open water. Missiles rained down. Submarine turrets returned fire. A hellfire missile rammed into one submarine and the explosion rocked a neighboring vessel. Metal groaned, water rushed into the breached hulls, and the submarines sank.

Down the road just beyond the battle, sunlight glinted off bronze wings flapping in the distance. Within moments, four figures alighted on the ground and unbuckled the metal wings from their backs. Rather than fall, the wings somehow remained balanced on the wingtips, no doubt thanks to clever gyros inside.

Layla gasped. "Clockwork wings?"

"Yeah, looks like it." Just when I thought the mechanists had run out of gadgets, they impressed me with something new. I zoomed my scope on the newcomers and hissed between my teeth when I saw the leader.

Both of her temples were shaved, leaving a long, thick purple mane down the middle. The right side of her face bore mild burn scars, pocking her brown skin with white marks. But it was Esteri, this world's version of Hannah.

Esteri ignored the Anubis soldiers and went straight for the boy unleashing sizzling yellow beams at the mechanists. The Apache helicopter rotated toward the new threat and launched a hellfire missile at her. One of Esteri's comrades, another young girl, uprooted a small tree as if it were nothing and threw it like a javelin. It slammed into the missile, diverting it from its path. The missile exploded in the nearby woods, showering the area with dirt and burning leaves.

The sun boy turned toward Esteri, cupped his hands, and directed a yellow ray of destruction at her. Esteri responded with white beams from her eyes and mouth. An explosion rocked the area when the two forces met.

The helicopter spun away from that battle as new threats loomed across the lake. A pair of mechanist airships streaked across open water. I'd seen diagrams of the vessels, but this was the first time seeing one in person. They were nothing like blimps, their airframes sleek and low profile, powered by corkscrew-shaped propellers. Rockets leapt from turrets on the gondolas, whistling like fireworks as they raced toward the enemy target.

The helicopter gunner panicked, firing the rest of his missiles and opening fire with the forward turret. He shot down one of the incoming missiles, but the other zipped back and forth, dodging his attempts. The pilot veered at the last minute, but it was too late. The whistling missile punctured the cockpit. Green gas poured inside, and the crew died.

The helicopter spiraled into the water with a great splash, blades thumping into the water until it sank out of sight. The airships altered course, heading toward the other fight.

"These bastards just made our job a lot harder," Layla said. "It might not be so easy sneaking around here when we come back."

I tore my eyes away from Hannah's doppelganger. "Then let's steal a sub and go. This place will be swarming with security once the battle is over."

"First things first." Layla looked at the six battle submarines that hadn't launched during the raid. When the first subs had been destroyed, the ramp leading from the shore had been destroyed, leaving the crews no easy way to reach the vessels.

I knew what she had in mind. Summoning my staff, I ignited the brightblade and cut the locks from several crates. We found what we were looking for in a beige crate a few feet away.

Layla examined the small torpedo. "I don't know how it works, but it should go boom."

"Yeah," I said. "It'll go boom." The submarines were moored only a few feet from the dock, so we hefted a torpedo and set it down next to the nearest sub, doing the same for two more vessels as the battle raged.

That was all we dared do. The other submarines were dangerously close to the battle and we didn't want to be spotted.

Layla tapped the hull of one of the battle submarines. "Maybe we should take one of these."

"They're big and cumbersome," I said. "We've got a better chance sneaking around in the *Archimedes*."

She pursed her lips. "Yeah, I guess I can't take one home with me anyway."

We crept back down to the end of the docks where the smaller submarines waited. I slashed the mooring lines for all of them, hoping that would help cover our tracks. They might think the *Archimedes* sank during the fight.

Once Layla was inside, I switched my staff to sniper mode and aimed at the furthest torpedo. In quick succession, I fired, shifted target, fired again. The three torpedoes we'd place exploded, ripping holes in hulls and sending more submarines sinking into the depths.

The battle was all but over. Dead Anubis soldiers lay at the feet of Esteri and her demis. Sun boy had backed up to the water's edge. Esteri screamed and charged him. White light poured from her mouth and eyes. The boy tried to block the attack, but his defenses melted under the onslaught. He cried out in agony for a brief instant as his flesh melted and burned.

I ducked inside the submarine and closed the hatch. Layla sat before a bank of controls that looked identical to the ones in the submarine we'd stolen from the mechanists on our world. She backed us slowly out of dock. Once we were clear, she spun the submarine around and pulled a lever. The forward hull split vertically, the sections folding in on themselves, leaving the entire section transparent.

A switch activated the exterior floodlights, penetrating far into the green gloom. The bridge was smaller than the one on our other submarine, but the mechanists had miniaturized most of the controls, meaning the levers were smaller and the switches were tiny. The navigation console, to use a term loosely, used a globe of Gaia mapped with travel tunnels and nodes called deepways. The globe on our ship only had hundreds. This one displayed thousands. Cthulhu had apparently shared the locations of them all. In addition to the globe of Gaia, there were three other small globes, lines charting the deepways.

An axis held each globe suspended from the bulkhead and allowing them to rotate. One of the globes was Feary and the other, Oblivion. The third globe had only one deepway highlighted, but there were no other markings to show landmasses or water. I didn't have time to puzzle over it since Layla needed to chart a path to the deepway in the lake. I rotated the globe, but the problem with it being smaller was that Lake Lanier was tiny and difficult to find.

There were banks of switches and levers on the navigational console, far more than the ones in our stolen submarine. Each bank lined up with its respective globe. I flicked the first lever. Clockwork ticked and a light glowed from within the globe, projecting the chart on a screen against the wall and magnifying it. I rotated the globe and found the deepway closest to us.

Layla glanced back. "Cain, you're doing it wrong. Find the destination, not the starting point."

"Oh, yeah, that's right." I began searching the Gaia globe for the deepway to Oblivion and then realized that was also the wrong way to do it. I switched off the projection for Gaia and turned on the one for Oblivion. Olympus Prime was marked on the map. I rotated the globe until the destination lined up in the center of the projection, then flicked the next switch.

A glowing reticle appeared on the right side of the forward window. Layla adjusted the heading of the submarine until the reticle lined up with faint lines etched in the window.

"Smooth sailing from here." She leaned back in her chair, one hand on the steering wheel.

"Don't get cocky." I knew from experience there was no such thing as smooth sailing.

Layla scoffed. "I wonder if your lake house is around here."

"I don't see why it wouldn't be." I stepped up next to her chair and gazed at the underwater landscape.

The lake was over forty miles long, but the mechanists had chosen the location of their docks because it was only a few minutes from the hidden deepway entrance. When we neared the entrance, a bell over the navigation console chimed. A single red button beneath the levers for the globes glowed red, so I pressed it.

Haunting whale song echoed in the water. The lakebed parted before us, four sections splitting apart to form a giant hole. A twisting vortex waited just beyond the lip of the hole, but its pull didn't affect the lake.

I strapped into a chair and braced my head against the headrest. Layla nudged us forward. The moment the front of the submarine touched the vortex, it sucked us inside at incredible speeds. Anyone not strapped down would be thrown violently across the bridge in the first instant, but once the initial g-force passed, a person could get up and walk around like normal.

Even so, it wasn't advisable. After travelling at high speeds for several minutes in the dark, rushing waters, another hole opened and light streamed in. The submarine reached the end of the deepway and slowed quickly enough to throw my body against the straps. Anyone foolhardy enough to have taken a stroll during the transition would have been thrown forward at bone-breaking velocity.

Amazingly, we hadn't had to learn that the hard way during our first journey in a submarine. I'd seen the first vortex and, as usual, played it safe. It was one more reason why I remained alive.

Our vessel floated in a spherical cavern that spanned miles. Phosphorescent algae covered the walls, casting the cavity in soothing white light. Hundreds of dark tunnel entrances pockmarked the walls, many leading to another node like the one we were in. Layla oriented the submarine and lined up the reticle with the next tunnel. We reached it and jetted through the passageway.

"Good work, Captain Layla."

She turned and flashed me a mischievous grin. "I wondered if you'd address me properly."

I snorted. "Half the time I don't know if you're being serious, or just trying to be a pain in the ass. I find it easier to just go along with it."

"Smart man." Layla grunted as we hit the next node and slowed.

I rotated my seat toward the navigational console so I could study the mystery globe until we reached the next tunnel. "The mechanists have deepways mapped on Gaia, Oblivion, and Feary."

Layla rotated her seat, keeping half an eye on the glowing reticle. "There are deepways on Feary? You'd think the fae would be all over that."

I rotated the globe. "There are ten of them. Maybe the fae haven't noticed yet."

She frowned. "What's the fourth globe?"

I shrugged. "Don't know, but it only has one deepway."

"Weird." She turned her chair around as we neared the next tunnel. "Must be another plane we've never heard of."

I rotated my chair forward and locked it in place so it didn't spin when we hit the vortex. "Must be something like that. But I only know of the three."

The vortex thrust us into darkness. "Ever wonder what happens if something is coming the other way through the tunnel?" Layla said in a strained voice.

"Why did you have to say that?" I gripped the armrest. "Now all I'm going to think about every time I'm entering a tunnel is if this is the time we ram into another submarine at light speed."

Layla burst into laughter. We hit the next node and her laughter abruptly died. It only took me a second to see why. The cavern was teeming with creatures large and small. Hundreds of squid-headed soldiers swarmed around us. Behind them were giant eight-legged beasts that looked like a cross between an octopus and a spider. And beyond them were two monsters that made my mind freeze in terror.

The army of Cthulhu was on the march, and we'd just run right into them.

Chapter 24

Layla's hands gripped the steering wheel, but her muscles seemed frozen in place. The squid people stared blankly at us, but easily swam out of the way of the submarine. The great eyes of the monsters in the back still held me frozen in place.

Why am I so afraid? I wondered. The creatures dwarfed elephants by a long shot. They were green-gray, with thick, quadruped bodies. Massive wings thrust them through the water as if they were flying in the air. Each monster had only one eye, a swirling void that seemed to draw in my very soul. It was like being swallowed into dark infinity.

That was it, I realized. They were infinity traps, similar to those employed by the giant crystal arachnids of Feary. The only way to avoid madness and death was to imagine an end to the emptiness.

I'd trained extensively to short-circuit psychological traps. Even so, the mere act of focusing took tremendous effort.

Find the end of the spiral.

I focused everything I had and blanked out the swirling pattern.

In that instant, my mind sprang free. I yanked the lever to close the window shield. The forward window closed, and Layla blinked from her stupor.

She tried to leap from her chair, but the straps held her down. She clawed at the straps, desperately trying to free herself. I gripped her arms and she screamed, thrashing like a madwoman.

"Layla!" I slapped her cheek hard enough to leave a mark.

She gasped. Wide eyes focused on my face. "What happened?"

"Malgorths." I took breaths to calm my racing heart. "They're greater minions of Cthulhu."

"Malgorths." She spoke the word as if testing it on her tongue. "How do you know about them?"

"Reading and studying everything about Cthulhu and other outsiders." I peered through a porthole at the massive army swimming past. They didn't seem to care about us in the least, probably because they assumed we were mechanists. "The squid-heads are salkos. The ones that look like a cross between an octopus and jellyfish are migyos."

"It's always about tentacles with Cthulhu, isn't it?"

I nodded. "Seems so." I went to the captain's chair and pulled down the periscope for a quick look through the binocular lens. I kept one eye closed in case I made eye contact with the malgorths again. Monocular vision prevented the brain from forming the complete pattern and lowered the risk of a trance.

The malgorths had already passed us, but the tunnel ahead continued disgorging more monsters, each one bearing more tentacles than the last. One thing they all had in common were feet and legs. These creatures were capable of traveling on land, meaning Cthulhu was preparing a land invasion.

I rotated the periscope to make sure none of them had taken more than a passing glance at us. "Line up the reticle."

Layla rotated the vessel until the glowing reticle lined up with the middle of the shielded window. I didn't want her looking outside in case more malgorths appeared. It was best to get out of here as fast as possible.

"Full ahead."

Layla followed my instructions without question. It was almost unheard of, but I had a feeling the encounter had shaken her up more than she'd ever admit. I strapped into the captain's chair just before we reached the tunnel. When we reached the next node moments later, I took another look through the periscope. We were thankfully alone.

"You can open the forward shield," I said.

Layla stared at the lever for several seconds before pulling it. She flinched when the glowing cavern appeared, as if afraid she might encounter the spiraling void of a malgorth's gaze. I knew from experience with the crystal spiders that some people had visions when they encountered the trap of a spiral gaze. Those visions varied from warming in the sun of a tropical paradise to being tormented by their worst fear.

I'd never been allowed such pleasures or endured such horrors as a child. Erolith had instilled a sense of unwavering duty in me. Hard work and constant training were all I'd ever known. All I'd seen during my first encounter with a hypnotic gaze was darkness. Erolith told me it was because I was trained to recognize it, stopping short of being drawn in by the psychological pull.

I knew Layla didn't want to talk about it, but I asked anyway. "What did you see?"

She shivered. One of her hands reached over her shoulders as if to touch something that was no longer there. "Please don't ask me, Cain."

I'd never heard such vulnerability in her voice. If ever there was a time to dig up Layla's past, it was now. Instead, I left the captain's chair and went back to the navigational console. We had two more jumps before the portal to Oblivion. The last node wasn't far off the coast of Greece. Not surprisingly, the geography of Oblivion was similar to that of Gaia, at least in some places.

Their original attempt to create a living, breathing world had failed, but they'd found some success in attempt number two. From every moment since then, the living had tried their best to tear everything apart.

I strapped down in the navigator's seat and let Layla pilot us in silence. It was kind of nice not having to deal with her constant smartass remarks, but the silence felt strange. I saw no need to fill it with anything and let the ticking of the clockwork engine fill the void. In less than an hour we were at the tunnel that would deposit us off the coast of Olympus Prime.

We shot through darkness and emerged in the orange glow of an underwater sun. Technically, the orange orb was a fragment of the fires of creation. It had been ejected from the forge beneath Olympus and taken an entire peninsula down with it during the war that destroyed most life on Oblivion.

From the underwater sun to the sunken columns of the dead city, everything looked identical to what we'd seen on Oblivion in our world. But when we reached the surface, the differences were clear. The dead volcano that was once Olympus Prime still stood. The dead city was still in one piece, not completely ravaged and turned to rubble as it had been when Hannah used Earthmaker to battle Torvin and Tidebringer.

A long pier extended from shore and into the water where two submarines similar to ours were docked. Construction crews in mechanist exo-armor worked on another pier not far from the first, and other crews were repairing the great domed building onshore. Hannah and Torvin had annihilated most of the structures during their battle in our dimension.

Layla finally spoke. "Those people aren't wearing breathing masks."

I'd noticed it too. Oblivion's environment was harsh and deadly. I'd spent months acclimating to it during training with the Oblivion Guard. The climate in this area was hot with dangerously low oxygen levels. I unstrapped from my chair and climbed the ladder to the hatch. I knew what to expect. Even so, I braced myself for the burning air to greet my face and scorch my lungs. But I found nothing of the sort. The temperature outside was mild, and my lungs didn't strain to find the proper mixture of gasses in the air.

"What the hell?" I climbed up and stood on the sail. Took in a deep breath of salty air. And felt perfectly fine. Fluffy white clouds filled the sky overhead, though dark storms threatened on the horizon.

Using the scope on my staff, I surveyed the shore. Some construction workers glanced our way, but none of them seemed concerned to see an unscheduled submarine coming to dock. Their auras were those of nubs, leading me to believe they were either stock humans or, at the most, another brand of mechanist without any magical abilities.

I went back down the ladder. "Let's dock at the end."

Layla nodded, once again uncharacteristically quiet. I picked up our uniforms where we'd hung them and slipped into the teal one, then climbed the ladder to the sail so I could tie us down. A pair of grays sprinted down the pier and reached us just as we pulled into the slot. Chests heaving, they coordinated to tie down the vessel and inflate large bladders to cushion the hull against the concrete.

I pretended they weren't there since it seemed to be typical of the hierarchy. The grays said nothing to us, but waited on the floating dock, eyes averted as we disembarked.

"How goes the construction?" Layla asked in a haughty voice.

"The nubs are ahead of schedule," one of them answered.

The other looked at her companion uncertainly but said nothing.

Layla sighed. "What is it, little one?"

The woman cleared her throat. "The climatologists are concerned about weather patterns forming around the bubble they created with Airbender. They think a super storm is possible at any time and could kill everyone."

The mild climate suddenly made sense. I pursed my lips. "Did they move more oxygen into this area, or did they completely change the composition of the air?"

The woman shrugged. "I don't know. The climatologists made recommendations and the magician made the changes."

Layla waved off the subject. "We must go to Olympus." She looked at a rugged off-road SUV where the pier met the shore. "Take us there."

I wasn't too sure about asking grays to chauffeur us around, but they made no complaints and hurried to obey. I was surprised to find the SUV wasn't mechanist made, but a gasoline powered vehicle. Layla and I climbed into the backseat and the grays drove us down a newly constructed asphalt road to the mountain.

"Where are the climatologists?" I asked.

The driver pointed up and toward Olympus where a radar dish and several antennas protruded from the mountain. "They're in the cave where the clockwork Cerberus was."

The horizon looked threatening in all directions. We were indeed in the center of a fragile bubble that could implode at any moment, unleashing horrific storms. They were like children playing with nuclear weapons, ignorant about the chain reactions their manipulations caused.

I hoped the next question didn't give me away. "How long ago did they change the climate?"

"The first adjustment was almost three months ago, sir." The driver glanced back at me. "They've made adjustments every week since then to keep it the same. Otherwise, the oxygen bleeds away."

They'd been messing with mother nature for quite some time then. The road continued through a neatly carved tunnel that took us through the outer wall and into the volcanic crater. A few minutes later, the SUV stopped outside the armory doors. The grays stepped out and opened the car doors for us.

I doubted they could help us, but I asked anyway. "We're tasked with recovering a clockwork owl from the armory. Which crevice did it fall inside?"

The grays looked confused. The driver stuttered an answer. "We're not allowed inside, nor are we allowed to ask questions about it, sir."

"Ah, of course." I pressed my lips together. "We just weren't given much information."

"I'm sorry we can't be of help, sir." His female comrade kept her eyes on the ground. "We'll wait outside for you."

I nodded. "Thank you." Then Layla and I stepped through the open doors. Aside from racks and shelves, the underground chamber was empty. The furnaces at the far end were dark since all the fires had escaped eons ago. The armory in our dimension had been reduced to rubble, and the floor was a treacherous maze of crevices that could swallow someone whole. This place had no such damage and no crevices that I could see.

Layla nudged me. "Try the whistle."

Her voice was so subdued that I flinched in surprise. "Good idea." I pulled it out of my utility belt and blew into it. A faint hooting drew my attention toward the shadows near the furnace. We walked that way with me blowing into the whistle every so often to keep oriented in the massive space. We wound through a maze of shelves until we arrived in an area behind the furnaces. The rock floor looked as if someone had beaten it with a giant hammer. A spider web of cracks turned into wide openings as they radiated out from the point of impact.

"Looks like someone used Earthmaker here," I said.

Layla nodded.

I blew the whistle and the hooting echoed from a crevice back near the wall. We carefully made our way across treacherous chasms until we reached the spot. I cast a light globe into the dark pit and let it fall. It reached bottom about a hundred feet down. Light glinted off brass and silver not far from where the globe landed.

I cupped my hands to my mouth. "Noctua, are you down there?"

There was no answer.

I blew the whistle and the hooting replied. "She must be completely defunct."

"She must have taken a hell of a blow to get damaged." Layla sounded more like herself. She considered the pit for a moment. "We need rope or chain."

I looked around but there was nothing of use anywhere that I saw. "Let's ask the grays to fetch us some."

Layla nodded.

We went back outside and heard conversation from the other side of the SUV. I walked around the front of the vehicle and froze at the precise moment the conversation stopped. Cruel eyes flashed with surprise and cruel lips twisted into a scowl. But there was no hesitation as the man reached for a weapon.

I leapt back from the vehicle, hand grasping up and behind me just in time to draw my staff and ignite the brightblade as the enemy slashed a killing blow at my neck.

Chapter 25

"Torvin!" I strained to hold his blow at bay. "Fancy meeting you here."

"Impossible!" he bellowed, eyes gleaming.

"Possible," I bellowed back. I dodged to the side, allowing his brightblade to slide free of mine.

He looked from his brightblade to mine. "I took this from you."

"I keep a few spares laying around." I whirled the blade, letting the electrical hum build in volume. With Layla by my side, we'd defeat him in no time.

The grays watched in horror, unsure what was going on. Layla stared blankly at Torvin, as if her mind had completely left her body.

I stepped closer to her. "Uh, Layla?"

She stared unblinkingly at Torvin, more precisely at his pointed ears.

Torvin saw the opportunity and pounced. I parried his blade in time to keep Layla's head attached to her body, then blocked another strike that would have skewered her. I powered my body sigils and donkey-kicked Layla back through the armory doors, then slammed them shut with a force spell. Torvin blurred toward me, brightblade slashing through four different attacks I barely blocked.

He locked blades with me and leaned closer. "It's better this way, Cain. I wanted to kill you myself, not leave it to some brat. I don't know why they didn't kill you or why you're free, but I will make sure the mistake is corrected."

I'd barely beaten the bastard the last time I met him, and he'd spent hours battling Hannah before facing me. It was the only time I'd won a duel with him.

Torvin spat in my face. I slid away and wiped it clean just in time to parry another flurry of attacks.

"Weak human vermin," Torvin growled. "You cost me everything, but now I have a world of my own."

I frowned. "Cthulhu gave you Oblivion?"

"And the tools to mold it into whatever I desire." His lips parted into a mocking grin. "Soon, I'll have my revenge on the fae as well. I have been promised the honor of slaying the fae queens themselves."

As he kept bragging, I realized this was not the same Torvin I'd slain only days ago. That Torvin had been fueled by vengeance and rage. He'd hated me so much he'd been willing to destroy the world so long as I died with it. This guy, on the other hand, was now the king of a world with the promise of that last pound of flesh he felt the fae owed him.

Now that he had the chance to kill me himself, this Torvin was practically giddy with happiness. The other Torvin had been a dark elf with nothing he cared about losing. This one had plenty to lose if he died.

"What did Hera think when you abandoned her to join Cthulhu?" I asked.

Torvin blinked. "I rarely spoke to her myself, but once Esteri joined Cthulhu, I sensed a powerful alliance to be made."

Keeping well away from him, I threw a wildcard into the pile. "You went from planning to trick me into helping you find the armory, to convincing the Pandora Combine to join Cthulhu."

Torvin didn't flinch, but his eyes betrayed surprise.

I kept going. "You had it all planned out. Norna, Bisbee and Dwight, that bar Shipwreck, and then getting Norna to kill me in Deepvale."

"How could you possibly know all this?" Torvin said. "I had only just approached Norna with the details, and she would never tell you anything."

I was sort of enjoying this, but I hesitated at telling him the truth. It seemed better I let him think I'd somehow survived Esteri, escaped, and was now here. "I came to kill you, Torvin."

His smirk flattened. "I think not, pathetic worm." His brightblade swung in precise movements, sparking against my blade so fast my eyes could barely keep up. As a dark elf, he had a physical advantage. Only my body sigils gave me the speed to keep him at bay. But long before he grew tired, my endurance would wane, making me a lamb to the slaughter.

My blade grew brighter with every strike just as it had in the first fight with Torvin. The replacement orb I'd taken from the armory had upgraded my staff in many ways I still didn't understand. Though he'd stolen the alternate Cain's staff, it still had the old orb on the hilt. An image flashed through my mind: excess energy spearing from the tip of my sword and into Torvin.

The staff had never communicated with me before the upgrade, but now it seemed to have a function that included tactical advice during a fight. The problem with firing the excess energy at Torvin, was that he could easily block it with his brightblade. Plus, extending the blade would leave me open to other attacks. He could simply sidestep my maneuver and cauterize my guts without me ever landing a blow.

Our blades danced, sparks flew, and the fight continued. Though I kept up with his attacks, I felt the inevitable slowing as my endurance waned. His deeper physical reservoir would easily outlast me if this continued much longer. I decided to go for the same maneuver I'd used on my Torvin.

We locked blades. Energy crackled violently. A light rain began to fall. Water hissed and steam rose where the rain touched our blades. A bolt of lightning struck high up the mountain. A boulder tumbled down the cliff of the outer crater, fell inside and smashed into the cave opening where Korborus, the clockwork clone of Cerberus had once abided.

A group of people I hadn't noticed before stood outside the cave watching the fight from afar. The boulder crushed them and collapsed the cave entrance. Their cries echoed and died almost immediately.

Before I could attempt my trick, Torvin disengaged and leapt back a few feet for a look up the mountain. The grays who still cowered near the truck also looked up in horror at the destroyed cave. Another bolt of lightning struck the mountaintop and another. More and more boulders tumbled and crashed down the cliff sides. It seemed our protective bubble was collapsing.

I took advantage of the situation and lunged at Torvin. He swiped down, batting away my blade. I put everything I had into my attacks, driving him back relentlessly. He finally stood his ground and took a stab at me. The moment he did, I released the energy in the blade in a single blinding flash directed at him.

At the same instant, I drove Carnwennan, the legendary Arthurian dagger, into his side. But instead of his ribs, it clashed with another dagger.

Torvin's lips spread into a clever smirk. "That trick won't work twice, Cain." He blinked and frowned as if confused for having said that, then just as suddenly shoved me away.

I was just as surprised. "You remember that, Torvin?"

"I-I was bleeding." He looked down at his side as if expecting to see a fatal wound draining his lifeblood onto the ground. "I died by your hand."

"How could you possibly remember that?" I circled him warily, keeping half an eye on the rockslides still pouring into the far side of the crater. The grays were scrambling up a path toward the cave entrance, as if they might rescue whoever had been up there.

"What's the meaning of this?" Torvin glared at me. "Insignificant vermin like you could never defeat me. It's impossible!"

I wasn't quite panting from exertion, but I was on the verge of it. This fight couldn't last much longer. I also couldn't simply back out and run. Noctua was just within reach, and all I needed was rope. There were hundreds of feet of it back at the docks. The only positive thing was that the grays hadn't known who to back—Torvin, or their mechanist masters.

Decisive, not reckless action was key here. Torvin was off balance, his mind filled with confusion. That had to play to my advantage somehow. I attacked again. He remained defensive, unwilling to commit an attack. Sheer reflex kept him in the fight as he fought whatever was going through his mind.

I thrust my blade at his stomach, a move he could easily parry, and ghostwalked behind him at the last instant. The blade sizzled into his back even as he spun, leg thrusting out to kick me. The move saved his life but cost him his leg. I swept the brightblade down, slashing through flesh and bone, cauterizing the wound before it could bleed.

Torvin, the master swordsman that he was, kept his balance, and hopped back on one foot, his face a mask of rage and agony. He growled and hissed, face burning red. "No!" he roared at the top of his lungs. "Impossible!"

"You keep saying that word," I said. "I don't think it means what you think it means."

"What trickery is this, Cain?" Torvin continued hopping backward on his remaining leg. "You never knew mind magic before."

"It's not mind magic," I said. "Somehow you're remembering what the Torvin in my dimension experienced just before I killed him."

His eyes widened. "Yours is the dimension we haven't yet conquered. The one in which we couldn't coordinate with our others."

"Because I destroyed everything in the armory in our dimension." I advanced on him. "Your people never took the Tetron there." Now that I had him at my mercy, gathering information seemed more vital than killing him. "How did you send the letter to Horatio with the Tetron?"

His lips curled into a fierce grimace. "I don't know. The scientists figured it out, but attempts to send through living beings results in their immediate deaths."

I slowed my advance. "How is it possible you remembered what happened to the other Torvin?"

"Perhaps because my death was only a moment away." Torvin grinned maniacally. "My fate was sealed by a dog." Then he sprang forward, his good leg strong enough to hurl him across the five feet separating us like a missile.

I'd seen his leg tense at the last instant and sidestepped. My blade swung down and took off his sword arm. His brightblade flickered off and the oblivion staff clattered to the ground. Torvin screamed and squirmed, desperately trying to rise with his remaining limbs. I slashed down and took off his head. His body twitched, and his mouth stretched into a soundless scream before the eyes went dark.

I picked up the other oblivion staff. I still felt a faint bond to it even though it had been separated from the other Cain for months. Sadness washed over me as I realized the true owner was gone forever from this world. I tried to banish it to its pocket dimension, but it resisted, needing more time to bond before it would readily respond to my commands. It was like being betrayed by my own body.

The grays were walking unsteadily back toward me. The rockslides had stopped, but the rain was growing heavier. I walked toward them, wondering what would happen next.

"What happened?" I asked casually, as if the fight between me and Torvin had never taken place.

They looked at what was left of his body and cringed.

The man gulped. "I've never seen an engineer fight like that."

"Torvin was plotting to overthrow Inventor Horatio," I said. "We came on a covert mission to stop him."

The woman nodded knowingly. "That sounds like him. He was always unnecessarily cruel to us."

I pointed up the mountain. "Any survivors?"

They nodded. "There's someone trapped in the rocks. We can't reach them without equipment."

I looked up at the storm clouds. "The bubble is collapsing."

The man nodded with a worried crinkle of his brow. "They've had to reinforce the bubble once an hour. With most of them dead, there's nothing holding back the storm."

"I need two hundred feet of rope for the armory." I pointed toward the mountain. "And I want three people in exos to start removing the rubble and freeing survivors, okay?"

They nodded eagerly, then jumped in the SUV and roared off.

I tugged open the armory door and found Layla sitting on the ground inside, her back against a shelf. I knelt in front of her and met her troubled eyes. "What's wrong, Layla? Stop with the tough-gal act and talk to me."

Her fists clenched and she shook her head. "That malgorth fucked with my mind. I can't clear my head."

I didn't know how to respond to that, so I went with my gut feeling. "What did you see? Was it a painful memory, or did something violent happen to you?" Everyone saw something different, at least when it came to the hypnotic spiders. Most people lived their worst fears or memories. For some reason, I always went back to a peaceful sunny field of flowers before my defenses kicked in and stopped the downward spiral.

Layla clenched her jaw and shook her head. "Just help me up, Cain."

I sighed, clasped her outstretched hand, and yanked her to her feet.

She inspected a burn mark on my arm. "You kill Torvin again?"

"Yeah." I told her how it had gone down. How he'd somehow gained the other Torvin's final memories.

"Makes sense," Layla said. "His thread was about to get snipped again by the same guy who killed his counterpart. That's got to fuck with the space-time continuum."

"Yeah, probably." I felt encouraged that she was starting to talk again, so I told her about the rockslide collapse and the storm outside.

Layla frowned. "How many lightning strikes?"

I shrugged. "A dozen. Must've been from them using Airbender."

"That doesn't sound right." Layla stepped outside and looked up. The blast marks were easily discernable by the blackened stone. "That's too precise for a storm."

"She's right." A deep baritone voice said from behind us.

I knew in that instant there was no defense that would prevail against the man behind us, because he could kill us in a heartbeat.

Chapter 26

Thor, god of thunder, emerged from the armory. He wore dark blue and platinum armor pocked with black marks and blood. Dried blood covered his thick biceps and his horned Viking helmet looked as if it had been dragged through the mud. He removed the helmet and tossed it to the ground. A scar ran across his left eye, down his cheek, and to his neck. His irises burned ice blue, flashing as if an inner storm raged.

I finally found my voice. "What in the name of the gods happened to you?"

"Divine war." Thor stood nearly seven feet tall, muscles rippling through his fair skin. He was a giant version of the man I'd met in Voltaire's. Some gods could physically change themselves to look more normal. I had no doubt he'd done that so as not to overly alarm the other bar patrons.

"Divine war?" Layla shook her head. "Who are you fighting?"

"I haven't much time, and I cannot let the others know I'm here." Thor motioned us back inside the armory. "The shielding here prevents us from being detected."

I was suddenly suspicious and summoned my staff.

Thor nodded. "A wise precaution. Look at me with true sight."

I flipped up the scope and peered at him. His aura glowed so bright it was almost painful to look at, but his physical being remained the same. He was not using illusion or glamour to hide his true appearance. Lightning raced through his aura, as if he himself were a storm barely contained by a shell. "You are who you appear to be."

"Now that's established, listen to me, and listen well." He glanced outside. "I cannot stop local time for fear of being detected, so I have only a few minutes. When the people in the cave attempted to use Airbender, it was an easy matter to piggyback the effect and cause the cave-in. They'd planned to aid Torvin, and you would have been defeated without my help."

I raised an eyebrow. "Thanks, I guess?"

"You're most welcome, Cain." Thor's tone indicated he was being completely serious. "The battle for Yggdrasil rages, but I found a moment of respite that allowed me to shadow walk here to aid you. I thought to leave immediately, but there is no reason I cannot tell you what's at stake."

I was intrigued by his use of the term shadow walk. I'd seen Hephaestus and other gods vanish into the shadows, so it obviously had something to do with that. But I simply nodded and let him speak.

"There is a dark conspiracy that we learned of too late to prevent the war across multiple universes." He absent-mindedly flicked dried mud from his cuirass. "The trickster gods, Loki and Dolos, banded with those from other pantheons to cause dissent among the divines. Blood was spilled and now war rages over the tree of life and the realms it connects. Meanwhile, their conspiracy caused a single moment of fate to go awry here, that they might unleash pandemonium on earth. We managed to employ safeguards that prevented Prime from meeting the same fate."

"What does that mean?" I said.

"It means that gods across many pantheons war with one another while the trickster gods wreak havoc on Gaia." He put a hand on my shoulder. "You are at the very crux of the battle for mankind. If Loki and the others have their way, it will spill over into your dimension. Once Prime is compromised, the other dimensions will fall to their sway like a stack of stones."

"You mean cards?"

"Do the gods span all dimensions, or are you separate from the Thor in our dimension?" Layla said.

"Some like me, Odin, Zeus, and Yahweh are single beings across all dimensions. There are others who are separate beings but with partially shared consciousnesses across dimensions. By causing chaos among the many realities, they gain new power that may allow them to unify their physical beings and gain far more power."

"What about Cthulhu?" I said. "Is he part of the lords of chaos?"

Thor shook his head. "No, but he has benefitted heavily from it. If he solidifies his hold on these dimensions, then it will benefit him and the tricksters. There will be a new balance of power across pantheons, and the balanced worlds we have striven to create will fall into chaos and anarchy."

"If you're so keen to help us, then shadow walk us to Noctua and then back to the Tetron so we can get back to our dimension," Layla said.

Thor sighed. "You do not understand."

I grimaced. "Oh, I understand, all right. You want us to do more than go back home. You want us to put a stop to Loki's plan in Alpha."

"Yes." Thor patted my shoulder. "Once you crossed the interdimensional barrier, you crossed the threads of fate from your world with this one. What was once a forgone conclusion is now a fate clouded in mystery." He patted my shoulder again. "Find the owl, save the world."

"Noctua is the key?" I said.

Thor nodded. "Hold out your hand." I did so. He squeezed his fist and a tiny drop of bright red blood fell into my palm. "You'll need that in a moment."

"Is this for the Tetron?" I asked.

The god glanced at the door, then turned and vanished into the shadows.

"Oh, hell no!" Layla ran after him, but he was gone. "How are we supposed to save the world if they don't give us better instructions?"

The grays stepped inside an instant later, thick coils of rope in their arms.

"The exos are on their way to move the rubble," he said. "Do you want us to help them?"

I shook my head. "We may have to leave soon. You're not to tell anyone of our mission here, understand?"

"Yes, of course," they said in unison.

"I want you to burn Torvin's body and bury it in the desert," I said, "or throw it in the sea."

"Yes, sir." They turned and left.

Layla managed a smile. "Feels nice to boss people around, doesn't it?"

"Yeah." I picked up the rope and carried it to the pit where Noctua had fallen. I tied it around a metal post near the furnace and tossed the coil into the pit. I didn't have a proper harness, but my utility belt worked in a pinch. I removed the uniform and threaded the rope into the belt, then rappelled into the darkness.

About halfway down, I cast a light globe and let it hover in place. The one I'd tossed in earlier had already gone out, so I dropped one to replace it so I could gauge the distance to the bottom. A few minutes later, I found a wide ledge where Noctua had fallen. The clockwork owl was dirty, but other than a few dents, didn't seem to have been destroyed.

Noctua was small, but not enough for me to fit her into a pouch on my belt. She was also much heavier than she looked. I put her inside my shirt and tucked it in. Her wings were folded, but still scratched my skin when I moved. I ignored the mild pain and used the rope to walk up the wall.

I was tired by the time I reached the top. The fight with Torvin and the long climb had really taken it out of me. I removed Noctua from beneath my shirt and set her on the ground next to me. The little owl didn't stir, nor did the intricate clockwork beneath her metal skin make any noise.

"Cain, I think she's dead." Layla picked up the owl and shook her, then thumped the head with her finger.

"Is that how you fix things?" I said.

"Maybe the mechanists can repair her." Layla set her down. "She's clockwork inside, right?"

"She was crafted by Hephaestus." I groaned and sat up. "Not even the best mechanist could repair one of his creations."

"Then what in the hell are we—" Layla gripped my wrist and turned my palm upright where Thor's blood stained the skin. She examined the owl, then rubbed the top of the head against my hand. Clockwork clacked and ground as if a worn cog was gumming up the machinery. A small dent in Noctua's side popped out and the grinding noise stopped.

Noctua's eyes blinked open. Her head spun in a complete circle and her wings fluttered. She looked at me and blinked again. "How may I be of service, master Hephaestus?"

I frowned. "I'm Cain, not Hephaestus."

The owl blinked several times. "My memory is not quite intact. It seems I suffered some internal damage." Her little legs worked back and forth, turning her in a circle. "Where is my pedestal?"

"It's gone," I said. "The mechanists stole the Tetron."

"Oh." Her tone remained matter of fact. Noctua wasn't built to take sides, but to observe and record. It meant she'd tell anyone just about anything unless she was prevented from doing so. She hadn't been able to tell us Hannah's origins, nor mine due to such limitations. "If you can return me to the Tetron, I can restore my memories, Hephaestus."

"Cain," I said.

She blinked calmly. "My apologies, Cain." She turned to Layla. "And you are?"

"Aphrodite," Layla said.

Noctua bobbed her body in a nod. "Apologies, goddess. You are, indeed, quite beautiful from an objective standpoint, but I was unable to connect the clues to your identity."

Layla blushed. "You're my favorite owl, do you know that?"

Noctua blinked. "I was originally built for someone else." Her head rotated slightly. "Athena, perhaps? But I would happily be your companion, oh, beautiful goddess."

Layla grinned from ear to ear. "Oh, do go on!"

I almost corrected Layla's lie, but Noctua's compliments seemed to have a healing effect on her spirit.

"Losing my memory is quite bothersome," Noctua said in a mildly annoyed tone. "I would be ever so grateful for your help."

"Well, at least you know how to speak English," I said.

"That is true." Noctua fluttered her wings. "Most of my base knowledge seems intact, but personal information is lacking."

"Then let's get you to the Tetron." I stood up. "It's on Gaia, so we've got a journey ahead of us."

"I am ready." Noctua fluttered on her metal wings, somehow hovering despite not flapping them nearly fast enough to remain aloft. She perched on my shoulder, but this time felt light as a feather compared to her dead weight.

We headed back to the exit. "I had to use Thor's blood to revive you."

"How were you able to obtain such a rare specimen?" Noctua asked.

"He gave it to me." I told her what had happened on the way out. Outside, we found the grays building a pyre and unceremoniously tossing Torvin's bits and pieces onto it. The sky was even darker now, and extremely threatening. I had a distinct feeling that Thor's interference with Airbender had probably kicked off one of those super storms the climatologists had worried about.

The grays were technically my enemies, but the construction workers were enslaved nubs and had no choice.

The grays looked surprised when they saw me approach with the gold and silver owl perched on my shoulder.

"That super storm the climatologists warned you about is going to hit soon." The pyre consisted mostly of broken up wooden crates since there weren't many trees growing in the barren terrain. "I want you to get everyone you can inside the armory right now." I looked up the mountain where mechanists in exo-suits were tossing boulders and rocks aside to free the survivors beneath.

"Yes, sir." The grays looked confused. "You want us to protect ourselves?"

I sighed. "I know most engineers and inventors treat you like you're trash, but there are those of us who view you as extremely valuable to the cause. And yes, I want you to preserve your lives and those of the other workers because the future of this world needs you."

They both straightened, smiling and almost proud.

Layla took their hands. "I believe the grays are our future. Teach them well, and let them lead the way."

I repressed a groan. "Show them all the beauty they possess inside?"

Layla nodded.

The two grays looked full to bursting with joy.

"We are proud to serve," the woman said.

The man saluted. "Very proud."

"Good," I said. "Is Airbender up in that cave?"

The man nodded. "Yes. Someone said there are some weather orbs up there as well."

We didn't have time to wait. "I want you to bring them into the armory with you, okay?"

They nodded.

I glanced at the sad remains of Torvin, then summoned my staff and ignited the brightblade. The grays looked startled but held their ground. I lowered the humming blade to the wood. It began to smoke and then caught fire. "May you burn in whatever hell awaits, you sick, murderous bastard." I continued to watch as the flames grew and consumed him. Then I banished my staff and turned toward the SUV. "Take us back to our sub."

Our new best friends dropped us off and then set off rounding up the construction workers and ordering them into the armory. The exo-suits gave the wearers incredible strength and speed, so most of the workers were halfway to the mountain by the time we walked down the dock to our submarine.

Pitch black clouds swirled to the north. Thick bolts of lightning rained down on the hills and plains. I realized I should have told them to take oxygen and other supplies because the storm might bring with it the hostile climate. But it was too late now. We climbed into the submarine and Layla got us underway.

I activated the light inside the Gaia globe and rotated it until the deepway beneath Lake Lanier was on the screen. I set the coordinates, and Layla steered us deeper, past the underwater sun to the hidden tunnel below.

Layla strapped in. "They'll have tightened security after the battle back at the mechanist compound. I hope we can still get to the Tetron."

"Me too." I strapped in and hit the whale sound button, or whatever it was called. The seabed opened and we entered the vortex.

Noctua seemed unaffected by the sudden acceleration, perched as she was on a railing near the captain's chair. Her counterpart in our dimension had managed the same thing, probably due to the god-built gyros and devices inside her.

"There is fighting on Gaia?" Noctua said.

"Yeah." Layla began to tell her everything that had happened since our arrival in this dimension. After we traveled through several nodes, her conversation trailed off. Her body tensed in apprehension and the submarine came to a stop outside the next tunnel.

I knew exactly what she was thinking. The underwater army we'd encountered was somewhere ahead of us, and we were about to travel back into their crosshairs. We hadn't been in Oblivion long and the creatures hadn't been moving very fast, so it was likely we'd overtake and pass them.

And Layla couldn't handle the mental strain again.

Chapter 27

Layla took a deep breath and looked back at me. She unstrapped herself and walked in circles, taking deep breaths.

I watched in silence and let her deal with the anxiety. Whatever she'd seen while in the grasp of those hypnotic eyes had shaken her to her very core. She needed to deal with it in whatever way worked best, because I couldn't afford having her freeze up like she'd done in the fight with Torvin.

Layla's face paled. She turned to me, lips quivering.

I knew that she needed my help but couldn't bring herself to ask for it. The Layla that had been and the Layla that existed now were at war. It was up to me to break the stalemate and suffer for it. I unstrapped and approached her. I took her hands in mine. "What do you need?"

A single tear rolled down her cheek. "Comfort."

I knew what comforted Hannah might not comfort Layla, but I tried it anyway and gave her a hug. Layla shuddered and leaned into my chest. She was no tiny thing, tall and muscular and naturally stronger than me because of her fae blood. But in that moment, she almost seemed like a child in my arms.

The moment lingered as long as it needed to, and then Layla backed away, the color once again returning to her cheeks. She removed the ivory uniform, then pulled off her shirt to reveal the athletic bra beneath.

I didn't know what was happening, so I remained still and silent.

Another tear escaped her right eye as she turned and displayed the scars on her back. The two on her opposing shoulder blades were the largest and deepest, as if intentionally done in the cruelest way possible.

"I had wings, Cain." Layla traced a shaking finger above one scar. "Most fae have them, even if they hide them behind glamour most of the time." Another shudder wracked her body. "I couldn't fly very well, but I could glide. The human who owned me didn't want me flying away, so he sheared my wings when I was a teenager." She looked at the floor. "It was the worst moment of my life and I relived it when I looked into that monster's gaze."

A tear burned its way into my eye and dripped down my cheek. "I'm sorry, Layla."

She nodded slowly. "You genuinely are, and I don't understand why."

I considered that for a long moment. "Because as much as you irritate me, I respect you and I like you." I reached into my well of emotion and tried to decipher what I felt. My adoptive fae parents had deprived me of human emotion, and despite binging on nub culture, I still had difficulty grasping it. But I knew from my experience with Hannah what it was that I felt for Layla.

She saw me hesitate and put a finger on my lips. "Don't say it, Cain. You've already shown it."

I remained silent.

Layla stepped closer, a new apprehension building behind her eyes. She leaned up and gently pressed her lips to mine. She tasted them again, then grew hungrier, pressing harder, her tongue finding mine.

Just as suddenly as it had begun, Layla backed away, a smirk on her face. "I'm ready to go face the monsters."

My throat was dry and my body was certainly ready to go in more ways than one. "Gods damn—" I bit my tongue. "Okay."

Layla pounced, shoving me against a bulkhead. We rolled along the curving wall, found the hallway, kissing and shedding clothes as we stumbled backward. I noticed Noctua's head turning as she quietly observed us. Then we found the bunkroom and I shoved Layla on the bed. We tore off the remainder of our clothes, our mouths hungrily exploring each other.

And then, at long last, after all the teasing and temptations, I pushed inside and we both gasped at the sensation.

Layla laughed. "Well, shit. We finally did it."

I grinned. "Oops."

Her grin grew hungry again. "Now, let's see if the wait was worth it."

Gods be damned, it definitely was.

I lost track of time, but a look at my phone told me that we'd whiled away two hours in carnal exploration.

Layla slid off the bed, then leaned over and kissed me. "If you tell anyone else about this, I'll cut your throat."

I stood and began dressing. "You don't have to worry about that."

She pouted mockingly. "We don't need to make it Facebook official?"

"Let's make the announcement on LinkedIn."

Layla snorted. "Stupid nubs and their social media."

"Yeah." I looked at her still naked body longingly, but we'd burned enough time.

She noticed. "Gods, you're hungry."

I nodded. "Curse of being a man."

Layla chuckled. "Get strapped into your seat, Cain. It's time to get that Tetron and get the fuck out of here."

"Even after what Thor said?" I was still trying to make sense of the thunder god's missive.

She shrugged. "If we get the Tetron, then we automatically save our world, right?"

"But do we save this one?" I absolutely hated having to stay here a moment longer, but we couldn't allow Umbra to spread the infection.

Layla shook her head. "Stealing the Tetron is enough, okay? Let Hemlock deal with her fuckups." She spat the name as if it were poison.

I knew I shouldn't ask, but I did. "Why did you get so pissed off at her for using that name?"

She worked her jaw back and forth. "Do you really think Layla Blade is my given name?"

I paused as the realization hit me. "Your real name is Hemlock Breakstone."

Layla scowled. "One more thing I'll cut your throat for if you tell anyone."

I scoffed. "Why don't you like that name? A deadly poison that breaks even the hardest substance? That describes you perfectly." I flicked my hand back. "Layla Blade has nothing on that name."

Layla pursed her lips. "I like that you like it, Cain, but there are other reasons I don't want to hear that name. Layla suits me just fine."

I sat down and strapped in. "Okay, Layla. Let's go."

She winked, turned around, and thrust the acceleration lever forward. The submarine jetted into the tunnel. We didn't encounter Cthulhu's army in the following nodes, much to our relief, so it came as a nasty shock when we surfaced in Lake Lanier and found the lodge grounds teeming with monsters.

Malgorths stomped across the land, leaving giant imprints in the soft soil. Their gray flesh quivered without the comfort of water surrounding it. Salko, the squid-headed humanoids, seemed the most comfortable out of water, while the migyos stumbled awkwardly on their tentacles, limbs unaccustomed to full gravity.

The docks were partially destroyed, just as we'd left them. The lodge and surrounding area were cratered and blackened from the fierce fighting. There were no mechanist forces to be found, and the rest of the undamaged submarines had moved out. I wondered if our theft had been discovered.

One thing was certain—we couldn't return to shore here. "Let's see if there's a place to dock near the waterworks."

Layla needed no prodding. She submerged the submarine before anyone took notice and headed southeast. It was dark by the time we reached the mainland near the waterworks, but we had no problem finding a dock at which we could moor the submarine. Every house along the lake had a dock, and most were built for houseboats or yachts.

She piloted into a dock while I climbed the ladder to the outside so I could tie us down. Once we were secured, I used the wireless to contact Hannah.

"We're back with the owl."

"Cain!" Hannah sighed with relief. "I've been so worried."

With the mechanists being on heightened alert, I didn't want to go into too many details about what we'd been through despite the point-to-point encryption. "Phase two is next. Expect us in a few hours."

"Are you sure? Maybe we should come help."

"Negative, Ghost Rider. Remain where you are."

Hannah scoffed. "You're using *Top Gun* references with me now?"

It was clear I needed to spell things out for her. "Firsters attacked the mechanists. They're on high alert. Can't say more."

"Oh." Hannah drew out the word. "Please be safe."

"We will be." I slid the radio onto my utility belt and turned it off. Then I climbed the submarine sail and used my true sight scope to scout the area. Aside from a few animals, no heat signatures appeared in the nearby forest. Our berth was less than a half mile from the waterworks.

Layla and I geared up and set off into the woods at a light jog. We reached the house neighboring the makeshift prison across the road from the waterworks and continued toward the concrete building. We slid off the backpacks we'd taken from the submarine's stores and unpacked the stolen mechanist uniforms. Layla once again wore ivory while I sported teal.

I scouted the waterworks. Instead of two constables, there were now nearly two dozen of them in exos patrolling the grounds. A pair of airships floated high overhead, their blinking lights giving away their positions. Security had been beefed to the max.

Layla grunted. "This ought to be interesting."

"Or suicidal." I tried without success to peer through the thick concrete walls of the waterworks building. "The mechanists don't care that much about protecting the observers. I think this much security means they're protecting something else."

"Like the Tetron." Layla leaned against a tree. "Even so, that's a hell of a lot of protection."

Her observation shifted my train of thought to another set of tracks. "Why would the Firsters attack the bulk of mechanist forces with such a small squad? Even with their impressive firepower, they didn't stand a chance of winning."

Layla mulled it over. "They were probing the defenses for a larger strike."

I nodded. "They wanted to see the response time of Esteri and her demis."

"It didn't take them long at all," Layla said. "The demis must be stationed nearby."

I nodded. "They approached from the north."

She pursed her lips. "Do you think the demis are stationed close to the apocalypse weapons?"

"Yep." I opened the maps app on my phone and scrolled to our area so I could look for possible origins. "It took them a solid ten minutes to get here from the time the fight started."

Layla pursed her lips. "Which means they came from the northern end of the lake somewhere. That's a lot of land to cover."

I turned off the screen and tucked away my phone. "I have better ways of finding their base."

"Why, exactly, do we want to find their base?" Layla's eyebrow rose in challenge. "We want to avoid them, snatch the Tetron, and leave."

I waggled a hand. "Eh, maybe."

Her eyebrows dove into a confused V. "The Tetron is in the waterworks building right now. Why aren't we making a move for it?"

I knew she wasn't going to like this next part. Hell, I hated what I was about to say, but if it meant keeping our dimension safe from invasion, then there was no avoiding it. "We need to follow the people who brought the Tetron here back to wherever they're keeping the other weapons. We raid that place, steal everything, and use the Tetron to take it to our dimension. Then we can take it to our Oblivion and melt everything down in the armory."

Layla shook her head. "You're fucking crazy, Cain. All we need to do is march in there right now and take the Tetron. We go home and leave these bastards to sort shit out themselves."

"You heard Thor," I said. "If we don't stop them in this dimension, they'll eventually be able to raid our dimension and it'll be game over. The best way to ensure we end their plans is to steal the apocalypse weapons and destroy them." I pointed at the guards. "Besides, I guarantee you that breaking in here won't be any easier than breaking into their armory."

"You're forgetting something." Layla folded her arms across her chest. "What if the demis are in the same base? We'll never get the weapons."

I pursed my lips. "I guess we'll just have to play it by ear."

Layla hissed through her teeth. "This isn't our responsibility."

"If we want Prime to survive, then it is." I held out my hands helplessly. "We have to stop the infection."

Layla glared at me for a long moment, then finally shook her head. "Gods damn it, Cain, you're too soft sometimes."

I nodded. "And I'm stronger for it."

She scoffed. "Fine. But I'm only agreeing to this because Thor said so."

"Whatever it takes." I began plotting how we were going to follow the people who transported the Tetron. It seemed another tracker was in order. It had been a while since I'd cast the last one, so I started patterning a new one with fresh sigils, weaving them into an encrypted mesh.

Noctua perched on a nearby branch. I turned to her and asked, "Noctua, is there a quicker way to find the other weapons stolen from the armory?"

"I do not remember." Her eyes clicked as they focused on the waterworks building. "I apologize."

"This is useless," Layla hissed. "What if this damned owl never remembers how to use the Tetron? Will we put some of Hannah's blood in the cube again?"

"Not if it means leaving the cube here," I said. "Leaving a doorway open between our dimensions would be catastrophic."

But until Noctua's memory improved, there was no telling when we'd get to go home.

Chapter 28

Hours later, a man in ivory emerged from the waterworks building with an escort of five constables. They vanished behind a line of parked police wagons before I could line up a shot. The other patrolling constables marched to the vehicles and began climbing into the back. The back doors faced away from us, so I couldn't tell which one the inventor occupied.

That left me little choice. I quickly tagged the driver of each vehicle as they climbed inside and hoped they were all going to the same place.

Layla smirked. "You didn't think this all the way through, did you?"

"Not entirely." I banished my staff. "I didn't think an inventor would ride in the back of a paddy wagon."

"I couldn't tell which one he boarded," Layla said. "Judging from the look on your face, you couldn't either."

"We'll need to follow them." I watched as the line of vehicles pulled onto the road, leaving behind a pair of police wagons and nothing else.

"Well, let's try our luck." Layla brushed leaves off her uniform and started walking toward the waterworks building.

I turned to Noctua where she still perched on a branch. "Go back to the submarine and wait for us there, okay?"

The owl fluttered away without comment.

I hurried to catch up with Layla. We were about halfway to the paddy wagon when Tony and Maria emerged from the building carrying a limp figure between them. A pair of constables followed them, bored expressions on their faces. The observers looked markedly sicker, probably from such a long exposure to the Tetron. I wasn't surprised to recognize the dead man as Howard.

I didn't want to draw their attention to us, so we altered our angle of approach to keep a shrub in the line of vision between us. They continued around the side of the building until we lost sight of them. I imagined they were going to dump the body in the woods since the mechanists had such low regard for nubs.

The constables escorting them were the same pair who'd been guarding the front earlier. With them out of the way, there was no one to see us waltz over to one of the paddy wagons and climb inside. Layla claimed the driver's seat and spun the ignition crank. The vehicle rattled to life and we took off after the convoy.

I used the tracker to sense the locations of the drivers and immediately encountered a problem. One of the drivers headed southeast while the other two went northwest back in the direction of the island lodges.

Layla slowed when she saw the expression on my face. "What's wrong?"

"One of the wagons is headed to the mainland and the others turned toward the islands." I looked the map app on my phone. "I was expecting them to stick together."

"Esteri and her little friends came from across the lake to the north, which means the weapons must be there too." Layla stopped at the intersection and looked at the map. "The only way to get there is by taking a road north around the lake."

I pursed my lips. "Not necessarily." I pointed right. "They might have come by boat."

"Ooh, you're right." Layla turned north and started driving.

I reconsidered our current course of action. "If they came by boat, we should go back to the submarine."

Layla hit the brakes again. "Damn it, Cain, make up your mind."

"I just did." I made a circle with my finger. "Turn us around and go back to the sub."

The two-lane road was narrow, and the paddy wagon wasn't designed for tight turns, so it took a moment to get pointed back the other way. Thankfully, there was no other traffic, so we made it back to the submarine without issue.

Noctua waited on the railing near the hatch. "That didn't take you very long."

"Change of plans." I opened the hatch. "Get in."

Noctua hopped inside, spreading her wings at the last instant to glide away from the ladder and out of sight. Layla and I followed her in and secured the hatch. I sat in the captain's chair and concentrated on the trackers. I didn't have a precise fix on them, but they were still northwest of us.

The water seemed darker and murkier than before. Even with the flood lamps brightening the way, disturbed sand and muck clouded the view.

"Does this thing have radar?" Layla said.

"You mean sonar." I examined the navigational console but none of the icons near the switches even remotely resembled sonar. I slid over to the tactical console and located an icon with little waves coming out of it. Hoping I didn't launch a torpedo, I rotated the corresponding knob beneath it and was rewarded with a vibrating hum in the hull.

Glowing lines on the forward window outlined the terrain before us, giving Layla enough time to narrowly avoid a boulder.

She glanced back at me. "I thought sonar made a pinging noise."

"Yeah, but this is mechanist tech." I shrugged. "They march to the beat of their own tambourine."

Layla steered us into a deeper area and increased speed. "I see what you did there."

A few minutes into our journey, the tracking signals stopped moving. I raised the periscope as we passed the lodge. Hundreds of grays in exos were cleaning up the wreckage in the docks and surrounding area. Cthulhu's soldiers were gone, presumably back into the water. Unbelievably enough, there was another party raging at the pool. The building itself hadn't suffered much damage and the mechanists apparently believed lightning wouldn't strike twice. I was surprised Cthulhu hadn't kicked their asses into gear after the drubbing they'd taken.

I oriented myself on the tracking signals again. "The marks are southwest." I checked the map on my phone. "Keep going around the coast."

Layla turned off the forward floodlights and sped up, apparently confident in the sonar's ability to warn us of collisions. As we rounded the island, I swept the periscope across the horizon, searching for anything on the water. In the few minutes it took us to catch up, the mechanists could have already launched a boat or submarine and carried the Tetron out of sight.

Lights blinked on at a dock. I zoomed the view through the scope and spotted the ivory uniform of the inventor I'd seen exiting the waterworks building. A constable next to him carried a small brass chest.

A breath of relief whooshed out of my mouth. "Target spotted on the island."

Layla slowed the submarine to a stop. "And?"

I watched as the inventor and constable walked to the end of the dock where a sleek bronze boat waited. The constable placed the chest into a locker and slid into the driver's seat while the inventor made himself comfortable in the back. The other constables remained onshore.

The driver steered the boat north by northeast which was about the same direction Esteri and the demis had come from. I turned a dial on the periscope handle and activated the night vision so I could continue to track the boat's progress. The driver reached down and pulled on a lever and two halves of a transparent bubble rolled out of the sides of the vessel and closed around the passengers.

Within seconds, the boat began to submerge until it vanished from sight.

"Well, now I've seen everything." I lowered the periscope. "The target is underwater heading northeast."

Layla didn't look impressed. Then again, with the submarine underwater, she hadn't been able to see what I'd seen. "They're in a sub?"

I shook my head. "A mechanist speedboat."

She did a double take. "You said they're underwater?"

"Yep." I pointed in their general direction. "That way."

Layla pushed the vessel to full speed. Moments later, the sonar began to pick up the strange outline of the submersible boat.

Layla scoffed. "Why in the hell would you even make such a stupid boat when you have submarines?"

"Because the mechanists aren't the most practical people." I shrugged. "It is pretty cool, though."

"It's stupid." Layla sucked in a breath and slowed the submarine. "You've got to be kidding me."

It took a moment for me to see the faint outline highlighted by the sonar. Something too symmetrical to be boulders on the lakebed. "Take us in slowly."

"Yeah, you think?" Layla eased forward the engine lever and took us deeper to follow the trajectory of the submersible boat. We passed through a cloud of murk and emerged in clearer waters nearly forty feet down.

A ring of bright lights around a structure made the sonar unnecessary. A vast bronze dome covered the lakebed as far as the eye could see. A series of pipes connected the dome to cylindrical structures. A portal door opened in the side of the nearest cylinder and the boat vanished inside.

Layla stopped the submarine, rotated her chair, and glared at me. "Are you kidding me right now? They're keeping the weapons in an underwater base!"

"No way." I stared in disbelief at the newest obstacle in our path. "Gods be damned. I've completely fucked us. We should have stolen the Tetron and run."

Layla cackled. "Oh, the look on your face!"

"Glad to see you're back to your normal self." I scowled at her and slumped in my chair.

"Let me use your scope." She held out a hand.

I summoned my staff and handed it to her.

Layla scanned the area. "I don't see any external docking ports which means those pipes are the only way in."

I considered what little I knew of underwater facilities. Most of that info came from movies, but that didn't mean it was totally inaccurate. "Take us to the lakebed so I can get a look at the bottom of the structure."

She dropped us until the submarine settled on the sandy lakebed, then used the scope again. "The dome doesn't sit in the lakebed." Layla pursed her lips. "The pipes run underneath the structure and curve up into it."

"Do you see any openings in the bottom?"

"Not from this angle." Layla handed me the staff.

I went to the window and got on my belly. It took a moment, but I spotted a submarine partially concealed by the distant gloom. It was parked beneath the dome, meaning there was an opening. The air pressure inside kept the water from flooding the building and allowed the submarines to moor in place with their sails protruding up inside the bay.

"What now?" Layla stood over me.

That was a good question. "Maybe we can dock and try our luck with the disguises."

"I like it." She shrugged. "Simple, stupid, and highly likely to get us killed."

"The other choice is to wait until they bring the Tetron back to the observers."

Layla shook her head. "Let's try your plan first. I'd rather die than sit around waiting." She dropped into the pilot's seat and took us forward. We hadn't gone more than twenty yards when a speaker on the bulkhead crackled.

"Identify yourself, unknown submarine."

I found the communications button on the arm of the captain's chair and pressed it. "This is the *Archimedes* coming in to dock."

"You will halt until clearance is confirmed," the voice demanded.

Layla grimaced. "So much for this plan."

The voice spoke. "*Archimedes* you do not have clearance."

I tried one more tactic. "The docks were destroyed. Where are we supposed to secure our vessel?"

"Report to the lodge and they will arrange something," the voice replied.

"Affirmative," I replied.

Layla turned us around and we headed in the general direction of the docks. It looked like my brilliant plan had completely and utterly failed.

"Head northeast." I stared out the window. "We're going to my lake house."

"Why?" Layla said.

"Because it's in an isolated part of the lake, and I want to get the others out here." I closed my eyes and considered the options before us. Somehow, we had to approach the underwater facility without showing up in their sonar. While I could camouflage our visibility, I had no spells that could conceal us from sound waves.

"The mechanists are insane." Layla steered us around a small island. "Out of all the things they could've done, they built an underwater lair in the middle of nowhere."

"Just because they can." I pursed my lips. "The question on my mind is whether Esteri and the demis are on that station or not."

"Doubtful," Layla said. "They're probably on land further north. The clockwork wings they used are too wide to fit into a boat and it'd take them too long to reach the surface by submarine in the event of an emergency."

I nodded. "That's our silver lining."

"Silver lining?" Layla scoffed then seemed to reconsider. "Yeah, maybe it is."

Once we were far enough away from mechanist activity, I had Layla surface so I could radio the others.

"Lone wolf to panda, come in."

Hannah answered immediately. "I was so worried. Are you okay?"

"Yeah, but we've hit a bump." I detailed what we'd found. "Gather everyone and meet me at the lake cabin. Hemlock should know how to reach it."

"Won't it be dangerous to drive there with the mechanists patrolling the area?"

"The cabin is isolated, and the mechanists are concentrated to the east. We'll be fine."

After I gave her a few more details, I went below and closed the hatch. Layla submerged and we continued to the destination. The *Archimedes* was small enough to fit beneath the boathouse canopy. I tied it down and we went inside the cabin.

Noctua fluttered to a perch in the wooden rafters. "I have determined that the only way I might recover my memories is to attempt deep meditation. This requires me to shut down most of my other functions, and I will be unavailable until I awaken."

"You can meditate?" I didn't understand how a clockwork being could do anything she did.

"That is the closest analogy to human brain function," she replied. "I will be searching my memories and attempting to reconstruct the damaged areas."

"Like a computer."

"Another passable analogy," she said.

I frowned. "How long will it take?"

"Unknown." Noctua blinked. "Perhaps hours. Perhaps days."

"Great." I dropped onto the couch. "What if you never wake?"

"If I cannot repair the damage, I will awaken myself." Her wings fluttered one last time then folded and her eyes clicked shut.

"Just dandy." Layla dropped onto the couch next to me. "What now?"

"We wait." I had a few ideas about passing the time, but Layla stood and stretched.

"I need some alone time." She rubbed my head. "No offense."

"Oh, um, me too." I resisted the urge to take her hand and pull her down next to me.

She winked and left the building. I took off my utility belt and set it on the floor, then lay on the couch and closed my eyes to get some rest. With so much going on in the past few hours, I hadn't slept in nearly twenty-four hours. Getting shut-eye was essential to surviving the next twenty-four.

Hannah sits next to me on the couch. We're back at home in Sanctuary, eating popcorn and watching a movie. She bursts into laughter. I turn toward the television, but the screen is dark. I frown and try the remote, but still nothing. Hannah howls with laughter.

"What's so funny?" I ask.

She turns toward me, teeth bared in a maniacal grin. The flesh on the other side of her face is burned and melted down to the bone. My Hannah isn't sitting next to me. It's Esteri.

"Why are you still alive, Cain?" Her voice rasps as if she can barely breathe. Power glows in her eyes. She opens her mouth and a torrent of energy consumes me. The pain is unbearable, but I grit my teeth and bear it anyway.

"Hannah, don't do this!" Darkness takes me.

I jerked awake, rubbed the sleep from my eyes and sat up. Sweat trickled down my forehead and into my eyes. Bad dreams didn't usually get to me, but that one seemed so real my skin felt raw. Dread constricted around my heart. Was my Hannah just a heartbeat away from becoming Esteri?

The thought filled me with despair. The house felt empty. I checked the time and saw I'd been asleep for three hours. "Anyone here?" I called out.

No answer.

I unclipped the radio from my belt. "Hannah, are you there?"

No answer.

I tried again. Waited. Tried again.

Still no answer.

An icy serpent of dread slithered through my guts, constricting my heart until I could barely breathe.

Layla burst inside, sweating and breathing heavily. She grinned. "Felt good to go through my routine again." She frowned. "You're white as a ghost. What happened?"

"I can't reach the others." I walked over to the kitchen counter.

Layla went to the kitchen and opened the pantry. There was a large selection of canned goods, but nothing fresh. She picked out a can of black beans and set it on the counter. "I'm sure they're fine, unless my idiot doppelganger ran into something she couldn't handle."

"She's perfectly capable." I unconsciously started pounding the flat of my fist against the counter. "Something's wrong. I need to go find out what happened."

"No, you need to stay in place." Layla put her hand over my fist. "It's slow going from all the way down there, remember?"

"Yeah, but why wouldn't they answer the radio?" I picked it up and tried again, with no more success than the last time.

I'd been an idiot for asking them to come up here. Layla and I should have gone back to the others instead. Besides, what could we possibly do to infiltrate an underwater base with just the five of us? It was stupid and impossible. Why hadn't I taken the Tetron when it was at the waterworks? I'd blown the entire operation and now the others were killed or captured.

I reclaimed my fist from Layla and punched a wall. "Fuck!" Despair filled me and it was all I could do to keep myself upright.

Lights flashed outside the window, and I realized the situation had become even worse. The others had been captured and given the mechanists the location of the lake house. We were burned and about to be invaded.

I was so furious I didn't even think to run. I summoned my staff and went out the back door.

"Cain," Layla hissed. She grabbed my shoulder. "What are you doing?"

"I'm going to kill the bastards before they know what hit them."

Her grip tightened on my shoulder. "You idiot, don't you hear them talking?"

I cocked my ear. "Sorry, I don't have superior fae hearing."

Layla groaned. "It's not a kill squad, if that's what you're thinking. I hear the girl babbling all the way from the front yard."

I blinked a few times. "You hear Hannah talking?"

She nodded. "If she's been captured, she sure is excited about it."

I ran around the front of the house and spotted Hannah and the others emerging from the detached garage. Hannah's eyes lit when she saw me. She ran across the distance and hugged me.

"Cain, I'm so happy to see you."

I hugged her back, unashamed to show that I'd been worried. "Gods damn it, why didn't you answer the radio?"

"I left it on all day and the batteries died." She smiled sheepishly. "I forgot to bring new ones when we left."

"And she wouldn't stop worrying about it the entire drive." Hemlock stepped out of the garage.

I backed away from Hannah. "What took so long? Two hours should've been plenty of time."

A hauntingly familiar voice answered. "I'm afraid that's because of me, Cain."

The man who stepped outside was the last person I expected to see.

Chapter 29

Aura and Grace emerged from the garage behind their surprise guest. They watched him uncertainly, and I couldn't blame them.

I finally found my voice. "How and why are you here?"

"I'm a scout, nothing more." Erolith regarded the cabin. "It seems you took exhaustive measures to hide this place from us, Cain. He knelt and touched the ground. "Silver, iron, and fae glamor. I wasn't aware you possessed the ability for such advanced magic."

"Never allow an enemy to glimpse your full potential." I raised an eyebrow. "I'm sure you remember that speech."

He nodded. "You nearly became everything I hoped you could be, child."

"Until I ruined it all by abandoning the Oblivion Guard." I scoffed. "Let's go inside. I don't want our voices travelling across the water."

"A wise precaution." Erolith preceded the others into the house without once glancing back at us. He went to the fireplace inside and flicked his fingers. A smokeless blue blaze ignited, and the room began to warm.

"Now that's handy." Layla dumped the can of black beans into a pan and held them over the fire.

Aura looked hungrily at the beans. "Where did you get those?"

"Use that elf nose and sniff it out yourself," Layla told her.

Hemlock snorted. "The pantry." She took Aura to it.

I dropped onto the leather couch and Hannah snuggled next to me. I considered telling Layla that the cabin electricity was powered by liquid mana. I simply hadn't turned on the generator yet. But she seemed to enjoy cooking over an open flame, so I remained silent.

Erolith raised an eyebrow and sat in a divan across from us. "I crossed over from Feary with my staff and have been scouting the Feary portals to see if the mechanists have missed any. Unfortunately, it seems they've placed deadly contraptions at the portals, ensuring a painful death to anyone who attempts to come through."

I shrugged. "That should be no problem for the Oblivion Guard to handle."

"I agree." He clasped his hands in his lap. "But the queens have told us to stay our hand for now. They believe it is in our best interests to let the humans fight the conflict. Their pervasive numbers on Gaia have whittled at its resources and dirtied the lands. A reduction in population would not be the worst thing."

"Yes, except the war won't stop at Gaia." I pointed in the general direction of the mechanist base. "Cthulhu and his allies possess the apocalypse weapons from the lost armory. They've hesitated to use them against the humans because they don't want to destroy this world. But they won't have the same hesitation when it comes to Feary."

"I agree with that assessment, but I am in no position to defy the queens." Erolith pursed his lips. "You are identical to my Cain in almost every way, but there's a certain edge to you. It seems sharper and less jagged. Then again, he was much different after the girl tried to kill him the first time." His eyes wandered to Hannah. "It's most unsettling to see you huddled against him like a lamb sheltering from a storm."

"It's always unsettling to see you," Hannah shot back. "Because you're a shitty dad."

Layla barked a laugh. "The girl's got a point."

Erolith looked unapologetic. "Raising a human child in a fae society allows for no compromises. It would have been fatal to the boy."

I leaned forward on my elbows. "See, I find that extremely puzzling. Why would high fae, of all people, suddenly take mercy on a human boy and raise him as their own? Why not dump me off at a human orphanage instead?"

Erolith's lips flattened into a line. "I suppose that does seem puzzling, given the way fae treat humans among them."

"That's not an answer." I sighed. "Not that I expected anything after all this time."

I looked back at Hemlock and Aura in the kitchen. "You ran into him when you were scouting the Feary portals?"

Hemlock nodded. "We nearly fought, but he noticed my ears."

A flicker of distaste flashed across Erolith's features. "It was an unsettling reminder that some of our kind will lay with the beasts."

I slapped my hand on the couch armrest. "Exactly! Why in the ever-loving hell would you adopt a beast? Was I an experiment? A pet?" I resisted the urge to run over and shake him by his shoulders.

Erolith crossed a leg and regarded me in silence until it became awkward. Even then, he said nothing.

He was a master at manipulation just like all the high fae, but the difference between him and other fae was that he preferred not to answer direct questions. Fae couldn't lie, but they could twist truths into something resembling an answer.

Erolith's steady gaze flicked to Hannah for the briefest instant. He'd used such subtle techniques to mislead me before. I guessed he was doing it to make me think he knew more about Hannah than he'd indicated in the past.

But this time, Erolith surprised me with an answer. "Your origins are shrouded for a reason, Cain. The fact that this and several other dimensions have been struck by war is a clear indication that the forces we protected you from will do anything to uncover the truth. It seems my Cain died before they learned his secrets, and that is for the best."

Hannah leapt to her feet. "You're saying an entire interdimensional war was started just because some bad guys want to know about Cain's past?"

"I'm saying that the forces of trickery and chaos wish to recreate the universes in their image." Erolith sighed as if he were simply discussing the weather over tea. "Cain's past has something to do with that, but by revealing it, I risk revealing far more." He looked at the darkness beyond the window. "Despite all the damage they've wrought on this world, they still haven't uncovered the weapon that may yet prevent them from reaching their desired outcome."

"Just admit you're being mysterious because it makes you feel superior to everyone in this room," Layla said. "Fucking high and mighty fae. I hope Cthulhu wipes out your world and feasts on your corpses."

Hannah scoffed. "That escalated quickly."

Hemlock nodded. "I've fantasized about that a time or two myself. But there are other creatures on Feary besides the fae, and I'd hate to see them killed as well."

"I don't suppose elves fit into that category?" Aura said.

Hemlock simply smiled.

Grace stepped inside a moment later. "According to the local wildlife and elemental, there aren't any other humans for miles around."

I nodded. "Can your elemental look underwater?"

She nodded. "I must warn you that it's not very good at descriptions. Elementals don't see things the same way animals do."

Since Erolith didn't seem any closer to revealing my origins, I pushed ahead with the main reason I'd brought everyone together. "After my little talk with Thor—"

Erolith flinched. "You spoke with the thunder god?"

I'd never seen such a strong reaction from him. "I've spoken with several gods. Hermes, Hephaestus, and Poseidon."

He nodded solemnly. "Very risky."

I shrugged. "It's not like I had a choice. They talk, I listen and hope they don't kill me on a whim." He didn't seem to have anything else to say, so I continued. "The mechanists have an underwater base where I believe they're keeping the Tetron and other apocalypse weapons."

"Underwater base?" Hemlock barked a laugh. "What's wrong with these idiots?"

Layla nodded. "That's what I said. They're insane."

Aura shook her head. "Cain, I know you want to help this dimension, but how are the five of us supposed to infiltrate an underwater base and steal the weapons?"

"Oh, it gets better," Layla said. "Somewhere out there is an army of terrifying Cthulhu minions. Last we saw of them they were in the lake."

Aura held her hands out helplessly. "And where's Noctua, anyway?"

I pointed up to the rafters. "She's hibernating in an attempt to recover her memories."

Erolith raised an eyebrow. "Where did you find the famed clockwork owl?"

"In the armory." I shook my head. "But she was damaged when the mechanists raided it. We need her to tell us how to use the Tetron to return to our dimension."

He nodded. "The scales were unjustly tipped. Fate has brought you to this dimension to right the imbalance caused by chaos. I promise there is nothing you can do to return to your dimension until the task is completed."

I'd heard this same old argument too many times. "I disagree. Fate is fluid."

He shrugged. "Perhaps. Fate is a lake of tar. You might be able to pull yourself from it if someone extends you a rope, but the harder you fight it yourself, the deeper you sink."

Layla scoffed. "There is no fate but what we make."

"We're getting off course." Grace clapped her hands together for attention. "I've got to agree with Aura. Infiltrating secret underwater bases is way out of my realm of expertise."

Layla scoffed. "Infiltration is infiltration. Cain and I could do it in our sleep."

"Agreed," Hemlock said. "Their base could be on the moon and it wouldn't make a difference."

Layla grinned. "There's my girl."

Hemlock grinned back. "I can tell my girl's been busy." She glanced at me, back to Layla, and winked.

Layla cackled with laughter. Thankfully, no one else seemed to get the reference.

I stood up and turned to face the room. "The underwater base uses sonar to scan all incoming traffic. We tried to approach in our submarine, but they warned us off. I don't know what defenses they have, but they'll be at least as good as the weapons on the submarines."

"All we have to do is steal that submersible boat." Layla used a flat hand to mimic a boat going underwater. "They'll think it's the same people and let us in."

"Doubtful, and the boat can't hold more than four people." I'd already considered several possibilities for infiltration and settled on what seemed like the easiest way in. "The docking ports have doors and I doubt we can force them open. The best bet is to sneak into the open submarine bay."

"What's the complement of the crew in the base?" Aura said.

I shrugged. "It could be hundreds for all I know. The place is at least a hundred yards in radius and two or three stories tall."

"How about we take the submarine, fire some torpedoes, and breach the hull?" Layla said. "While they're distracted, we can blow open another door."

"I'd bet the hull of that place can easily withstand anything we throw at it." I turned to Grace. "Which is why I need your help to get inside."

Grace's eyebrows rose. "Me? I'm not even an especially strong swimmer."

"I don't even need you to go underwater." I wasn't quite ready to detail the plan, not with Erolith in our midst. I turned to him. "Perhaps you should be on your way."

He raised an eyebrow. "You don't trust me."

"Oh, I trust you'll do exactly what duty tells you to do, and I'm telling you right now, the fae won't get their hands on the apocalypse weapons."

Erolith nodded. "That is not their intention. They would rather the weapons be hidden forever from mortal eyes."

I hated the idea of making a bargain, but if there was one thing about my adoptive father I could rely on, it was his sense of honor and duty. He wasn't what I would consider a typical high fae, but that didn't mean he would make me a fair deal.

But I tried anyway. "I would have you agree that you will allow us to take the weapons back to our dimension for disposal."

Erolith frowned. "These weapons were hand-forged in the fires of creation."

"Yes, and those fires were scattered across Oblivion." I let that sink in a moment before continuing. "But we relit the forge with the fire and melted all the weapons to useless slag."

He remained silent for a long time, perhaps contemplating how to dissuade me from doing the same with these weapons, or if this might be a ploy for me to gain the weapons for myself. "Cain, I am impressed."

I rocked back on my heels at that statement. It was only the second compliment I'd ever received from him. I steeled myself too late to conceal my surprise, so I rolled with it. "Then you agree to the bargain."

He nodded. "Provided the Tetron is left with us."

"We need the Tetron to return home."

Erolith nodded again. "You may use it to return home. I will come with you and use it to return here."

"So the fae can use it to see everything across dimensions?" I shook my head. "That's not a thing." I pointed to the door. "Please go."

Erolith sighed. "I can summon the Oblivion Guard to aid in the attack. Would you forgo such a powerful force?"

"I'd rather fail and die than give the fae the Tetron." The device was simply too powerful to trust with them. "Unless you agree that none of the items from the armory will go into the custody of the fae, I don't want you around."

"I see," he replied.

"Does making such a bargain conflict with an existing bargain?" I'd learned to ask such questions after growing up among the fae. Extricating the truth from a people who could not lie was like squeezing blood from a stone.

"No bargains conflict with it."

"Do you have direct orders which conflict with it?" I asked.

He shook his head. "The queens have not mapped a strategy for fighting on Gaia and thus have not issued orders with regards to the weapons. But possessing the Tetron would greatly aid the success of the Oblivion Guard."

I shuddered at the thought of them possessing it. "Then I see no reason for you to resist."

Erolith gave no outward indication that he was seriously considering my proposal, but his lack of immediate response gave me hope.

"Erolith Sthyldor, I would bargain with thee."

His eyebrow quirked at the formal tone.

I continued. "Swear that all items forged in Hephaestus's armory on Oblivion will be safely conveyed to my dimension for destruction and that no fae will attempt to take or keep any of them. Swear that the Oblivion Guard will aid us in our fight until I have given them leave."

Erolith stood. "You will destroy everything from the armory post-haste?"

"Yes."

"Agreed, agreed, and thrice agreed." Erolith glanced up. "Thus is the bargain sealed."

The cold rush of magic felt like ice against my soul as his words took effect. I followed his gaze and realized why he'd looked up. It was clear in that instant that Erolith had two goals in mind—securing the Tetron and another valuable source of information.

I had just agreed to throw Noctua and the Tetron into the furnace.

Chapter 30

"Gods damn you, Erolith." I scowled. "I did not agree to throw a living thing into the furnace."

"The owl is clockwork and not alive." He shrugged. "The bargain is sealed, and you must abide. When I saw your determination to keep me from the Tetron, I knew also that you would not let me keep the owl. Her vast library of history and information would have been invaluable. But I also do not wish you to have it."

Hannah gasped and rose to her feet. "He's going to make you kill Noctua?"

Erolith shook his head. "The bargain will compel him to. Should he break it, his power will suffer."

Noctua was going to have a rude awakening when I told her about the bargain.

"No!" Hannah shouted. "Why would you kill a sweet little owl?"

"I have sworn the Oblivion Guard to your cause," Erolith said. "Do not forget that."

"I swear to burn your balls to ash if you don't take back that bargain right now!" Hannah's eyes began to glow, and a white nimbus surrounded her body.

Erolith shook his head solemnly. "It may not be rescinded, child."

"Hannah, calm down." I put a hand on her shoulder despite the heat emanating from her skin. I looked her directly in the eyes. "Trust me."

Body shaking with anger, Hannah took deep breaths. "If Noctua dies, Erolith dies with her."

Erolith remained stony-faced, but a slight tic in the corner of his eye told me he took that threat very seriously.

Aura dug into a cabinet and pulled out the liquor supply. "I feel like we just sold our souls to the fae all over again, and I didn't even make the bargain."

"Damned right we did." Layla scowled at Erolith. "We don't even need your help, fae."

I held up my hands to stop all the cross-chatter. "The deal is made, and yes, we need all the help we can get. Now we need to plan the attack."

"Which somehow involves me?" Grace said.

I nodded. "Can you talk to the fish in the lake?"

She frowned. "Yes, but what good would that do? Throwing every largemouth bass and rainbow trout in the lake against the mechanist base isn't going to help."

"What's the largest fish in the lake?" I said.

She shrugged. "I have no idea which species is the largest. I'd have to talk to the elemental and see what it tells me."

"Can you do that right now?" I glanced out at the docks. "It's important that I know so I can plan accordingly."

Grace gave me a puzzled look. "Sure, but I'm going to need more details before I agree to anything else."

I nodded. "Definitely."

I turned to Layla and Hemlock. "Can you raid the other nearby boathouses and look for supplies?" I jotted down a list and gave it to them.

Layla grinned. "Oh, we're doing this James Bond style, aren't we?"

"Whatever it takes," I said.

She turned to Hemlock. "Let's go, loser."

Hemlock raised the eyebrow above her missing eye at me, then followed her counterpart outside.

Aura finished mixing a drink and slid it across to me. "How can I help?"

I took a sip and moaned in satisfaction. "Just like this."

"I'll get started with my task too." Grace left for the dock.

Erolith stood. "I need to return to specific coordinates so I can cross over to Feary and gather my troops. It will take me several hours to do so."

I tossed him the keys to the car my counterpart kept in the garage. "If you don't show, the bargain is broken."

"I am well aware of that." Erolith looked uneasily at Hannah, then left.

"Asshole." Hannah stood and paced, fists clenched. "Cain, tell me why I shouldn't kill him."

I took her hand. "Hannah, trust me, okay?"

She sighed. "Not when you go making shitty bargains like that!"

I couldn't blame her for her anger, but Erolith was right. Noctua's knowledge was a dangerous tool in the wrong hands. Of course, if she didn't remember how to use the Tetron, then we might never get home anyway.

I'd already formulated our plan in my head, but everything hinged on Grace. After finishing my drink and eating some canned food, I walked outside and went down to the dock to see how things were coming. It took a moment for me to see her standing in the water, the moonlight casting her in silhouette.

I didn't want to disturb her, but she seemed to sense me coming. I saw her shadow form wave me over. I took off my shoes, rolled up my pants, and waded in next to her. When I was close enough, I realized she wasn't wearing a stitch of clothing.

"Why are you naked?"

Grace didn't seem the least bit embarrassed by her nudity. "I didn't want to get my clothes wet."

"Oh." The water was freezing but there were no tell-tale signs it affected her.

Grace swished the water with a hand. "There are four giant catfish in the lake, and thousands of bass and other species. I believe they're willing to help us."

I forced myself to maintain eye contact though my gaze wanted to wander lower. "Good." I turned and headed back to shore.

She touched my shoulder. "Cain, why do you need them?"

I kept walking until I was back on dry land. I turned around and saw her standing right behind me, hands on hips.

"Cain, I asked you a question."

"Yeah, but your body is distracting me."

She rolled her eyes. "Deal with it."

"Are those catfish strong?"

Grace nodded. "Very strong."

"Good." I told her exactly what I needed. "How does that sound for a plan?"

She grinned. "It's brilliant. I really like it."

"Glad to have your approval." I enjoyed one last look at her naked form. "Thanks."

"For the help or letting you gawk?" she said.

"Both." Then I went back inside.

Layla and Hemlock returned after midnight looking mighty pleased with themselves. They'd filled the back of a pickup truck with the supplies I'd requested.

I hadn't expected such a haul. "How did you find so much?"

Layla grinned. "There's a school right down the road."

Hemlock put an arm over her doppelganger's shoulder. "Easy peasy."

It felt as if I were talking to a different person than earlier. "I see our Layla has finally corrupted you."

"She's always been like this," Layla said. "The apocalypse had her down."

Hemlock smirked at me. "We had a nice talk too."

There was no question what the subject of their talk had been. Hemlock had been intimate with the Cain of this world. I supposed she was happy that her counterpart had finally taken the plunge.

I had nothing to say, so I started unloading the pickup and carrying the supplies to the submarine. Once that was done, it was bedtime. There were plenty of rooms for everyone, so I went into the master suite and locked the door. I didn't know if that was to keep Layla out or to keep me in. The more I thought about what we'd done, the more I wanted to do it again.

Now wasn't the time to be distracted with such things. I had to sleep well to be ready for a busy day tomorrow. As I lay in bed staring at the ceiling, I thought I heard someone outside my door. A part of me hoped it was Layla while another part of me also hoped it was Layla. Whoever it was left after a moment and I regretted not opening the door.

I knew I'd never get to sleep if I kept thinking about it, so I resorted to deep meditation. Then I finally drifted to sleep.

Erolith returned the next morning. The first thing I noticed was that he was alone. That meant nothing since the guardians might be hiding in the woods.

"Did you bring them?" I asked.

He nodded. "The queens have blessed your efforts and wish you gods speed."

I grunted. "That doesn't sound like them."

"They understand the dangers of war with Cthulhu." Erolith glanced at Noctua where she sat on the rafter. "Especially when he has such mighty weapons at his disposal."

"Are they aware of the other war being fought right now?" I went to the kitchen and searched the pantry for something to eat besides beans.

"They are but have not committed forces to aid either side." Erolith walked to the kitchen island. "As you're aware, the queens are not of the same mind."

"Oh, but they are when it comes to the gods." I finally found hermetically sealed melba toast and opened the package. "They'd both be fine with a power vacuum at the top. After all, their official stance is that the gods are dead."

Erolith avoided the jibe altogether. "Do you have any tea?"

I rooted out a container of dark seed tea leaves and set them and an elven teapot on the counter.

His eyebrows rose. "Interesting that you would have this particular species."

"It's your favorite." I tested the corner of the melba toast and found it mostly edible.

He took the teapot to the kitchen faucet and filled it. "I'm surprised my tastes have any bearing on your decision."

"I was barely walking when you took me in and raised me." I found a jar of preserves and broke the seal on the mason jar. "I was heavily influenced by everything about you." I shook my head. "I even have a humidor with orcish pipe tobacco. For some reason, I picked it up in case I ever needed to host you."

"Do you really, even here in this safe house?"

I nodded. "I usually duplicate everything I keep at home unless it's perishable."

Erolith produced a small ivory pipe from his robes. "Would you mind?"

I shook my head. "Be my guest." I told him how to find the humidor since it was hidden behind a secret opening in the basement. I didn't have milk or eggs to make a proper breakfast, so I took some canned sausages and the melba toast to the back deck and ate breakfast while watching the sun rise.

Erolith sat in the chair next to me and began packing his pipe.

I watched him as I crunched the rock-hard toast. "In retrospect, I've found it hard to understand why a being of absolute discipline would enjoy a vice such as pipe smoking."

"No being is always at work." A flame from the tip of his finger ignited the tobacco. "The most disciplined especially must break from structure for a time to allow the soul the freedom it needs."

"In other words, everyone needs to go crazy every once in a while?"

He nodded. "That was why I never said anything about your proclivity for exotic females, though it is abhorrent for me."

I rolled my eyes. "Sex with anyone besides a fae is abominable in your eyes?"

"It is, Cain. Not because of prejudice, but because it is like laying with animals."

"I'm an animal in your eyes."

He said nothing.

"You don't say a damned thing about the gods fucking humans."

Erolith drew on his pipe and puffed rings of smoke without any special effort on his part. "It is no less disgusting to me."

"In fairy tales, the fae have no such aversion." I spread jam on another piece of toast. "Are they wrong, or is this something that changed?"

"It is simply a truth recognized by the high fae of our time."

I didn't see it as important enough to argue about and tried to enjoy my breakfast even as it viciously attacked my palate.

"This is a nice moment, son." Erolith sighed in contentment. "Two beings merely existing outside of duty."

"You have the strangest way of thinking." I pondered his statement. "Why would it be remotely pleasant for you to spend time with a lowly human?"

He continued puffing his pipe without answering.

There was a certain truth in his silence—an answer waiting for me to reach out and grasp it. A chance, perhaps, for me to know where I'd come from and why my family had been slaughtered. The only thing I could infer from his refusal to discuss it was that there was something he didn't want me to know. I wondered if perhaps he had something to do with the death of my family. But if that were true, why adopt me?

I finally voiced the question. "Why won't you tell me anything about where I'm from?"

"It's vital that it remain unsaid, for only a scant few know the truth." He turned to me. "Trust me on this. Not even the gods, the fae, or that owl know where you came from. If certain agents knew, they would hunt you to the ends of the earth."

His sudden honesty confused me. "I lived among those who hated me and hid from those who hunted me for over ten years."

"You learned well. But not even you can hide from the gods." He leaned back in his chair and stared at the sun. "Does my counterpart know you keep his favorite tobacco and tea on hand on the off chance that he will visit?"

"No, but he tried to arrest me on suspicion of murder."

Erolith nodded. "Were you guilty?"

I shook my head. "No." I told him the short story of betrayal that led me to destroy the apocalypse weapons in our dimension.

"He did not truly believe you guilty," Erolith said. "He simply did not want you reaching the armory."

"Noctua knows my origins," I said. "But something prevents her from talking about them."

"Destroy the owl in your dimension too, Cain." He took a last puff on his pipe and then stood and knocked the ashes onto the ground. "When the time is right, you'll know what you need to know." Once he tucked the pipe into his robes, Erolith reverted to his disciplined form. "I am ready to hear your plan."

"I'll come inside and tell everyone about it in a moment." I walked to the water's edge and listened as it gently lapped the shore. The sky was clear, and only a slight breeze rustled the pine needles overhead. The surface of the water was calm, almost flat as a sheet of glass.

If my plan worked those calm waters would betray nothing to those on land. But if it failed, these blue waters would run red with the blood of my enemies and comrades alike.

Chapter 31

No one particularly liked my plan when I spelled it out.

Well, except for Grace. Mainly because it didn't involve asking the fish to hurl themselves into battle.

"We have no idea how many people are in that base," Layla said.

Hemlock nodded in agreement. "There could be a garrison of constables."

"For once, I agree with Layla," Aura said. "It's suicidal taking only three people with you."

"Hold up." Layla threw up her hands. "Two of me can handle anything you throw at us."

"Mostly." Hemlock seemed slightly less sure which made sense considering all she'd lost so far.

"I want to be in the first wave." Hannah glared at Erolith as if the plan were all his fault.

Everyone but Erolith and Grace started shouting each other down, but no one introduced a better plan.

I held up my hands. "Silence!"

The others flinched at my sudden outburst but stopped shouting.

"I will go in alone if I have to," I said. "We have no other way to determine what's in there unless we kidnap someone from the facility and beat the information out of them."

Hannah raised a hand. "Let's do that, then."

"We don't have time." I looked around the room. "The presence of Cthulhu's army means one thing. They're about to throw everything at the front lines of the resistance. If that fails, then they'll bring out the apocalypse weapons which are probably being kept in the underwater base. We need to act before the weapons are moved."

"We don't even know for sure the weapons are there," Layla said.

I shrugged. "I'm willing to bet they are."

"The plan is sound, and I believe the risk is lower than the others seem to think." Erolith ignored Hannah's glare. "Provided I can get my troops inside, there is little the mechanists can do to resist."

Layla sighed. "Fine. But it's one of the dumbest plans I've ever heard."

"Thanks, I appreciate it." I clapped my hands together. "Everyone into the sub."

With a great deal of grumbling, my crew filed toward the dock. Erolith stepped outside and raised a fist. Camouflage illusions melted away, revealing a dozen guardians stationed at various intervals in the woods around the house. I already knew they were there thanks to the extensive wards and security in the area.

By the time I boarded the submarine, it was nearly packed to capacity. The guardians occupied the tail section and bunk rooms while the others lined the corridor leading to the bridge. Hannah sat at the helm while Layla instructed her on piloting the craft. Aura sat in the captain's chair. Hemlock and Grace occupied tactical and navigation.

Hannah looked up at me when I stepped next to Layla. She offered a wan smile. "I learned to pilot a submarine before driving a car."

"Everything's a downgrade from here," Layla said. "Except maybe airships."

"Everyone's in," I said. "Let's get underway."

"Aye, aye, captain." Hannah slowly shifted the lever into reverse.

Layla watched closely but didn't mock Hannah when she messed up. Layla's lack of pettiness worried me. She'd already explicitly said the plan was garbage. Maybe she was even more worried than she let on.

I hated to admit it, but Erolith's faith in the plan bolstered my confidence. He might be an awful father, but he was an excellent strategist. That both worried and calmed me at the same time.

We left the offshoot of the lake where my cabin was hidden and set off to the southeast. We reached the desired coordinates about half a mile from the underwater base within the hour. I grabbed my equipment from the storage closet and climbed the ladder to the hatch. Only the sail and the top of the submarine protruded from the water, keeping a low profile so we wouldn't be spotted. I pulled on flippers then strapped on an oxygen tank and scuba mask.

Layla, Hemlock, and Grace filed out after me and put on their equipment. Grace sat where the hull curved into the water and closed her eyes. "They're waiting here already."

Four catfish rose to the surface. To say they were large was an understatement. They were monstrous, nearly six feet long with mouths wide enough to swallow a man whole.

Hemlock whistled. "Gods be damned, I didn't know catfish grew that big!"

"How are we supposed to hold onto them?" Layla raised an eyebrow in my direction.

The fish had no dorsal fins and their skin was smooth and slick. But I'd already worked out a solution. I knelt next to the first catfish and traced a sigil on its back. I put my hand on that area and it suctioned into place. No amount of pulled or twisting would remove it.

"Brilliant, Cain." Layla scoffed. "Now you're glued to the fish?"

I wiggled my index finger three times and my hand popped free. "Suctioned, not glued." I traced the sigil on the remaining catfish.

Hannah stood atop the sail, face masked with concern. "Cain, don't die, okay?"

"Just wait for my signal, and everything will be all right." I slid into the water and chose a catfish. Layla, Hemlock, and Grace followed suit. I put on my facemask and tested the seal underwater. The view was green and murky, but the catfish knew where they were going. I turned on the oxygen tank and made sure I could breathe.

Once the others had done the same, I slapped a hand on the catfish and let it suction in place. Grace did her Aquaman thing and the catfish dove beneath the water, powerful tails propelling them much faster than I would have thought possible.

I would've preferred sharks just for the wow factor, but they weren't exactly available in a freshwater lake. Besides, if everything went to plan, the mechanists wouldn't even see us coming.

Covering a half mile took longer than expected, but we finally reached the outskirts of the base. The lone submarine was still docked where it had been yesterday. A pair of submersible boats patrolled the perimeter, indicating they'd increased security since yesterday. I didn't know if it had anything to do with our attempt to approach the base or not, but I hoped it didn't mean the complement of constables inside the base had increased.

If the sonar from the base operated anything like it did in the submarines, their security would immediately notice the outline of humans attached to fish. That was why I'd planned a phase two.

As the catfish continued swimming, a dark swarm approached from behind. The next part was about to get uncomfortable, but since illusion couldn't fool the sonar, this was the only way to do it.

Just as we neared the perimeter where the sonar had pinged us last time, a school thousands of fish strong engulfed us. I could only imagine what the sonar displayed. I just hoped the idiots didn't open fire.

Surrounded as I was by every species of fish the lake had to offer, I couldn't see a thing. A sudden downward pull on my hand alarmed me as the catfish dove. The fish swarm parted as a slender torpedo zipped past and shot into darkness. A moment later, the water rumbled as it detonated.

The mechanists were even bigger idiots than I thought. A torpedo wasn't designed to detonate from striking a fish. And even if it did, what was their goal? I didn't think security had spotted us. If anything, they were probably trying to scare the fish and keep them from coming closer.

I caught a glimpse of our goal—the docked submarine. I also noticed the submersibles zipping toward us. They would be a bigger problem than random torpedoes, especially if they entered the swarm and found us. Unfortunately, I couldn't talk and there were too many fish concealing us for me to hand signal the others.

Grace already had things in hand. Hundreds of fish split off and swam toward the submersibles, diverting them away from us. The swarm pressed around me, making it impossible for me to see anything else for a time. When it thinned again, we were nearly to the underwater bay.

I'd trained for unthinkable scenarios but being escorted by a massive school of fish certainly hadn't been one of those. My skin felt slick and slimy from the constant press of fish bodies against me. At long last, we reached the docked submarine. I wiggled my finger and unlatched from the catfish.

Despite my desire to get above water, I rose slowly toward the bay, making sure I didn't see anyone standing over the water. The submarine blocked part of the view, but it would also conceal me from anyone on the other side. I surfaced gently in the underwater bay, careful to keep noise to a minimum.

I shouldn't have bothered.

A mechanist naval officer scrubbing down the bronze hull of the submarine stepped into view at the same instant, and his eyes went wide when he saw me. He went stiff and toppled over, face-planting against the hull and sliding into the water. One of Layla's daggers protruded from his back. Unfortunately, he wasn't the only one in there.

I powered my sigils and gripped the side of the bay to pull myself up as over a dozen sailors came to the realization they were under attack. One of them went for a lever on the wall. The red symbol below identified it as an alarm. I summoned my staff and blind-fired. A blast of magic slammed into the man's thigh and he went down screaming.

Layla and Hemlock flung blades, taking out more sailors before they could reach for weapons or escape. I activated my brightblade and slashed through the barrel of a mechanist gun, continued the swing, and took off the sailor's legs. I spun, kicked one attacker, beheaded the other, then drew a dueling wand and fired a shot behind me. A gurgling scream told me I'd hit home.

The wand slid back into its sheath as I ducked beneath a swinging rifle. I slashed in a circle and took out two more rifles. The brightblade hummed as it cut through metal and flesh, but there was almost no blood spray since the heat cauterized the wounds.

Within minutes, bodies and dismembered limbs covered the floor.

Layla looked at one of the sailors I'd beheaded. "No mess, no fuss. I need a brightblade."

Hemlock nodded. "It's an amazing weapon."

That reminded me of something I hadn't told her. "I recovered Cain's staff from Torvin. I can show you how to use it if we make it out of this alive." I banished my staff.

Her eyes brightened. "Y-you have it?"

Layla scoffed. "This is no time to get sentimental." She kicked aside a head. "We need to get to the control room before someone stumbles in here and finds all the bodies."

"Gods, what a slaughter." Grace stared at the bodies, a look of horror on her face.

I slid a wireless communicator from my waterproof pack and handed it to her. "Just be ready to pilot this submarine out of the way when I send the signal."

She composed herself and nodded. "Three beeps."

I climbed on the submarine and opened the hatch. If anyone was hiding inside, they were being silent. I dropped inside, wand at the ready. The bridge was clear, so I skulked down the main corridor checking the bunks, the mess, the heads, and engineering. There weren't many places to hide on the submarine and I checked them all to be sure. It would be disaster if someone surprised Grace during the next phase of the operation.

Once I was sure the submarine was clear, I climbed out gave her a thumbs up. "You're good to go."

Grace climbed up the sail and stood near the hatch. "I'll wait here until you send the signal."

The docking bay looked like a slaughterhouse, but it couldn't be helped. There were simply too many bodies and too much blood to clean up, and we couldn't dump them into the bay because the sonar would probably pick them up immediately.

Layla pulled three uniforms from her waterproof backpack, two teal and one ivory. She put on the ivory and handed the others to us. We slid into them and went to the metal door. The door slid open with the push of a button and we stepped into a bare metal corridor. A pair of sailors came down the hallway toward the door we'd just exited, making it obvious they were about to go inside.

A quick stab of the brightblade through the heart would make minimum mess and we could drag the bodies inside. Thankfully, Layla was well ahead of me.

She stepped in front of the sailors, face drawn into a scowl. "Why is this vessel not ready for departure?"

Confusion and fear flashed across their faces. The first one stiffened at attention. "Inventor, there should be a crew already assigned to it!"

"Yes, but they have been shirking their duties." Layla narrowed her eyes. "You will lock this door and allow no one to enter or leave until I return. Do you understand?"

He nodded. "Yes, inventor."

Layla's scowl deepened. "Do not even so much as open this door to look inside, or I'll have you scrubbing decks for the rest of your days."

"Yes, inventor!" Trembling with fear, the sailor lowered a lever that apparently locked the door, and then he and his comrade positioned themselves to either side.

Layla rubbed her hands together like an evil mastermind. "Excellent." She looked down the corridor. "Where is the control center?"

The sailors looked confused, but the same one answered. "The bridge is at the very top, inventor. Has no one given you the tour?"

"We just arrived from the front lines." Layla clasped her hands behind her back. "But it is of no matter. I will find my way around." She looked around uncertainly.

The other sailor pointed down the curing corridor. "Take a right at the fourth corridor and it will take you to the central lift."

I gave the sailors a hopeful look. "Are the demis stationed here? I haven't met one yet."

"No, sir." He shook his head. "They're stationed north of the lake in a secret location."

"Ah." I sighed.

"This way," Layla said imperiously to me and pointed down the corridor.

Hemlock had faced away the entire time, presumably to keep them from noticing how similar she looked to Layla. She began walking in that direction and Layla followed at a casual pace. I gave the sailors an apologetic shrug and followed.

The first corridor on the right went into a large cafeteria where I estimated fifty people were eating. The next corridor led to barracks. I couldn't see inside, but I counted a few distinct voices inside. By the time we reached the aforementioned corridor, I'd counted nearly eighty souls aboard the base. That seemed a high number considering there was only one submarine parked here. It strengthened my assumption that the weapons were being kept here.

A pair of constables stood before the elevator doors, neither of their faces displaying fear or concern at the approach of an inventor. One held out a hand as if expecting us to hand him something. "We have been ordered to verify the identity chits of anyone entering the elevator."

"We just arrived," Layla said. "No one said anything about identity chits."

"Then I must apologize, inventor, because we've been instructed to escort anyone without chits to security for questioning." He reached for his sidearm, but both he and his comrade were dead by daggers an instant later.

Layla hit the button and the elevator doors slid open. She and Hemlock shoved the bodies inside and I followed. When the doors closed, the women sat the bodies on the floor, keeping them upright to minimize bleeding.

I examined the buttons on the wall. "Let's hope they don't have a hundred people on the bridge."

"I'm betting no more than twenty," Hemlock said.

Layla grunted. "Fifteen."

I imagined the bridge of the first submarine we'd stolen and estimated how many stations an underwater base would have. It wouldn't have navigation, but it would have weapons stations and more. I threw out my guess. "Ten."

Layla hit the top button and the elevator bounced into motion. "Let's see who wins."

The lift was exceedingly slow, because it took us a full minute to reach the top floor. The doors slid open silently which was a good thing because it was in the middle of the bridge. A transparent dome granted a view of the murky green water outside, but not much more. Eight people in navy blue uniforms occupied stations before us.

One with extra-large shoulder pads and several gold circles stitched below them turned at the hiss of the door. We stepped out keeping our shoulders together to block his view. It seemed to work, but a sudden gasp from the left drew my attention to a woman who stared in horror at the corpses.

The gig was up.

Chapter 32

I sighed and summoned my staff. Daggers flew and people slumped over their consoles. I knocked a brass pistol from the hand of the officer and twisted his arm behind his back while Hemlock and Layla incapacitated the rest of the bridge crew. They made a full circle around the lift but found no one else.

"Nine people." Layla grunted. "Cain wins this time."

I shoved the officer into a chair. "Where are the apocalypse weapons kept?"

He stuck out his chin. "You'll have to kill me because I'm not talking."

Layla and Hemlock dragged two more living crew members next to the officer's chair.

"First one to talk lives," Layla said.

Trembling in fear, they remained silent. I took a walk around the bridge, examining the consoles and looking for clues, but everything looked much as it did on the submarines. There were no written logs or anything that might offer hints.

Layla put a dagger to the throat of the officer. "Count of three and you die."

"Go ahead." Fear shone in his eyes. "I will never talk."

She counted down, the dagger digging deeper with every second. Sweat poured down the man's face, but he didn't break. I jabbed two fingers into his neck and released a shock of magic to knock him out.

His comrades gasped and cried out, apparently thinking he was dead. Layla went to the next one. "Your turn."

Urine pooled in the crotch of his uniform. "I don't know anything! Not even the commander was privy to such information!"

His female comrade cowered. "He's telling the truth. Only the inventors know where the weapons are kept."

I leaned forward. "But they're on this station?"

She nodded vigorously. "Possibly on the command level."

Hemlock raised an eyebrow. "This isn't the command level?"

"No, the woman replied. "It's the level below the bridge."

"You're going to kill us, aren't you?" The man looked ready to drop a deuce in his uniform any minute.

I shook my head. "No, but you'll be taking an extended nap." With that, I jolted him and the woman in the neck and sent them to dreamland.

Hemlock rotated some dials and flipped down a lever. "The sonar is off. Let's get everyone else onboard."

I took out the wireless and clicked the Morse code button three quick times. Grace responded with two beeps. Hannah responded with four beeps. So far, so good. Provided the weapons were onboard, we might actually pull this off.

"Why is there a navigation console?" Hemlock stood in front of a console filled with switches, knobs, and levers.

"They copied the layout of the submarines almost exactly," I said. "Maybe it's easier to keep everything the same." I opened the elevator and we stepped inside. Layla and Hemlock tossed the bodies of the constables out to make more room, then I hit the second button from the top. Clockwork gears clanked and the elevator dropped as slowly as it had risen. When it stopped on the next floor, the door slid open to reveal yet another metal door.

A speaker box in the corner of the elevator crackled on. "Password."

We looked at each other in dismay. I waved the others back and summoned my staff. The brightblade crackled on.

The speaker crackled again. "Password now, or the lift will be sent to the docking ring."

I jammed the brightblade into the crack at the edge of the door and slid it up. Someone on the other side cried out in surprise. The latch holding the door snapped and gears clanked as the door slid open.

A pair of constables reached for rifles in a metal cabinet in the next room. Layla and Hemlock downed them before they even got close. The security room was little more than a metal box with another door behind the constables. I hit a button and the next door slid open to reveal a curving corridor. We were higher up in the dome than the docking ring, so the corridor was shorter, making it difficult to see very far down it in either direction.

I hit the button to open the first door. Behind it was an ornate suite with a long, round window looking out at the green water.

"The concept of an underwater base sounds cooler than it actually is." Layla shook her head. "Because the view is garbage."

"Be right back." Hemlock vanished into the bathroom and closed the door. A few moments later, she stepped out. "I left them something to remember us by."

Layla smirked. "Did you drop a load in his toilet?"

Hemlock returned the smirk. "A lady never tells."

"Gods, I thought one Layla was bad enough." I stepped back into the corridor, listening carefully for any signs of life, but all was quiet. We quietly slinked to the next room. It was also a bedroom. As was the next and the next. Since all the doors looked the same, it felt as if we weren't making any progress.

"Where is everyone?" Layla whispered.

"I don't think many inventors use these rooms." I pointed up. "They're too busy enjoying the poolside benefits at the lodge."

A door down the corridor slid open and a bearded man stepped out. Laughter and music filtered into the hallway behind him. He roughly pulled a young woman behind him, his hand wrapped around her wrist. Black eyeliner was smeared down her face and what little clothes she wore were torn.

"I know it's here someplace," the man said drunkenly.

We pressed our backs to the wall and slid sideways to keep out of sight behind the bend in the corridor. The man pounded a button to open the door to the next room and yanked the woman in behind him.

Layla touched my clenched fist. "Keep it calm, cowboy."

Hemlock raised an eyebrow. "Nah, let's fuck them up."

I nodded. "I'm in."

Layla snorted. "Gods, you two are soft."

I wrapped my hand around her neck and squeezed. "Can you stop me from doing this?"

She nodded. "In a heartbeat."

"Exactly. But that woman is powerless. You ever wish someone helped you when you were powerless?"

She pursed her lips. "At the time, yes. But it forged me into a weapon."

"Not everyone is you, Layla." I caught a smirk from Hemlock and corrected myself. "Not even the other versions of you are you. So how about you put that weapon to use for a good cause?"

Layla's lips spread into a wide smile. Her hand reached up and rubbed the fingers that held her throat. "You're going to have to choke me harder than that, Cain."

I rolled my eyes and let go of her throat then crept to the door. I touched the button and the door slid open. The bearded man had pinned the woman's arm to the floor with his knees. She squirmed and cried out in pain, but it only seemed to excite him more.

"Careful, darling." He leaned over and licked the woman's face. "Don't wear yourself out."

Hemlock stepped behind him, gripped his long, scraggly hair, and yanked him off. He shouted in pain and surprise, then suddenly found himself beneath Hemlock's knees.

I helped the girl up and put a finger to my lips. "Not a word."

She trembled in fear but nodded.

Layla stepped inside and the door closed behind her.

"Get off me!" the man howled.

Hemlock clamped a hand over his mouth. "Quiet now, sweetie. I don't want you to wear yourself out."

His eyes bugged with fear.

"I recognize the bastard." Layla knelt next to him. "It's Darby."

Darby's gaze flicked between Hemlock and Layla. The eyepatch did little to disguise their identical features.

"Well, this is quite a bonus." I squatted behind the man's head and looked down at him. "Darby, where are the apocalypse weapons?"

He squirmed like a rat, face red with exertion, cheeks puffing as he roared impotently.

I put a finger to my lips. "Quiet, good man. Just answer my question or things will get truly unpleasant."

Hemlock reached behind her to his crotch and smirked. "Oh, how cute. I wonder if Darby will mind losing his package one parcel at a time."

Darby's face blanched. His eyelids fluttered and, for a moment, he passed out. He blinked awake a moment later and terror returned to his eyes. He stopped squirming and nodded.

Hemlock removed her hand. "Where are the weapons, Darby?"

"The vault," he said in a harsh whisper. "Four doors down from this one. The door looks different than the others."

"Is there a code to get inside?" I said.

He nodded. "I'll only tell you if you let me go."

"From the sounds of that party, there's another room full of people with the answer." Layla smoothed his sweaty hair back. "I promise we will let you live, but we will leave you tied up in this room, okay?"

"And we'll be back if the code doesn't work," I said. "Honesty really is the best policy."

Darby gulped. "Get off me, woman, and I'll tell you." A pompous tone cut through the drunken slur.

Hemlock stood and backed up. She held out a hand and Darby took it. A quick yank brought him easily to his feet.

He regarded me silently. "You're Cain, but you're not our Cain, are you?"

I frowned. "How is that even a question since the Cain of this dimension is dead?"

Darby flinched. "Yes, of course."

"The code." Layla narrowed her eyes.

Sensing that he had some small measure of power over us, Darby looked down his nose at her. Since she stood a head taller, it only made him look ridiculous. "The code is in four parts, and I only possess one."

I resisted the urge to backhand him. "No more lies, Darby. What's the code?"

"I am not lying." He sat gingerly on the edge of the bed, using the bedpost to steady himself.

I leaned threateningly over him. "Then how do you put the Tetron back into the vault when you're done with it?"

"We don't put it in the vault," he said. "We keep it in a lead box in the room next to the vault."

"Who has the four parts of the code?" I said.

"Me, my man Boris, Horatio, and Chadwick." Nervousness crept back into his voice. "At best, I can give you two of the four symbols."

I frowned. "Is the door secured by a sigil pad?"

He nodded. "You must trace the symbols in order."

I took out my phone, slid the stylus out of the holder, and opened a drawing app. "Draw the symbols you know."

Darby scowled at the sight of nub tech but took the stylus and sketched the symbol.

I saved it. "Don't pretend you don't know Boris's pattern." I opened a new slate. "Draw it too."

He looked ready to disavow all knowledge, but finally sketched out the symbol. They weren't sigils, but mechanist symbols, some of which I recognized from blueprints and diagrams.

"Are Horatio and Chadwick on the station?" I said.

Darby shook his head. "No, and they won't come here anytime soon."

I sensed he was telling the truth. "If you know their code symbols tell me now."

"I swear I don't." He held up his hands in surrender. "Horatio and Chadwick don't like me very much."

"I wonder why," Hemlock growled.

"What is the order of the symbols?" I said.

"Horatio, mine, Chadwick, and Boris," he replied.

My wireless beeped twice. Grace had moved the other submarine out of the way. I needed to have access to the mechanist armory by the time Hannah docked, or we'd be way behind. I turned to Layla. "Keep an eye on him. I'm going to get the Tetron."

She raised an eyebrow. "Don't waste time, Cain. Let's take what we need and go."

"Is that how you reached our dimension?" Darby said. "You used the Tetron from your dimension?"

I looked down at him. "What's the grand plan? Take over the worlds and then use the Tetron to help Cthulhu defeat our dimension?"

Darby's eyebrows rose. "That's what you think this is about?" He giggled like a boy caught doing something naughty.

Hemlock's forehead pinched. "What else would it be about?"

Darby looked genuinely amused and delighted to know something we didn't. "Oh, how rich and unexpected!" He leaned on his elbows. "Cthulhu is not our ally, nor is he the one directing this war."

The revelation rocked me back on my heels. "Then why in the hell are his troops on the move?"

Darby's delight grew brighter. "Because we command Cthulhu."

Chapter 33

I nearly rocked back on my heels at his claim.

"That's impossible." I shook my head like a dog shedding water. "I eavesdropped on your meeting. You yourself said that Cthulhu was tired of dithering in place."

"Why, yes, I did." He tutted. "Not everyone is aware of the grand scheme, Cain. Only Horatio, Chadwick, and Brunhilda know, and that is by design. We use the threat of Cthulhu as a prod to keep the underlings hard at work."

"But, how do you control him?" I couldn't imagine under any circumstances that Cthulhu would allow himself to be commanded by anyone.

"Perhaps I'll tell you if I feel the urge." Darby feigned a yawn. "But not today, you filthy peasants."

The door slid open and constables wielding brass pistols poured inside, forming a semi-circle to block us in. Darby had somehow activated a silent alarm. He tried to get up from the bed, but I twisted his arm behind his back and put a hand at his throat, putting him between me and the constables.

"Futile," Darby wheezed through a constricted windpipe. "Let me go, and I'll allow you to live."

The woman he'd brought in with him slipped into the bathroom, taking her out of the equation. Layla and Hemlock stood absolutely still, hands poised to draw daggers. No matter how quick they were, there was no way to avoid bullets in such an enclosed space.

I glanced back at the large window behind us. "Start shooting and you'll bring the entire lake crashing in here."

Darby scoffed. "Their bullets will do nothing to the glass. It's the same we use on the submarines."

I'd hoped that was the case, but his words confirmed it.

A constable with four golden pips on his shoulder stepped forward. "Release the inventor or die."

"Darby will die one way or the other, unless you let us pass." I ran calculations in my head trying to find the path out of this predicament. There were eight constables crowded into the room, each of them with a clear shot on me and my allies. But there was no way for them to kill us without killing Darby. He might not be the most popular guy on the mechanist payroll, but if a constable shot an inventor, they wouldn't be earning any promotions.

The chief constable certainly wouldn't risk his career by ordering a shootout that would kill Darby either. We still had the advantage even if Darby didn't realize it yet. The only other question was how many more constables would be waiting outside the door by the time we got past these? Or was this the entire complement of guards on the entire station?

I threw out my strongest demand first. "Clear a path and let us pass, or Darby dies."

"You will not," Darby wheezed.

I squeezed his throat harder. "Think again."

He shook his head. "I will not be held hostage!"

I dug my fingernails into his flesh, drawing blood and the attention of every opposing eye. I glared and scowled, keeping all eyes on me while at the same time picturing where the bullets from all those guns would emerge when they opened fire.

Layla and Hemlock stepped away from me ever so slightly, drawing the aim of four pistols with them. I adjusted my calculations, patterning sigils with the hand no one was paying attention to. And then, everything was ready.

"I'm done bargaining." I violently shoved Darby straight at the four constables targeting me. As I'd thought, none of them fired. But the ones staring down their sights at Layla and Hemlock unloaded immediately. My calculations were almost perfect.

The small shields before the muzzles of their weapons sent bullets ricocheting back in their faces. Two constables screamed as the heat of exploding liquid mana washed back over them. Even before the four constables caught Darby, I had my brightblade in hand. Two quick swings separated three heads and lopped the chief constable's head in half.

He fell screaming, his brains sizzling in an open skull. Layla and Hemlock rolled beneath the shields I'd cast, thrusting daggers up into crotches, and then into the hearts of their targets. Within seconds, the only living mechanist in the room was Darby.

During those moments of consideration, I'd also seen through his earlier ruse. There was likely no code guarding the armory. He'd activated the alarm and bought as much time as the constables needed to get here.

I examined the bedframe, but the switch wasn't there. It was on the bedpost he'd grasped. "I'm an idiot."

"None of us saw it," Hemlock said.

Layla merely scoffed as she reached down to yank Darby off the floor.

This time the inventor was truly afraid. It wasn't so much how he looked, but how he smelled. The man had shit himself.

"Gods be damned, he stinks!" Layla shoved the man against the bedframe and put her nose inches from his. "Tell us where the gods damned armory is, or I'll gut you this instant!"

Crying and shaking, Darby shook his head. "Don't kill me!"

Despite the loud music emanating from next door, I knew we had little time before someone came to investigate the multiple gunshots. The mechanist bullets didn't make as much noise as standard bullets, but they were still plenty loud.

"I'm going to lockdown the other room." I put a hand on Hemlock's shoulder. "Come help."

Layla nodded grimly. "I'll get answers from this bastard."

Stepping around the bodies, Hemlock and I reached the hallway just as a pair of half-clothed men exited the neighboring room, both of them staggering drunkenly. I recognized them as inventors from the earlier meeting.

They gasped in surprise and fell over each other as they ran back into the room. The doors slid shut. Four slashes from my brightblade brought it crashing down. Men and women screamed in alarm and the music stopped. I noticed four people, three women and a young man who would never scream again, their pale bodies discarded in a pile across the room.

The inventors were easy to differentiate with their pale, untoned bodies. I raised my brightblade threateningly. "All the men over here!" I pointed the blade to the left. "Women over here." I indicated the place behind me."

A mechanist staggered through the throng. "Who the bloody hell—"

My blade blurred and his head bounced on the floor. "No more fucking questions," I said in a deadly voice. "Do as I say or die."

I'd never seen people move so fast. When all the men were on one side, I separated the athletic ones from the others and put them in another group. Then I turned to the women. "Tell me if there are any mechanists among you, or other non-mechanists with the men."

A woman with two black eyes and bruises all over her neck limped forward. "These women are mechanists."

A pair of thin women were shoved from the group.

The bruised woman pointed out two more men who were not mechanists and finally the room was sorted. There were far fewer mechanists than there were nub men and women.

I dragged one of the few clothed mechanists from the group. "What is the complement of constables on this station?"

"Forty-three," he whimpered.

I nodded. "How many other mechanists are on this station?"

"Twenty-eight sailors, eight bridge crew, and twenty grays in engineering."

It was nice having someone answer my questions for once. "Where's the armory?"

"In the vault three doors down from here." The man trembled violently. "You're Cain!"

"Don't sound so surprised." I glanced at Hemlock. "Keep an eye on them. I'll be back."

She nodded.

I dragged the man into the hallway and paused for a moment to listen. I didn't hear the sound of running feet, so it seemed the silent alarm only brought the chief constable and his men running up here. That didn't mean we wouldn't have to fight our way back out. I took the man to the door. It did indeed have a sigil pad, and the door was made of mithril. I wouldn't be cutting through it anytime soon.

I hoped Darby had been lying about the four codes. "Open it."

He quailed. "I don't have the symbols!"

I gripped him by the throat and slammed him against the wall. "Don't lie to me!" I roared.

He screamed. "I'm not!"

"Well, shit." I shoved him to the floor. "Stay there." The wireless beeped twice, paused, then twice more. Hannah and the others were here. I beeped back six quick times, telling them to remain in place and expect trouble, then slipped the wireless back into my utility belt and withdrew revealer mist. I was going to have to do this the old-fashioned way.

The mist picked up clear traces of finger oil. Darby's and Boris's symbols were there, superimposed over two more. But I couldn't infer a pattern from unfamiliar symbols. I could only make out the different parts that weren't part of the symbols I knew.

I opened the app Darby used to draw the symbols and showed them to the inventor. "What do these mean?"

With a trembling finger, he pointed to the one Darby had drawn. "It's the symbol for the element pleuron."

I knew of pleuron, a magical element that strengthened metals far beyond their normal values. "And this one?" I indicated the other symbol.

"The element glief," he said.

Another magical element, this one found in pixie dust. It was the catalyst for making liquid mana. I'd hoped for a common theme to link the patterns, but there were too many elements that Horatio and the others might have used as their symbols. But I wasn't done yet.

I used my stylus to trace the revealed patterns that weren't part of the other two. "Do you recognize any elemental symbols in this?

He nodded. "Yes. One is phytus and the other is lead."

"The mechanists have their own symbols for ordinary elements?" I said.

He nodded. "Of course. We wouldn't stoop to using nub symbols for any reason."

I gave him the stylus. "Draw both symbols."

He sketched them in perfect lines and handed back the phone. I knew the correct order, but the missing piece of vital information was determining which symbol belonged to Chadwick, and which one was Horatio's. "What is phytus?"

"An element found in certain plants on Feary. It allows them to grow faster."

I pursed my lips. "Do you think Chadwick or Horatio would choose that element as their symbol?"

"I have no idea." He shivered. "I don't know either of them well enough to say."

"Has Chadwick ever invented anything?" I said.

"I'm sure he has, but I couldn't say." He scooted away from the door.

This man was too tied up in Darby's filthy little world to care about anyone outside of it. It was obvious, however, that he expected something terrible to happen if I entered the wrong combination. I dragged him back to the door. "What happens if I get the combination wrong?"

He shuddered and looked at thin slits in the ceiling. "Shutters will close off the area and poisonous gas will fill it."

Apparently, the mechanists weren't fucking around when it came to securing the armory. I took a moment to consider my next actions. I knew nothing of Chadwick and had only cursory knowledge of Horatio. I closed my eyes and thought of the few times I'd seen him. He wore ivory like the other inventors, but there was nothing else about him.

I rewound my memory then played it back. The last time I'd seen him, we discovered he'd stowed away on the submarine and come back to Gaia with us. I'd knocked him out and thrown him in the trunk of my car, and later tossed him into a cell beneath Sanctuary. I backed up the memory to when he was in the trunk and then I saw it. An amulet on a chain of cogs had fallen out of his uniform. The amulet was carved into the symbol of lead.

Why that was important to Horatio, I had no idea. All that mattered was I knew the final parts of the puzzle. Even so, I wasn't going to take chances. I drew my brightblade and readied it. The mechanist tried to squirm away, but I gripped his hair and dragged him back.

"Please let me go!" he begged.

"Shut up and act like a man for once." I hit him in the neck with a jolt and let him sleep on it. Then I traced the symbols. Gears clanked and clockwork ticked. It seemed I'd done it right.

And then the shutters slammed down, locking me into a small section of corridor. I rammed my brightblade against the shutter to my right, but it was also made of mithril. Cutting through it would take far too long. I'd be dead from poisonous gas well before then.

Chapter 34

I wasn't ready to die just yet. I tested my brightblade on the wall. It wasn't made of mithril, but it was thick and dense. Depending on how fast the gas filled the space, I had little time to carve an escape route.

But then the vault door swung inward, and bright lights illuminated the room beyond. That was when I realized I wasn't about to die. The shutters dropped into place whenever the vault door was open, probably to keep people from making off with unauthorized weapons. I went inside and looked around. I certainly didn't remember everything that had been in the armory on Oblivion, but it looked as if everything was here except for Tidebringer and Airbender.

Though the mechanists' security plan was sound, they obviously hadn't accounted for the weapons inside the vault. I located the weapon I needed hanging from a rack on the wall among the other swords in the collection. Soultaker claimed the soul of anyone it killed, adding them to an army of the undead. But there were other aspects to the weapon that made it perfect for what I needed.

I shoved the point into the wall and wasn't disappointed when it sliced right through it. It wasn't quite as easy as cutting warm butter, but it made my brightblade feel like a dull butter knife by comparison. I carved a new exit, bypassing the closed shutters.

"Now, for my next trick, I'll make these weapons disappear," I muttered to myself. There weren't any carts or bags handy to make cleaning out the armory any easier, but Hannah and the others had brought some on the submarine, provided they could get to us without incident.

A klaxon blared and red lights flashed in the corridor. It seemed the gig was up. I slid Soultaker into its special sheath and buckled it to my side as I jogged back to the room with Darby's pals.

When I opened the door, the first thing I noticed were the trails of blood leading to the bathroom and the screams and moans coming from inside. The sex slaves were gone.

I stopped in my tracks. "What the hell?"

Layla and Hemlock looked pleased as punch.

"We sent the nubs to another room then castrated Darby and his friends," Hemlock said matter-of-factly.

I pointed toward the hallway. "You do hear that klaxon, right?"

"We're not deaf, Cain." Layla folded her arms over her chest. "What did you screw up this time?"

"Nothing. Hannah docked the submarine a few minutes ago. They must have run into trouble." I went back into the hallway. "Everything secure here for now?"

The pair nodded.

"Then let's go." I ran down the corridor to the elevator and we piled inside. It took us to the first floor at a leisurely pace while the alarms continued to blare. The corridor outside was empty, but shouts and gunfire echoed from the far end.

We jogged to the intersection and peered out. Bullets whined past. I didn't see the shooters because they'd been fired from around the curve. Mechanist bullets were winged, giving them some directional control. I drew my staff and powered the brightblade then dashed to the left toward the submarine bay.

A constable lay on the floor gasping, an arrow protruding from his chest. He looked up at us with horror just as the last breath rattled from his mouth. We came upon a group of constables behind a makeshift barrier of tables. One of their comrades lay on his back, an arrow jutting from his eye. They held their guns over the top and fired without aiming, apparently too afraid to risk even peeking over, lest they end up like he did.

I slashed through two of them before they knew what happened. Layla and Hemlock snapped the necks of the others, and we pushed through the barricade. Aura emerged from a doorway, an arrow nocked in a bow.

She breathed a sigh of relief when she saw us. "Thank the gods. I didn't think we'd ever break through the barricade."

"Where are the others?" I said.

"Fighting the rear." She motioned us to follow and we jogged toward the submarine bay. "Erolith and his people are somewhere on the other side of the docking ring fighting constables."

Bullets whined around the bend. I slashed one from the air and Layla intercepted another with a dagger. Apparently, the projectiles would keep flying until they ran out of propellant.

Hannah and Grace hunkered behind crates. Not far away, another group of constables hid behind metal tables, popping up on occasion to fire a volley. I deactivated the brightblade and switched to longshot mode.

Stomping boots echoed and the constables behind the tables cheered as a fresh complement of their ilk came into view around the bend. This group bore rifles, but grenades and other ordnance dangled from their belts. We could retreat, but at this point, we had no choice but to clear out the enemy forces so we could steal the armory weapons.

I turned to Layla and Hemlock. "Grab duffel bags from the submarine and start gathering the weapons. We'll clean up here and help soon."

"Making us do grunt work while you enjoy all the fun?" Layla smirked and ducked inside the submarine bay.

A deafening explosion shook the floor. The entire base seemed to shift on its foundations. Metal groaned and anyone standing struggled to remain upright. I braced myself and took advantage of the confusion. I aimed and fired at the flailing constables. I didn't aim for the head. Instead, I struck the grenades.

Liquid mana detonated. Men screamed. Body parts flew. The base shifted again and then slammed back down on the lakebed. My ears rang in the sudden silence that followed. The overhead lights blinked off for a moment and then flickered back on. A distant shouting drew my attention. I followed the sound back down the corridor and into the submarine bay.

Layla struggled with a metal beam. Smoke and fire filled the room. Our submarine was missing, and debris filled the bay. I realized in shock that Hemlock lay beneath the beam. Her eyes were closed, and she wasn't breathing.

"Cain, help!" Layla's powerful legs strained as she tried to lift the beam.

I unsheathed Soultaker and slashed the beam in two places, leaving only the portion atop Hemlock. Then I sheathed it and helped Layla move the remaining metal. The beam hadn't crushed Hemlock, but a jagged piece of metal protruded from her lower left abdomen.

Hemlock's eyes fluttered and she drew a gasping breath. She managed a smile, revealing blood-flecked teeth. "Well, shit, Cain." She grasped my hand and squeezed. "Looks like this is it, love."

Layla cradled her doppelganger's face and forced her to look at her. "It's not over, moron. Shut up and live!"

I studied the wound. It was probably fatal by most human standards, but Hemlock wasn't entirely human. I got down on my stomach and looked at the other side. I couldn't get to it easily, meaning the only choice was to gently pick her up. I produced Soultaker once more and carefully cut off the protruding part, then put it away again.

"Help me lift her." I reached beneath Hemlock's shoulders.

She smiled up at me. "This is a nice last view."

"Shut it," Layla growled. She put her hands under Hemlock's back to either side of the wound.

Aura appeared through the smoke. She quickly assessed the situation and slid her hands beneath Hemlock from the other side.

"One, two, three." We lifted.

Hemlock gritted her teeth and laughed. Blood bubbled in her mouth.

"I think it nicked her lung," Aura said.

"Yeah, you think?" Layla sidestepped in unison with us as we moved Hemlock to a bare spot of floor and set her down.

"What happened to the sub?" I said.

Layla wiped blood and soot from her face. "No idea. It blew up the moment we came inside. Must have been a torpedo."

"Someone set off the general alarm. I can only assume reinforcements are coming." I looked around the blasted bay. "They won't be docking in here, though."

"There's a medical bay not far down the hallway," Aura said. "Let's get Hemlock in there."

Hannah and Grace entered the bay, coughing from the dust and smoke.

Hannah's eyes flared. "What happened to the sub?"

"It's gone." I checked Hemlock's pulse. It was faint and weak. "Is the hallway clear of hostiles?"

Grace nodded. "But how are we getting out of here now?"

"I don't know." I slid my arms under Hemlock's back. "Everyone help move her. She's in bad shape."

Hemlock's eyelids fluttered, but she looked unconscious.

Everyone knelt beside her and lifted as a team. We made our way back to the corridor and found the medical bay.

"I have some healing knowledge," Grace said. "Leave her with me while the rest of you figure out how to get out of here."

I led the others back into the hallway and started pacing. "Where do the submersible boats dock?"

Layla shrugged. "Those pipes lined up beneath the base, so the bays are probably behind one of these doors."

"Let's start with those." I walked toward the destroyed bay and pointed to the icon on the door, a square with water waves in the center. "Look for other doors with his symbol." I pointed back the way we'd come. "Layla, go that way. Hannah, Aura, and I will go this way."

Layla took off without being snarky. Aura nocked an arrow in her bow, and I readied my staff as we trotted down the corridor. We reached the first door with the docking bay icon. I hit the button to open the door, braced myself, and slipped inside. The pool inside was round and just large enough to hold a boat. This one was empty.

I went to the water's edge and looked down. The giant pipe that connected the bay to the cubes was misaligned. The explosion from our submarine had shifted the station off its base. It was a good bet the other docking stations were offline as well.

Hannah sighed. "We're not getting out of here are we?"

"On the bright side, no one else is getting in." I led them back to the hallway and we continued around the big circle. Another squad of constables came around the corner. Aura downed one before they reacted.

We couldn't afford a protracted siege, so I charged them before they could raise their rifles. My brightblade slashed through guns and flesh alike. Hannah grappled with a burly man nearly twice her size. She twisted free of his grasp, ducked low, and hammered his crotch with an uppercut. When he grabbed his aching balls, she gripped his hands and yanked them between his legs. His nose crunched against the deck.

I jolted him in the neck and let him sleep on it.

"Shouldn't we kill him?" Aura said.

Hannah shook her head. "Not in cold blood."

"He'll be out for hours," I said. "Let's go."

We found the next docking bay in no better condition than the last. Whoever had destroyed our submarine had blocked us in and everyone else out. I'd been running a tally of the constables and figured we'd taken them all out by now. I hadn't seen a sign of the grays or teals and assumed they were hunkered down somewhere hiding.

Dozens of bodies were sprawled in a neighboring cargo bay. Erolith and his squad of guardians were inside.

I looked around appraisingly. "I wondered where you were."

"Advancing and clearing," he said simply. "We'll ensure there are no enemies at our backs."

I told him about the submarine and our efforts to find a way off the station.

He nodded. "I'll take my people up a level and begin clearing it. Keep me apprised."

I left them to finish their business in the cargo bay and moved on down the hallway.

Layla appeared around the bend, a few new splashes of blood on her outfit. "The other docking bays are wrecked. There's a boat in one, but it's pinned between the pipe and the ledge."

"Same over here." I stopped and considered our next moves. "Maybe I can cut the boat free with Soultaker."

She shook her head. "It's toast, Cain. The bubble is cracked."

"Then we'll swim for it or get Grace to call the catfish back to us." I marched back toward the medic bay.

"Then we'll have to leave Hemlock behind," Hannah said. "We can't move her, much less carry her underwater."

I stopped and turned. "Well, I'm open to suggestions."

Aura shook her head sadly. Layla stared blankly at me, and Hannah's face furrowed in concentration.

"That's what I thought." I started to walk away, but Hannah grabbed my arm.

"Let's get Tidebringer!" Her eyes were wide with excitement. "I'll empty the entire lake or just make the water carry the base to shore."

"Two problems," I said. "The base is too heavy for the water to carry it. You'd have to gather all the water and then slam it against the hull to make it move. There's no way to lift it."

"Oh." Hannah frowned. "Then I'll move the water out of the way."

"And we walk?" I shook my head. "The mechanists have airships. They'll blast us from overhead."

"I can tunnel through the water," Hannah said. "They'll never see us leave."

I considered the plan. "It's a long walk, but maybe it'll work."

"How are we supposed to tote everything from the armory and Hemlock?" Layla shook her head. "Remove all the water around the base to clear out the debris. When another submarine tries to dock, we'll take it."

It wasn't ideal, but it was the best plan I'd heard. "We don't know how many subs are out there." I pointed up. "Let's go the bridge and see what the sonar says."

"I'm going to look through the other rooms on this deck and see if there's anything else we can use," Aura said. "We'll need some way to carry the weapons."

"Good thinking, elf." Layla slapped her on the ass.

I slid Hannah's wireless from her belt and gave it to Aura. "Stay in touch." Then we ran for the elevator. I imagined submarines circling the station like sharks while the mechanists plotted the best course for getting inside the crippled station. I was amazed it hadn't sprung any leaks after the explosion. It was certainly made of super strong materials.

The elevator took its sweet time getting us to the top level. Layla went to the sonar station and flicked the lever to activate it. Low vibrations hummed and outlines of objects in the water appeared on the window. There were two submarines slowly circling down near the docking ring.

Red arrows pointed to the area behind the elevator. I went behind the shaft and saw another smaller submarine patrolling there. But the submarines were nothing to be frightened of compared to what lurked behind them—the hulking forms of malgorths. A squirming mass of bodies swam our way, too many to differentiate the forms, but it was the same army we'd passed on our way to Oblivion.

Within minutes, ganthagons, migyos, and salkos would swarm through the open bays on the bottom of the station and fill the corridors. We might be able to hold them off for a little while, but they'd eventually overwhelm us, or simply trap us somewhere and starve us out.

Not even Hannah's underwater tunnel plan would work. There was no way to escape here with the weapons, but we might have a chance to get out with just the Tetron. Either way, I didn't see a course that gave Hemlock a chance of surviving if she wasn't dead already.

Layla went to the weapons console. "I'll fire everything we have at the monsters. Then we can grab the most important weapons and make a run for it."

I nodded. "Hannah, you'll control Tidebringer, okay?"

Hannah ignored me and sat down at a console. "Dude! How did you not include this in our options?"

I blinked. "What are you talking about?"

She flicked several switches. Lights blinked from red to green and the entire station shuddered beneath us. Gears clanked and her seat raised up several inches, forming a platform with a pair of raised pedals and several more levers. The station shuddered again and began to rise.

Layla grabbed a console to steady herself. "What in the hell is happening?"

The entire station buckled as if it were about to fall apart.

Chapter 35

Hannah grinned and shouted above the rumbling of the station. "The base is mobile!"

"You mean the navigation console has a purpose?" I couldn't believe a contraption of such immense size was moveable. "What about the connected docking bays?"

The station began to rise. Most of the lights on the console turned green, but a pair blinked red.

"The doors close on the docking bays." Hannah flicked the switches next to the blinking red lights. "Some of them are jammed, but I think that's okay."

The station continued to rise for several more seconds before shuddering to a stop. Then it sank a few feet before stabilizing. Outside the window, I saw the bent joints of insectoid legs. There were two more on the other side. Hanna gripped a pair of levers and pushed them in opposite directions. The entire base began to rotate. Sand and dust clouded the windows until the only way to see anything was with sonar.

My wireless crackled. "What in hades is going on?" Aura shouted.

"Hannah just figured out that the base can walk," I said. "Hold on for a bumpy ride!"

Layla blinked out of her stupor and manned the weapons console. "Gods be damned, Hannah, I'm starting to like you."

Hannah beamed. "I still don't like you very much, but thanks!"

Layla barked a laugh. "Head south by southeast away from the monster army. If I have to look another malgorth in the eyes, I'm going to kill myself."

Hannah adjusted the heading. A pair of submarines altered course to intercept. The slim outline of torpedoes appeared on the sonar.

"Shit!" Layla looked over the console. "I don't know if this thing has countermeasures."

"This one." I slammed the palm of my hand on a button above an icon that resembled glitter. Dozens of bubble streams trailed out from the hull. Small drones shot toward the incoming torpedo and intercepted it. The explosion rocked the base. Four more torpedoes launched. The remaining drones stopped one, but the other slipped past.

I raced to the window and looked at the saucer-shaped hull just as the torpedo made impact. It exploded down near the docking ring. Our forward momentum slowed as the station rocked back on its four feet. Then Layla hit another button and grinned. "Enjoy that, you bastards."

A pair of torpedoes streaked in the opposite direction. The submarines turned tail and began racing away. If they deployed countermeasures, they were too small for the sonar to pick up. Either way, it gave us time for Hannah to move us closer to the distant shore.

"Keep it up," I said. "I'm going below to get the Tetron. I want it in my hand just in case everything goes to shit."

Layla turned to me. "Good idea."

"Be careful." Hannah reached down from her elevated seat, so I took her hand and squeezed it.

"Maybe we should get you a learner's permit next time we have the chance."

She giggled. "I'm overqualified at this point."

"I don't know. You still haven't driven in Atlanta traffic." I released her hand and stepped into the elevator. The last thing I saw was Layla blowing me a kiss when the doors closed.

Screams of terror emanated from the room where Layla and Hemlock had locked in the newly castrated Darby gang. I continued past it and into the opening I'd carved in the wall. I went to the other wall and carved an opening into neighboring room. Just as Darby claimed, a lead-lined brass box sat on a table inside the empty room.

I picked it up and went back into the armory. I considered taking Tidebringer and Earthmaker, but it seemed wiser to wait and hope Aura found satchels or something to carry the weapons in.

The wireless crackled. "Cain, there are some rooms I can't get into. Can you bring that magical sword?"

"On the way." I was already reconsidering my decision to fetch the Tetron. Without a satchel to carry it in, the lead-lined box was cumbersome and heavy. As far as I knew, it didn't emit radiation when it wasn't in use, so I opened the box and regarded the mystical device. The cube, pyramid, and sphere were arranged in that order on plush royal red velvet. Touching them didn't cause my fingers to tingle, and the tiny clockwork behind the golden mesh wasn't moving, so I assumed they were inactive.

Each piece was just about the right size to fill a pouch on my utility belt if I crammed them in the right way. I emptied three pouches of hopefully non-vital items, stuffed the pieces of the Tetron inside, and zipped them shut.

Having wasted too much time on the task, I rushed to the elevator and hit the button for the first floor. It thumbed its nose at me, clanking down two levels at the slowest speed possible. When the doors opened, I sprinted out and raced around the docking ring. Aura was on the opposite side, standing outside a heavy-duty door I'd seen during our earlier search.

"No luck in the other rooms?" I said.

She shook her head. "I found some crates, so if worse comes to worst we've got those. Otherwise, I haven't found anything useful."

"Well, let's see what we've got here." I thrust Soultaker into the door. It penetrated a fraction of an inch and clanged to a halt. I flinched in surprise.

Aura's eyebrows rose. "What's wrong?"

I tested the wall to the right of the door and encountered the same problem. Turning the blade sideways, I shaved off the outer layer of metal and found what had stopped the blade. The core of the door and wall was plated with bronzed mithril.

Aura ran a finger over it. "Why does everything have to be brass or bronze with these people?"

I examined the sigil pad next to the door, then sprayed it with revealer mist. The pad had seen a lot of use, making it difficult to discern even one pattern from the mess of oil residue. Mithril was a rare alloy found mostly on Feary. It was expensive to purchase and illegal to import to Gaia.

The fact that the mechanists had hardened this room even more than their armory made me extremely curious what they were hiding inside. It might be where they stored their conventional weapons. The station shook and the floor tilted. Aura and I slid across the hall and hit the wall. Explosions resounded against the hull and the floor tilted the other way.

The entire facility seemed to sway, wobbling as it if it were trying to find purchase on slick ice. I sheathed Soultaker before I accidentally slashed off an arm or a leg. "Let's go to another room. I can't get into this one right now."

Aura nodded and we staggered down the moving corridor to the next locked room twenty yards down. Soultaker easily slashed through the door, but behind it were crates upon crates of non-perishable provisions like toilet paper, canned foods, and soft drinks.

A mechanist exo unit was strapped to the wall near the door. I imagined they used it to ferry goods from the docking bays to this room. "If we don't find anything else, we can load everything into a crate and use this exo to move it."

"That thing won't fit in the elevator," Aura said. "We'll have to bring everything down a few pieces at a time."

I stepped into the corridor. "What's next?"

She led me to a door on the inner ring. The sound of gears and clockwork emanated from inside. I slashed open the door, already suspecting what I'd find on the other side.

A catwalk led into the bowels of the beast, or as the mechanists would call it, the engine room.

I shook my head. "Definitely not in there." Another idea occurred to me. "Did you search the barracks?"

Aura frowned. "Why would I look in there?"

She obviously didn't understand the life of a soldier. We made our way down the hall despite the heaving motion of the floor. It was in the constable barracks that we finally found what we were looking for—large black duffel bags designed for carrying small arms.

Aura and I emptied the ones we found and ran back to the elevator. The station tilted nearly forty-degrees, slamming us against the wall. The elevator ground to a halt and I thought for a moment we were stuck. The station leveled out and the lift once again clinked to life.

Aura held onto me for support. "What in hades is going on out there?"

I shook my head. "No telling, which is why we've got to hurry."

We made it to the armory. I took the longest duffel bag and shoved Tidebringer, Earthmaker, and long objects inside. Aura filled another with orbs, armor, and bulky items. Because of the violent rocking of the station, items littered the floor. Some had spilled out into the hallway and the neighboring room thanks to the holes I'd cut in the wall.

"Why didn't they use mithril walls in here?" Aura said.

I shrugged. "They must have run out after using it on that other room."

"But wouldn't this room be more important to protect?" She shoveled more items into a new bag.

"Maybe they thought it was already more secure being on the command level." I crammed as much as possible into my bag, picking another rack bare. "It's not really important at this point."

"Yeah, you're right." Aura stood and surveyed the empty room. "We did it!"

I looked at the row of bulging duffel bags. "Now we have to figure out how to get them off the station." I carried a couple into the corridor and set them next to the elevator while the floor rocked like a boat on rough seas. "I'm going to the bridge to see what in the hell is going on."

Aura braced herself against the wall to keep from falling. "Me too."

The elevator crept to the top, threatening to stop every time the station pitched too far. The doors opened and I staggered out, grasping the nearest console to keep from sliding away. Gone were the green waters of Lake Lanier, replaced with blue skies and sunshine. A pair of airships floated overhead, raining missiles upon us.

The bridge was just above the treetops while the base of the station mowed down pine trees by the dozens. A bomb from an airship slammed into the docking ring and the station staggered sideways. The hull was pitted with holes and blackened from attacks.

Layla grinned wildly as she ran to a seat near the domed window and strapped in. "Grab a gunnery station!" she shouted. "Shoot the bastards down!"

I chose another one and hit a button on the side of the chair. A section of the saucer-like hull rose just outside the window while a control stick appeared from the floor between my legs. I twisted it and the turret outside rotated. I pressed the button and flurry of bullets flashed into the air.

Layla unleashed on one of the airships. Sparks flashed along the nacelle where the bullets struck. The vessel shifted course, but it wasn't fast enough. Flames spurted from the sides and it began to drift in slow motion toward the ground. I lit up the other airship. It slowed and stopped pursuit.

I unstrapped and ran back to Hannah. "Where are you taking us?"

"I don't know!" She surveyed the horizon and her eyes widened. "Oh, no."

I followed her gaze and found the next big threat. From this distance, they were only specks. I summoned my staff and peered through the scope. I counted seven people streaking toward us on clockwork wings with Esteri in the lead. To her left was another unmistakable face—Sigma.

"I thought she killed that little bastard!"

"Who?" Hannah said."

"Sigma is with them." I grimaced. "Once they get here, it's game over."

Hannah's eyes flared. "What do we do?"

"Back to the water!" I ran to the front of the bridge for a better look. We'd entered the campgrounds and the lake was falling behind us. "Turn this thing around!"

Hannah shifted levers and the lumbering juggernaut rotated. I looked through my scope at the incoming threat. They were only a few minutes out from us. The lake appeared ahead once again, and Hannah pushed us at full speed back to the relative safety of the water. We might be trapped down there, but it was better than facing a squad of demis led by her insane counterpart.

A pair of the small, sleek airships swooped down and strafed the outer edge of the saucer. It quickly became apparent they weren't targeting the hull, but the legs. Rockets exploded, sending shockwaves throughout the station. Metal fragments flew into the air, but the leg held. The airships came in for another pass.

Layla and I manned turrets. Aura took a cue and hopped in one on the other side. Layla proved she was just as expert a shot with the turret as she was with arrows, leading one of the airships with a trail of bullets. It fell from the sky and burst into flames in the forest. I took down the second one but not before it launched another barrage.

The leg buckled under the onslaught. The third airship retreated, leaving a trail of smoke behind it. The leg was still functional but dragging. Our forward momentum slowed to a crawl. There was no way we'd make it into the water before the demis reached us. It was time to make a desperate decision.

I took out the wireless. "Erolith, are there any safe transition zones around here?"

His response came a moment later. "A mile southwest of here."

It was a long way off, but it was better than fighting Esteri. I went to the communications console and hit the button for the medical bay. "Grace, how is Hemlock?" I held my breath, afraid for the answer. Layla and Hannah turned my way.

"My gods, what's going on up there?" Grace said. "I've barely been able to work with the floor trying to throw me on my ass."

"We're under attack and it's about to get worse," I replied. "What's Hemlock's status?"

"She's stable," Grace said.

I blew out a sigh of relief. "Can she be moved?"

"I patched her lung with magic, so yes, but I can't guarantee it'll hold if things get too rough."

"Take her to the submarine bay. We'll meet you there shortly."

"We're evacuating?"

"Yep." I disconnected and used the wireless again. "Erolith, we're abandoning ship and making a run for the transition zone. I've got fourteen satchels and we need help carrying them. Meet me on the third level."

"On the way," Erolith replied.

I tucked away the wireless and examined the controls for the mobile base. "Can you lower the base while it's moving?"

Hannah bit her lower lip and pulled a lever toward her. "Let's find out."

The saucer-shaped body dipped while the legs continued to move. The damaged leg caused the station to tilt toward that side, but it wasn't enough of an angle to cause a problem yet. We were well below the tree line when the saucer was as low as it could go. The bottom was probably still several feet off the ground, but it'd have to do.

I didn't know how many mechanists were still alive, but I needed some way to add to the confusion of our exodus. I also wanted to give any living nubs onboard a chance to escape. I pressed the ship-wide PA button. "Abandon ship. I repeat, abandon ship. We have suffered critical damage and are going down. We have dropped as low as possible so you can escape through the docking bays."

Layla raised an eyebrow. "What are you doing?"

"Anything and everything." I turned back to Hannah. "Do you have to manually move the legs?"

She shook her head. "As long as the acceleration levers for both sets are pushed forward, it'll keep going."

"Oh, shit." Layla opened fire with the turret. Esteri and the other demis easily dodged the gunfire on their nimble wings and landed on the hull.

They were here.

Chapter 36

"Into the elevator!" I shouted. "Go, go, go!"

Layla, Aura, and Hannah abandoned their stations. I cast the illusion of a mechanist in the pilot's seat and ran to the elevator. The light above the door showed the lift was on level one. Erolith and his people were probably using it. I cursed and ran to the backside of the shaft, pulling Hannah and Layla with me to stay out of sight of the demis.

Esteri pounded on the transparent dome. "Stop this station right now, or I'll burn you to a husk, you traitorous bastard!"

The illusionary mechanist didn't even look at her. It wasn't designed to have responses. She thought it was ignoring her.

There was no way to check the elevator from this side, but I calculated it'd take several minutes for it to ferry the guardians to level three. The only way down was to carve a new path. I slid Soultaker from its sheath, then paced a few feet from the back of the elevator shaft and plunged it into the floor all the way to the hilt.

It sliced through. Gears ground and springs sprung. Smoke and oil hissed from the floor plate. I had no idea why there was machinery beneath the floor, but cutting a hole down a level wasn't going to work.

Esteri stood on the window above the pilot's seat, eyes glowing white, and unleashed her fury on the dome. I didn't know if the enemy would see us or not, but we had no choice. Staying low, I ran to the window at the rear of the bridge and slashed a hole with Soultaker.

The material was nearly as thick as the sword was long, but that made it no harder for the mythical sword to handle.

Esteri and the demis were so intent on killing the fake mechanist they hadn't noticed our departure. I slid down the outside of the saucer and stopped at the windows for command level. Soultaker made short work of the window and we climbed inside a bedroom packed with the nubs that had been in the party earlier.

Men and women screamed and cleared a path. We made our way to the door and opened it. Erolith and some of his people were just getting off the elevator. He hadn't been able to fit everyone inside We hurried to meet them.

Erolith frowned. "What were you doing in there?"

"The elevator is too slow." I pointed to the room. "Use the window in there. I'll cut another hole in the hull on the docking level."

"Very well," he said.

I hefted the duffel with Tidebringer and Earthmaker inside. Erolith had made a bargain, but I still didn't quite trust him. Aura, Layla, and Hannah each grabbed a bag and we went back to the bedroom where the nubs still cowered.

I stopped near the window. "We're abandoning this station. If you want a chance at freedom, follow us. If you want to die, stay here."

The fear on their faces grew, but a few women with determination etched into their expressions pushed through the crowd and approached the window. I stepped outside. The angle of the hull was just steep enough to make sliding the fastest way to travel, but it wasn't so steep that I couldn't stop.

The edge of the saucer turned down ninety degrees forming a flat edge for the docking ring. I stopped well before the edge since the unsteady gait from the station's damaged leg made footing treacherous. I stabbed down into the hull and cut out a circle. The metal fell inside with a loud clang.

I dropped several feet into darkness penetrated only by the shaft of light from the hole in the ceiling. The drop was only about six feet due to stacked crates strapped down to the floor. I summoned my staff. The brightblade hummed to life, casting light for several feet around me.

The air reeked of feces and I wondered if I'd ended up in the sanitation section of engineering. After casting several glowing orbs, I was finally able to discern my surroundings—a long room about fifty feet wide. Besides the crates there was nothing else in the room except a gray stone column rising from the floor in the center. It stood five feet tall and was half as wide, almost like a native American totem pole.

Something about it tickled a memory in the back of my mind.

Layla's head appeared at the hole. "Found a way out?"

One of my light globes had reached the other wall. I recognized the mithril enforced door we'd been unable to breach earlier. I was inside that room. The mechanists hadn't thought anyone would even think of breaching the outer hull, since the station spent most its time underwater.

"Hang on." I jogged to the door and found a button. One press and the door opened. I went back to the hole. "Come on down."

Layla dropped inside followed by several nubs, then Hannah. I walked around the pole and examined the carvings. Icy tendrils of dread snaked around my bowels. I'd seen this thing just outside Cthulhu's citadel when Fred took me on his little tour. Had the mechanists taken this from the real R'lyeh?

Just like the one in the dream world, this ring of etchings bisected the column, each one of them depicting Cthulhu in various poses. He stood with arms upraised in one, in the next he crouched. No matter which way his body was oriented, his face always looked out, as if to say Cthulhu was always watching. In the center carving, only his head was visible, eyes closed slits.

Erolith and his people began dropping through the hole in the ceiling, each toting a duffel bag. After them came more and more nubs. Some looked grateful while others looked just as terrified as they'd been earlier.

A young woman with prematurely gray hair fell through the hole and was caught by a pair of young men who were aiding the more fragile among them. The woman saw the cylinder and burst into screams.

"Not this place! No, please, no!"

The nub men tried to comfort her, but she started pounding on the far wall as if she could break through it. Several puzzle pieces aligned, and I suddenly had a good idea why this room had been so secure. I approached the woman and gently reached for her hand. "Calm down. I promise I'll get you out of here."

She pressed herself against me, body trembling, the smell of urine and sex thick in her hair. These people had been through pure horror, used as disposable sex toys for Darby and his sick friends, but this woman had seen something the others hadn't.

"What happened in here?" I said.

Tears poured down her face. "Don't touch it. It will drive you mad."

"Did someone make you touch it?" I asked.

She nodded. "Darby brought me here. Wanted to tie me to it while he had his way with my body while my mind went mad." Her knees wobbled, but I kept her from collapsing. "Don't touch it."

I guided her out of the room and into the corridor where she started to regain some control. "I need to know what happened."

"He said it was why the beast slumbers." She gulped. "They control him through his dreams."

"Gods be damned." I stared at the object. "What did they call it?"

"Rlhala," she said in the guttural tone of someone who'd heard the word pronounced in its native tongue, had it seared into her mind where it would remain until her dying day. "Darby touched it, but it didn't scare him."

"He didn't do anything special before he touched it?" I asked.

She shook her head. "He touched the head."

"The head of Cthulhu?" I pointed back to the cylinder. "Where it's etched on the surface?"

She nodded. "Yes."

"Anything else you can tell me about it?" I said.

"He pushed me against it, and I saw the beast. I saw his eyes staring into mine." She began to shake again. "He was in my mind!" she screamed "My mind!"

I decided that was enough torment for the poor woman. "Don't think about it. Go with the others, okay?"

She backed away casting furtive glances into the room, then ran after the others.

I went back inside the room and searched near the doorway until I found a metal light switch. A flick of it and lights snapped on all up and down the room. With the room fully illuminated, I noticed something on right and left walls that I hadn't noticed before—bronze levers. I went to the nearest one on the right and pulled it down. A crack appeared in the wall and a hidden door slid open.

The stench of body odor redoubled, and I stumbled back, hand over my nose.

Layla stood beside me. "Gods be damned. What's that smell?"

A light flickered on, revealing an elderly man. It took a moment before I realized who it was. "That's Clayborn Higgins, the mechanist Master Inventor."

"Not so grand now." Layla pinched her nose. "Horatio must have taken political prisoners after he came to power. I'm surprised the old man lasted this long."

Clayborn groaned and his eyelids cracked open. "Kill me, please."

The odor was awful, but I did my best to ignore it. We were quickly running out of time, but this man might have vital information. "Clayborn, look at me."

He shielded his eyes from the light. "Why would you do this to me, Horatio?"

"What do you know about the Rlhala?" I said.

"End my torment!" he wailed. "Even the gods are not so cruel, Horatio."

"He's mad." Layla shook her head. "We need to go, Cain."

I walked away and studied the Rlhala without touching it. If it truly controlled Cthulhu, then I couldn't leave it. But I didn't dare attempt using it without understanding how.

"Forget it, Cain." Layla grabbed my arm. "We've got the apocalypse weapons. Now isn't the time to lust after something else."

"It controls Cthulhu, Layla." I dropped my duffel bag. "I can't leave without it."

"Why?" She stepped in front of me. "So you can save your little ragamuffin girl?"

I turned my gaze on her. "Don't pretend you don't care about anything, Layla. Help me."

She threw up her hands. "Gods damn you, Cain! Can't you see I've been helping all this time?"

I nodded. "Can't you just once make it easy?"

Layla shook her head. "Never." She took off her backpack and removed the ivory uniform. It was covered in blood, but that didn't seem to concern her. She slashed the uniform into two wide strips and handed me one.

"Good idea." I approached the Rlhala and touched it with my boot. Nothing happened, so it apparently required skin-to-stone contact. A groove in the floor held the object upright. Turning a handle released the clamp inside, and the Rlhala began to wobble with the erratic movements of the station.

I wrapped a strip of cloth twice around the bottom and pulled up. It budged just enough to topple it over. I held my breath, fearing it might shatter to pieces. It clanged against the metal without so much as chipping.

Layla worked her cloth strip beneath the other end and lifted. Arms and legs straining, she eased it back down. "This thing must weigh five hundred pounds. We'll need more muscle."

"I can help," Hannah said.

Aura held out a hand. "Give me something to lift with."

The station rocked and tilted. The Rlhala rolled across the floor and slammed into the wall a few doors down from Clayborn's cell. The old man had wandered out and now lay on his back helplessly.

I looked around for Erolith, but he and the others had already left with their duffel bags. I opened my bag and tucked Soultaker inside, so the scabbard wasn't hanging from my hip.

Layla slashed the remains of the robe in half again. "I don't think the cloth is strong enough to hold it."

"Wait!" I staggered back and forth as the floor tilted crazily. "The rest of you go. There's an exo in the cargo bay down the hall."

The Rlhala rolled across the floor toward us. We leaped over it to avoid being pancaked by its immense weight.

Layla rolled her eyes. "Now you tell me."

I shooed them toward the door. "Get to the docking bay. I'll be there soon." I ran into the main corridor and got my bearings. The cargo bay wasn't far down the hall to the left. I made my way there, staggering side to side as the station pitched back and forth drunkenly. Piloting the exo would be no easier, but I had to try.

Some of the crates in the room had shifted, forcing me to climb over boxes and pallets. I reached the exo-armor and unstrapped it from the wall. It was as if someone took the metal body of a terminator, enlarged it slightly, hollowed out the body and, in mechanist fashion, had fashioned it in bronze.

I clamped my feet into the metal clamps halfway up the armored legs. Another shift in the station nearly caused the exo to topple over, but a nearby crate caught it in time. I strapped in my legs and midriff, then slid my hands into metal gauntlets located just before the elbow joints in the suit.

When I tried to move, the suit didn't budge. I freed my hands, unstrapped my body, and climbed out. After a quick examination, I found a crank on the back of the suit. A few quick rotations ignited the liquid mana. Clockwork ticked, gears clacked, and the suit came to life.

I strapped back in and slid my hands in the gauntlets. This time when I flexed my arms, the exo moved with me. I started walking toward the door, the metal feet stomping. Despite the tilt of the floor, the footing remained sure, probably due to magnetized soles.

There was a slight lag to my movement, and I couldn't move as fast as I wanted to, but I covered the distance back to the other room surprisingly fast. The Rlhala had rolled to the front left of the room. The remaining cell doors were open. Clayborn and another old man wandered aimlessly in the bay. The body of a younger man lay in a pool of blood. Judging from the blood spatter on the Rlhala, it seemed he'd gotten in its way as it rolled around the chamber.

It seemed Hannah had freed the prisoners before leaving. I navigated the exo to the Rlhala, reached down, and grasped it in both metal hands. Gears whined, and the suit lifted the Rlhala with little problem. I clomped toward the exit, urging the suit to move as fast as my legs were trying to, but unlike the combat exos, this one wasn't designed for speed.

On the other hand, the feet barely slipped despite the crazy pitch of the floor. Blood painted the floor and walls where fallen enemies had rolled back and forth. I navigated around them and was nearly to the submarine bay when metal screeched and gravity vanished. The exo-suit remained attached to the floor, but my stomach rose into my throat as the station entered freefall.

I braced myself just as the hull slammed to earth with a deafening rumble. The pitch of the floor was suddenly forty degrees and the exo's feet began to slide ever so slightly. Aside from the ringing in my ears, I felt unharmed, but now the docking ring was halfway on its side. I pushed out my right foot and braced it on the wall, leaving me juxtaposed between it and the floor.

The submarine bay door was just ahead. Walking awkwardly with a foot on the floor and wall, I made it to the door on my right. Thirty yards of open space separated me from the hole in the floor. Due to the extreme angle, walking wasn't an option. I'd have to hope the magnetized boots would allow me a controlled slide. I had no idea what was on the other side of the hole. It might be a two-foot drop to sand, or a ten-foot drop to rocks.

There was only one way to find out.

Chapter 37

I waddled to the door, angling the Rlhala so it didn't get stuck on the side, and then put my right foot on the floor inside the doorway. That, at least, was the plan. The right foot didn't plant correctly, and I tumbled sideways. The Rlhala clanged. The exo clanged, and my teeth rattled inside my head.

A monstrous face filled my vision. Tentacles squirmed around my body. Glowing eyes penetrated me to my soul. Just as suddenly as the vision struck me, it was gone. I was in freefall for an instant and splashed back-first into water. With the weight of the exo and the Rlhala, I sank like a rock.

The exo settled onto the lakebed. A cloud of sand rose around me. The surface of the lake rippled no more than six feet above. I had only a small breath of air in my lungs. Despite the water, the exo still functioned. One of my hands had come free from the gauntlets and hung near the Rlhala. I'd probably brushed against it during the fall, causing the terrifying vision.

Resisting the urge to gasp for air, I slid my hand back into the gauntlet and threw the Rlhala to the side. I slid both hands free, unstrapped my waist, my legs, and unclamped my feet. My lungs screamed in agony. I pushed toward the surface, but my right foot was caught. I tried to see what held it, but the cloud of sand concealed it.

I reached down with my hands, fumbling with the jammed clamp. I couldn't hold my breath a moment longer, so I clenched my teeth as tight as I could and held on for one second more. But it was too late. Spots filled my vision and consciousness faded.

I coughed. Water sprayed from my mouth. I gasped and tasted sweet oxygen, then coughed uncontrollably, heaving water from my lungs. I rolled onto my hands and knees, coughing until I could draw breath without pain.

"Cain!" Hannah knelt beside me. "What happened?"

"I saw him fall into the water," a familiar voice said. "I ran back to help him."

I blinked water from my eyes and turned my head slowly. A mirror image looked back at me. "Gods be damned." I wanted to rub my eyes, but sand coated my hands. "Cain?"

He nodded. "If you think you're surprised right now, imagine how I felt when Hannah opened the cell door and didn't want to torture me."

The other Cain wore a ragged orange jumpsuit like Clayborn's. His arms were thin but muscled, as if he'd continued to exercise even during confinement. Burn scars ran up and down his arms, but his face was untouched. He reached down and helped me to my feet.

I managed to speak again. "I know how Layla felt when she met Hemlock."

Cain snorted. "Yeah, this is fucked up."

Explosions echoed from the other side of the fallen mechanist station. The demis were still blasting away at other side. It would only be a matter of time before they realized they could enter through the docking bays on the bottom.

I waded back into the water. "I need the Rlhala.

Cain's eyes flared. "That's what you were carrying." He glanced at Hannah and regret flashed through his eyes. "Hannah, catch up with the others, okay?"

"But—"

I held up a finger. "No buts. Just do it."

Her brow furrowed. "This is too weird." She backed up, then turned and ran into the woods.

"Where are the others going?" I said.

"The cabin. We're about a click out. Hannah—my Hannah—doesn't know where it is."

"She calls herself Esteri," I said.

Cain shrugged. "She'll always be Hannah to me." He stepped to the water's edge and pointed ahead. "The Rlhala is about twenty feet straight out from here."

I nodded and waded out, trying not to disturb the sand, then went underwater and swam in the indicated direction. The exo still lay on its back and the Rlhala was next to it. I checked to make sure the exo was still running, then clamped in my feet and slid my hands in the gauntlets. I didn't want to strap in all the way in case I had to get out fast.

Using the powerful arms, I pushed myself upright and planted the feet. Then I reached down and grasped the Rlhala. I turned to shore and walked until my head finally broke water and I could breathe again. Despite the rocky underwater slope, I made it back to shore without incident. Cain had already gone deeper into the woods, scouting ahead.

The explosions ceased. I imagined Esteri and her gang had breached the hull or discovered the hole I'd carved in the back. I hoped they took the time to investigate inside before realizing we'd evacuated.

I tromped through the woods, weaving between trees and trampling bushes while Cain led the way. I already recognized the terrain and knew where I was going, but another part of me was fascinated seeing my scrawny twin in the lead.

The air whistled overhead. I looked up and saw a sleek airship flying low over the treetops. I had little doubt they saw the trees moving when I bumped into them. Our time, it seemed, had just about run out.

The cabin came into view. Erolith stood outside near a pile of duffel bags. The other guardians were, no doubt, forming a perimeter and preparing for an attack, because the airship had followed me.

I set the Rlhala down near a stack of logs at the back of the cabin and unstrapped from the exo. We walked around the cabin toward the others. Erolith's eyebrows lifted in what was a sign of extreme surprise for him. He apparently didn't know his Cain still lived. My eyebrows rose when I saw the group of people standing on the porch behind him.

Nathaniel Church and Agatha Moon watched our approach with apprehensive eyes. I'd heard quite a bit about Church. He was a brash playboy mage with a bad temper, but he was also highly protective of his home turf. He had a reputation for being one of the most powerful mages alive. Though I'd never met him, I understood why the other Cain had recruited him.

I'd also never crossed paths with Agatha Moon, but I'd heard she was a thief. That was about as much as I knew. "Did Harry or Caolan survive?"

Cain shook his head. "I don't know. Hannah refused to tell me. But if they weren't locked up, it means they escaped or died." He looked at Church and Moon and frowned. "They told me you were dead."

"Rumors of my demise were greatly exaggerated." Church waltzed off the porch and smirked at us. "I must have had too much to drink. I see two Cains." He turned to the other Cain. "Does this mean Layla can finally have the threesome of her dreams?"

Cain grunted. "We're about to have guests. I suggest you start thinking with your other head, Church."

The other man grinned. "I can think with both at the same time, Sthyldor."

It felt strange to hear my last name since I never used it. Erolith glanced at the other Cain when he heard it but didn't remark. "How far is the nearest transition zone?" I asked Erolith.

"There's a small clearing nearly five miles away." He looked at the duffel bags. "It's possible we could make it, but someone will need to run interference to keep the mechanist airships from shadowing us."

I jogged to the garage. A motorcycle was the only source of transportation. I went back to Cain. "We need a pickup."

"I know." He pointed west. "There's a campground with a heavy-duty truck abandoned next to a camper trailer. I could probably jolt it to life. Might be some cargo straps laying around we could use for that thing." He jabbed a thumb at the Rlhala.

"Well, at least we're on the same wavelength." I looked down at the stone etchings. "Did they tell you anything about it?"

Church walked around it. "No, they never mentioned it."

"I don't think it's anything important," Agatha said. "Just a souvenir."

Cain scoffed. "Hardly unimportant. Darby used to brag about how he could control my Hannah with it. She didn't know the mechanists control Cthulhu with the help of that thing."

Agatha feigned a yawn. "Just bragging, I'm sure."

Cain shook his head. "No, it was more than that. Darby said they found it not long after raiding the armory. Their navigator plotted an incorrect route and they stumbled upon it just outside a deepway entrance in the middle of the Pacific."

"Looks like a decoration for a haunted house." Church shrugged. "Darby is a windbag. He'd take me from my cell simply to brag that he had the biggest dick in the mechanist order."

Agatha burst into laughter.

Cain frowned at them as if they were crazy. "Someone didn't do well in confinement."

Church frowned. "I'm afraid none of us did."

"I dunno," Hannah said. "You and Agatha must have been fed better because you don't look nearly as bad as Cain."

"How many more prisoners were there?" I asked Hannah.

"I don't know." She traced a circle with her finger. "I unlocked all the prison doors, but we didn't hang around to see who came out of them."

"It was quite a surprise," Church said. "The door opened, and I followed the exodus of people to here."

Agatha nodded. "Same."

I turned back to Cain. "How do you use this thing?"

"I don't know." He knelt and examined it. "Darby didn't give me instructions."

If the woman I'd questioned earlier was correct, it had something to do with touching the head in the center. Just brushing my hand against the surface had given me a glimpse of madness. I couldn't risk driving myself insane with the mechanists and Esteri's demi squad on the way.

He said my Hannah didn't even know about it. They stole it from the temple of the Outer Gods.

"I heard Darby telling someone it was all lies." Church spat on the ground near the Rlhala. "Now, I suggest we vacate the premises forthwith, before the entire mechanist army shows up."

"Agreed." Agatha looked to the skies. "Esteri and her little minions will burn us to ash if we dither too long."

Layla emerged from the cabin in fresh clothing. Her gaze traveled between me and the other Cain. Aura stepped out behind her.

Cain walked to Aura. "How is my Layla?"

"Grace said she's still stable, but not conscious."

He bit his lower lip and took her hand. "Thank you."

Aura seemed surprised by the gesture. "Oh, okay."

Layla stared blankly at him for a moment, then over to me, eyes troubled.

"We will shortly have a mechanist army on our doorstep," Erolith said. "Not to mention Esteri and six other demis. Fighting them will be problematic, so I suggest we formulate an exit strategy."

"We need that pickup truck for starters." The other Cain turned to me. "I'll get it and we can make a break for the transition zone." He turned to Erolith. "Have your people take the weapons and get a head start. You can move fast enough to make it on foot."

Erolith nodded. "A sound strategy, but one that will leave the rest of you exposed."

I nodded. "Yes, but getting the weapons away is the most important thing. Look, if we don't make it, you can destroy the weapons on Oblivion. You just need to go to the Kameni Desert where you'll find a fragment of the fire of creation. Use Earthmaker to create channels back to the forge and ignite the furnace. Throw in everything and melt it."

Erolith's eyebrows rose. "This goes outside the border of our bargain, Cain."

I nodded. "Well, Father, I just suppose I'll have to trust that you know what's best for this world."

Cain snorted. "Father knows best as long as it's in the interests of the fae, the world be damned."

I shrugged. "Well, maybe it'll be enough."

"Watching the two of you trash your dad is surreal," Hannah said. "But I kind of like it."

Erolith made a gesture most people wouldn't notice, and the guardians began fading into view as their camouflage dissipated. They hefted the bags, some of them taking two. None of them seemed to like having two of me nearby, which made sense given my disgraceful resignation from the guard.

"Perhaps you could utilize Earthmaker or Tidebringer to even the odds," Erolith said. "If we remain and fight, our odds of winning would be much better."

"Disagreed," Church said. "Running is for the best. Leave the damned weapons and go far away."

"We lost handily the last time we tried to fight," Agatha said. "It's foolish to go for another round."

"You lost your edge, Church." Cain shook his head. "Did they break you in that prison cell?"

"You've got to know when to fold 'em." Church held out his hands helplessly. "Live to fight another day."

"Pussies." Layla scowled. "Your reputations are lies if this is what you're really like."

Agatha feigned a yawn. "As if you know either of us very well."

I didn't know either of them very well either, but they certainly weren't acting how I'd expected.

Cain pursed his lips at the same time I did. We looked at each other and nodded. Both our guts pointed to the same conclusion. Despite what Church and Agatha said, fighting with the apocalypse weapons was our best chance. I found the duffel with Earthmaker, Tidebringer, and Soultaker inside.

I held Soultaker out to Agatha. She held up a hand and shook her head. "I can't accept that."

I turned to Hannah and gave her the trident and the hammer. "You've already proven that you're better with these than we are. Just try not to kill us in the process, okay?"

Hannah's eyes gleamed with inner light. "I'll make you proud."

Layla pouted. "I wanted to try Earthmaker this time."

"I thought you'd use Apollo's bow again." I rummaged through a duffel bag. "It's around here somewhere."

Erolith opened a bag and removed the golden bow.

Layla grimaced as if she were accepting an unwanted gift from a hated family member. "You don't mind giving it to an abomination?"

He tilted his head slightly. "You are a tool for the greater good no matter how lowly your birth. I would give a horse a saddle if it meant victory."

She snatched it from his hand. "Maybe I'll put a saddle on you, you sanctimonious fae scum."

Erolith nodded. "I welcome the challenge, should we emerge victorious."

Cain grinned but his smile quickly faded. "I don't know how much good I'll be. Torvin took my staff."

"Oh, well there are a few things you don't know. Wait here." I dashed inside and grabbed his staff from the bedroom then went back outside and handed it to him. "Torvin Rayne is dead in both our dimensions."

He grinned. "Wow, I guess I owe you a mangorita."

I grinned back. "Deal." My grin faded as I remembered Voltaire's was no more in this world.

Cain took the staff and touched the brightblade sigil. It hummed to life. He stepped into the yard and went through the practice exercises. His joints looked stiff and he was a little slow, but all in all, it wasn't too bad considering how long he'd been locked up. I felt proud and wondered if I was proud of him or me.

He finished the exercise, nodded at me, and went inside, no doubt to spend a moment with Hemlock. Esteri and her comrades would be here in minutes, so it was probably the only chance he'd have to deliver any parting words.

I went inside and found Noctua still inactive. We couldn't afford to chance leaving her here, so I picked her up and took her outside to the duffel bags. If she didn't recover her memories, we'd be stuck in this dimension unless we used just the cube the same way that had brought us here. That didn't appeal to me in the least, but it was something at least.

Aura fished through one of the bags and pulled out a battle axe. "This must do something good," she muttered.

I didn't remember seeing it in the other armory, but we'd been tossing weapons into the furnace by the cartload so I'd probably missed it. I held out a hand and she gave it to me. Despite its size, it was light, much like Earthmaker. I swung it at a tree. It cut deep but didn't lop through it as easily as I'd expected.

"Without Noctua, there's no telling what it does." I handed it back. "Melee weapons aren't exactly your specialty."

Aura raised an eyebrow. "Cain, I wasn't always a handler for Eclipse. I used to be a pretty good bounty hunter too."

"Yeah?" I glanced at the bow slung across her back. "You certainly know how to handle one of those, but I haven't seen you fight with a sword, much less a battle axe."

She whirled the axe until it was a blur, then slashed through the remaining half of the sapling. "I guess we'll just have to see."

The distant clack of clockwork motors grew closer. I stepped out to the dock and looked across the lake. A dozen or more mechanist boats were a few hundred yards out. I looked through my scope and saw Esteri standing at the stern of the lead boat, her face twisted with rage. She'd probably scoured the wrecked base and discovered Cain and the Rlhala missing. I saw nothing of the Hannah I knew in her eyes, only madness. It made me sad to think about what could have been. A single bird had altered the outcome of an entire dimension and destroyed so many lives.

I might have to kill the Hannah of this world, but do it I would, if it meant ending this insanity.

Chapter 38

"You look like you just swallowed a bug, Cain." Layla stood next to me. "Planning to kill Esteri yourself?"

"If I have to." I summoned my brightblade and circled it above me. "Gather up."

Hannah, Nathan, Agatha, and the others grouped up.

Nathan sighed. "This is a mistake. We should go now."

"Go where?" Layla said. "We can't outrun the airships, even in vehicles."

"Best to try." Agatha frowned. "We can make it if we abandon everything and run now."

"What's wrong with you people?" Cain glared at them. "Did imprisonment completely kill your spirit?"

I held up a hand. "Run if you want, but we're standing our ground with the apocalypse weapons."

Hannah jammed Tidebringer into the water. "I'm ready."

I put a hand on her shoulder. "Try to limit the destruction."

She nodded. "Won't be a problem."

The flash of bronze caught my eye. I focused on the incoming boats and found the origin. Esteri and the other demis were buckling on clockwork wings. She looked straight at me and drew Airbender. It seemed someone had brought it to them from Oblivion. A male demi held what looked like an ancient cloth sling. If it was something from the armory, I didn't remember seeing it.

"Hannah, destroy the boats," I said.

The water out near the boats began to swirl faster and faster, catching the vessels before the drivers knew what was happening. Esteri and the other demis shot into the air, propelled by clockwork wings as the hapless mechanists fought to keep their boats from being sucked to the depths of the lake.

Esteri spun Airbender, and a whirlwind appeared above the whirlpool spinning in the opposite direction and negating the pull of the water. Mechanists caught in the middle hung on for dear life and cried out in panic. Hannah gritted her teeth and the maelstrom slowed. Waves began to rise, rocking the boats violently.

Gusts of wind batted down the waves, clearing a narrow channel of relatively calm waters for the boats to traverse. Though water was a powerful force, so was the air. Esteri knew how to counter whatever Hannah threw at the mechanists.

"Fuck her!" Hannah shouted. "I should easily be able to fight air with water."

"You don't have enough momentum," Agatha said. "Build a giant wave in the distance and draw it toward them. The sheer weight alone will be too much for any amount of air to blow away.

Hannah frowned. "I've got a better idea." She slammed Earthmaker to the ground...and nothing happened. She blinked and stared at the ground in confusion. "It's not working!"

Nathan laughed. Agatha snickered like a child trying to repress her mirth. I suddenly got a very bad vibe coming from them and leapt back. They looked at each other, a pair of kids caught being naughty. I looked through my true sight scope. At first, they looked normal, but the upgraded orb began to melt away the powerful glamour disguising the truth. Nathan's features paled and his hair went from short and brown to long and black. Agatha's eyes shaded to lavender and her hair turned frosty white.

I had no idea who the woman was, but the other I knew all too well by now. "Loki!"

He sighed and threw up his hands. Both his and Agatha's glamor flickered away. "I'm sorry, but the looks on your faces was simply too much."

"What do you mean?" Hannah rose and faced them. "What did you do?"

"Quite simply, we've leveled the playing field." The woman opened her hand to reveal an orb of darkness so absolute, it was like staring into infinity. "No one claimed the Nullstone from the armory, so we helped ourselves."

Cain glared at them. "What happened to Nathan and Agatha?"

I turned my scope on him, but he was who he appeared to be.

Loki shrugged. "I have no idea. They escaped your encounter with Hannah and were never taken prisoner. But you didn't know that so we thought it might be fun to join the team."

Layla scowled. "No wonder you wanted us to run."

From what Thor had told me of the trickster revolt, I finally realized who the female had to be. "You're Eris, aka Discordia."

"Very good, Cain Prime." She smiled. "I'm not as well-known as my Nordic counterpart, especially not to outsiders."

Cain looked at the Nullstone. "I take it that orb disabled the weapons?"

Eris nodded. "That ugly brute, Hephaestus made it at the request of Ares who thought that war might be more interesting if no one could use supernaturally enhanced weapons. It turns out that war is incredibly boring without explosions, so Ares discarded it in the armory after the first trial run."

I glanced out at the lake. The mechanists were still coming, but they'd slowed considerably. The look on Esteri's face told me she'd realized Airbender was no longer functioning. She'd soon realize our weapons weren't working either and the onslaught would resume.

"If you could take the Nullstone, why didn't you take Soultaker? What's the reason for any of this?"

"Isn't it obvious?" Loki spread his arms wide. "Though we can directly affect our worshippers, it's far more effective to let mortals carry out our plans." He looked at the demis circling above the lake on their clockwork wings. "In this case, I think the battle will be far more entertaining without the weapons."

"I'm simply dying to see who comes out on top." Eris smiled at Hannah. "You or your insane counterpart."

"Considering that Esteri is backed by an army of mechanists and more demis, I think it's a foregone conclusion." Hannah threw Earthmaker and Tidebringer to the ground. "If a slaughter is what you want, then that's what you'll get."

"Let's see if luck is on your side as it has been before," Eris said.

"That's all you care about?" I glared at them. "Chaos and death?"

Loki smirked. "Let us just say that Prime will be much easier to manage without you around."

"Why me?" I still didn't understand what made me so important to their plans.

I'd been so embroiled in getting us back home that I hadn't taken a step back to look at the big picture. It was the way Eris emphasized luck that I began to surmise how events had turned so sour in this dimension. Loki and Eris might be gods of devious manipulation, but in the end, they couldn't directly control the paths of mortals who didn't worship them. Sometimes, a far more subtle method of nudging events was more useful.

"You've been cheating even worse than usual, haven't you?" I glanced again at Esteri and the mechanists. They still idled far out in the lake, probably assessing the situation since Airbender stopped working. I turned to Loki and Eris. "Tell me, is Fortuna on your team, or did she grant you a favor?"

Loki flinched, but quickly recovered. "That's quite a speculation."

"Why bother covering for her?" Eris rolled her eyes. "The poor girl wants the same thing we do, but once the deed was done, remorse overwhelmed her sensibilities."

"You used the Tetron and found an instant where bad luck could cause the most drastic outcome possible." I shook my head. "Fortuna altered chance and the outcome fractured the timeline."

Loki shrugged. "We didn't expect Prime to split the way it did, but here we are." He looked around as if appraising the world. "I rather like it."

Layla's eyes flared. "Are you saying that bitch caused the bird to fly into my dagger?"

I nodded. "That's exactly what happened. It wasn't supposed to happen at all, but when it did, it split our dimension into Alpha and Beta."

Aura brandished the battle axe threateningly. "This is why the gods must die."

Loki spread his arms open. "Please try, little elf."

I gripped her arm. "Don't do it. He'll be free to react if you try to strike him."

Aura dropped the axe onto the pile of duffel bags. "What's he going to do, kill me?"

"Knowing Loki, probably far worse."

Layla looked puzzled. "So I'm the one who threw the dagger, but when Fortuna altered chance, it caused a split in our dimension?"

I nodded. "There was only one of you until that instant and then there were three."

"Why three and not two?" Hannah frowned. "Was there a third outcome?"

"I don't know." I smirked at Loki. "I'm guessing they didn't realize this would happen either."

"Direct intervention is frowned upon," Loki said. "This has happened before, and it will happen again." He looked out at the lake. "Your fate approaches."

The mechanists had resumed course and would be upon us in minutes.

I picked up Earthmaker and Tidebringer and shoved them into a duffel bag. I didn't know if the Nullstone disabled Noctua, but I checked on her anyway. I picked up her still form and held it to my ear. Clockwork ticked gently beneath her metal skin, meaning she wasn't affected, but still wouldn't be of any use.

Loki and Eris vanished from sight, presumably behind god-level glamour. I was certain they'd watch from nearby, actively rooting against me and Hannah. My mind still grappled with the scope of their plan. Out of all the events to manipulate in the world, why had they chosen us as the focus? There were plenty of other demis who seemed more than willing to wreak havoc. Daphne and the Firsters would have been perfect for them. But for some reason, they saw Hannah as the biggest threat on their radar.

Admittedly, switching Hannah to the dark side had completely flipped this dimension on its head. Even so, the Firsters and their demis had held the mechanists at bay. It seemed evil Hannah wasn't quite enough to give them the world domination they so desired.

The mechanist boats reached the shore. Esteri and the other demis landed and unbuckled their clockwork wings. Sigma held up his hands and lightning flashed across the sky. He alone was strong enough to kill us all. I had no idea how we were going to emerge from this alive.

There was only one chance and it was slim. We had to stop the fight before it began.

"Wait here." I held up my hands and walked through the woods toward the shore. "Esteri, I want to talk."

Her eyes gleamed with anger and a cruel smile spread across her face. She glanced toward the other Cain who was now some distance behind me. "Coward!" she cried out. "Who did you disguise to look like you?"

Keeping my hands raised, I called back, "Esteri, we're both Cain. I'm from Prime."

Her eyes snapped back to me. "Prime?" Her mouth dropped open. "But how?"

"It was an accident." When I was within thirty yards of her, I stopped. "What happened to you wasn't supposed to happen. Loki and Eris used Fortuna to alter chance. The bird that flew in front of Layla's dagger was because Fortuna manipulated chance. The event split Prime into three parallel dimensions."

Sigma smirked at me. "Cain and his stories."

I glared at him. "Stay out of this."

"Blaming the gods now?" Esteri laughed mirthlessly, voice tinged with madness. "It doesn't matter." Her eyes flashed toward Cain. "What matters is that he gave me to Cthulhu to get rid of his disease. He used me. I will never forgive him for that."

"You would have died otherwise." I held my hands out pleadingly. "He wanted you to live and that was your only chance."

"Please listen to him," Hannah said.

Esteri flinched as if she'd been struck when she saw Hannah. "You're me from Prime."

"Yes." Hannah held out her hands. "Please don't fight. Cain loves you. He was faced with losing you forever and did the only thing he could to save your life."

"It's true." Cain approached. "Please, Hannah, don't do this. I'll figure out a way to free you from Cthulhu, I promise."

Tears trickled down Esteri's cheeks. "I loved you, Cain. You were like a father to me." Her tears sizzled and steamed as her eyes began to glow. "And then you betrayed me!" A scream of madness and rage tore from her throat. "Bastard!"

Brilliant white beams speared from her mouth and eyes. Cain whipped out his staff and deflected the energy at the last instant. The energy sheared through dozens of trees in an instant. She unleashed another barrage at me. I deflected the beams back at her.

Esteri screamed and dove to the side. One beam sliced through a mechanist in an exo suit. He gurgled as his innards fried. There was a pause as everyone on both sides watched the man writhe in agony until he toppled over in the exo and went still.

Esteri pushed up from the ground, body shaking with sobs. She turned her furious gaze on us and pointed. "Kill them!"

Sigma cracked his knuckles and electricity flashed across them. "Gladly."

The forest filled with the sounds of clacking gears as forty or more mechanists in exos marched toward us. The enemy demis lined up behind Esteri. Far off in the lake, the water frothed and bubbled as a new threat—probably Cthulhu's army of the deep made its way to shore.

Cain's brightblade sizzled to life. I activated mine and turned to Hannah. "Get to the back. I don't want you up here."

"But Cain—"

I put a hand on her cheek. "I don't care what happens, I want you to get out of here alive, okay? Go with Erolith if you have to, but don't do anything stupid."

Tears trickled down her face. She kissed my hand and nodded. "I love you, Cain. Never forget that."

The other Cain wiped at his eyes. "Gods damn it, this is not the time to be emotional."

I laughed. "Enjoy it while you can, because it might be your last chance."

Cain nodded. "Never can they say we died for naught, but for goodness, freedom, and a world without tyranny."

"Quoting old fae proverbs now?" I said.

"Yep." He assumed a fighting stance as the mechanists and their clockwork armor closed in on us. "It's a good day to die."

Hannah backed away slowly, then turned and ran toward the cabin.

"Should anything happen to you, I will care for the girl," Erolith said, appearing from behind fae glamour at my side.

"Thanks, Dad." Cain and I smirked at each other, and then the mechanists were upon us.

Guardians sprang from the trees, fae camouflage vanishing an instant before brightblades slashed through the metal frame of exos and into flesh and bone. Mechanists screamed and died. Whirring cannons like Gatling guns sprang from the arms of the exos and sprayed bullets through the forest.

My brightblade became a blur, slashing projectiles from the air as I worked my way closer to the next target. I cast small shields in front of the nearest weapon. The bullets ricocheted back at the shooter, some sparking off his bronze armor, others filling his gut. Incendiary bullets lodged in trees, exploding. Flames crawled up trees and across pine straw, but the ground was damp enough from recent rain to prevent a massive blaze from erupting.

The guardians flashed in and out of camouflage, leaping from trees, dashing behind mechanists, and slashing through their legs before they knew what hit them. I ghost-walked past another exo and separated his head from his shoulders, then turned the robotic frame on his allies, spraying bullets into the masses.

Within minutes, the mechanists were down to the last two men. They screamed and ran toward Esteri and the demis. She sneered and cut them to pieces before they were within twenty yards.

Then the demigods came for us.

Not far offshore, hundreds of squid-heads appeared above water. The giant wings of malgorths sprayed water as their massive bodies began to rise from the deeps. I didn't see how we'd win this, especially in a direct fight. The odds of beating the demis was already slim enough, but if we could just drive them back a little, it might give us time to plot an escape.

Layla hadn't shown herself yet, presumably because she'd seen us handle the mechanists with ease. Even without the golden bow, she was deadly. I hoped the element of surprise netted us a victory.

Because this would be the fight of our lives.

Chapter 39

The guardians switched their staffs to sniper mode and unleashed a volley of kinetic energy at the small group of demis.

Esteri glanced at one of her companions. "Luxo!"

A teenager with long blond locks spread his hands, and a translucent dome intercepted the threat. He smirked at us. "Have to do better than that, mortals."

"Altair, give them a taste," Esteri said.

A young man with dark skin rammed his fist against the ground. The earth shook beneath our feet. A spike of rock nearly emasculated me before I jumped back out of the way. Cain, Erolith, and the others dodged similar earth spikes.

"Rania!" Esteri called.

A girl who looked no older than ten ripped a medium-sized pine tree from the earth and hurled it at us like a spear. We scattered out of the way an instant before it splintered against a nearby tree.

Esteri laughed. "Your turn, Sigma."

He sneered at us and raised his hand, then closed it into a fist and slashed it toward the ground. A bolt of lightning obliterated a tree.

"Why in the hell are you fighting for the mechanists?" I shouted. "Are all of you bound to Cthulhu?"

"Yes," Esteri said. "I pulled them into the fold. He will soon be master of Gaia."

"Look, we don't want to kill you." I held out my hand pleadingly. "It's not too late to turn this around and rebuild."

"Oh, it's far too late." Esteri's eyes glowed. "Besides, my companions know if they try to leave, I'll kill them. Not even Luxo's shields can protect him against me."

That was good to know. Unfortunately, my Hannah's abilities didn't work on command and throwing her in front of these lunatics wasn't part of the plan. These kids might have superpowers, but they were still just kids without training. They all looked incredibly smug right now, but maybe if we rattled them, we could talk them down.

One girl still hadn't demonstrated her powers. She was average height and size with plain brown hair and freckles on her young face. She looked as if she wanted to be anywhere but here. I suspected she was an ace in the hole.

Esteri watched me and my counterpart and it suddenly hit me. "You trained her, didn't you?" I said to Cain in a low voice. "Taught her tactics?"

He nodded. "Yeah, training with golems, shadow dancing, everything."

"Oh, shit." I turned to Erolith, but he'd vanished, presumably to initiate a strike against the demis.

There was only one reason Esteri hadn't made another move. She knew and understood Oblivion Guard tactics and was waiting on them to attack. Luxo's shield was down and the others just stood watching us, a prime target.

I shouted into the forest, "Erolith, wait!"

My warning was an instant too late. The unknown girl's eyes turned black. She threw out her hands and a wave of darkness spread through the trees, casting outlines around camouflaged guardians who were rushing in for an attack. Their bodies slowed, weapons upraised as if caught in tar. Time literally slowed. Esteri turned in slow motion and screamed. White beams speared through one guardian and burst through the elf's back. Esteri rotated, slicing another guardian in half.

Rania caught a guardian in mid-air and ripped off his arm. Blood spray filled the air in slow motion as the man cried out. Sigma summoned bolts of lightning, burning two guardians to ash. Luxo encased another in a spherical shield, squeezing his hand to make it smaller until the dark elf was crushed.

Erolith somehow slashed his way through the black mist, moving fast despite the slowed time, no doubt due to his fae magic. His brightblade slashed through Rania's throat, and whipped toward the unknown girl, but Luxo caught his arm in a shield.

I didn't know what I planned to do, but I raced forward. Arrows rained down from a tree where Layla perched. Aura fired a salvo of arrows alongside Layla's. Cain raced by my side. We hit the black mist. It was like struggling through mud. I slashed at it with my brightblade, but it did nothing.

The black mist caught the arrows and Sigma incinerated them with blasts of lightning.

I focused on the area near the unknown girl and ghostwalked. I flickered into place behind her and raised my blade. Esteri spun and donkey-kicked me. I flew backward through the air and the mist caught me once again.

Erolith spoke in Alder and cast a glittering wave of magic in a circle. The mist dissolved and time resumed its normal pace. His wings unfurled and he rose into the air, dragging Luxo and his shield into the air with him.

Cain ghostwalked behind Luxo and thrust his brightblade into the kid's back—or tried to. The blade struck an invisible barrier and sparked. Beams speared toward Erolith from Esteri's mouth and eyes. Erolith blocked with his brightblade, but Sigma called down lightning, stunning him. He went limp and fell to the ground. Cain ducked beneath an attack from Esteri, grabbed Erolith, and flickered away with another ghostwalk.

I collected myself off the ground and took cover behind a tree. Rania's head lay a few feet from her body. One demi was dead, but at the cost of every guardian, but Erolith. These weren't just kids with powers, they were a team trained to work together. Only a high fae had penetrated their defenses, and he'd nearly paid with his life.

We couldn't shoot them from a distance. We couldn't get close using stealth. They'd keep coming at us until we were dead. Without the guardians, we couldn't even take all the weapons and run.

"Looks rather hopeless, doesn't it?" Loki stepped from behind a tree. "Perhaps you should just give up."

I really wanted to take off his head, but directly attacking him would allow him to strike back. I wasn't nearly strong or fast enough to take down a god.

"Once Cthulhu sank his claws into Esteri, it was over. She recruited demis from all over the world and they spent months training." Loki smirked. "Your Hannah is nothing more than a babe lost in the woods."

"You couldn't bear the thought of an outsider god having so much power." I ducked behind a tree to stay out of sight of Esteri. "So, you helped the mechanists."

"Guilty as charged." Loki's gaze brightened. "They're coming your way, Cain. Run or die, it doesn't matter to me. Regardless of what you do, you'll be out of my way."

He was right. The others and I might survive, but we'd be trapped and powerless to stop whatever Loki planned to do in Prime.

"Better run for it now, Cain." Loki vanished but he continued to speak. "I'll even distract them for you if you'd like."

I held in a retort, not wanting my voice to give away my position as Esteri and the demis began advancing slowly. The unnamed girl stalked behind them, eyes black as pitch. I suspected she could see or sense the presence of beings even through glamour, which was how she knew the guardians were about to attack. She could probably see Loki too, provided he wasn't behind a tree.

I looked toward the cabin and hoped Hannah was hiding inside. The battle was over. We had no choice but to run. Nothing we said or did would matter. Despair filled me at the thought of the bleak future ahead not just for this realm, but for Prime. Chaos would rip through order and leave nothing behind.

The weight grew so heavy, I could hardly bear it. That was the moment I knew it wasn't coming from me. Loki's team was larger than he'd let on. "Oizys, leave me be." I struggled against the painful tide of anxiety and despair tearing at me. Only the goddess of misery could tear through my defenses so easily.

All I could think about was fleeing, even though I knew that wasn't what I wanted. Somehow, we had to fight back, but how? I dragged myself through the underbrush, my heart so heavy I could barely move. If Esteri didn't kill me, it seemed my heart might implode and do the job for her.

Someone gripped my arm and flipped me onto my back. I looked into Esteri's eyes and knew it was over. But there was no hate in those eyes, only concern and fear. I blinked and realized it was Hannah.

"Leave him alone!" she screamed.

Despite the crushing weight of anxiety, depression, and despair, I turned myself on my side and saw Esteri and her gang only a few yards away.

Tears pouring down her cheeks, Hannah stepped between me and them. "After everything Mom did to keep you safe, do you really think she'd be happy to see you now, Hannah?"

Esteri froze. "Don't you bring her into this. She killed herself and tried to kill me. She abandoned me in a cruel world. I suffered abuse after abuse until Cain came along. Just when he'd earned my trust, he abandoned me to Cthulhu."

Sigma held up a fist. "Join us. The world deserves payback for what it did to us."

Hannah trembled and shook her head. "No." A white nimbus glowed around her body. "All you want to do is kill and destroy. You have the chance to create something new, something wonderful, but you're too blinded by hatred."

"Humans are trash," Luxo said. "They don't deserve to live."

"Everyone deserves a chance to live." Hannah's voice grew soft and calm. "Cain taught me that. He gave me a chance to live while others tried to kill me because they feared what I might do with my powers." Her shoulders straightened and she faced Esteri. "And now I see that they were right."

Esteri's eyes began to glow. "I'm glad I didn't turn into the pathetic dog you are."

"And I'm sad you don't see the truth about yourself."

Esteri's lips spread into a cruel smile. "Well, then do me a favor and die." White hot energy speared from her eyes and mouth.

"No!" I shouted. I ghostwalked in front of Hannah and cast a shield. My shield shattered like glass the moment the attack hit it. Darkness folded over me and I floated in oblivion. Despite the darkness, I felt warmth all around me. I realized this must be that final moment of life where the last second stretched for an eternity. I'd tried and failed to protect Hannah. There was no way either of us had survived the blow.

The darkness receded. I stood outside the cabin. My knees buckled, but I managed to stay upright because someone held me from behind. I looked down at the hands, turned and found Hannah hugging me from behind. She released me and looked up, tears sparkling in her eyes.

"W-what happened?" I shook my head. "Are we dead?"

"No." Hannah looked around. "I tried to ghostwalk like you. I think it worked."

Something else caught my gaze. I blinked and rubbed my eyes, but when I looked back, the spectacle was still there. A ring of huge glowing flowers stood where we'd been a moment ago. Esteri and the others gawked at them, apparently trying to decide if we'd transformed into flowers or not.

I grabbed Hannah's arm and pulled her behind the cabin. Layla and Aura appeared from behind the log pile, faces tight with concern.

"Cain, you know I hate to lose, but we're fucked if we stay here a second longer." Layla grasped my hand. "We need to go."

Aura nodded. "I hate agreeing with Layla, but she's right."

I frowned. "Did either of you see what happened?"

Layla raised an eyebrow. "I was trying to figure out how to save your ass, but you vanished."

"Hannah saved me." I pinched the bridge of my nose because my head ached. "She ghostwalked me away from Esteri."

Aura's eyes widened. "Wow, really?"

"Yeah, it's neat and all, but we need to go." Layla tugged my sleeve. "Now."

Water splashed and rumbled as Cthulhu's army began to wade ashore. Salkos and other creatures clambered onto the dock and the shoreline behind the cabin. If we didn't run now, we'd be surrounded and outnumbered. I didn't want to rely on Hannah's unreliable powers to get us out of another mess.

I sighed. "Yeah, it's game over." I pointed west. "Let's find that pickup truck Cain mentioned and run for it."

"And leave the apocalypse weapons here?" Aura grimaced. "Gods damn it, this was all for nothing."

Hannah slumped. "God, I suck so much! If I could control my powers, I could stop them!"

I shook my head. "You aren't filled with the kind of hate it takes to be like Esteri." I put a hand on her shoulder. "And I'm proud of you for that."

"What a sweet moment," Layla said. "Can you shut up and run?"

I was about to nod when what Hannah said lodged in my mind. There was one obvious solution but if I screwed up, I'd die for sure. But if it worked, we might just save the world.

Chapter 40

I ran toward the log pile.

"Cain, what in the hell are you doing?" Layla tried to grab my arm, but I slipped from her grasp.

"Hold off the monsters, I need a minute." Before anyone could stop me, I put my hand on the only thing that could stop the juggernaut—the Rlhala. My hand covered Cthulhu's head and the world vanished. I tumbled forward through a vortex of water, unable to shout or scream lest water fill my lungs.

I settled to the sandy bottom of the ocean. My lungs threatened to burst from lack of oxygen. I looked up, desperate to find the surface, but there was nothing but endless water all around me. In the back of my mind, I remembered this wasn't real. I had entered the slumbering mind of Cthulhu, which meant I could breathe water as freely as air.

Pushing aside my primal fear was something I'd trained to do since childhood, but even so, it didn't come easily. I forced myself to breathe. Oxygen filled my blood, but it wasn't because I'd filled my lungs with air, but because the gills on my body drew it from the water. I looked at my body. It seemed as human as it had moments before, but this dream state made it something else.

A city of crooked spires and spikes, of oblong angles and uneven surfaces stood in silhouette against a faint glow from somewhere ahead. A road of skulls and skeletons paved the way. I didn't know how long a moment in the dream state was in real life, but I couldn't afford to linger a moment longer.

I'm a fast swimmer, I thought to myself. *Like a dolphin.* I launched myself through the water, propelled faster than possible with human feet, even though I hadn't magically grown flippers or a tail. Within moments, I reached the edge of the city. The crooked spires and structures made me dizzy. There was no east, no west, no up or down. It was as if someone had taken a city and jumbled it into a chaotic mess before dropping it into place.

On land, it would have been impossible to navigate without being intimately familiar, but underwater, I swam between structures encircled with the bones of long-dead monsters and over twisted constructions that defied my ability to comprehend them.

A crooked spire in the center of the city caught my eye. It was the temple Fred had shown me. The Rlhala jutted crookedly from the silt as it had during my last dream visit. I swam inside the massive opening and entered an empty chamber. I looked around, puzzled. If the beast wasn't here, where was he?

I continued further into darkness and bumped into something slimy. Glowing red orbs lit the water. Massive tentacles writhed around me, and I realized I'd just run into Cthulhu himself.

Before I could react, his gaze settled on me.

I can't move. Can't see. People shout and muffled screams echo.

"Every last one," a cruel voice hisses. "Not a single one must remain."

After an eternity, there is silence. I struggle to free myself, but my body hasn't the strength to dislodge the weight. I hear more voices, but I can't understand them. They speak in the language my parents sometimes used when they didn't want me to know what they were talking about.

"Help! Help!" I shout until I'm hoarse and can hardly breathe.

The weight shifts. Sunlight glares in my eyes and fresh air relieves my lungs.

"One still lives," says a calm voice. "The gods in their unjust wrath failed."

"What good is it if only one lives?" a female says.

"I do not know, but their lineage is too precious to let them all perish."

The woman grunted. "I agree."

"Then we will take him as our own," the man said. "Raise him."

"We will be shunned and looked down upon," the woman said. "We will be shamed."

"A price worth paying. I will make him worthy."

My eyes adjusted to the light and I saw the two figures standing over me.

Erolith reached down and cradled me in his arms. "You come from those even greater than the gods themselves, little one. I am unworthy of you, but I will do my best."

I blinked and stood once again in Cthulhu's presence. *What was that?*

A dream of your past, he said in my mind. His voice was subdued, almost submissive compared to the other times I'd spoken with him.

Was that my origin?

I do not know, he replied.

I finally recovered my wits and realized I was in Cthulhu's dream. I had no idea how much time had passed in the real world, so I had to make this quick. *Your army will respond to my commands now.*

It is so, he replied dully.

Esteri and the demis will also be under my command.

It is done.

Just like that? I asked, stunned that it could be so easy.

Yes.

I realized that I wasn't sure what to do next. *How do I wake up?*

You are awake, Cthulhu said. *The Rlhala rests beneath your palm.*

I felt the cold touch of the artifact and sensed my body in the real world. I pulled my hand away and the dream world vanished. I stood and looked around.

A pair of dead salkos and several migyos lay a few feet away. Layla and Aura were breathing heavily and covered in guts and slime. The rest of the army stood still, their fish eyes watching me.

"What the hell happened?" Layla said. "They stopped fighting."

"Return to the lake," I said.

Grinding squeaky sounds emerged from the salkos' orifices as they turned for the water. The migyos pulsated and glowed like jellyfish before waddling back to the lake. The monstrous malgorths met my gaze, but their eyes didn't grasp me with madness as they had the last time.

Yes, master. Their words filled my mind in the same alien language as Cthulhu's but I somehow understood them. Beating their great wings, they carried their massive bodies back into the depths. The ganthagons with their tentacle legs struggled on dry land but eventually made it to the water.

Esteri and the other demis stood not far from the cabin, their faces twisted in fear and frustration.

"Wait here," I told the others.

Hannah put a hand on my arm. "You control them too?"

"They're tied to Cthulhu, so let's hope so." I approached the demis.

Esteri's face contorted with rage. Tears poured down her red face. "What did you do, Cain? Did you strike another bargain with Cthulhu?"

She didn't know the mechanists had controlled him, and it was probably for the best right now. I didn't want her trying to use the Rlhala herself. "I did what I had to do," I said.

Luxo raised a fist, but when he tried to close it, he cried out in pain. "Shae, do something!"

The unknown girl shook her head. "Nah. You people forced me to join Cthulhu. Deal with it."

I studied the girl. "Shae, where did your powers come from?"

"They told me I'm a distant relative of Nyx, goddess of night and darkness." She shrugged. "I'm cursed with true sight and a bunch of other awful stuff."

"Esteri forced you to join Cthulhu?"

She nodded. "She threatened to kill my family if I didn't."

"You were a loser Goth kid when I found you." Esteri held a fist to her face. "I did you a favor."

"Don't threaten her," I said.

Esteri lowered her fist and glared at me.

I looked back at Shae. "Can you reveal that which is hidden?"

She nodded.

"Then do so, please."

Esteri screamed. "Just kill me and get it over with, you bastard! I'll bet you enjoy controlling me like a puppet."

I'd presumably broken the control the mechanists had over her and the others when I used the Rlhala, meaning I suddenly had all these lives in my hands. And the thought of it made me sick to my stomach. But I couldn't simply cut them loose. Free to do as she willed, Esteri would probably kill us on the spot.

As much as I despised having this power, the responsible thing wasn't to relinquish it until I could be sure Esteri wasn't a danger to everyone.

"No!" Loki faded into visibility, pacing back and forth in front of Eris. "That insignificant little speck will pay for this. I swear it."

Eris and a very depressed looking woman appeared next to him. I guessed she was Oizys, goddess of misery. "I tried everything, but something protects him."

Eris pursed her lips. "We must get him to act directly against us so we can strike him down."

"He's clever." Loki tapped a finger to his chin. "But no mortal is cleverer than me."

The trio continued speaking, apparently unaware that we could see and hear them thanks to Shae's powers.

We watched them go back and forth about how to handle me for a moment before Loki flinched comically and did a double-take once he realized we were staring at them.

"Well, fuck." He hooked arms with the goddesses. "I'll just show myself out for now."

"I hope the other gods make you pay for what you've done." I glared at him. "Millions dead and for what?"

He shrugged. "It was amusing while it lasted." They stepped into the shadows of the shed behind the cabin and vanished, shadow walking out of this world.

A troubled look creased Esteri's brow, but she said nothing.

"I need help!" Cain struggled from the woods, Erolith cradled in his arms.

I ran to him and took our adoptive father in my grasp. "Grace is still inside with Hemlock."

Cain sighed. "I took him and hid. I'm sorry I left like that."

"It's okay." I waited for him to open the door. "The demis are under control for now."

He nodded. "I saw."

Grace wasn't inside, but Hemlock lay on the couch, face pale. Cain checked her neck and sighed with relief.

I lay Erolith on the table and looked around, but Grace was nowhere to be found. The front door opened, and she stepped inside, eyes wide. "What happened? I tried to gather animals to help us fight, but it looked like we were done for."

I waved off her explanation. "It's fine. Erolith needs your help."

She examined him. "He's been badly burned inside and out."

"Lightning struck him," Cain said.

Grace hissed. "I can't help him. The damage it too extensive."

"We need to get him to Feary," I said.

Erolith drew in a ragged breath. "Too late, I'm afraid." His burned eyelids cracked open. "You are alive."

I took that as a question and told him how I'd used the Rlhala to control the enemy.

Erolith nodded sagely, no pain showing on his face despite the severe injuries. "I am proud."

Cain and I both flinched at the unexpected compliment.

"Surely you can be healed on Feary," Cain said.

Erolith shook his head. "I feel the final breath coming. But I have fulfilled my destiny."

"By saving me," I said. "When I used the Rlhala, I saw you saving me from a pile of bodies. You said that I came from those even greater than the gods. What does that mean?"

Erolith raised an eyebrow. "You will know in time." He shivered violently.

"He's going into cardiac arrest!" Grace placed her hands on his chest. "His heart is too damaged. I can't heal it."

A final breath rattled from Erolith's throat and he went still.

"Fuck." Cain backed away and turned to me. "After everything that son of a bitch put me through, and he won't even give us answers on his deathbed?"

I smiled. "He was nothing if not consistent."

Cain sighed. "True." He looked at me. "Tell me about this vision."

I gave him the details. "Maybe using the Rlhala again would show me more."

He pursed his lips. "Maybe, but we've got bigger decisions to make." He jammed a thumb toward the back door. "What do we do about them?"

I gave it some thought. "I think it's time to bring the mechanists to heel so we can start rebuilding. Esteri and her little friends will play a major role in reconstruction."

"The Firsters are still out there," Cain said. "I have no doubt they'll try something again."

I shrugged. "Well, why don't we go home and think about it?" I turned to Grace. "Can Hemlock be moved?"

"Carefully." She examined the other woman. "She's mending pretty well now, but it'll be a few days before she's on her feet."

Cain knelt next to her and kissed her forehead. "Let's not move her. There's plenty of room here at the cabin for a few days."

I shrugged again. "Sounds good, but I call dibs on the master bedroom."

"Gods, you're a bad houseguest." He snorted. "Remind me never to invite you to our dimension again."

I left him with Hemlock and went outside to the others. Esteri was already in a shouting match with Hannah and anyone else who looked at her. I decided to lay some ground rules. The road to reconstruction wouldn't be just about buildings, but about communities and lives. Unless and until Noctua remembered how to use the Tetron to traverse dimensions, we were stuck here.

"Esteri, you will not harm anyone by any means at your disposal. You will not use magic unless given express consent." I turned to the other demis. "This goes for all of you."

Shae breathed a sigh of relief and wiped tears from her eyes. "Thank you."

"Soft little bitch," Esteri muttered.

I sighed. "Is anyone hungry?"

All the demis raised their hands, including Hannah, Layla, and Aura. I looked across the lake at the setting sun. "Well, let's have a cookout, then."

"We save the world and you want to cook out?" Layla snorted. "It's perfect."

I didn't sense an ounce of sarcasm in her statement.

The deep freezer had plenty of food. Hannah took charge of organizing everyone into their own work details. All the demis but Shae complained, but most of them seemed to get into the spirit once I set out the potato chips and soft drinks.

Layla elbowed me when I was at the grill turning over the burgers and hot dogs. "Shit, Cain, you went from having one kid to five."

I chuckled. "Gods, I'm ready to go home."

She nodded. "Me too. I didn't think we were going to make it out of this one."

"Me either." I impulsively put an arm around her waist and just as quickly retracted it.

Layla winked. "Don't get domesticated on me, Cain." She slapped my ass and left to help Hannah set a table.

Esteri was the only demi who didn't look eager for a hamburgers or hot dogs when the food was ready to serve. Despite her scowls and glares, I considered it a huge success for a post-apocalyptic barbeque.

It was dark by the time we finished eating. I'd half-expected another contingent of mechanists to show up to ruin the festivities, but they were a no-show. I assumed they'd discovered they couldn't control Cthulhu anymore and were making a run for it before the new master decided to end them.

We put sleeping bags in one of the guest rooms so the demis without a bed could sleep in those, then I sent them off to bed with a simple command. I knew from experience that having kids was a million times harder when they weren't bound to Cthulhu and forced to follow commands, but it felt like some kind of accomplishment to see them obey without too much resistance.

Even Sigma relaxed once he realized I wasn't planning to summarily execute them.

Then Cain, Grace, Layla, Aura, Hannah, and I carried Erolith's body into the forest to lay it to rest. Grace knelt and put her hands on the ground and the local elemental slowly pulled his body into the ground.

"Maybe we should have sent it back to Feary," Cain said. "And what do we do about all the slain guardians?"

I shook my head. "I'm leaving that on your shoulders."

He snorted. "I figured."

The day felt like it had gone on forever. Considering all we'd done, there was literally no accounting for our survival. But Loki and his coconspirators were still out there, and things would probably get worse before they got better.

Chapter 41

The first thing next morning, we invaded the mechanist compound at the lodge. Unbelievably, the place was still packed with inventors and other leaders. Apparently, they'd been so sure of victory that they'd partied until the wee hours of the morning. The people who could have reported what happened were all dead.

We approached using the boats the mechanists had invaded with yesterday. The constables onshore didn't even suspect anything until we pulled into the dock. When they saw Esteri and the other demis with us, their eyes went wide with fear.

I stepped out of the boat and held up a hand. "I control them now. Surrender or die horribly."

They threw down their weapons and raised their hands.

I shook my head. "Pick up your weapons. I need you to do something for me." The constables looked conflicted about my next orders, but they complied without comment. They loaded up their paddy wagons and preceded us to the lodge. By the time we arrived, they'd gathered all their comrades into the largest ballroom in the hotel.

Darby and his pals had probably died on station, but I sent some constables to the wreckage to recover anyone still alive.

"What is the meaning of this?" Horatio wailed when his own constables dragged him in. His eyes flared when he saw our party. "Esteri, kill them this instant!"

She looked at the floor. "I can't."

"I stole the Rlhala," I said. "I'm the captain now."

Layla snorted.

"The what?" Esteri looked back and forth between us.

"Do you remember the stone column kept near the prisoners?" I said.

She frowned. "Yeah, it was an artifact."

I nodded. "An artifact that allowed the mechanists to control Cthulhu. Everything you've done was because they commanded it."

Her eyes flared. "That's how you control us?"

"Yes." I countered her gaze. "And you're all forbidden from getting near it."

Her lips curled into a sneer, but she looked down instead of responding.

"Gods be damned." Horatio wilted.

"Umbra answers to me." I gripped his chin and forced him to meet my eyes.

Tears poured down his cheeks. "Yes. Umbra is yours."

I turned to the others and shouted, "Swear fealty, all of you!"

The other mechanists knelt and swore their obedience to me and Cain.

I nodded. "Everyone, take a seat."

There weren't enough seats, so many ended up on the floor. Then Cain and I outlined our propositions. First, they would gather all mechanists, even those not part of Umbra or the Pandora Combine. Second, they would formulate a plan to rebuild the destroyed city of Atlanta, but in an orderly mechanist style. And third, they would release all prisoners and employ the willing ones in their efforts by first constructing homes for the survivors.

Our demands were simple, but met with positivity, especially from the engineers. We had just given them all an equal stake in rebuilding a world they'd torn apart.

"I am dissolving the inventor hierarchy," I said. "From here on out, all leadership positions will be determined by merit and equal opportunity."

Inventors cried out. Some even cried. The engineers seemed excited, at least until Cain stated the rest of the directive.

"This means the grays will no longer be treated as indentured servants." He raked his gaze across the mechanists. "Even they will have a stake in this bold new world."

Cheers erupted near the back of the room and echoed out into the hallways where those in gray uniforms stood.

One of the constables gave me an uncertain look. "What about us, sir?"

"What would you like to do?" I asked.

"I want to learn to build, but they said I didn't have a knack for it."

"Do what makes you happy." I didn't really care about his happiness except that it would lend itself to a peaceful reconstruction. Or so I hoped.

We continued detailing our directives, and by the end, the mechanists seemed sad, but willing under penalty of death, to do what we required.

"Everyone here is free to submit a general outline for the rebuilding of Atlanta," I said. "We will choose a winner and move forward immediately."

Excited murmurs rose across the room, and even a few grays looked ready to test their skills in the contest. I was happy that Cain would be the one in charge of this mess. Having this much control of so many lives was not a feeling I enjoyed.

Once we were done, we returned to the cabin. There were still several more tasks that needed immediate attention.

Cain and I used the Rlhala to enter Cthulhu's dream world. I'd told him what to expect beforehand, so it wasn't quite a shock when he found himself underwater with me.

We visited Cthulhu and I gave us joint command over all his minions while keeping me the supreme leader just in case. Cain rolled his eyes at the caveat, but since he was me, he understood my reasoning. Unfortunately, neither of us had a vision like the one I'd had during my first visit. Cthulhu had no information to offer about how we could relive that moment of our shared past.

Once we were done, we took some time to sit back in the cabin and relax since the past twenty-four hours had been a whirlwind. Cain went to his bedroom and I snoozed in the easy chair.

Someone prodded me awake. I blinked open my eyes to Hemlock. "What did I miss?" she asked.

I grinned. "Everything." I stood and held out my hand.

She frowned but took it. When I started walking toward Cain's bedroom she slowed. "What are you doing?"

"I want to show you something."

Her frown deepened. "I'm not going to fuck you, Cain."

I sighed. "Just shut up and follow me, okay?" The door wasn't locked, but Cain was up the instant I opened the door.

Hemlock stepped inside and gasped. "Cain?"

"Layla." He said the name with such tenderness it shocked me.

Hemlock shoved me roughly out of the room, closed and locked the door before I knew what happened.

Layla snorted from behind me. "Well, aren't you just the matchmaker?"

I turned to her. "That was weird."

She nodded. "Yeah. Don't expect me to ever get that mushy."

"Me either." I walked away from the door. "It's dangerous."

Layla nodded again. "Never let your guard down."

"I won't." I stroked her cheek and pulled her in for a long kiss.

She laughed softly. "It's just physical, Cain. Never forget that."

I took her hand and led her into the other bedroom. "Then let's get physical."

Three weeks passed, by which time reconstruction was slowly getting underway. A small team of engineers and grays had devised the winning plan. Not a single inventor came anywhere close. It was obvious that once they rose to that level, they ceased doing anything useful.

The wearing of the old inventor uniforms was forbidden, and it was amusing to see Horatio and his ilk walking around in jeans and t-shirts.

As part of the plan, the mechanists were devising great recycling machines that would grind up structures, separating concrete, metals, and plastics with a magical process dwarves used in their forges. The new city would be nothing like its predecessor. With magic no longer a secret to the nubs, all bets were off the table.

"I don't know about you, but I'm tired of sharing space with so many people," I told Cain as we returned to the cabin from overseeing the demolition of downtown Atlanta. "Do you mind if I relocate to Sanctuary?"

He shook his head. "Go ahead. Layla—uh Hemlock—and I can stay here."

I nodded. "I'll leave the demis with you unless you don't want them."

He rubbed his hands together. "I've got big plans for them to clean up the lake."

"They're gonna love that." I glanced at the locked room where we stored the duffel bags of apocalypse weapons. "I think it's best if we store those at Sanctuary as well."

"We could make a trip to Oblivion and melt them," Cain said.

I sighed. "It may come to that. I'm just not looking forward to the hassle of lighting another forge."

Cain laughed. "Yeah, you've been to Oblivion more than anyone in their right mind would want."

We'd ordered the evacuation of Oblivion since the overuse of Airbender had turned the climate into an even bigger apocalyptic nightmare than it had been before. Those workers were now involved with the rebuilding of Atlanta.

I went outside to gather the others. Shae sat next to Hannah on a bench near the grill, a forlorn look on her face. She'd been shunned by the other demis for not being a team player before I'd taken control. She'd been the only one of them to despise what the mechanists made them do. Hannah had tried making friends with the other girl, but overwhelming guilt and depression weren't easy to penetrate.

Hannah saw me coming and grinned. "Cain, I made another grove of flowers today!"

I craned my neck to take in the giant glowing flowers. They dwarfed nearby trees. "Yeah, they're kind of hard to miss." I shook my head. "Maybe until we know the significance of these flowers you should take it easy on growing them."

"I like them," Shae said in a soft voice. "Their auras hum softly in my ears."

"Oh." I didn't have a response for that. "Hannah, we're headed to Sanctuary. Grab your things."

Shae spun, eyes wide. "Let me come with you, please."

"Oh, can she?" Hannah batted her eyelashes.

I nodded. "Go get packed."

I found Grace and Aura picnicking on a beach not far from the cabin. The pair had grown close over the past few weeks and had taken to sneaking away. It was the worst kept secret that they'd become romantically involved, but nobody cared enough to tell them we knew.

They straightened their clothes when they saw me coming.

"Why are you out here, Cain?" Aura stood up and pulled down her dress, unaware her panties were down around her ankles. I looked down and snorted. "We're headed to Sanctuary. Pack your things if you want to come. Cain and Hemlock are staying here with the demis."

"It'd be nice to have a change of scenery," Grace said.

"You two can even have a room all to yourselves." I turned to walk away.

Aura touched my arm. "You're not upset, are you?"

I frowned. "About what?"

She looked unsure of herself. "You had a thing for me once."

"Yeah, I did." I shrugged. "But it doesn't matter what I think. Your life, your decisions. I've got no power over that."

Grace chuckled. "Cain, you are such a Cain."

"Maybe the other Cain is such a Cain." I jabbed a thumb at my chest. "I'm Prime, remember?"

They both laughed.

"Cain El Primo." Aura flourished a bow and suddenly saw her panties at her feet. "Oh, gods!"

I burst into laughter and walked away.

Layla was already packed by the time I returned to the cabin, and we were all on the way within the hour. It was a relief to reach Sanctuary. I took a moment to stand outside and bask in the sunlight before starting the chore of relocating everything to the basement. The mechanists had constructed a sturdy bronze case for the Rlhala and secured it with a sigil lock. Shae had confirmed they'd built no backdoors into it so only I had access.

In mechanist fashion, the case could also sprout four legs and walk itself wherever it needed to go. They might serve me out of fear, but they never failed to do a top-notch job. I followed the walking case down to the basement and guided it into the side room with the other weapons while the others went back upstairs.

When I finished checking everything over, I found Shae staring at a blank wall at the far side of the library.

"What's wrong?" I said.

She walked slowly toward the wall, uncertainty and fear mingling in her eyes. "Some kind of strange energy is behind the stone."

"A cult once ran this church," I said. "The farmer who used to own it said he destroyed everything."

"Maybe not everything." She walked to the wall and put a hand on it. "Something is hidden behind this."

The stonework matched perfectly with the wall around it, so if there was a hidden door, I couldn't find it. The farmer had probably walled up secrets he couldn't destroy. I could have used my brightblade, but it didn't cut through thick stone very well. Instead, I grabbed Soultaker and slashed a neat doorway into the rock, then cast a glowing orb into the room.

The room beyond was small, no more than six feet squared. It might have once been an alcove and not a room. A pair of stone obelisks with Alder symbols inscribed on them sat on square stone blocks about a foot apart. One obelisk was black and the other white. Centered on the floor behind them was a larger gray obelisk with an eye in the middle of the top part.

Shae stared at it unblinking. "I think it's an altar."

I'd seen plenty of bizarre obelisks, so these probably weren't any different than the ones I'd seen utilized by other cults. The Alder on the gray obelisk said *Overgod*. The Alder on the black obelisk translated to *Cha* and on the white obelisk, *Ord*.

"What does it say?" Shae asked.

I told her. "I've seen variations on this cult. They believed an overgod is responsible for making the gods and everything else."

"I've never heard of that. Then again, I was just an ordinary nub before the mechanists kidnapped me." She knelt before them. "Regular gods are too powerful already. I can't imagine what an overgod could do." She leaned forward and pressed the eye on the gray obelisk.

Sparks flew from the top of the obelisk, splashing the room with a strobe effect. We jumped back as the fireworks continued for several seconds and then died away, leaving the room smoky.

"I don't think it was supposed to do that." I backed out into the library to escape the smoke.

Shae grimaced. "It's definitely broken."

I summoned my staff and examined the area with the true sight scope. A stone centered between the three obelisks sat over a small container of liquid mana that had apparently gone bad. Replacing it might fix the problem.

I walked to the storage room to see if the other Cain kept a supply like I did, but the faint clinking of metal drew my attention to the duffel bags. Something was moving inside. I cautiously unzipped the bag and leapt back when Noctua sprang from inside and fluttered around the room.

She settled onto a shelf and blinked her eyes at me. "Where am I?"

"Sanctuary." I offered silent prayers to no gods in particular as I asked the next question. "Do you remember how to use the Tetron?"

Noctua blinked again. "For what purpose?"

"To go back to my dimension," I said.

"You are not of this world?" She blinked several times. "That is quite unusual."

"Wow, that's so cool." Shae stared at the little owl. "Is that Bubo?"

"Her name is Noctua," I said.

"Oh, yeah, the mechanists talked about her all the time, but I didn't know they meant a clockwork owl."

I turned to Noctua. "You were damaged and lost your memories. I came from Prime by accident and the only way back is to use the Tetron from this world. How do I use it to return to my dimension?"

Noctua looked around the room. "The process is quite simple. Bring me the Tetron and I will illustrate." She looked down at the bag she'd come from. "Goodness, are those weapons from the armory?"

I rummaged through the bags and found the Tetron. "This thing apparently puts off harmful radiation. Do I need to worry about that when I use it?"

"That is because the device wasn't properly configured." She fluttered her wings. "If anything is out of alignment, it will leak god particles."

"So, looking into other dimensions, and so forth is safe if it's properly aligned?"

Noctua bobbed her body in a nod. "Correct. Now, hold the Tetron in the palm of your hand and follow my instructions."

She directed me to rotate, shift, and perform various manipulations of the three parts of the Tetron. After the last step, the device clicked and hummed. "What now?" I asked.

"Touch the Pyron and it will allow you to view the dimensional threads," Noctua said. "Once you find the proper dimension, lock onto it by rotating the Cubon until it clicks and hums. Then pull out the Spheron until it snaps into place. At this point, the device will begin to whine. Press in on the Pyron and it will take you to this place in that dimension."

I touched the Pyron. My body soared straight up through stone and ground as if I were a ghost. I continued though the top of the chapel and into the sky. Within seconds, I found myself looking down at Gaia from space. But she wasn't alone. More and more Gaias appeared, each one shrinking down until there was a sphere made of layers of worlds.

Some of the worlds were black and dead. Others were covered in green or brown hues that looked unnatural. Some sparkled with city lights that spanned from pole to pole. In the very center of the sphere was a blue-green marble that looked perfectly normal. It was orbited by a pair of nearly identical planets. I sensed a blip on one of those worlds that indicated where I was.

I was looking at the multiverse.

Chapter 42

It was bizarre seeing all the variations of Gaia that existed, some far out in the fringes that must have changed millions of years in the past to be so completely different. But something nagged at the back of my mind telling me that there was more than this. Past the outer ring of dimensions, there was nothingness, but there was something more beneath the surface.

I reached toward the super-sphere and flicked it. It rotated and replaced Gaia with the multicolored hues of Feary. Another flick revealed the dead world of Oblivion. For every iteration of Gaia, there was also an iteration of Oblivion and Feary, except for a few blank spots on the far fringe. It seemed something catastrophic had occurred making the creation of those worlds impossible.

But there were more worlds lurking beneath these, worlds I'd never realized existed. I switched among them, stunned by how many there were. I felt as if I were losing myself in a sea of worlds, unable to find the way back to my origin. In my panic, I focused on finding Gaia and suddenly, it was there again.

I was ready to return to my current location, eager to fetch the others and take us home. But something nagged at me, something off to the side of the super-sphere of dimensions. I turned to the side and another universe was there. Another turn and I found yet another universe. Beyond that, I saw nothing else. But neither of those universes had more than a dozen or so dimensions, barely enough to create even an outer layer around their prime.

"What in the hell?" My voice echoed in the void. I sensed another presence, something out there with me, lurking but not speaking. Fear was normal, but for the first time in a long while I was absolutely terrified. I turned back the other way, past the two dead universes and found Gaia.

Something cold, something so ancient that it defied all reasoning brushed against my senses. I fled back to earth, flying straight down through the chapel, into the ground and ended up back in the room where I'd started. I stumbled away from the Tetron, gibbering like a madman, fell to the ground shivering uncontrollably, unable to form a coherent word.

"What's wrong?" Shae cradled my head in her lap. "What happened to him?"

"I don't know." Noctua blinked curiously. "I have never witnessed this before."

"Get Hannah!" Shae shouted. "Now!"

"I am not familiar with this place." Noctua fluttered away through the door. "But I will do my best to navigate." Moments later, running footsteps closed in.

Hannah dropped next to Shae. "What happened?"

"I don't know." Shae wiped tears from her eyes. "The owl was telling him how to use the Tetron. He touched it for a minute, then fell down screaming his head off."

"Cain, screaming?" Layla knelt in front of me, hand caressing my face. "Cain doesn't scream."

"Whatever happened, it terrified him." Shae's eyes went pitch black and she shuddered. "Oh, god."

"What?" Hannah gripped my hand. "What do you see, Shae?"

I tried to talk, but gibberish was all that emerged. I felt them tear off my shirt and gasp at what they saw.

"Is that a bruise?" Layla said.

"No," Shae replied. "It's some kind of magical energy I've never seen before." She gasped. "No, that's not true. It looks like what I saw in the obelisk room."

Layla frowned. "The what?"

"Over there." Shae pointed in the general direction of the other room.

I finally stopped shivering and my racing heart began to slow. "I saw everything."

Layla's eyes widened. "Babe, are you okay?"

The room went silent.

Layla must have seen the shock on my face because she frowned and did a double-take. "What the fuck is everyone looking at?"

A faint smile touched Hannah's lips. "Nothing, babe."

Layla groaned. "I call everyone that ironically."

Hannah's smile widened. "Whatever you say, babe."

I finally found the strength to struggle to my feet. "I saw more universes than our own, but they were dead."

"Fascinating." Noctua fluttered to a shelf. "I have never been able to look beyond our own sphere, but according to information I possess, there were several failures before our own."

Hannah shuddered. "Freaky. I don't want to know what else is out there."

My back ached as if someone applied a hot-cold patch with far too much heat and ice, but I did my best to ignore it. "I have the feeling curiosity almost killed this cat." I shook my head. "I just want to go back home. We can sort all this later."

Layla nodded. "Agreed."

I used a wireless communicator the mechanists had given me to speak with my counterpart and let him know we'd found a way home.

"Well, shit. What happens if I need to get in touch?" he said.

"I'll figure out how we can both have working Tetrons so it won't be a problem," I said. "Keep doing the work here and everything will be fine."

He snorted. "Yeah, sure it will. Especially with Loki, Oizys, Eris, and the gods of chaos working against us."

"Hey, it's better than it was," I said.

He chuckled. "That's for damned sure."

Hemlock spoke. "Tell Layla that I'm proud of her progress."

Layla frowned. "Don't sass me, bitch."

Hemlock snorted. "I'll sass you as much as needed."

Everyone said their goodbyes over the wireless. There was no need to go do it in person. And then we prepared to go home. I tested the dimensional shift by myself first and carried over a duffel bag. The Tetron was still in my hand when I appeared all alone in the same storage room back in Prime. I'd been fearful of encountering whatever touched me in the void the last time, but in the brief time I spent travelling, it left me alone.

By touching me, the others were able to travel as well. Soon we had all the duffel bags transferred. I returned to the empty room in the alternate dimension and found Shae and Noctua the only ones waiting next to the last item I was bringing with me.

Shae wiped her eyes. "What do you want me to do now?" Tears trailed down her face. "Do I have to go back to the others?"

I felt bad for her. "You can come with us if you want."

Hope crept into her face. "But there's another me over there, right?"

I nodded. "Yeah, but I think there's room for one more."

She hugged me, sobbing. "I see why Hannah loves you. You're a good person, a savior."

I cleared my throat. "Look, Shae, I'm not a good guy. I've got so much blood on my hands, I'll never be clean."

She shook her head. "I don't care. You saved me. You saved my world." She looked up at me with big eyes. "I want to be on your side."

"Gods almighty, Layla's never going to let me live this one down." I sighed. "Just take it easy on the sentimental stuff, okay?"

She laughed. "Deal."

I turned to Noctua. "I'll return in a few days."

"I am remembering some things that were said during my hibernation." She blinked her clockwork eyes.

"You heard what we were talking about while you were asleep?"

"Naturally. I did not completely cease to function." She blinked again. "Erolith demanded I be destroyed with the armory weapons."

I grimaced. "Yeah, about that—"

"It is a bargain freely made," Noctua said. "I do not wish death, but I will not force you to break the bargain. The price is too high."

"Erolith is dead," Shae said.

"The bargain still exists," Noctua said.

"Yeah, well about that." I explained about the nuances of fae bargains and what that meant for her future. "Think about that until I return."

Noctua fluttered her wings and bounced around. "You out-bargained a fae? That is most unheard of for a human."

I shrugged. "Some of us just have skills." I took Shae's hand and had her grasp the lever on the Rlhala case. Then I shifted us over to Prime. Like the others, she screamed in fear when the we shot out into the void and screamed again when we hurtled back to Gaia. Layla was the only one who hadn't screamed, but she had held onto my hand extra tight. And I'd liked that.

Hannah looked worriedly at me when Shae and I appeared in the basement of Sanctuary Prime. "Where's Noctua?"

"Still in her dimension," I said.

"Do you really have to destroy her?" Hannah took my hand. "Erolith is dead so we don't have to do it, right?"

Shae smiled. "I wouldn't worry about it too much." Then she walked out of the room.

Hannah's forehead creased. "What does that mean?"

"Noctua was damaged when the mechanists fought Korborus for the armory." I folded my arms. "It damaged her memory."

Hannah nodded. "Okay, but what does that have to do with it?"

"I told Erolith I'd destroy anything forged in the armory and he agreed."

"Because he wants you to destroy Noctua and the Tetron!" she said.

I nodded. "But Noctua wasn't forged in the armory and neither was the Tetron." I grinned. "They, along with Korborus, were forged on Mount Olympus in Gaia. Otherwise we never could have damaged them."

"Oh!" Hannah dragged the word out for a couple of seconds. Her eyes brightened. "You outsmarted him!"

I nodded. "At least, that's what I'd like to think. But maybe he let me have a win for once."

"It's good to be home." Hannah slumped and began to sob.

I put a hand on her shoulder. "What's wrong?"

"I've loved being around you so much. It was like having family again. I'm going to miss you so much."

"Miss me?" I said.

She nodded. "I'm way overdue reporting back to Cthulhu."

"Yeah, about that." I took her hand. "Let's take a little trip, shall we?"

I opened the case containing the Rlhala and prayed it worked in this dimension as it had in the other one. I told Hannah what to expect and we touched the etching of Cthulhu's head on the stone. Despite my warnings, Hannah freaked out when we plummeted underwater. When she gasped, however, the only surprise on her face was that she could breathe just fine.

I talked in a normal voice. "We're not really underwater."

"You can talk like normal?" she said.

I snorted. "Duh." Then I took her hand and we swam into the city of R'lyeh.

Almost to the temple, Hannah released my hand and stared around. "I've seen all this before when he spoke to me and initiated me." She shuddered. "It's so surreal seeing it like this."

I nodded. "Yeah, it's creepy."

We entered the temple and Cthulhu opened his eyes, glaring at me with glowing red orbs. Tentacles thrashed as he spoke, the alien language of the Great Ancient Ones emerging even as I heard the translation in English in my head. *I am displeased, mortal. You hid the girl and my minion from me. I should kill them both so you understand the price of such deception.*

"How about you shut your tentacle mouth?" I said.

Cthulhu's great orifice closed. His eyes widened in outrage and then fear.

"I have the Rlhala." I grinned. "What is yours is now mine."

Cthulhu shivered in impotent rage.

"You will release Hannah from your service. She is a free being once again. You will also free the minion named Fred and the girl named Shae."

It is done all but the last, for she is not under my control. Cthulhu's voice echoed in my head even though his mouth didn't move.

Apparently, Shae belonged to the Cthulhu in the other dimension. There was so much more I wanted to do, but that was enough for this trip. Hannah and I snapped from the dream world and grinned at each other in the real world. She laughed and hugged me.

"I'm free!" She backed away, spinning and dancing. "I'm free!"

I mussed her hair. "Yep. Ready to go back to high school?"

She froze in place, a look of horror on her face. "God, no!"

I chuckled. "Home schooling it is, then."

We went upstairs and made the announcement to everyone.

"This is the perfect excuse to have cake," Grace announced. "And ice cream."

"Party!" Aura said.

Layla mocked a yawn. "Sounds like a boring party, but sure, I'll attend.

Shae grinned happily at Hannah. "I'm so happy for you."

"It was like someone lifted lead weights from my soul." Hannah looked down. "Cain tried to free you too, but the Cthulhu in this dimension doesn't control you."

Shae gasped and looked at me. "You were going to free me even though I just literally helped kill all your allies a few weeks ago?"

"I think you've proven that you're not one of the bad guys." I patted her shoulder. "Why don't you and Hannah go with Grace into town for some ice cream?" I turned to Aura. "And make sure you bring some mangoes back. I'm dying to have a mangorita."

Aura grinned. "I'll still bartend for you, Cain."

The water in Fred's pool splashed. I turned, expecting to see the octopus emerge. I wondered if he'd felt something lift from him when Cthulhu freed him. But it wasn't Fred that emerged from the pool. The creature was light brown with two huge blue eyes and a mouth surrounded by small tentacles. It stumbled from the pool on four legs, a small tail dragging the ground behind it.

"Oh my god, it's so adorable!" Hannah scooped up the infant-sized creature.

"Hannah, be careful!" I lunged toward her, but the creature cooed, its eyes wide with pleasure.

Hannah turned to me. "I can hear it talking in my head."

The little creature looked at me and reached out a tiny hand. I touched it and Fred's voice filled my mind. *When Grace blocked me from Cthulhu, I began to mature, but I have not changed at all for several days, so my growth may have been limited.*

"I don't understand. What's happening to you?"

I am a spawn of Cthulhu. This is what I would have looked like long ago had he not stunted my growth. I fear I will never grow beyond this.

I did my best not to laugh, but it was just too hard. "Fred, you're Baby Cthulhu."

Layla groaned. "Gods be damned, you went from having one teenager to two and now you've got a fucking baby outsider god to take care of too?"

Everyone burst into laughter. Even Fred made amused cooing sounds.

It was seriously fucked up, but a part of me kind of liked it.

My world had changed in ways I'd never imagined. I'd been to other worlds and other dimensions, but there was no other place I'd rather be than right here, right now. And I planned to make the most of it.

####

I hope you enjoyed reading this book. Reviews are very important in helping other readers decide what to read next. Would you please take a few seconds to rate this book?

Please consider joining my Facebook group at https://www.facebook.com/groups/overworldconclave

Or my mailing list at http://johncorwin.net

Books by John Corwin-

<u>Books by John Corwin</u>
Join the Overworld Conclave for all the news, memes and tentacles you could ever desire!
https://www.facebook.com/groups/overworldconclave
Or get your tentacles via email: www.johncorwin.net
Fan page: https://www.facebook.com/johncorwinauthor

AMOS CARVER THRILLERS
Dead Before Dawn
Dead List
Dead and Buried
Dead Man Walking

CHRONICLES OF CAIN
To Kill a Unicorn
Enter Oblivion
Throne of Lies
At The Forest of Madness
The Dead Never Die
Shadow of Cthulhu

Cabal of Chaos

Monster Squad

Gates of Yog-Sothoth

Shadow Over Tokyo

THE OVERWORLD CHRONICLES

Sweet Blood of Mine

Dark Light of Mine

Fallen Angel of Mine

Dread Nemesis of Mine

Twisted Sister of Mine

Dearest Mother of Mine

Infernal Father of Mine

Sinister Seraphim of Mine

Wicked War of Mine

Dire Destiny of Ours

Aetherial Annihilation

Baleful Betrayal

Ominous Odyssey

Insidious Insurrection

Utopia Undone

Overworld Apocalypse

Apocryphan Rising

Soul Storm

Devil's Due

Overworld Ascension

Assignment Zero (An Elyssa Short Story)

OVERWORLD UNDERGROUND

Soul Seer

Demonicus

Infernal Blade

OVERWORLD ARCANUM
Conrad Edison and the Living Curse
Conrad Edison and the Anchored World
Conrad Edison and the Broken Relic
Conrad Edison and the Infernal Design
Conrad Edison and the First Power

STAND ALONE NOVELS
Mars Rising
No Darker Fate
The Next Thing I Knew
Outsourced
Seventh

About the Author

John Corwin is the bestselling author of the Overworld Chronicles and Chronicles of Cain. He enjoys long walks on the beach and is a firm believer in puppies and kittens.

After years of getting into trouble thanks to his overactive imagination, John abandoned his male modeling career to write books.

He resides in Atlanta.

https://www.facebook.com/groups/overworldconclave

Join the Overworld Conclave for all the news, memes and tentacles you could ever desire!

https://www.facebook.com/groups/overworldconclave

Or get your tentacles via email: www.johncorwin.net

Fan page: https://www.facebook.com/johncorwinauthor

ENJOYED THE BOOK?

JOIN MY READER GROUP ON FACEBOOK
HTTPS://WWW.FACEBOOK.COM/GROUPS/OVERWORLDCONCLAVE

Made in United States
Cleveland, OH
01 December 2024

11061499R00226